The Bestse TOM CLANCY

RAINBOW SIX

John Clark is used to doing the CIA's dirty work. Now he's taking on the world. . . .

"ACTION-PACKED."

—*The New York Times Book Review*

EXECUTIVE ORDERS

The most devastating terrorist act in history leaves Jack Ryan as President of the United States. . . .

"UNDOUBTEDLY CLANCY'S BEST YET."

—*The Atlanta Journal-Constitution*

DEBT OF HONOR

It begins with the murder of an American woman in the back streets of Tokyo. It ends in war. . . .

"A SHOCKER CLIMAX SO PLAUSIBLE YOU'LL WONDER WHY IT HASN'T YET HAPPENED!"

—*Entertainment Weekly*

THE HUNT FOR RED OCTOBER

The smash bestseller that launched Clancy's career—the incredible search for a Soviet defector and the nuclear submarine he commands . . .

"BREATHLESSLY EXCITING."

—*The Washington Post*

continued . . .

RED STORM RISING

The ultimate scenario for World War III—the final battle for global control . . .

"THE ULTIMATE WAR GAME . . . BRILLIANT."

—*Newsweek*

PATRIOT GAMES

CIA analyst Jack Ryan stops an assassination—and incurs the wrath of Irish terrorists. . . .

"A HIGH PITCH OF EXCITEMENT."

—*The Wall Street Journal*

THE CARDINAL OF THE KREMLIN

The superpowers race for the ultimate Star Wars missile defense system. . . .

"*CARDINAL* EXCITES, ILLUMINATES . . . A REAL PAGE-TURNER."

—*Los Angeles Daily News*

CLEAR AND PRESENT DANGER

The killing of three U.S. officials in Colombia ignites the American government's explosive, and top secret, response. . . .

"A CRACKLING GOOD YARN."

—*The Washington Post*

THE SUM OF ALL FEARS

The disappearance of an Israeli nuclear weapon threatens the balance of power in the Middle East— and around the world. . . .

"CLANCY AT HIS BEST . . . NOT TO BE MISSED."

—*The Dallas Morning News*

WITHOUT REMORSE

The Clancy epic fans have been waiting for. His code name is Mr. Clark. And his work for the CIA is brilliant, cold-blooded, and efficient . . . but who is he really?

"HIGHLY ENTERTAINING."

—*The Wall Street Journal*

continued . . .

TOM CLANCY'S HAWX

Tom Clancy's Ghost Recon

GHOST RECON
COMBAT OPS
CHOKEPOINT

Tom Clancy's EndWar

ENDWAR
THE HUNTED
THE MISSING

Tom Clancy's Splinter Cell

SPLINTER CELL
OPERATION BARRACUDA
CHECKMATE
FALLOUT

CONVICTION
ENDGAME
BLACKLIST AFTERMATH

Created by Tom Clancy and Steve Pieczenik

TOM CLANCY'S OP-CENTER

OP-CENTER
MIRROR IMAGE
GAMES OF STATE
ACTS OF WAR
BALANCE OF POWER
STATE OF SIEGE
DIVIDE AND CONQUER
LINE OF CONTROL
MISSION OF HONOR
SEA OF FIRE
CALL TO TREASON
WAR OF EAGLES

TOM CLANCY'S NET FORCE

NET FORCE
HIDDEN AGENDAS
NIGHT MOVES
BREAKING POINT
POINT OF IMPACT
CYBERNATION
STATE OF WAR
CHANGING OF THE GUARD
SPRINGBOARD
THE ARCHIMEDES EFFECT

Created by Tom Clancy and Martin Greenberg

TOM CLANCY'S POWER PLAYS

POLITIKA
RUTHLESS.COM
SHADOW WATCH
BIO-STRIKE

COLD WAR
CUTTING EDGE
ZERO HOUR
WILD CARD

Tom Clancy's
NET FORCE®
POINT OF IMPACT

Created by
Tom Clancy and Steve Pieczenik
written by Steve Perry

BERKLEY BOOKS, NEW YORK

This is a work of fiction. Names, characters, places, and incidents are either the product of the author's imagination or are used fictitiously, and any resemblance to actual persons, living or dead, business establishments, events, or locales is entirely coincidental.

TOM CLANCY'S NET FORCE®: POINT OF IMPACT

A Berkley Book / published by arrangement with
Netco Partners

PRINTING HISTORY
Berkley edition / April 2001

The Penguin Putnam Inc. World Wide Web site address is
http://www.penguinputnam.com

ISBN: 0-425-17923-0

BERKLEY®
Berkley Books are published by The Berkley Publishing Group,
a division of Penguin Putnam Inc.,
375 Hudson Street, New York, New York 10014.
BERKLEY and the "B" design
are trademarks belonging to Penguin Putnam Inc.

PRINTED IN THE UNITED STATES OF AMERICA

10 9 8 7 6 5 4 3

ACKNOWLEDGMENTS

We would like to acknowledge the assistance of Martin H. Greenberg, Larry Segriff, Denise Little, John Helfers, Robert Youdelman, Esq., and Tom Mallon, Esq.; Mitchell Rubenstein and Laurie Silvers of Hollywood.com, Inc.; and the wonderful people at Penguin Putnam Inc., including Phyllis Grann, David Shanks, and Tom Colgan. As always, I would like to thank Robert Gottlieb, without whom this book would never have been conceived. But most important, it is for you, our readers, to determine how successful our collective endeavor has been.

PROLOGUE

Saturday, October 1, 2011
Atlantic City, New Jersey

"We should go outside and enjoy the sunny weather," Mary Lou said.

Bert snickered. "Right. We'z drove alla way from da Bronx to Atlantic City to take the goddamned sun? I can sit onna stoop at home, I want to get hot. No thankyuz, I'm happy right here."

Bert fed another dollar into the slot machine and pushed the button. He didn't like the new electronic machines as much as the old mechanical ones, like those in the back rooms of the New Jersey bars where his father used to sneak off with him when he was a kid. Those had been fun, with the big arm you pulled down and the real wheels going round and round. Cost a quarter, was all. He didn't quite trust the new ones to pay off—it'd be too easy for some computer geek to rig 'em so they'd keep every damned dime you put in—but it was what it was. Hell, he was up seventy-five bucks, he should complain?

Around him, the machines flashed colored lights,

hummed and whirred and played crappy music, and now and then dropped tokens into a metal tray.

Mary Lou said, "There's something you don't see every day."

The slot's computer screen whirled to stop on a cherry, a bar, and a picture of some dead rock star. Crap. Only seventy-four dollars ahead now.

Irritated, Bert said, "What?"

"Over there. Lookit."

He glanced in the direction Mary Lou was pointing. He saw right away what she meant. There was a fat, white-haired old guy, maybe sixty-five, walking into the casino. Way he moved, he was like a man with a mission, nothing real unusual there, except the dude was in a tiny red Speedo and nothing else.

"God, I'm trying to win money here, you wanna make me puke? There ought to be a law against a suit like that if you're thirty pounds overweight."

"Prolly there is. I'm pretty sure the casino rules say no swimsuits without a robe and some kind of sandals or shoes. There you go, see, the security guard is gonna toss him out."

A big uniformed guard, six five, two sixty, easy, angled toward the fat guy in the red Speedo. This might be worth watching. You didn't get to see a guy in a bikini bottom get bounced up by a casino guard real often. In fact, Bert had never seen it before.

Speedo smiled at the giant guard, grabbed him by the arms just under his shoulders, picked him up, and threw him like the guy was a toy. The guard smashed into a slot machine with a loud, rattling crash.

"Holy shit!" Bert said.

He wasn't the only one to notice Speedo at this point. Two more guards came running, pulling out those expandable steel batons they carried as they ran.

Speedo didn't seem concerned. He took a couple of steps to the nearest slot. It was bolted to the floor, so Bert didn't know what the guy thought he was gonna do with it.

Still smiling, Speed wrenched the slot from the floor with a sound like a nail being pulled from wet wood, and threw that, too. Made a helluva noise.

Bert stared, frozen. This wasn't possible. He hit the gym two or three times a week, kept in shape for a man pushing forty, could bench two fifty for reps, and there was no way this flabby old Q-Tip–haired dude had the muscle to do what he'd just done, no way! Nobody was that strong.

The second security guard to get there let fly with his expandable night stick, took a good crack at Speedo's white head. Speedo reached up, almost in slow motion, grabbed the baton as it came down, jerked it from the guard's grip, and threw it. The thing whistled as it whirled away, so fast Bert couldn't even track it. Speedo shoved the guard one-handed, and the guy just *flew* into two by-standers and knocked all three of them down.

Mary Lou stared at Speedo, frozen like a deer in head-lights. Bert understood that. It was like he was hypnotized himself. He couldn't look away.

The third guard, seeing what had happened to the other two, dropped his baton and went for his pistol. Bert thought this was a real good idea.

Speedo took a couple of quick steps—really quick steps—and caught the guard's wrist before he cleared leather.

Thirty feet away, Bert heard the sound of the man's arm bones breaking.

Oh, *man!*

The guard fell to his knees, screaming in pain, and

Speedo stepped around him like he was doggy doo on the sidewalk.

Then things really got going. Speedo waded through the casino like Sherman through Georgia, breaking stuff, throwing it, tearing the place up. He knocked over slots, he upended card tables, he flipped a roulette wheel table completely over. People scrambled to get out of his way.

He was a human wrecking ball, he was *smiling* while he did it, and Bert couldn't begin to understand how he was doing it. He just stood there and watched.

It seemed like a long time, but it couldn't have been more than a minute or two before the local cops showed up. Six of them in full battle array.

The first couple of cops to reach Speedo tried to whack him with their batons and collar him. You'd think, after seeing what the guy had done, they'd have better sense, but they didn't, and Speedo grabbed one and used him like a club on the second.

The other four cops were smarter. One of them fast-drew his pepper spray, another pulled an air taser, and both let loose.

Speedo ran at the cops. Through the pepper fog, and from where he stood, Bert saw the two electric taser needles in the old man's chest, and if either the fog or the juice bothered him, you couldn't tell. Either one should have stopped him, had him gagging or jittering like a spider on a hot stove, but he never slowed. Speedo slammed into the next two cops, knocking them sprawling. He went down himself, but he was up in a heartbeat. He looked pissed off now, and he scooped one of the cops from the floor—a big black dude who probably went two hundred pounds—and shot-putted the cop at a thick plate glass partition that separated a cafeteria hall from the casino floor.

The partition had to be six, eight feet away, easy.

The partition shattered, shards of glass flew everywhere, and the cop who went through it would be lucky if he wasn't slashed to hamburger.

"Everybody down!" one of the two remaining cops on his feet screamed. "Down, down, down!"

People hit the floor, but Speedo wasn't one of them, and Bert stayed up watching, too.

The two cops had their pistols out by now—big ole Glocks—pointed at the old man.

Speedo looked at them and smiled, a kind of sad smile. Like he felt sorry for them. He started walking toward the cops.

"*Stop,* asshole!"

He didn't.

Both cops fired, couple, three times each.

Speedo kept coming, and they kept shooting.

Bert *saw* the hits on the old man, saw dark puckers appear in his arms and chest, wounds that oozed blood, but he kept going.

People screamed bloody murder, but the cops kept blasting away. In some corner of his mind, Bert tried to keep count of the shots, but there were too many of them. How many rounds did those guns hold? Fifteen? Eighteen? They were going to town.

It was like some monster movie. The old guy in the red bathing suit just kept shambling toward the cops. He was hit at least six or eight times, but he wouldn't stop.

"Fuck!" one of the cops yelled. He turned and ran.

The other cop clicked empty, then, when Speedo was almost on top of him, he threw the Glock at the old man.

Yeah, right. Guy takes a whole shitload of bullets and a plastic pistol is not gonna bounce off him like a cotton ball? Bert stared at the cop. Whaddayuz, stupid?

The old man grabbed the cop, managed to get him five or six inches off the floor—

—then the old man finally ran out of gas. He dropped the cop and fell, landing on the floor facedown.

It got real quiet in the casino then.

"Ho-ly *shit,*" Bert said softly.

"Amen, sweet Jesus," Mary Lou said. "Amen."

1

Alex Michaels grunted as the socket slipped off the hex nut and his hand shot forward, scraping his knuckles on the rocker-arm cover.

"Ow! Crap!"

At such times, he was wont to blame the nut or the wrench, but since he had put the bolt in himself, and the wrench and socket were both fairly new Craftsman tools, he knew he had nobody else to blame.

From the kitchen, he heard Toni call out. "You okay?"

Must have yelled louder than he'd thought. "Yeah, yeah, I'm fine. Stupid piece of crap Chevrolet!"

Toni drifted into the garage doorway. He was leaning over the fender on the passenger side, under the hood, so he saw her. Five months pregnant, in one of his T-shirts and a pair of drawstring sweatpants, she was, if anything, more beautiful than ever.

She smiled. "That's not what you said when you were convincing me you needed to have it. 'A fifty-five Bel Air convertible,' you said. 'A classic.' "

"Yeah, well, that was before I had a chance to spend time with it. Thing is engineered like a tank."

"Also a selling point, if I recall."

He looked at the nut. It was tight enough, he decided. He put the wrench down, grabbed a red rag and some of the pungent lanolin hand cleaner and started wiping grease off his fingers. Well, it *was* a classic car. Created by the chief engineer of General Motors in the post World War II years, Edward Coles, with legendary designer Harvey Earl, the '55 introduced the small block V-8 engine, the 265, later the 283, and then the 327. These engines became the standard against which all others were measured for more than forty years. A convertible in top condition would cost $60,000 to $75,000, easy. Even one in so-so shape like this one wasn't cheap.

He smiled back at her. "I thought it was your job to keep me from running off half cocked."

"I don't recall that part of the marriage vow."

He walked toward her. "How did your *djuru* practice go?"

Her smiled disappeared, and frown lines wrinkled her forehead. "Terrible. I'm all off-balance! I try to do the turnaround, I almost fall down. When I sweep, it's all I can do to keep from falling over. When I dropped into the squat for *djuru* five, I *farted!*"

He couldn't help it; he laughed.

Her face clouded up, tears welling. "It's not funny, Alex! I feel like a big fat *cow!*"

Michaels hurried to her. He hugged her to him. "Hey, it's all right."

"No, it's not! Nobody told me this was going to happen! If I can't practice my *silat,* I'll go crazy!"

This was not the time for him to point out that her doctor had told her to avoid exercise because of some bleeding early in the pregnancy. Everything seemed to be all right, but just to be sure, Toni was supposed to take it easy. That theoretically included Toni not doing the short dances of the Indonesian martial art in which she was an expert. No, definitely not the time to bring that up. A wrong word, and she'd start crying, which was so unlike her that it still amazed him every time. It was just hormones, the doctor had said, a normal part of pregnancy, but Michaels still hadn't gotten used to it. Toni could kick the crap out of most men, even some who were fairly good martial artists themselves—he had seen her do it a few times—and for her to well up and cry at the drop of a hat was, well . . . it was spooky.

"Maybe you should just, you know, take a break from *djurus*. It's only another four months until the baby is born."

"Take a *break?* I've done *djurus* almost every day since I was thirteen. Even when I had pneumonia, I only missed three days. I can't just *give them up* for four months!"

"Okay, okay, it was just a suggestion."

Maybe it was better if he just kept his mouth shut. It had been a long time since he'd been around a pregnant woman. When his first wife Megan had been carrying their daughter, Susie, he had still been working in the field and was gone quite a bit, sometimes for a couple weeks at a time. He'd missed a lot of the experience, and at the time he'd been sorry he had. Now he was the commander of the FBI's elite subunit Net Force, and maybe he might be spending a little more time at the office until things settled down at home.

He immediately felt guilty at that thought.

"I know it's not your fault," Toni said. "Well, okay, it *is* your fault, technically speaking." She grinned. "But I don't blame you."

He smiled back at her. Her mood swing was instant, zap, just like that, from angry to happy.

"Go on back and finish installing your carburetor," she said. "You putting in the four-barrel?"

"I decided to go with three deuces," he said. "You know, pep it up a little."

She shook her head. "You've been watching that old movie *American Graffiti* again, haven't you? Boys and their toys. You won't be able to afford to run it, you know. It'll get what? Ten miles a gallon? You'll have to take out a loan to fill the tank."

"Well, I really am going to sell it. Eventually."

"Uh-huh. Go on, go scrape some more skin off your hands and curse the guys who made that big chunk of Detroit iron. I'm going to sit down and see if I can't get your son to stop kicking my bladder."

"You sure are pretty when you're pregnant," he said.

"Forget it. One baby: That's my limit."

Toni went to her computer and slid the VR band down over her eyes, adjusting the earplugs and olfactory bulbs so they were comfortable. The set was wireless and had a pretty good range, so if her ankles started to swell, at least she could go lie down and prop her feet up on a cushion while she was on-line. She put on the tactile gloves and was ready.

She allowed the system's default scenario to play, and there was a small moment of disorientation as the virtual reality program took over and constructed a shopping mall in place of the small office that had been the guest bedroom. She found herself in front of a virtual elevator, the door of which opened. She stepped inside, along with other shoppers.

"Arts and Crafts, please," she said.

Somebody tapped a button.

The sensation was of rising rather than falling. After a moment, a chime sounded and the door opened. Toni alighted from the elevator and looked at the sign a few feet away. YOU ARE HERE pulsed in a pale green light. *No, I'm at home in my office with my shoes getting tighter.*

But the suspension of disbelief that was VR was easy enough to accept. She found the place she was looking for listed: Hergert's Scrimshaw. It was not far away—though it could have been if she wanted a long walk in VR—and she headed toward it.

When she and Alex had been on their honeymoon in Hawaii, they'd gone to an art gallery in Lahaini, on the island of Maui. There had been some world-class work in the gallery, in all kinds of media and materials—everything from pencil drawings to oil paintings to sculptures in wood or bronze or even glass. Seascapes and dolphins and whales were big, but what had impressed her the most was a small display of microscrimshaw. There were pictures engraved on small bits of fossilized ivory, old piano keys and billiard balls, even a couple of sperm whale teeth. Some of the images were smaller than her thumbnail but, when viewed under magnification, showed a wealth of detail she would not have thought possible. There were sailing ships and whales, portraits, nudes, tigers, and several with fantasy elements. She had been particularly impressed by a tiny black-and-white rendering of a long-haired, naked woman sitting in a lotus position and gazing up at the heavens, but floating two feet above the ground. The image had been done on a pale ivory disk the size of a quarter.

"How do they do that?" she'd asked Alex.

He'd shaken his head. "I dunno. Let's ask."

The gallery manager was happy to explain: "There are different ways," she said, "but in this case, what the artist did was to polish the ivory smooth, then use a very fine-pointed instrument, probably something like a sewing needle, to put thousands of tiny dots into the material, it's a process called stippling. Then he rubbed the color onto it. This is a Bob Hergert piece, and he prefers oil paint to ink. I believe he uses a shade called lampblack.

"Once the piece was covered with paint, he wiped it clean, and the oil paint filled up the stipple marks but came off the polished part. It has to be done under magnification, of course, and it is, as you might suspect, rather painstaking work."

"I can only imagine," Toni said. "It's beautiful."

"Yes, Bob is one of the better artists working in the medium. We handle some other scrimshanders who are also very good—Karst, Benade, Stahl, Bellet, Dietrich, even Apple Stephens—but Bob's work is not only beautiful, it's still reasonably priced. He does a lot of custom commissions on things like knife handles and gun grips."

"How much?" Alex asked.

"Eight hundred for this one."

"We'll take it," he said.

"No, Alex, we can't—"

"Yes, we can. It'll be your wedding present."

"But—"

"I made a good profit on my last car restoration. We can afford it."

As she packaged the scrimshaw and ran Alex's credit card, the manager said to Toni, "If you are ever interested in seeing how he does it, Bob teaches an on-line course."

At the time, Toni had nodded and murmured something polite, not thinking such artwork would ever be something she'd have time for.

As she walked through the virtual mall, she smiled to herself. Well, she had time now. Plenty of time. She was supposed to sit around and twiddle her thumbs for the next four months, and even if she wanted to practice her *silat,* she was, for all practical purposes, a beached whale. She'd just flop around on the sand if she tried to do any-

thing physical, she could already see that, and she was
only five months along. At seven or eight months, dropping into a *djuru* turn was just not going to be in the
cards. But sitting at a table and scratching on a piece of
faux ivory with a pin? She could do that, and the idea of
creating something anywhere close to as beautiful as that
tiny scrimshaw Alex had bought for her was appealing.
Of course, she didn't really have much artistic talent, but
maybe she could learn. It was worth a shot.

She arrived in front of a small shop. On the window it said,
Bob Hergert, Microscrimshaw—www.scrimshander .com.

Toni took a deep breath, let it out, and walked into the
shop.

Inside, the place was neat and well laid out. There were
glass-topped cases with pieces of ivory on black velvet,
everything from knife handles, gun grips, and billiard
balls to larger framed pieces. Several magnifying glasses
on little stands had been set up on the glass so that the
smaller pieces under them were easier to see.

An electric guitar hung on the wall behind the longest
counter. Toni didn't know from guitars, but there was an
ivory plate on the body of the instrument, and she recognized the man's face lovingly engraved upon the plate.

A medium-sized man with a thick mustache came out
of the back and smiled at Toni. "The King," he said.
"When he was in his prime. About 1970 or so, the television concert where he wore the black leather suit."

Toni nodded. "I bought one of your pieces in Hawaii,"
she said. "A naked woman sitting in a lotus pose, floating
in the air."

"Ah," he said. "Cynthia, the Goddess of the Moon. I
enjoyed doing that one. How can I help you, Mrs. . . .
ah . . . ?"

"Michaels," she said, still feeling somewhat strange about using Alex's name that way. "Toni."

"Toni. Nice to meet you."

"I understand you give lessons in how to do this." She waved, taking in the shop's interior.

"Yes, ma'am, I surely do."

"I'd like to sign up, if I could."

"No problem at all, Toni."

They smiled at each other.

2

"You look like hell, Julio."

"Thank you, General Howard, sir, for your astute observation."

"What happened?"

"I was up half Sunday night feeding the baby. Your godson."

"I thought Joanna was breast-feeding."

"Yeah, she is. But somebody told her about a little pump that lets you take mama's milk out of the original container and put it into little bottles. That way the father can be part of the suckling process."

"Don't look at me, I didn't tell her."

"No, it was Nadine, your lovely wife, who was the snake in the garden."

Howard laughed. "Well, you know how women are. Never let a man spend too much time getting by with something."

"Amen."

"So, what are we looking at this fine morning, Sergeant Fernandez?"

"Three new items of field gear unrelated to weaponry, sir."

Howard glanced around the inside of the small storage warehouse. There were crates, boxes, and items covered with tarps, the usual.

"Proceed."

"Over here, we have our new tactical computer units, supposedly shockproof backpackers that will plug into the SIPEsuits. Seven pounds, more FlashMem, DRAM, and ROM than a high school computer lab and faster than greased lightning. Ceramic armor and spidersilk webbing, all bullet-resistant and waterproof and like that. I turned one on and dropped it on the floor from chest height, and it still ran fine. Twelve-hour batteries the size of D cells, so you can carry a few days' backup without recharging, no problem."

"Good, about time they came up with something that didn't go down every time somebody sneezed. What else?"

"Right this way. This here is our emergency broadcast jammer, which will supposedly make any radio inside a ten-kilometer circle spew static and nothing else. Doesn't work on LOS infra or ultra headcoms. They say it'd stop KAAY in Little Rock at its peak, but I haven't tested it yet."

"Bad guys use LOS, too."

"What can I say? This is RA stuff. You know how they are."

Howard nodded. Regular Army did have its own whys and wherefores. He'd been there, done that, and was much happier being the head of Net Force's military arm, such as it was. He had expected it to be a lot more quiet than when he was a colonel in the RA, but in the last year or so, it sure had been anything but that. In fact, after his last fracas, he'd been thinking about retiring. He still ached from his wounds when it got chilly, and the idea of not being around to see his son grow up bothered him a lot.

Julio kept talking:

"And under this here cover, we have the toy of the week. Ta-da!" He pulled the lightweight tarp off, revealing what looked like a table with four jointed arms sticking up from it, two in the corners at one end, two more in the middle. The thing had wheels and a closed compartment under it.

"And what is this? A high-tech electric golf cart?"

"No, sir, this is Rocky Scram—that's R-O-C-C-S-R-M, the acronym standing for Remote-Operated, Computer-Controlled Surgical Robotic Module."

Howard frowned. "We talking about a doc-in-the-box?"

"Actually, a surgeon-in-the-box, only this is just the box. You're gonna love this one, it actually might be useful."

"Talk to me."

"Here's the deal. You need a surgical PA, couple nurses, and orderlies. They set this sucker up in a field hospital. Guy comes in, all shot up, needs fixin'. The PA—that's physician's assistant, for those of you who missed the medical personnel lecture—does a triage, examines the guy, and makes a quick diagnosis. They plunk him on the table, get him prepped, and dial up a first-class REMF surgeon, who can be up to a thousand miles away, give or take. He cranks up his unit—that part is over here, come look."

They walked to another covered unit, and Julio removed a tarp from it. There was a chair, a computer screen mounted in front of it on a platform, and some odd-looking appendages on the arms of the chair.

"Your surgeon sits here and slips his fingers into the surgical controls, that's these rings here. He uses his feet on pedals down on the floor, one each, with a freeze pedal in the middle, kind of like a brake."

Julio sat in the chair and slipped his fingers into the jointed ring arrangements. The computer screen lit up. "These control the waldos, those are tools you can connect to those arms on the operating table. Left foot runs the endoscope, which holds your light and your camera. Right foot works various clamps and suction things. The hand tools will hold scalpels, hemostats, suture needles, scissors, and a bunch of other things."

"You're telling me a surgeon can operate on a patient from a thousand miles away using this gadget?"

"Yes, sir, that's what the RA medicos say. The surgeons who qualify have to cut up a bunch of pigs and cadavers and RA soldiers before they let them work on real people. They've repaired bowels, done blood vessel grafts, stitched up torn hearts, all kinds of things. Nurses and the PA assist, just like in a regular OR. RA medicos say a guy good with this toy can pick up number-six BBs and never drop one."

Julio waggled his fingers, and there was mechanical hum from the nearby table as the surgical arms moved around.

"It's all self-contained, battery backup if you can't get a generator going. Wheel it out there, slap 'em on the table, and you cut and paste."

"Good Lord."

"Yessir, I expect He is impressed."

"Downside?"

"Heavy, expensive—million and half a copy—and you need a repair tech who's qualified to service 'em if they break down. Still, RA figures it's cheaper than training and replacing a surgeon who catches a stray round on the way to do his cutting."

"Good point."

"There's a civilian model been around for a while, but it's not so compact, and it ain't portable."

"Amazing."

"Ain't it, though? Now, if the general is through being impressed with modern hardware, I'd like to go catch a nap."

"Go ahead, Sergeant. Oh. Wait. Hold up a second. I got something for you." Howard grinned. He was going to like what he was about to do. He was going to like it a whole lot.

Julio paused, and Howard tossed the small plastic box at him. Julio caught it, started to open it. "Not my birthday. What's the occasion?"

Howard didn't say anything, just kept grinning.

When Julio got the box open, his eyes went wide. "Oh, shit. No!"

"Oh, shit, yes. And we're skipping right over shavetail and going to right to first.

"Congratulations, *Lieutenant* Fernandez."

"You can't do this, John. Gunny'll never let me live it down."

"Already done, Julio. Paperwork is signed, sealed, and delivered."

"John—"

"More money, which you need with a new baby. Plus now you don't have to take orders from your wife. Well, no more than any of the rest of us have to take orders from our wives." Julio's wife was Joanna Winthrop, and a lieutenant in Net Force herself, although she was on extended leave at the moment.

"But . . . but . . . who can you get to replace me?"

"Nobody will be able to replace you, Julio. But there

are some new recruits who can manage a top's chores if you show them how it is done."

Julio shook his head. "I'll be damned."

"No doubt, but at least you can tell the devil you earned your money for part of your career before you got the free ride."

Julio nodded slowly, then looked up. "All right. Thank you, sir."

"Don't look so sour, Julio. Welcome to the officer-and-a-gentleman club. Or at least the officer part of it."

"Yeah, right."

Under the bitching, Howard was pretty sure that Julio was pleased. They'd been working together for more than twenty years, first in the regular army, then in Net Force. Julio had known about Howard's promotion to general before Howard himself had, and there were times when the two of them were practically telepathic. Julio didn't have the educational background of a lot of officers, but when a situation went hot, he was the man you wanted covering your back. He had another few years before he was going to think about retiring, and the higher his grade, the bigger his pension. He was a married man with a baby; he needed it.

"Go take your nap, Lieutenant."

"Yes, sir."

Washington, D.C.

Normally, at seven in the morning, Jay Gridley would be at Net Force HQ, plugged into his computer and making war on the bad guys. He'd be hunting lubefoots who'd dumped the latest ugly virus into the world's e-mail, or searching for clues to some computer fraud, or trying to track down some sicko posting kiddie porn on church web sites. Now and then, there'd be a big shark cruising the virtual waters of the net, like the mad Russian or the crazy Georgia redneck or the British genius who'd been using a quantum computer to try and restore England's lost glory, though those were relatively rare. But a few months ago, Jay had finally met his on-line guru who had been helping him recover from a stroke, an old Tibetan monk named Sojan Rinpoche. And as it turned out, the old man was actually a young and beautiful woman. Saji, she liked to be called, and one thing had led to another, which had led to another, which had led to her lying beside him in the bed.

Now, there were days when he called in sick and never left that bed except to pee.

He giggled.

"What is funny?" Saji asked.

He smiled at her. "You. Me. This. Us."

"What time is it?"

"Who cares?"

"No, you don't, goat-boy. I'm teaching an on-line class this morning."

"You don't have to get up to do that. You can lie right there."

She laughed. "I don't think so. I remember the last time I tried to do that. Somebody kept distracting me."

"You're a master Buddhist, you're supposed to be able to meditate and tune out little distractions."

"Yeah, but the problem was, the little distraction kept getting bigger every time I looked at it."

They both laughed.

"Work is dead. I could stay home. It's totally boring there these days. Seriously."

"Seriously," she said, "no, you can't."

"You are a party pooper."

"Life is full of suffering, haven't you learned that yet?"

Jay rolled out of the bed, scratched his chest, and padded toward the bathroom. "You'll be sorry when I'm gone. You'll finish your class and be all alone in this big old condo, and you'll wish I was here."

"I'll try to be brave."

"You want to shower?"

"Yes. After you leave."

"You don't trust me. I'm hurt."

"I can see that. Go on. I'll cook supper when you get home."

"What, roots and twigs?"

"You said you liked my cooking."

"That was before you threw me out into the cold," he said.

"It's supposed to hit seventy-two today," she said. "Not so cold."

"I was speaking metaphorically."

"Go and shower, Jay."

He grinned at her. Boy, did he like having her around. Really. A lot. More than anything he could think of. He headed for the shower and considered for the hundredth time the proposition he'd been working on in his head for the last couple of weeks. Was it possible to make it permanent? Legally permanent? As in getting married? Would she go for it?

There was only one way to find out, but he was hesitant. What if she said no?

That would be . . . bad.

The hot water began to steam up the bathroom. He called out to Saji: "Hey—?"

"No," she cut him off. "Definitely not."

But he was rinsing the shampoo from his hair when the shower door slid open and Saji followed the draft of cool air in, gloriously naked and grinning.

"Why, Sojan Rinpoche! What are *you* doing here?"

"I came to wash your back is all."

"Uh-huh."

"Turn around."

"Yes, ma'am."

He turned around. She reached out, and her soapy hand began rubbing him.

However, the hand was definitely *not* stroking his *back,* nope, no sir, no *indeedy!*

He laughed, and she laughed with him.

Yep, he was going to be late to work, no two ways about it.

"Hey, I think you missed a spot there."

"I didn't miss it. I was ignoring it. Easy to do, it's so . . . small."

"Ooh. You are a cruel woman. Cruel."

"Suffer, big daddy, suffer. . . ."

3

Robert Drayne looked up from his mixing bench in front of the big picture window as a pair of young women in thong bikinis jogged past on the hard-packed wet sand, just at the water line. No rain today, the sky was clear, the Pacific Ocean a nice blue and fairly calm, and the two honeys were blond and tan and bouncy. Not bad for a Monday. He grinned. He loved this town.

He looked back at the bench. He had a batch ready to time and encapsulate, only six hits, and where the hell was Tad? You didn't want to start the clock ticking and then have the stuff sit on the table for an hour or two. That might cut things a little close. Even with a master such as himself, the timing could get a little tricky, could be an hour either way.

As if in response, the door alarm *ching-chinged* as somebody disarmed it and entered the house.

That had better be Tad. . . .

Drayne dumped a bit of catalyst into the white compound, stirred in the fine red powder so that the resulting

mix started turning pale pink. Drayne worked by sight and
smell, he kept adding catalyst until the right shade was
achieved—a shade somewhere between titty and bubble
gum—and that sharp, cherry-and-almond odor drifted up
and told him it was about right, too.

Ah, there we go. . . .

"About fucking time," Drayne said. There was no real
anger in his voice, just making a comment was all.

"Traffic is bad on the Coast Highway," Tad said by
way of explanation. "The tourists are all slowing down to
look at the house coming down in the mud slide. How's
it coming?"

"Catalyst mixed, as of thirty seconds ago."

Tad looked at his watch.

Drayne grabbed one of the big purple gel caps, a special
run he'd had made three years ago by a guy in Mexico
who was, unfortunately, no longer among the living. Well,
what the hell, he had more than a thousand caps left.
Worry about it when he ran out.

He opened the cap and scooped up the mix with both
halves, expertly judging how much so that he could put
the cap together again without overfilling it. He looked
up and smiled. This was the easy part. The real work was
in the creation and mixing of the various components.
That had to be done in a lab, and the current one was an
RV parked in a dinky burg on the edge of the Mojave
Desert, a couple of hours away from here. By tomorrow,
it would be parked a hundred miles away, the old retired
couple driving it looking about as illegal and dangerous
as a bowl of prunes. In this biz, appearance counted for
a lot. Who'd pull over Ma and Pa Yeehaw in their RV
with Missouri plates for anything but a traffic ticket? And
Ma could talk her way out of that by making a cop think
about his sweet little ole granny. And if the cop got really

horsey, Pa would cap him with the .40 SIG he kept under the seat.

Tad Bershaw was Drayne's age, well, actually, he was a year younger at thirty-one, but he looked fifty, rode hard and put up wet, like Drayne's grandma used to say. Tad was black-haired, skinny, pale, and had dark circles under his eyes, a real heroin-chic kinda guy. He always wore black, even in the middle of summer, long sleeves, long pants, pointy-toed leather boots. And sunglasses, of course. He looked like a vampire or maybe one of the old beatniks, because he also had a little patch of hair under his lip.

Drayne, on the other hand, looked like a surfer, which he had been: tanned, sun-bleached dishwater blond hair, still enough muscle to pass for a gymnast or a swimmer. He had to admit, they made an odd-looking couple when they went out. Not that they went out that often.

Drayne put the finished cap down and picked up another empty. He had enough mix for six. Five for sale and one for Tad. At a thousand bucks each, it wasn't a bad day's work, not bad at all, given that their costs were about thirty-five dollars a cap.

"You heard about the guy in Atlantic City?" Tad asked.

Drayne worked on the third cap. "Olivetti?"

"Yeah."

"No. What happened?"

"Hammer ate him. He ran amok, tore up a casino, beat the shit out of some rent-a-cops and local police before they cooked him. DOA."

Drayne shrugged again. "Too bad. He was a good customer."

"We got a guy coming from NYC says Olivetti referred him. Are we interested?"

Drayne finished the fourth cap. Found one of the special-special empties for number five. "No. If Olivetti is dead, the reference is dead. We don't sell to him."

"I figured," Tad said. "Just checking."

"You shouldn't have to check. You know the deal. A vetted customer vets a newbie, always. First time we get a guy we can't check out, that will be a narc, you got to figure it that way."

"I hear you."

Drayne finished the fifth cap, reached for Tad's empty. "How are you working today's produce?"

"Three off the net, FedEx Same Day as soon as we get the payment transfers to the dissolving account. One is a pickup, three-messenger drop. One is hand-to-hand."

"Who's the hand-to-hand?"

"The Zee-ster."

Drayne grinned. "Be sure to tell him we want tickets to his next premiere."

"Already in the pipe."

"Okay, here you go. Last one is yours, be sure the double-special, that's number five, goes out."

"You're crazy, you know that," Tad said, as he took the caps.

"Yeah, so what else is new?"

The two men smiled at each other.

"What's cold?" Drayne said. "I need to sit on the deck and watch the waves roll in."

"Got a bottle of the Blue Diamond, one of the Clicquot, and one of the Perrier-Jouët in the little fridge. Dunno what's in the garage."

"The Diamonte Bleu, I think," Drayne said. "You want a glass before you take off?"

"I'm not rotting my liver out, thank you."

They laughed again.

"I'm gone."

"See you later," Drayne said.

Tad left, and Drayne went to open a bottle of cham-

pagne. He had three-quarters of a million cash in a suitcase hidden in a floor safe under his bed, another two
hundred and some thousand dollars in a safe-deposit box
in a bank in Tarzana, and five cases of assorted but all
high-quality champagne in the cool room downstairs.

Life was pretty damned good.

Tad swung his souped-up, reconditioned Charger R/T
Drayne had given him out into the road the locals called
the PCH and stomped the gas pedal, heading south toward
Santa Monica. The big motor roared and laid five hundred
miles worth of expensive rubber compound behind it, tires
squealing and smoking. Tad grinned as the car acceler-
ated. No big deal. The radials were good for fifty thousand
miles, and he didn't expect either the car or himself to be
around when the tires' warranty ran out.

He never expected to live past thirty, maybe thirty-five,
max. Depending on how you looked at it, he was either
four years shy or a year overdue for the big sleep, and it
didn't much matter to him which it was. He'd been on
borrowed time for years.

He roared past a white four-runner with out-of-state
plates, a middle-aged couple in the front, and a pair of
big old German shepherd dogs looking out the windows
in the back. Goddamned tourists. He cut sharply in front
of the car, but the tourists were too busy looking at the
ocean to even notice. Dogs were probably smarter than
the people in that car.

That Bobby, now there was a smart one. He was a
certified fucking genius, no shit. IQ way up in Mensa
territory, one sixty, one seventy, something like that,
though you'd never guess he was anything more than a
big ole dumb surfer dude by looking at him. He could
have gone into any kind of legit work and made a mint,
but he had these quirks: One, he hated his old man, who

was a retired FBI agent, and two, the guy he most wanted to be like was some flower-power drug guru from the sixties, a guy named Owsley, who came out of the psychedelic movement. Owsley was so long ago that when he started making LSD, it was still legal. Problem was that he kept making the stuff after it got to be illegal, and got busted, but Bobby thought the sun rose and set in the guy's shadow.

Bobby wanted to be the Owsley of the twenty-teens. An outlaw to the core.

Tad patted his pocket for the fourth time, making sure the five caps were still in there. The other cap—*his* cap—was tucked away in his private stash bottle in the special pocket in his right boot, right next to the short Damascus dagger he carried there.

He lit up a cigarette, inhaled deeply, and coughed. His lungs were bad, never had gotten much stronger after the TB was cured and he got out of the sanitarium in New Mexico, and smoking only made 'em worse, but the hell with it, he wasn't gonna live long enough for cancer to get him anyhow.

The air conditioner blasted the smoke away as he reached for the music player to crank up some volume. Something with a lot of bone-vibrating bass, but none of that techno-rap junk the kids were listening to today.

He glanced at his watch. Still had half an hour before he had to make the first delivery.

He rolled the window down, took a final drag off the cigarette, and thumbed the butt out the window. He couldn't do the Hammer today, too much work, so it would have to be tonight or tomorrow. He knew when he needed to drop to get off. He didn't want to miss that window. Sure, Bobby would make him another, but it would be such a waste there was no way Tad was gonna let it happen.

Tonight, definitely. He could become Thor, and he would swing the Hammer high, wide, and anywhere he damned well pleased.

Oh, yeah—

Some asshole in a low-slung Italian something or the other whipped around Tad, caught rubber as he upshifted, and blew past. Guy looked like a movie star, might even be one: tan, fit in a tank top, designer shades, and a big expensive smile when he flashed his caps to show Tad there were no hard feelings.

The way he felt right now, Tad wouldn't bother chasing the guy. Even if he caught him, the guy would certainly be able to stomp his butt for his trouble.

Come back and see me tonight, pal. See how your SoCal pretty-boy tough-guy act plays when I'm swinging Mjollnir high, wide, and repeatedly. Be a different story then, old son, a whole different story.

4

Michaels was on the way to his office when his virgil blared out the opening chords for "Mustang Sally." He smiled at the little electronic device. Jay Gridley had been at it again, reprogramming the attention call. It was one of Jay's small delights, to do that every so often, usually coming up with some new musical sting Michaels never expected.

He shook his head as he unclipped the virgil—for virtual global interface link—from his belt and saw that the incoming call was from his boss, Melissa Allison, director of the FBI. Her image appeared on the tiny screen as he said, "Answer call," and activated the virgil's voxax control.

"Good morning, Alex."

"Director."

"If you would please stop by my office on your way in, I would appreciate it. Something has come up that I think Net Force needs to address."

"Yes, ma'am, I'm on my way. I'll be there in fifteen minutes."

She looked at something off-screen, then said, "I see you're on the freeway. You might want to take an alternate route. There's an accident a couple of miles ahead of you. Traffic will start backing up pretty fast."

"Thank you," he said. "Discom."

It used to bother him that they could GPS him that way, using the virgil's carrier sig to tell exactly where he was. Then he reasoned if he wanted to keep his whereabouts secret, all he had to do was kill the unit's power. That is, if there wasn't some hidden internal battery that kept the carrier going, even if the thing looked like it was turned off.

He smiled at his thought. Paranoid? Maybe. But stranger things had happened in the U.S. intelligence service, and he wouldn't put anything past certain factions, nothing.

The man was big, he was stark naked, and he had an erection. He walked through the hotel hallway, got to a window at the end, and stopped. The window was closed, one of those that couldn't be opened, and from the skyline visible in the distance, it was fairly high up.

The man put his hands on the window and shoved.

The window exploded outward. The man backed up a few steps, took a short run, and dived through the shattered window, looking like he was diving off the Acapulco cliffs or maybe pretending to be Superman.

Melissa Allison said, "Agent Lee?"

The man who'd been introduced to Michaels as Brett Lee, of the Drug Enforcement Administration, shut off the InFocus projector and his laptop computer, and the image of the broken window faded.

"This was taken by security cameras in the new Sheraton Hotel in Madrid," he said. "The man was Richard

Aubrey Barnette, age thirty, whose Internet company License-to-Steal.com earned him fourteen million dollars last month. He fell twenty-eight stories onto a cab, killing the driver and causing a traffic accident that killed three others and injured five."

Michaels said, "I see. And this is related to the casino owner who trashed his competitor's place of business before being killed by local police?"

"Yes."

"And to the woman who attacked a gang of construction workers who whistled at her and put seven of them into intensive care?"

"Yes," Lee said. "And to others of a similar nature."

Michaels looked at his boss, then at Lee. "And I take it that, since you are DEA, you think drugs were somehow involved?"

Lee frowned, not sure if Michaels was pulling his chain or not. Which, Michaels had to admit to himself, he was, a little. Lee seemed awfully stiff.

Lee said, "Yes, we are certain of that."

Michaels nodded. "Please don't take offense, Mr. Lee, but this concerns Net Force how?"

Lee looked at Allison for support and got it. She said, "My counterpart at DEA has asked for our assistance. Naturally, the FBI and any of its subsidiaries are happy to help in any way we can."

"Naturally," Michaels said, knowing full well that interagency cooperation was more often like competing football teams than the least bit collective. Rivalries among the dozen or so agencies that comprised the intelligence community in the U.S.—everybody from CIA to FBI to NSA to DIA to NRO—were old, established, and more often than not, nobody gave up anything without some quid pro quo. Yes, they were all technically on the same team, but practically speaking, an agency was happy to shine its own star any way it could, and if that included using another agency's shirt to do it, well, that's how the game was played. Michaels had discovered this early in his career, long before he left the field to take over Net Force. And DEA wasn't a major player anyhow, given its somewhat limited mission.

Michaels said, "So how is it that Net Force can do something here DEA can't?"

Lee, a short man with a fierce look, flushed. Michaels could almost see him bite his tongue to keep from saying what he really wanted to say, which was undoubtedly rude. Instead, Lee said, "How much do you know about the drug laws, Commander Michaels?"

"Not much," he admitted.

"All right, let me give you a quick and rough overview. Federal drug regulation in the United States comes under the authority of the Controlled Substances Act—that's CSA—Title II, of the Comprehensive Drug Abuse Prevention and Control Act of 1970, with various amendments since. Legal—and illegal—drugs are put on one of five schedules, depending on what uses have been established for them and on how much potential for abuse they have. Schedule I is reserved for dangerous drugs without medical applications that have a high potential for abuse, Schedule V is for stuff with low abuse potential."

"We're talking about the difference between, say, heroin and aspirin?" Michaels said.

"Precisely. The CSA gets pretty specific about these things."

"Go ahead, I'm still with you."

"In the last few years, there has been a resurgence in so-called designer drugs, that is to say, those that don't slot neatly into the traditional categories. Variations and combinations of things like MDA and Ecstasy and certain new anabolic steroids, like that. The government realized that certain individuals were trying to circumvent the intent of the law by adding a molecule here or subtracting one there to make a drug that wasn't technically illegal, so there is a provision for analog drugs not addressed by the code.

"So, basically, any salt, compound, derivative, optical or geometric isomers, salts of isomers, whatever, based on a drug that is regulated become automatically de facto regulated the moment it is created."

Michaels nodded again, wondering where this was going.

"And in case we have a really clever chemist who comes up with something entirely new and different—which is pretty much unlikely, if not impossible, given the known things that humans abuse—the attorney general can put that on Schedule I on an emergency basis. This is done if the AG determines that there is an imminent hazard to the public safety, there is evidence of abuse, and there is clandestine importation, manufacture, or distribution of said chemical substance.

"Basically, the AG posts a notice in the Federal Register, and it becomes valid after thirty days for up to a year."

Michaels nodded again. He thought Lee was a stuffed shirt, and he decided to give another little tug on his chain. "Very interesting, if you are a DEA agent. Are we getting to a point anytime soon?"

Lee flushed again, and Michaels was fairly certain that if the director hadn't been sitting there, the DEA man would have lost his temper and said or maybe even done something rash. But give him credit, he got a handle on it.

"What it means is, we have some pretty specific tools we can use to get dangerous, illegal drugs off the street. But in this case, we can't use them."

Ah, now that was interesting. "Why not?"

"Because we haven't been able to obtain enough of the drug to analyze it properly. We know what it does: It makes you fast, strong, mean, and sexually potent. It might make you smarter, too, but that's hard to say from our samples, since if they were that smart, they ought not to be dead. We know what it looks like; it comes in a big purple capsule. But we can't make it illegal if we don't know what it is *in* the cap."

Michaels grinned slightly. He could hear that conversation: *"Yes, sir, this is the vile stuff, all right. Could you put it on the list so we can bust the guys who made it? What's in it? Uh, well, we don't exactly know. Can't you, uh, you know, just make big purple capsules illegal temporarily?"*

Be interesting to hear the AG's response to that one.

"And where does Net Force come in?"

"We have evidence that the makers of the drug—they call it Thor's Hammer, by the way—are using the Internet to arrange delivery."

"If the drug isn't illegal, then using the net to distribute it isn't illegal, either," Michaels said.

"We know. But if we can find them, we can damn well ask the miscreants making it to give us a sample. So to speak."

Miscreants? Michaels didn't think he'd ever actually heard that word used in a conversation before. He said, "Ah, pardon me for asking a stupid question, but wouldn't it be easier just to buy some on the street and analyze it?"

"Believe it or not, Commander, that thought did occur to us, it being our job and all. It isn't a common street drug. The cost of it is extremely high, and the sellers are very selective about who they sell it to. So far, none of our agents have been able to make a connection.

"We did manage to seize one capsule after the death of one of the people that we know took the drug. Unfortunately, the chemist in this case is very clever; there is some kind of enzymatic catalyst in the compound. By the time we got the stuff to our lab and analyzed, the active ingredients had all been somehow rendered . . . inert. There is some kind of timing mechanism in the drug. If you don't use it fairly quickly, it turns into a bland, inert powder that doesn't do anything but sit there."

"You can't tell what the drugs were?"

"Our chemists can infer what they were, sure. There are residues, certain telltale compounds, but we can't document for certain what the exact precursor drugs and percentages of each were, because they are essentially gone."

"Huh. That must be frustrating."

"Sir, you do not know the half of it. The common thread running through all the sudden insanities is money. Every one of the twelve people we feel certain died as a result of having ingested this drug is—or was—rich. Nobody on the list made less than a quarter million a year, and some of them made fifteen or twenty times that much."

"Ah." Michaels understood that. You might lean on a criminal street pusher, threaten him, rough him up a little, to get what you wanted from him, but millionaires tended to come equipped with herds of lawyers, and a man with big bucks in the bank didn't get hassled by street cops who wanted to keep their jobs. Not unless the cops had enough to go into court and get a conviction, and even then, they tended to walk with more care. Rich people had recreations denied to the common folk.

"Precisely. So until we can get a sample before the enzyme is added, or get to one fast enough to beat the decomposition, we're stuck. We need your help."

Michaels nodded. Maybe the guy wasn't that bad. In his place, he could understand how he might feel. And things around Net Force were as slow as he had ever seen them. "All right, Mr. Lee. We'll see if we can't run your dope dealers to ground."

Lee nodded. "Thank you."

5

Toni smiled at the UPS man as he left—he was late to-day—then took the latest packages into the garage. Alex had told her she could have half the workbench, though she only needed maybe a quarter of it, and she had already started putting her stuff there. So far, she had the mag-nifying lamp set up, the alcohol burner and wax cauldron, a couple tubes of lampblack oil paint, and some rags and cleaning supplies. There wasn't really much else left she needed. The new packages should have the pin vises, some assorted sewing needles, lens paper, lanolin hand cleaner, and a couple of X-Acto knives and some blades. Plus the jeweler's special wax and some polishing com-pound. She already had some fake-ivory slabs, some old piano keys, and some little rectangles of micarta, which looked like real ivory but was much harder. She didn't need the heavy-duty saws and buffing wheels, Alex had a Dremel tool that would work for polishing small stuff. And while the stereomicroscope like the one her teacher used was really neat, she couldn't justify spending eight or nine hundred dollars on it—not unless she got to the point where she was selling pieces, which would probably not ever happen—especially given she wasn't sure she even wanted to try that.

Toni had never thought of herself as having much artistic talent. She'd done okay in art courses in school, could draw a little, but according to Bob Hergert's online VR class, while being a world-class artist wouldn't hurt, it wasn't absolutely necessary. Given the wonders of the modern computer age, there was a lot technique could do to make up for talent. And given what she'd learned so far, you'd be able to fool a lot of people into thinking you knew what you were doing when you didn't.

She opened the packages, removed the tools and supplies, and set them out. Being pregnant wasn't at all like she'd thought it was going to be. Sure, she'd heard about morning sickness and mood swings, but the reality of those things was something else. And it wasn't as if she were really a whale, not at five months, but she'd always been in shape, her belly flat and tight, her muscles firm, and having to lie around and watch herself balloon up was, well, it was scary. Having something to do that needed concentration and skill, like scrimshaw, might be just the ticket to help her get past this. The morning sickness—which lasted almost all day and any time she was around any food more spicy than dry soda crackers—had finally stopped. Supposedly, the hormone swings got better after the sixth month.

Supposedly.

She had some ideas of what she might like to try first, and for that she needed to go back to her computer. There were lots of places to find pictures in the public domain, and if those weren't good enough, lots of places where you could license an image for personal use for a small fee. Later on, if she got better at it, she could try some freehand drawings of her own, but at first, she wanted to keep it simple.

Toni looked at her corner of the workbench. The rest of it was covered with Alex's tools and car parts, all laid out neatly. He was much more orderly than she was about such things. So far, her investment in scrimshaw supplies had run less than what it cost Alex for a good set of wrenches. If it turned out to be a total waste of her time, at least she wouldn't be out much money.

She sighed. Before she sat down at the computer and went shopping on-line, she needed to go pee again. And that, she understood, was not going to get better as her pregnancy progressed. She sure hoped having Alex's son was worth all this aggravation.

John Howard bent from the waist and tightened the laces on his cross-trainers, finishing with the double-loop runner's knot that theoretically kept the laces from coming untied. Finished, he straightened, bent backward and stretched his abdominals, then shook his arms back and forth to loosen them.

Normally, he ran at the base or around the Net Force compound, but today he felt like taking a tour of his own neighborhood. It was warm for early October, and muggy, so he wore running shorts and a tank top, though he did have a fanny pack holding his virgil, his ID, and a small handgun—a little Seecamp .380 double-action auto. The tiny pistol made the Walther PPK look like a giant, it only weighed maybe eleven or twelve ounces and was awfully convenient if you were wearing summer clothes or work-out gear. True, the .380 wasn't exactly an elephant-stopper; the gun didn't have any sights, liked only one brand of ammo, and it tended to bang your trigger finger pretty good when it recoiled. No way it compared with his primary side arm, the Phillips & Rogers Medusa, but it did fulfill the first rule of a gunfight: Bring a gun. Point it at somebody in your face with a knife or a broken bottle and pull the trigger four or five times, and it certainly would offer them major incentive to back off. With the fanny pack strapped on tightly enough so it wouldn't bounce around much, it was doable. He used to carry a little can of pepper spray to discourage loose dogs, but realized that if he stopped running and said "Bad dog! Go lie down!" in a loud voice, the dog would stop, frown, and leave. At least they had so far.

A bit more limber, Howard started to jog up the street.

The leaves were falling—they'd all be down by Halloween, first good wind that came along any time now would finish 'em—and while the sun was warm, there was that subtle difference between spring and fall, that sense of impending winter.

He passed old man Carlson working in his yard, using the blower to herd leaves into piles. The old man, eighty if he was a day, smiled and waved. Carlson was a tanned, leathery old bird who was the ultimate Orioles fan. He'd retired after forty years with the Post Office, and there wasn't a street in the district he couldn't locate for you.

Howard reached the corner and turned right, planning to loop in and out of the cul-de-sacs that fed the main road through the neighborhood, staying on the sidewalk and ducking low, overhanging trees.

Tyrone had called today from his class trip to Canada. He was going to be gone for another ten days, two weeks in all, on a visit for his international relations class, something new at his school. Howard thought it was a good idea, getting to know other cultures. Better than learning it the Army's way. He smiled, remembering the old slogan his first top kick had posted over his desk when he'd first joined up: "Join the Army and See the World! Travel to exotic, unusual locales! Learn about other cultures!

Meet diverse and interesting people—and kill them."

He picked his pace up a little, stretching out, getting into a longer stride and rhythm. Just inside his breath, barely.

The scars were formed up pretty good where he'd had surgery after the shooting in Alaska. Pretty much nothing hurt most of the time—well, no more than usual after he worked out—but the memories hadn't faded at all. Being out in the middle of nowhere, exchanging gunfire with some real bad men, giving better than he'd gotten, but almost dying—those kinds of memories didn't go away in a few months. Every firefight—and he hadn't had that many—was as clear in his mind as the day or night it had happened. The thought that he might have bled to death in the woods and been eaten by scavengers wasn't so horrifying in itself. Hell, he was a professional soldier, getting killed went with the territory. But dying and leaving his son, just hitting his teens on his way to manhood, that bothered Howard more than it ever had. All it took was a real possibility he might actually buy the farm. Before, he'd been lucky. Never made it to a real war, and when he finally started seeing some action in Net Force, the bullets had zipped here and there, missing him. Julio had taken a round in the leg during the recovery of the stolen plutonium from the sons-of-whoever. Some of his troops had eaten frags from a mine or bullets from the mad Russian's hit man, Ruzhyó, the former *Spetsnaz* killer. Intellectually, he knew it was just chance and maybe a little skill that he'd never gotten hit; emotionally, he'd felt invulnerable, at least to a degree. Like God was watching over him because he was worthy. Yeah. Until that long shot in the darkness had plowed into him. A round from a handgun at rifle distance had killed that feeling of being bulletproof, oh, yes, indeed, it had.

Even Achilles had his heel, and waking up in a hospital

full of tubes did make a guy stop and consider the idea
he wasn't gonna live forever.

And while he wasn't afraid to go into battle—at least
he didn't think so—he didn't want to die and leave his
wife and son. They had become more precious to him
when he'd realized he might lose them. He believed in
the Kingdom of Heaven, and he tried to live his life in a
moral and upright manner, but going there wasn't at the
top of his to-do list for this year.

He opened up a little more on the run, starting to
breathe through his mouth more heavily now, as he
looped into the next street over from his and headed for
the circle at the end.

He remembered another joke his father had told him:

"So the preacher stands up in front of the congregation
and says, 'How many of you want to go to Heaven?'

"And all the hands in the church except Brother
Brown's go up.

"And the preacher looks at Brother Brown, who was
known to drink a little even of a Sunday morning, and he
says, 'Brother Brown! Don't you want to go to Heaven
when you die?'

"And Brother Brown says, 'When I die? Well, sure,
Reverend.'

"And the preacher says, 'Then, how come you didn't
raise your hand?'

"And Brother Brown says, 'Well, I thought you was
gettin' up a busload to go *now*.' "

He looped around the circle and headed back up toward
the main street. A toy poodle in a fenced yard raced back
and forth inside, barking wildly at him. *Fish bait,* his
Daddy would call it. *A waste of dog space.*

He could, Howard knew, become an armchair general,
an REMF who directed operations at a distance. Net Force
would prefer it that way, and probably nobody would

think less of him for it, not those who had been on ops with him before, anyway. But sending a man somewhere he wasn't willing to go himself didn't seem right, never had.

That left the other option, which was to retire. He could muster out with his current rank of general, draw a fair retirement, and get a job consulting somewhere, teaching, whatever. Probably do better moneywise than he was doing now. And be a lot more certain of being around when his son graduated from high school, from college, got married, and brought home grandchildren. Sure that was ten, fifteen years away, maybe, but he didn't want to miss it. And he didn't want to leave Nadine. If something happened to him, he'd always told her to remarry, find a good man, because she was too precious to waste away alone. And he meant it, too, but on a real, deep level, he had to admit to himself that the idea of Nadine laughing and loving another man wasn't at the top of his list of fun thoughts, either.

But he was a soldier. A professional warrior. This was what he did, who he was, and he liked it.

So he had to puzzle this out. It was important. Not easy, maybe, but something he had to do.

He picked up his pace again, now close to top speed for his run. He tried to get in four miles a session, at least four or five times a week, and while he was past the days when he could run 'em in five or even six minutes a mile, he could still manage six and a half or seven minutes.

That is, if he didn't get to thinking so hard he forget to keep the speed up.

Run, John. Think later.

Malibu, California

Tad Bershaw drove back to the beach house, poking along, in no hurry now. He had made his deliveries, collected the money, and decided what the hell and taken the purple cap half an hour ago. It would be another few minutes before it started to come on full force, but even now he was getting patterns, geometric overlays of complicated, pulsing grids on everything. That was from the psychedelic components of the drug. It made driving real interesting.

Bobby was cagey about his chem, he never told *any-body* exactly what was in it, but Bershaw had sampled enough illegal stuff over the years to have some pragmatic knowledge about such things.

There was some kind of MDMA/Ecstasy analog in the Hammer's alloy, with maybe a bit of mescaline; the body rushes got pretty intense an hour or so in, and just *breathing* was orgasmic when it got to circulating.

His experiences were not based on any formal knowledge of chemistry, but he knew it when he felt it. Though it didn't really matter, he had poked at it mentally a few times, what he thought Bobby had created. The psychedelics—*entheogens*, Bobby called those—for sure. That would be the MDMA, mescaline, or LSD, or maybe even some psilocybin from magic mushrooms. Maybe all four. That gave you that sense of being in contact with your inner self and loving the world and all, *entactogenesis* and *empathogenesis*, Bobby called them. Also picked up the sensory input, made everything feel really, really intense.

It had smart drugs in it, he knew that, because he was quicker, sharper, able to make choices better when the Hammer was at full pound, no question. He didn't know much about nootropics, stuff like deprynl, adrafinil, provigil, shit like that, but Bobby did, and he knew how to tweak 'em for an immediate response.

For sure it had some kind of speed—cylert, ritalin, dex, maybe; some tranq to balance it so you got the fast mind but not bad jitters. It definitely had painkiller in it, or a way to kick in the body's own opiates, and Tad guessed some kind of animal tranq and steroid mix, though he didn't see how those would do much in the short run. And something like Viagra was in it, too, because it gave you a hard-on that wouldn't quit. The Zee-ster once took six women to bed while tripping, and none of them could walk the next day. Supposedly made women horny, too.

Past that, Bobby definitely had some secret ingredients about which Tad knew zip. He knew what they did to him, but not why or how.

The total combination was synergistic—that meant more than the sum of its parts—and the bottom line was, it didn't really matter how it did what it did, only that it *did* do it.

There was a bright flash of orange to Bershaw's left but, when he glanced over that way, no cause for it. He grinned. Yeah, he was coming on. Hallucinations, real hallucinations you could talk to and have them answer back, he'd never had those while riding the Hammer, but light flashes, visual distortions, little shifts in reality, those were par for the course. Your motor ran at full speed, no governor and no idle.

He took a deep breath, and chills frosted him all over, despite the still-warm late afternoon Santa Ana wind blowing in through the open window.

Hoo, what a rush!

Seventeen times he had swung Thor's hammer, and not once a bad trip. One in five or so went bonkers, like the guy in the casino. Something in their body chemistry maybe, or the way their brains were hardwired, Bobby didn't know which, but whatever it was, Tad didn't have it. Seventeen times he had become more than he was, practically turned into a superhuman. Stronger, faster, smarter, pain-free, fatigue-free, a guy who could walk into the local kung fu school and kick its collective ass.

And, oh, yeah, there was the sex, though that never seemed to call to him much. Yeah, he got the iron woody and all, but he never seemed to have time to put it into anybody, too much else to *do* to lie down and be still . . . or relatively still.

Though right at the moment, he felt pretty mellow, the desire to shuck the car and get physical was ahead, he knew. Maybe he'd go for a walk on the beach after it got dark. Or a swim. He was usually a crappy swimmer, but once he'd swum out half a mile or so and back without any problem with the riptide or anything. He'd been look- ing for a shark; he'd had a kitchen knife in his hand, and he wanted to see if he could take a shark out with it. Hadn't found one, which was probably good. Away from the Hammer, you knew you had limits. Swinging it, you didn't. But hell, maybe he could have sliced Jaws up into cat food. Who could say?

Another rush enveloped him, and he was glad the house wasn't too far away. It wasn't that he couldn't maintain control enough to drive during the early stages of the trip 'cause he could, but it took too much effort, and he didn't want to waste effort on piddly shit. He would get home, shuck the car, and go outside. After all, outside was only a bigger inside, right?

He grinned. It was like the time he realized that choc- olate wasn't the opposite of vanilla. They were just two different flavors. That had hit him like the secret of the universe. Shit, for all anybody knew, that *was* the secret of the universe.

6

Michaels was almost home and wishing he was already there. What he had in mind was a nice, cold beer, his bare feet propped up to watch the news hour, maybe falling asleep on the couch. Might make a sandwich, if he felt up to it. He was tired. It had been a long day, made longer because it was dull and mostly uninteresting, and just as he was about to leave, they'd had a small crisis over some hacker who was flooding every church web page his autopost-bot could find with obscene pictures taken during an orgy in a Thai whorehouse.

There was a threat to the republic.

Graffiti had certainly changed from simple spray-paint tags on the fence next to the local drugstore when it went electronic, but it was still stupid. Who gained anything by such foolishness? Did the idiot posting think people were going to see the pictures and abandon their faith? Run screaming into the streets?

No, probably he just thought it was funny. Which right off indicated a somewhat retarded sense of humor.

The church fathers and mothers were not the least amused, of course, and there were plenty of them in high enough government positions to get Net Force's attention in a hurry, including the president himself, and what was worse, a minor annoyance suddenly became a priority project.

Find whoever was doing this and stop him. Now.

Turning the other cheek didn't apply when the cheek was below the waist, so it seemed.

The e-tagger called himself The Tasmanian Devil, and as it turned out, that was a major clue. Net Force ops traced the postings to the north coast town of Devonport, Tasmania, overlooking the cool waters of the Bass Strait. The tagger was clever, he'd found some meltware that got him through a lot of firewalls, but he slipped up. His anonymous reposter was six months out of date, and in this business, six months was ancient history. Jay Gridley's team ran the cable sig to a house, informed the local constabulary, and they went round and knocked on the door. There they found a sixteen-year-old kid running a six-year-old IMac.

The boy was the son of a local minister, which probably explained a lot.

It had taken a while, and when it was done, Michaels called several heavyweights and told them they could rest easy, then left the building.

He was only a mile or so away from home when his virgil came to life.

He was tempted to ignore it, but it might be Toni, so he pulled the device from his belt and looked at the ID sig.

It was blank.

Michaels frowned. FBI com-watchware was supposed to circumvent any commercial ID blocker, so the only people who could reach out and touch him at this number without him knowing who they were would have to be somebody with federal-level blockers. He thumbed the connect button.

"Yes?"

"Commander Michaels, this is Zachary George, with the National Security Agency. Good evening. I hope I'm not interrupting your dinner?" The voice was smooth, even, just deep enough to sound authoritative. There was no picture transmission. The tiny screen was blank.

"Not yet. What can I do for you, Mr. George? Oops, can you hold on a second? I have another call."

This was not true, but it gave Michaels a few seconds to key in a trace, which he did. He didn't like not knowing to whom he was talking.

"Sorry about that. Go ahead."

"Sir, we understand your agency is involved in a joint investigation with the DEA. We'd like to speak to you about this, if we could."

"You can set up an appointment with my assistant, Mr. George. Although I'm not sure why NSA would have any interest in such a thing if it was so . . . and I wouldn't confirm it over the com in any event."

The incoming diode lit, that would be his trace. He tapped it, and a number scrolled up on the view screen, with an ID: George, Zachary, National Security Agency. Well. At least that much was true.

"I understand your reluctance, sir, and I will be happy to explain it all to you when I see you. This was just a courtesy call to let you know of our interest." There was a pause. "Ah. I see you've traced the call and confirmed my ID. Excellent. I'll be contacting your assistant for an appointment at your earliest convenience, sir. Thank you. Discom."

He went away. Michaels frowned again. What did NSA want with the drug investigation? And why was their stealthware better than the FBI's, to know they had been traced? He was going to have to talk to Jay about that. Maybe he could come up with a better program.

He dropped the virgil onto the seat and shook his head. Two more blocks to go.

Beer. Couch. Television. Soon . . .

Not that easy, of course. When he walked in, Toni was all aglow over her new hobby, so of course he had go into the garage and admire her toys.

Well, what the hell, it made her happy, that made him happy. With all the mood swings lately, anytime she was smiling was good, better make the most of it.

". . . and this is the pin vise, see, you put the needle in here and twist it, like so, and it holds it. I glued a fishing weight—this lead ball here—onto the end to give it some heft, so when I stipple, I won't have to use so much muscle."

"Such a clever girl," he said, smiling.

She smiled back at him. "And look here, this is the magnifier. . . ."

He listened with half an ear, not being that interested in the artwork per se. When she ran down, he smiled again. She couldn't drink, given her pregnancy and all, but maybe she could take some vicarious pleasure out of watching him enjoy a cold one.

"Not yet," she said.

"Huh?"

"You need to work out first. Do your *djurus.*"

Michaels wanted to say a bad word, but he wisely refrained. Toni wasn't just his wife, after all, but also his *silat* teacher, and that was the hat she had just put on. If he tried to beg off, that would be bad.

"Oh, yeah, sure, that's what I meant. *After* I work out."

That didn't fool her for a second, she was way too

sharp, but hey, you had to give it a shot. Might catch her dozing.

She said, "It takes a few thousand repetitions to get the moves down, Alex. Latest scientific research I read says somewhere in the fifty- to one-hundred-hour range."

He did the math mentally. "So, for eighteen *djurus*, I need to practice for nine hundred to eighteen hundred hours before I get them? At thirty minutes a day, that works out to about one hundred and eighty hours a year, so we're talking about ten years?"

"Well, to get them really smooth, it'll take maybe another five years."

"I'll be retired by then."

"Good. Give you more time to practice."

He laughed. "You are a slave driver."

He went to the bedroom, shucked his street clothes, and put on a pair of sweats and a T-shirt. He didn't need any shoes since he was inside. He went back and sat down in the living room and began to do some basic yoga exercises Toni had showed him. Stretching was a luxury you wouldn't get in a real fight, but for somebody over forty, it was better to do it before working out than not. A street fight might last ten seconds; a workout was gonna run thirty minutes to an hour, depending on how ambitious you were, and the older he got, the longer it took for a strain to heal.

As he was doing spinal twists, Toni wandered back in from the garage. "So, how was your day?"

Given that she had been his assistant and knew as much about his work as he did—more in some areas—it was natural for her to ask and just as natural for him to tell her.

"Dead calm," he said. "Except for a flurry at the end with a kid hacker posting porno."

"Oh, boy. And me here missing it all."

"Well, there were a couple of things mildly interesting." He told her about the drug stuff and about the cryptic call from the NSA guy.

She watched him, said, "Keep your back straight when you turn." Then, "So what does Jay say about tracking down the dope dealer?"

"He said it was going to be a bitch. Apparently, drug sales over the Internet have always been a problem. Back in the early days, a lot of it was technically illegal but not prosecuted."

"How so?"

"Well, suppose you were seventy years old and living on social security in North Dakota or maybe south Texas. If you got sick and needed medicine, a prescription might cost, say, fifty bucks a bottle. Suppose you had to take two or three bottles a month for years. That could cut way into your food budget. So you'd hop a bus to Canada or to Mexico, where the same drug might cost sixteen or eighteen dollars. A local doc writes you a scrip based on your existing one from the U.S., and even with twenty bucks for that, you still come out way ahead in the long run."

"Yeah?"

"So with the net and cheap home computers or access through cable TV or whatever, you don't even have to take the bus ride. You log onto a site, order what you need, maybe answer a couple of questions over the wire to keep things more or less legal in Canada or Mexico, and your prescription shows up in your mailbox in a day or two, assuming you are dealing with a reputable outfit."

"All the way down," she said. "And keep your knees straight."

He chuckled. "Being pregnant has made you mean, woman."

"Oh, you think so? Just wait. So the DEA didn't leap

all over these folks for importing medicine illegally?"

"Ha! Think about that for a second. Here's somebody's little old granny on a pension who's got a bad heart after working forty years teaching grammar school kids. Would *you* want to be the DEA guy in charge of arresting her for buying her nitroglycerin or whatever across the border to save enough money so she doesn't have to eat dog food? Imagine how many federal prosecutors would want to hop on *that* career bandwagon. The press would swarm you like a cloud of starving locusts. Can't you just see the headlines? 'Grandma Busted for Heart Meds!' "

"It could be a political problem," she said.

"Oh, yeah, it could. Then there are the drugs that are legal in other countries but not approved by the FDA, which, according to Jay, is another whole can of worms. Let's say you want to take Memoril, one of the new smart drugs that improves your short-term memory something like seventy percent. The FDA is still out on that one, but it's been legal in most of Europe for a couple of years. So, you log onto a web page in Spain, give them your credit card number, and order a hundred tabs. A few days later, you get a package from Scotland that looks like a birthday gift from your Uncle Angus, and inside is your drug, made by a pharmaceutical company in Germany. And all of this is perfectly legal in Spain, Scotland, and Germany, and it's not their concern about laws in the U.S.

"If Customs happens to guess what's in the package, they'll confiscate it, because technically it is illegal, but it's a gray area. If you went to Spain and got the stuff from a doctor there, you could bring it home for your own personal use. What's the difference if it comes by mail or you carried it home in your pocket? It's *malum prohibitum*—bad because it's illegal—not *malum in se*— bad in itself."

"When did *you* start speaking Latin?"

"Since I asked our lawyers about all this."

"Watch your shoulder."

"And then we get to the illegal stuff, which is easier to prosecute, assuming you know what it is and know for sure that it *is* illegal, which is the problem here. Big purple caps aren't illegal in themselves."

"Ipso facto," she said.

"Talk to me about Latin," he said. "So, there you have it. It's really the FDA's problem, only the boss made it mine. She probably owes somebody over there a favor, and this is it. And the NSA listens to everything on the air or over the wire, so I can understand how they know about it, but I don't see why it should interest them. Fortunately, I have plenty of time to think about it, things being slow. I wish you were still working there. It would be more interesting. We all miss you at the office. Me most of all."

"You're loose enough. Up. Do your *djurus*. You'll feel better after you work out."

He came to his feet. That was true. He almost always did feel better afterward. It was the damned inertia that was so hard to overcome sometimes. Good that he had Toni here to prod him. Among her many other virtues.

7

Malibu, California

Naked, Drayne padded into the kitchen to get the rest of the bottle of champagne from the freezer. He really ought to get a little fridge for the bedroom, save him a walk.

Life was *so* hard.

Not that the girl would miss him. What was her name? Misty? Bunny? Buffy? Something like that. He'd say, "Honey," and call it good. She was out, and she ought to sleep pretty hard, too, given the athletic encounters and the first bottle of bubbly they'd just split. She was an actress—all of them around here were actresses—early twenty-something, tight, fit, perky. A natural redhead, he had discovered to his delight, once the itty-bitty black silk bikini undies had come off.

Ah, youth, nothing like it.

He'd picked her up at the gym, which is where he found most of the girls he brought home. Jocks tended to be fitter, had less risk of disease, and were able to play longer before they wore out. He didn't like his women with too much muscle, so he stayed away from the hard-core lifters, but there was always a Misty-Bunny-Buffy working the aerobic bikes and the light weights, and it never took long for him to make a connection with one. He wasn't bad-looking, and the twenty-thousand-dollar diamond ring and drop-top Mercedes two-seater usually impressed them. He even had some business cards that said he was an independent movie producer—Bobby Dee Productions—and that would usually be enough to clinch the contact if they were about to walk away. "Oh, sorry we couldn't get together. Here's my card. If you are in Malibu, give me a call sometime."

Sex was always available, and not just to movie guys in this town. And Mama Drayne's little boy Bobby had more than a little endurance in that area, and without any chemical assistance, either—well, unless you counted good champagne. He didn't use the drugs he made, never had. Maybe someday when he got old and couldn't get it up anymore, he'd whip together a batch of some custom-made dick hardener, but frankly, he didn't think that was ever gonna happen. He'd never once had a failure in that particular arena, thank you very much, and four or five times a night was nooo problem. Then again, he was not thirty-five yet. Maybe when you hit sixty or seventy it *was* different.

As he turned from the hallway toward the kitchen, he saw Tad standing on the beach, staring at the ocean.

Drayne shook his head. Tad rode the Hammer, crazy fucker that he was. It was gonna kill him someday, no question. He was in such crappy shape, it was a miracle it hadn't killed him already, should have long since blown a blood vessel in the man's brain, stroked him blind, crippled, and stupid, not necessarily in that order. A night running with Thor was worth a week's recovery for somebody in pretty good physical condition, maybe more. Tad ought not to be able to recover at all, and yet he had swung the Hammer more than anybody alive and some-how managed to keep breathing. Of course, Tad had a portable pharmacy he gobbled, snorted, or shot up after he came off a Hammer trip. Probably more drugs than blood circulating in him at any given time. Somehow, he had managed to stay a step ahead of the reaper. Pretty damned amazing.

Drayne opened the freezer, pulled the second bottle of champagne out. He lifted it to his lips, thought better about that, and grabbed one of the chilled glasses on the freezer rack. Drinking it from the bottle was for barbarians. The bubbles didn't get released.

Had to be civilized about this, didn't we?

He poured the icy wine into the icy glass, watched the liquid turn to foam and fountain up, then slowly begin to settle down.

Time waiting for champagne bubbles to settle didn't count.

Out on the beach, near the water line, three hulking big jocks ran past, working on their aerobic fitness. Drayne glanced at Tad, worried. If Tad decided he didn't like the way the guys looked, he'd go for them, and big and strong as they were, they wouldn't have a prayer, Tad would twist them up like soft pretzels, if that's what he felt like.

But the trio jogged past, and if Tad even saw them, Drayne couldn't tell it from here. Watching Tad when something like this happened was like watching a Roman emperor. Thumb up or thumb down, and nobody knew which it'd be.

He shook his head. Sooner or later, Tad was going to step wrong and draw the law's attention. It had been a while since he'd done it last, and fortunately, it hadn't led back to Drayne that time. Plus, the house was clean, that wasn't a problem, he never kept anything illegal on hand for longer than it took to mix it and get it out again, but he didn't need the local deputies knocking on his door and asking about the crazy asshole dressed in black who suddenly turned into the Incredible Hulk and laid waste to the beach. Low profile was the way to go. If they didn't know about you, they wouldn't be able to bother you.

He finished filling up the glass, topped it off, and put the bottle back into the freezer. He walked to the deck, sipping at the cold champagne. Yeasty, with a hint of apple, good finish, no bitter aftertaste. Not the best, but after five or six glasses, there was no point in wasting the best; you couldn't taste the really exotic flavors and subtle stuff anyhow. As long as it was good enough not to irritate your stomach, that was all you needed for the second bottle.

There was a guy they called the Wine Nazi, up just north of San Francisco, way out a winding road in Lucas Valley, who made the best champagne on earth. Grand Brut, dry as the Sahara, and he sold *futures* in it, you bought what you could afford, he would call you when it was damned well ready, and if you didn't like it, too fucking bad. Worked out to about five hundred bucks a bottle—if you bought a case—and you couldn't buy more than one case a year. Six thousand bucks a case, and that was the nonvintage stuff. Sometimes it took eighteen months for the last batch to ripen to his satisfaction. The *really* good stuff ran two grand a bottle, and you had to get on a waiting list for that, too. Drayne's name hadn't gotten to the top of that list yet, but next year, he was pretty sure it would.

Drayne had done a tour there once. The winery was tiny, a hole-in-the-wall place, and before he was done, the Wine Nazi had him climbing up on barrels to taste the whites and reds right out of the casks, sucked it out with a long rubber tube and dribbled into a glass. And after a few sips of that, the guy had him helping hand-riddle the champagne bottles. They had to be turned so much every day, so the silt would settle and all.

Drayne was an appreciative audience. The guy was a certified genius when it came to wine, no question, and the champagne was the best of the lot. Of course, the Wine Nazi wouldn't let him call it champagne, since technically that meant it had to come from that particular region of France, so he called it sparkling wine. Even though it made the average good vintage of the French stuff taste like stale ginger ale.

That was the stuff you saved for special occasions, definitely first-bottle, and not something you shared with Misty-Bunny-Buffy just to get laid. He had six bottles left, and six months left before he could buy another case. If he was lucky. So he had to ration it, one bottle a month, no more, and even then, he might have to wait. Terrible situation.

He grinned. He sure had a lot to complain about, didn't he? Living in a big house on the beach in Malibu, good-looking naked woman in his bed, a shitload of money, six bottles of the best champagne anybody in *this* town had. Hell, it really didn't get much better than that, did it?

Since it didn't look like Tad was going to go ballistic and destroy the neighborhood, maybe he should go back to bed and nudge Honey awake. He was sure he could think up something new for them to try.

Yep. That seemed like an *excellent* idea. He lifted his glass in a toast to his own cleverness. *Hi, ho, Bobby. Away!*

He headed back toward the bedroom.

Tad felt the power.

It coursed through him like an electric current, filling him with pulsing flashes of juice, set him humming like a dynamo at full spin.

He was a god out here, deciding the fate of all who passed. At his whim, he could strike them down, become Shiva the destroyer, changing the very configuration of the planet with a mere wave of his hand. At his whim, which was how gods operated, far as he could tell.

He took a breath, and the sensation made orgasm seem pale in comparison. The thrills ran through his entire body, he could feel it everywhere at once, in his hands, his body, even his toes. *Man. What a rush!*

He was a god. Able to do anything he wished.

And what he wished to do right now was . . . walk. To stride down the beach, to pass among his people, disguised as a reedy, tubercular man all dressed in black, but beyond comprehension to mere mortals.

As far above them as a man was above an ant.

They couldn't know. He felt sorry for them, being so weak, so stupid. So pitiful.

He started to walk, feeling the sand like a living thing under his boots, hearing the soft *chee-chee-chee* squeaks it made with each step. He was aware of the evening breeze touching his skin, the smell of salt and iodine from the sea, the taste of the very air. He was aware of *every*-thing, not just on this beach, but radiating out to galaxies a billion light-years from where he walked. It was all his territory, all of it. If he reached up his arms, he could encompass it all in his grasp.

He laughed.

Ahead, somebody finished up a Frisbee game and headed for their towels. A beach volleyball game wound down. Traffic roared past on the highway, the cars and trucks taking on the aspect of dragons: fearsome creatures in their element, but creatures who knew better than to cross his path. He was Tad the Bershaw, and any being with enough sense to see him would know he was to be feared.

He walked through his kingdom, feeling for the moment benevolent in his omnipotence. He would suffer them to live.

For now, anyway.

Jayland/Quantico, Virginia

Jay Gridley had always been a man who enjoyed moving fast. When he slipped into his sensory gear and the net blossomed before him, infinite in its possibilities, he had always chosen speed as his vehicle. If he drove, it was a Viper, a rocket with wheels that smoked everything else on the road. Sometimes he flew—rocket packs, jets, copters, whatever. He created virtual scenarios that he zipped through like rifle rounds, clean, fast, slick as a tub full of grease.

Oh, now and then he would do period. He'd make a Western town and mosey into town on a horse. Or a boat. But getting there in a hurry was his pleasure, and most of his programs reflected that. Getting business done had always been about getting it *done,* not about the trip.

Not today. Today, Jettin' Jay was out for a stroll, through an Eastern garden. It wasn't strictly accurate, his program, it had mixed elements in it: Right where he was at the moment stood a Japanese tea house with a little brook running past it. Just ahead was a Zen garden, three rocks in a bed of raked sand. But over to the left was a Shaolin temple, monks out front doing kung fu, and to the right, a second temple, straight out of Bangkok, with traditional Siamese dancers moving like snakes. The Taj Mahal was past that, and there were even some pyramids off a ways behind him. It was a veritable theme park of Eastern religious thought.

The sun shined brightly, the day was warm with a little breeze, and the smell of jasmine and sandalwood mixed with roses and musk.

Welcome to the land of the happy, nice people, Jay. Your kind of place.

He smiled, walking slowly, not in the least bit of a hurry. What he wanted was here somewhere, but you know what? He would get to it when he got to it.

To be honest, he hadn't exactly embraced the tenets of Buddhism. The eightfold this, or the four ways of that. But there was an energy about what Saji did and how she related to it that he did find worth thinking about. He'd never considered himself much of anything, other than a computer jock, but this go-with-the-flow stuff—that was Taoism rather than Buddhism, right?—well, here of late, it had a whole bunch of appeal.

Thank Sojan Rinpoche for that, along with her other, more earthy talents.

A bee flew past, buzzing, looking for pollen.

Ah, yes, what could be better than a stroll in the cosmic gardens—

"Hey, Jay, you awake?" came the somewhat dissonant voice, intruding on his scenario.

Jay dropped out of VR, and was at once back in his office at Net Force. Standing in the doorway were two coworkers, Alan and Charlie.

"That door is supposed to be locked," Jay said, mildly irritated.

"Yep, and if you hadn't wanted somebody good enough to rascal the sucker, you'd have hired somebody other than us," Charlie said. He waved his key card. "You ought to change the codes every year or two, Jay."

"Would that do any good?"

"About as much good as me changing the codes on my bike did," Alan said.

Jay laughed. He had broken into the comp on Alan's fuel-cell scooter and programmed it so it wouldn't go faster than nine miles an hour. Well, that was the old Jay. He was a new man these days. No more sophomoric games.

"C'mon, we're going to Pud's for burgers and beer."

Jay spoke without thinking. "Nah, I'll pass. I'm giving up eating flesh."

Both Alan and Charlie stared for maybe two seconds before they cracked up. They laughed. They laughed harder. They fucking *howled*.

"Flesh? *Flesh*, you said? Ah, hahahaaa!"

"Gee, Jay, we wouldn't want you to kill and eat the waitress or anything. Flesh? Oh, yeah, I can hear that: 'Excuse me, ma'am, could I get a fleshburger on an onion bun, and could you sprinkle it with a little ground-up human skull?'"

"I dunno, Charlie, come to think of it, maybe we ought to skip Pud's and go to that new place, you know, Cannibal Moe's, instead. I hear they have a real good chicken fried thigh there."

"Nah, Alan, I think we should go to the new Donner's Pass Pizza, and pick up a pizza with fingers and nipples. Or maybe the spaghetti and eyeballs."

"Fuck off and die," Jay said. "You know what I mean."

The two men looked at each other and shook their heads in mock sadness.

"Tsk, tsk, tsk," Alan said. "The man is in *love*. Next thing you know, he's gonna be wearing a cowled robe to work and doing Gregorian chants up and down the halls."

"Yeah, and sprinkling rose petals everywhere and smiling at everybody like a fool."

"Go away," Jay said.

They did, cackling down the hall as they went.

Well. That certainly went well, didn't it? Maybe you

might want to be a little bit more low key in your conversion to vegetarianism, hmm?

Too late now. By tomorrow morning, this would be all over the building. He knew the jokes would be coming, and he had better recode his lock and his access, or his computer would be full of crap, too.

Still, he grinned. He could stand a little ribbing. He was, after all, the new, improved Jay Gridley, much more mellow than the old Jay had been. Much more.

8

Toni came up from sleep all of a moment. She looked at the clock on the bedside table. Two A.M., and she was wide awake, not a trace of drowsiness. Well, wasn't that terrific?

What, she wondered, had awakened her? Another hormone-fueled dream she couldn't remember?

She glanced at Alex, who slept soundly, tangled in the sheet and a couple of pillows. Sometimes he snored, and that might do it, but while he was breathing deeply, he wasn't making any noise to speak of.

She listened carefully, but the house was silent. No footsteps skulking down the hall, no creaks of doors being stealthily opened. No feeling of intrusion.

Was it because she needed to go pee?

No, not really, she *always* needed to go pee these days, and the urge wasn't particularly strong. She had fallen asleep plenty of times needing to go more than now. Still, as long as she was awake . . .

She got up, went to the bathroom, did what she needed

to do, and padded back to bed. Alex didn't stir. You could come in and walk off with the place, and he wouldn't wake up, he slept heavy. He had told her he hadn't done that before they got married, but now that she was here, he could could relax. That amused and pleased her on one level; on another level, it was mildly irritating. So she had to be responsible for their safety after hours? Not that she wasn't qualified, but still . . .

She slipped carefully back into bed and began practicing her *djurus* mentally, going through them step by step in her mind's eye, striving to capture all the details of each move. That usually would put her to sleep before she got very far along, but it wasn't working tonight. She managed to go all the way through the eighteen on the right side, and was halfway through doing them on the left when the phone rang.

It managed less than half a cycle before Toni grabbed it. "Hello?"

"Toni? It's me, Mama."

Toni felt her bowels and belly twist suddenly. Mama would never call at two in the morning unless somebody was seriously injured or dying. "Is it Poppa?"

"No, dear, Poppa's fine. But I'm afraid it's Mrs. DeBeers."

"Guru? What happened?"

"She had a stroke. About fifteen minutes ago."

Toni glanced at the clock again. Exactly when she had awakened. Was this some weird coincidence, or were she and her elderly teacher psychically connected as Guru sometimes said?

"She's on the way to the hospital," Mama continued. "When it happened, she managed to reach her medical alert button, and the paramedics and ambulances woke us all up. Poppa is going to the hospital with your brother. I thought you'd want to know."

Alex finally woke up. "Toni?"

She waved him quiet. "Which hospital, Mama?"

"Saint Agnes."

"Thanks for calling me, Mama. I'll talk to you later." She cradled the phone. Alex was sitting up. "Who—?"

"Guru had a stroke," she said.

"How bad?"

"I don't know."

He nodded. "I'll drive you to the airport."

She blinked at him. Just like that, no question, he knew she was going. "Thank you, Alex. I love you."

"I know. I love you, too. I'll call and get you a flight while you get dressed."

Toni nodded, already up and headed for the shower. Guru had been her teacher for more than fifteen years. Toni had started learning the art of *pentjak silat* from the old lady when she was already past retirement age, and she was eighty-three now. Guru was still built like a squat brick, but even so, she was not a young woman. *A stroke.*

Dear God.

She turned the shower control on and waited for the water to warm up. Was she supposed to fly in her condition? Well, supposed to or not, she was going. Guru was like her own grandmother; whatever was happening to her, she wasn't going to suffer through it alone.

Alex was mostly quiet during the drive to the airport, though he did offer to go with her.

"Nothing you can do to help," she said.

"Not her. But I can be there for you."

She smiled at him. "I knew there was a reason I married you. Keep the home fires burning. I'll call as soon as I know what's happening."

It was hard to think about Guru dying. She had been so much a part of Toni's day-to-day life from her early teenage years until she left for college. Every morning, they'd practice before Toni went off to school. Every afternoon, after she had done her homework, Toni would head across the street to the old woman's place, and they would practice the Indonesian martial art for an hour or two. Guru DeBeers had become part of the family, was included in all the gatherings: Christmas, Easter, Thanksgiving, birthday parties, weddings, graduations. She had finally given up smoking that nasty old pipe, but she still drank half a gallon of coffee a day and ate whatever she pleased. And even though she was in her eighties, Guru could still give most big strong men fits if they bothered her enough. She was slower and frailer, but her mind and skills were still sharp.

Toni hadn't been to Mass except with Mama on home visits for a long time, but she offered a silent prayer: *Please let her live.*

9

Michaels hadn't managed to get back to sleep after Toni left for New York, so he was a little tired. Fortunately, as slow as things were, he could probably take off early.

He had a partial staff meeting scheduled, and when he got there, his people were already at the conference table. John Howard, Jay Gridley, and the just-promoted Julio Fernandez. A few months ago, Fernandez's wife, Joanna, would have been there, as would Toni. He missed seeing them.

"Good morning," he said.

"Commander," Howard and Fernandez said in unison.

"Hey, I thought it was your turn to bring the doughnuts, boss," Jay said as Michaels sat. This was an old joke; they never ate doughnuts at the morning meetings.

"You didn't give up sugar when you gave up flesh?" Fernandez said.

"Very funny, Julio."

Michaels raised an eyebrow.

Fernandez answered the unasked question: "Our computer wizard here is turning Buddhist. No more eating *flesh* for him. Gonna step around ants on the sidewalk, too, I expect, chanting *om mani padme hum* while he does."

Michaels shook his head. *Never a dull moment around here.*

"Okay, what do we have? John?"

General Howard led off with his weekly report. New gear, new troops, old business. Things were slow. They'd be taking various units out on training runs over the next couple of weeks, unless something came up.

Jay didn't have a lot to report, either. "Nothing on your dope dealers," he finished. "The DEA's info was pretty sparse and dead-ended quick. I'll run some other things into the mix and see what comes up."

Michaels turned to Howard. "I sent a report your way, but in case you haven't had a chance to read it, we're helping the DEA run down some kind of new designer drug that turns the users into temporary supermen. And sometimes it makes them jump off tall buildings."

Howard said, "Yes, sir, I saw the report. Thor's Hammer."

Michaels said, "Here's another little twist. I got a call from an NSA guy yesterday. He's made an appointment to come see me today, in about an hour, my secretary tells me. He says it's about this designer drug thing. I'm curious as to why."

"What's his name?" Jay asked. "The NSA guy?"

"Last name, George, first name, Zachary."

Jay shrugged, but tapped it into his flatscreen's manual keyboard. "Never heard of him, but I'll scope him out."

"John?"

"Doesn't ring any bells with me, either," he said. "I can check with my Pentagon contacts."

"Why would the National Security Agency be interested in this?" Michaels asked. "Dope isn't in their mission statement, is it?"

Howard said, "Mission statements aren't worth the paper they are written on, sir. Everybody stretches them to fit whatever they need."

Michaels smiled. He had done that himself more than a few times, and everybody here knew it.

"I suppose I can wait until the man gets here and ask him, but I somehow doubt he'll be entirely forthcoming. Anybody have any thoughts I might pursue?"

"Overspent their budget and need a little extra cash?" Jay said. "Wouldn't be the first time an agency sold drugs to make up a shortfall."

"I thought Buddhists weren't supposed to be cynical."

"Nope, not according to Saji. You can be pretty much anything and still be a Buddhist. Cynical works."

"Except, apparently, a flesh-eater," Fernandez said.

"Well, actually, that, too. Some parts of the world, like Tibet, where food is scarce, meat is okay. As long as you do it with the right attitude."

Fernandez laughed. "Yeah, I can see you praying over a Whopper, chanting and all. Bet they'd love that at BK."

"You obviously have never been to a D.C. Burger King," Jay said. "You could do a Hawaiian fire dance over your fries there and nobody would look twice."

Fernandez laughed. He looked at Michaels and said, "Maybe one of their people is into drugs. Could be they are looking at some kind of internal security."

Howard blew out a small sigh. "There's another possibility that springs immediately to mind. Military applications."

Michaels looked at him.

Howard continued. "If you have a compound that makes a man think he's faster than a speeding bullet and more powerful than a locomotive, when you put a weapon in his hands and point him at an enemy, you could have something of military value, assuming there are controls in place."

"Didn't the Nazis try that kind of thing?"

"Yes, sir, and other armies have tried it since, from speed to steroids. Nobody has come up with something cheap and dependable enough yet, but if they did, it would certainly have useful applications."

"Would you use such a thing, General?"

"If it was safe, if it was legal, and if it would give my people an advantage over an enemy? Bring more of them back alive? Yes, sir, in a heartbeat."

"From what the DEA has given us, this stuff is neither safe nor legal."

"But it might be made both. Legal is the easy part, if it's useful enough. Safe might be harder, but it might be possible to make it so, and a lot of services would be willing to explore the possibility. And there are some armies with fewer scruples about testing things on their own people than we have."

Jay said, "When did the U.S. military develop scruples, General? Remember *The Atomic Café*? 'Here, men, put on these goggles when you look at the nuclear explosion. And don't worry about that glowing dust if it gets on you, just brush it off, you'll be fine.' "

"That was a long time ago," Howard said.

"Yeah? What about Agent Orange in Vietnam, or the vaccines against nerve gas and biowarfare in Desert Storm? Or the new, improved, supposedly safe defoliants in Colombia?"

Before Howard could respond, Michaels said, "Give it a rest, Jay. We didn't come to argue about the military's checkered history. And whatever happened, we can hardly blame General Howard, can we?"

Jay shut up, having expressed his standing liberal attitude.

"All right. If there's nothing further, I've got a ton of files to review."

Forty-five minutes later, as Michaels sat developing eyestrain scanning computer files using his new sharp-goggles, supposedly designed to keep the letters so clear you wouldn't get eyestrain, there was a tap at his door.

"Jay."

"Boss. I uploaded what I could find on this George guy. I didn't know if you'd get to it before he showed up."

"Thanks, Jay, I appreciate it."

After Jay left, Michaels found the file and read through it. Not much. There was a brief bio on Zachary George, place and date of birth, education, family, and shorter work history. Seemed Mr. George had been with the NSA since leaving college fifteen years ago, and the only references to his status there was a GS number only a grade below Michaels's own before he was booted upstairs.

"Sir?" came the voice of his secretary over the com. "Your nine o'clock is here."

Well, speak of the devil. "Show him in."

Mr. George wasn't particularly impressive upon first look. Average height, average weight, brown hair cut short but not too short, fair skin, and clothes that were standard midlevel bureaucrat: a gray suit expensive enough to look decent, not so expensive as to stand out in your memory. Black leather shoes. Put him in a room with four other people, and he'd be invisible. The guy in the corner who looked totally average? No, no, not him, the guy *next* to him.

Michaels stood and extended his hand. "Mr. George."

"Commander. Good of you to see me."

"Well, we like to keep relations good with our fellow agencies. Spirit of cooperation and all."

"With all due respect, sir, bullshit. Almost anybody at my agency would cut the throats of everybody at yours if they thought it would gain them two brownie points at review time. And that's pretty much my experience with all the security agencies I've dealt with."

Michaels had to smile at that. "Don't sugarcoat it that way, tell me what you really think."

George returned the smile, and whatever he was up to, he was interesting.

"Have a seat."

The NSA man sat, leaned back, crossed his ankle over his knee. "You figured out what it is I'm up to yet?"

"I have some thoughts. Why don't you just tell me?"

George smiled again. It started on the right side and worked its way across his face. "Well, sir, I don't want to make it too easy for you."

"Much as I'd like to fence with you, I do have a couple of other things on my plate. Twenty questions isn't high on the list. Talk or walk."

George nodded, as if that was what he expected to hear. "Sir. You may be aware that there are qualities connected to this drug we spoke of that might be of use to certain of our military organizations."

"That thought has crossed my mind."

"As it happens, my agency has a . . . research facility engaged in studying certain pharmaceutical aids for possible use in . . . field operations."

"Really?"

"More information is need-to-know, I'm sorry. Suffice it to say, we would be very interested in speaking with the chemist who has come up with this compound when you find him."

"Why aren't you talking to the DEA?"

George smiled. "We have. Frankly, we don't think the DEA has much of a chance of catching the guy."

"It is their area of expertise, isn't it?"

"Then why did they come to you for help?"

That was a good point, but Michaels didn't speak to it. Instead, he said, "And why didn't you just go after the dealer on your own? NSA has a finger in just about every pie there is, don't they?"

"True. And as a result, we are stretched somewhat thin. Net Force has had some excellent results in its short history, and continuing to speak frankly, your computer operatives are better than anybody else's. Including ours. You probably know we've tried to, ah . . . recruit some of them."

Michaels smiled. He knew. "No luck?"

"Oh, yes, plenty of luck . . . all bad. Your organization seems to engender a very high degree of loyalty."

"We try to treat our people right."

"So it seems. But the bottom line is, we think you'll uncover this dealer before either the DEA or our own ops will, and we'd like you to keep us in mind when you do."

Michaels leaned back in his chair and steepled his fingers in front of his face for a second, then quickly put his hands down on the desk. He'd read somewhere that steepling your fingers was a sign of feeling superior, and while he certainly felt he had the upper hand in this discussion, he didn't want to give anything away. He said, "Even if we did, what good would it do you? DEA has jurisdiction. We turn the information over to them, they make the arrest. End of our participation."

George hesitated for a second, then said, "Of course. We wouldn't want to usurp the DEA's legal position. But a heads-up from you would allow us to, ah . . . begin negotiations with that agency from a position of knowledge. I'm sure we can convince them that the nation's best interests would be served if we were allowed to question the criminal before he was locked away to await a long, drawn-out trial."

Michaels smiled again. George would know this conversation was being recorded, and he didn't want to say anything that sounded remotely illegal, but it was easy enough to read between the lines here. One developed a certain expertise in verbal fugue working in Washington. You said one thing, you meant something else, and you used expression or tone or gestures to make sure your listener got it. Tape recordings missed visual clues, and even videos couldn't pick up between-the-lines stuff.

George's fugue was simple: You give us the dope dealer, we rattle his cage real good and get what we want, *then* we turn him over to the DEA.

Interesting.

Michaels's immediate gut reaction was to tell Mr. Zachary George to scuttle back to his NSA hole and not let the door hit him on the way out. But he had learned a thing or two about political survival in this town, and peeing in somebody's corn flakes was not a smart move, especially when they had clout. NSA knew where a lot of bodies were buried, some figurative, some no doubt quite literally, and a direct confrontation, while it might be emotionally satisfying, was not the smart move. It wasn't just Michaels, it was his agency, and he had to keep that in mind. A hard lesson, but one he was learning better and better all the time.

"Well, I suppose we could keep you in the loop," Michaels finally said. "As a courtesy to a brother agency." There was no real fugue here, he wasn't going to give them squat, but he strived to leave that impression: *Why, sure, we'll scratch your back. What will you do for us?*

George flashed his crooked smile again. "We would

appreciate it, Commander. I'm certain we can return the favor in some small way."

The meeting was over, George had said what he came to say, and it was but the matter of another minute to exchange good-byes before the man left.

Interesting, indeed. So the National Security Agency had some kind of clandestine operation involving drugs. Not really that big a surprise, when you thought about it. There were more sub-rosa operations going on at any security agency than you could shake a stick at, some well-known in the trade, some hinted at, and some surely buried so deep that nobody had happened across them yet. Net Force was fairly public, but they didn't air certain articles of their laundry in public. And for sure the FBI had its own black-bag ops skulking about in the shadows. It was all part of the game. You couldn't sneak up on somebody if you had to yell at him through a bullhorn and flash your warning lights. Even local police departments knew you sometimes had to use unmarked cars.

When and if they came across the drug dealer, then Michaels could decide whether to let NSA know about it. Probably they wouldn't. Almost certainly not in time to do anything nasty with the knowledge. If NSA swooped in and grabbed the dope dealer from under the DEA's nose and someone figured out that it was Net Force who gave the guy up, heads would roll.

Right now, it was a moot point anyhow. They didn't have anything to give.

Before he could get back to his reading, the intercom cheeped again.

"Sir, Agent Brett Lee is here. He doesn't have an appointment, but he seems, ah . . . quite insistent on seeing you."

"Show him in."

Lee arrived in a huff, glowering. "What the hell is Zach George doing here?!"

"Nice to see you, too, Mr. Lee."

"You didn't answer my question!"

"Nor do I intend to. What goes on in my office is none of your damn business."

Lee stepped forward, as if he planned on doing something physical.

Michaels was tired and cranky. He came to his feet, ready to move. *Go for it, pal. Let me show you what my wife taught me!*

But Lee stopped, having apparently realized that throwing a punch at the head of Net Force might not be a smart career move.

Too bad. Michaels felt like decking him. This clown had no right storming into his office demanding anything.

"You and George are up to something, and I'm warning you, it better not get in our way! My boss will be calling yours," he said, still red-faced and angry.

"I hope they have a pleasant conversation, Mr. Lee. But right now, I'm busy, so if you'll excuse me, I have work to do." He sat and reached for his viewer.

In another second, Brett Lee was gone, leaving an angry wake behind him.

This was a *very* interesting development. Much more fun than reading reports on a dull morning.

10

Malibu, California

When Drayne shuffled into the kitchen with just the tiniest headache from drinking most of two bottles of champagne, he saw Tad sprawled on the couch and dead to the world.

Good. One of these trips, Tad wasn't gonna come back, but he was glad it wasn't this time. He'd miss the guy. Tad was balls-to-the-wall and full-out, not too many like him. And loyal; you couldn't buy that.

Drayne opened the cabinet over the microwave oven and dug through the vitamins until he found the ibuprofen. He shook four of the brown tabs into his palm, swallowed them dry, and put the bottle back. There were rows and rows of vitamin bottles there, he was a big believer in such things, but he wouldn't take those until he had some food in his stomach. He took so many vitamins and minerals and assorted other healthy supplements that doing so on an empty belly was apt to make him nauseated. His normal intake each morning amounted to maybe twenty, twenty-five pills, caps, caplets, or softgels.

Two grams of C, two caplets; three E's, 1200 IUs; 120 mg of ginkgo biloba, two caplets; two Pain Free tabs, that was 1,000 of glucosamine and 800 of chondroitin combined; couple of fat-burners, mostly chromium picolinate and L-caritine; 705 mg of ginseng, three softgels; 50,000 IUs of beta-carotene in two gelcaps; 100 mg of DHEA, that was four pills; couple of saw palm—he didn't really need that yet, but better to get a head start on prostate problems, as much screwing as he did—two gels, 320 mg; five mg of Deprenyl to keep the gray matter from rotting; and however many creatine caps he thought he needed when he was on the cycle, those varied from day to day, depending on how hard he hit the weights.

He waited until bedtime before he took the multiple and his melatonin, plus a couple of other odds and ends. That many pills down the hatch every day, dry-swallowing four ibuprofen was nothing. The stack seemed to work for him, and as long as it did, he'd keep it up. Prevention was better than a cure.

Champagne was his only vice—well, unless you counted sex—and he made sure he was covered on the health stuff. He ate pretty well, exercised regularly, even wore sunblock these days. He planned to live a long, rich, full life, unlike Tad, who'd be dead in a year, tops, and probably a lot sooner.

He'd tried to talk Tad out of them, the Hammer trips, but Tad was who he was, and if he did quit, he'd turn into somebody else. Drayne could live with the guy running at half speed, but Tad couldn't, and that was that.

Misty-Bunny-Buffy was gone, slipped out in the night sometime. He figured she had a steady boyfriend or a husband she had to get back to, sleeping with a producer to maybe get a job didn't really count, especially not if you were home before dawn. He was done with her, anyhow. She'd been great, but she'd only be new once, and there was no point in going spelunking in caves where he'd already been, was there? Unless they were spectacular—and past a certain point, they didn't seem to get much better—why bother? Might be a better one just ahead.

He looked at his watch, one of those Seiko Kinetics that you never had to wind or replace the batteries in; it ran off some kind of tiny generator that charged up a capacitor or something every time you moved your wrist. Watch would run as long as you could wiggle your arm a little, guaranteed for life. And if things got to the point where he couldn't wiggle his arm a little, there wouldn't be any reason to worry about what time it was.

At the moment, it was almost ten A.M.

He sighed. Too late to get in a workout or a jog on the beach. Better go take a shower and then get rolling. He had to drive out to the desert to restock his mobile lab, and it was a couple hours each way, even if the traffic was good. He could take his vitamins with him, get something to eat later. He needed to be back by six, he had a dinner with the Zee-ster, that was always good for some laughs. If Tad had been mobile, he'd have sent him, but he wasn't and that was that, too.

Well, at least it looked as if the weather was okay. Once he got past the smog curtain, he could drop the top and enjoy the sunshine. Great thing about SoCal was that you could pretty much do that year round. Yeah, it rained in the winter and actually got chilly a couple times in season, but he'd spent many a January day lying on the beach cooking under a warm sun. Sure, the water got colder, but with a wet suit, you could surf any time. Not that he'd done much of that lately. Too busy working. Have to remedy that pretty soon.

He grinned. He wondered what his father would say if he knew how much money little Bobby had tucked away.

Or how he had earned it. The old man would blow a gasket, that was certain, you'd be able to see the steam coming out his head for fucking miles. Thirty years with the Bureau, as straight an arrow as ever put on a suit, his old man, a guy who'd always paid his own parking tickets rather than flash his FBI badge at a meter maid.

And for what? What had all that nose-to-the-grindstone, johnny-be-good crap gotten his old man?

It had gotten him retired to a condo in Tucson, Arizona, just him and that little terrier of his, Franklin, living on a pension and bitching about how the world had gone to hell in a handbasket. Actually, Drayne kinda liked the dog. Best thing his old man had done since Mom died was get a dog, not saying much. First week he'd had the beast, it had come back inside carrying a big ole dead rat it had caught. Rat almost as big as the dog, and you'd have never thought by looking at the little barker that he had it in him. Drayne liked that.

It had been more than a year since he had gone to visit his father. Franklin must be pushing nine or ten by now, probably middle-aged in dog years.

Drayne often wondered, if his old man found out what he was doing, would he turn him in? Some days he was sure that former Special Agent in Charge Rickover Drayne, RD to his friends, most of whom were feds, would do it, no question. Other days, he wasn't so sure. Maybe the old bastard had a soft spot for his only son. Not that Drayne had ever been able to see it.

As far as the old man knew, Bobby worked for a small chemical company that produced plastic polymer for use in industrial waste containers, earning a decent salary, just a hair more than his father had made in his last year before retirement. This was done so the old man would think all that tuition money for the chemistry degree hadn't been wasted. He might have his differences with his son, but at least he could say the boy had a legitimate job making decent money.

Of course, that was as much for Drayne's protection as for making his father proud. He had gone to some lengths to create the PolyChem Products company, duly incorporated in Delaware, to set up a modest history in a few selected computer banks, and to make sure he was listed as an employee. Just in case his father checked it out. He wouldn't put it past the old man to do that. Paid taxes on the paper job salary he showed, too, and FICA and all that shit. IRS didn't care what you did as long as you paid taxes. He could have declared his income from dope sales and paid the feds their cut, and the IRS would never say anything to the DEA about it. People had done it before.

The government, in whatever form it manifested, was plainly stupid. He could dick around with them all he wanted, and they'd never catch him.

Drayne wandered into the bathroom and cranked up the shower. It was a big sucker, room enough for four or five people, all pale green tile and glass bricks, with a dozen shower heads set all over: high, low, in-between. With the jets turned on full blast, it was like being stabbed by wet needles. Used a shitload of water—he had a pair of eighty-gallon water heaters in the garage—but when you came out of it, you felt clean and rejuvenated, that was for sure.

He stepped into the shower and gasped at the force of the spray.

Tad would be out for probably eighteen or twenty hours, maybe longer. He'd still be on the couch when Drayne got back. Maybe even still breathing. And he'd spend most of the next week or so on the couch, lying on the floor, or, if he made it that far, a bed. Recovering from the Hammer was a chore. It got harder each time.

Drayne stopped thinking and let the hot water take him.

The Bronx, New York

Toni sat in the chair next to Guru's bed, watching the old woman sleep. Mrs. DeBeers had been lucky, the doctor told her. The stroke was mild, and she was in otherwise remarkable health for an eighty-three-year-old woman. There was only a slight effect on her grip and speech, no real paralysis, and they expected she'd make a full recovery. There were still tests they had to run and medications they had to administer and monitor for a couple of days, but pretty much they thought she was out of the woods.

The doctors only told her that because Guru had listed her as next of kin, even though that wasn't true.

Toni was more than a little relieved. Guru DeBeers had been a part of her life since Toni had seen her, at sixty-five, clean the clocks of four neighborhood toughs who tried to give her a hard time. Toni had been amazed at the sight and had known immediately she wanted to learn how to protect herself against physical attacks that way. Men tended to take women for granted physically, and even at thirteen Toni had known she did not want to be at the mercy of some man who decided he wanted something from her she didn't want to give. The training in *pentjak silat,* starting with the simple *bukti negara* style and progressing to the more complex *serak,* had been a part of Toni's world ever since. She still went over to see her teacher whenever she went home to visit her parents, and the trip across the street had never gotten dull.

Old as Guru was, it was impossible to imagine her gone.

"Ah, how is my *tunangannya* today?"

Toni smiled. *Best girl.* There was the smallest slur to Guru's voice, hardly noticeable. "I'm fine, Guru. How are you feeling?"

"I've felt worse. Better, too. It would be nice to have some coffee."

"The doctors won't let you do that, not after a stroke."

"I have outlived three sets of doctors so far. I will outlive this set if they wait for coffee to kill me. And if does kill me, at least I die happy."

Toni smiled again, and reached into her purse. She brought out a small stainless steel thermos.

The old woman's smile was radiant, if a trifle saggy on the left side of her face. "Ah. You are a dutiful student."

"It's not fresh," Toni said. "I didn't have time to go by your place and grind your grand-nephew's beans and make it. I got it at Starbucks more than an hour ago. I'm sorry."

Guru shrugged. "It will do. Raise the bed."

Toni operated the controls, and the motor hummed and raised Guru into a more-or-less sitting position. Toni poured the coffee into the thermos's cup and passed it over.

Guru inhaled deeply through her nose. "Espresso?"

"Of course. The darkest they had."

"Well, stale or not, it is welcome. Thank you, my best girl." Guru brought the cup to her lips and took a small sip. "Not bad, not bad," she pronounced. "Another hundred years or so, and Americans might learn how to make a decent brew. And certainly it is better than nothing." She took another sip, then smiled again. "And how is our baby doing?"

"Fine, as far as I can tell. Mostly he elbows me in the bladder or rolls around and tries to boot my stomach inside out."

"Yes, they do that. And he is tiny yet. Wait until you are eight or nine months along, and he kicks you so hard your pants fall down." She chuckled.

"There's a pleasant thought."

"You are worried because you cannot train," Guru said.

Toni shook her head. How could she know exactly what was going through her mind?

"I had four children," Guru said. "All after I began my training. Each time, I had to alter my practice."

"So I'm discovering."

"You can do *djuru-djuru* sitting down," she said. "Your *langkas* will need to be sharpened, but there is no reason to stop upper body movements."

Toni nodded. The Indonesian martial art forms Guru taught were divided into two parts, upper body, or *djurus,* and lower body, or *langkas.* You usually lumped them together and called the whole thing a *djuru,* though that was not technically correct.

"I have some things in my house for you to take home with you when you go. I have packed them into a big box by the front door."

Before Toni could protest, Guru continued, "No, it is not my time yet, and I am not giving you your legacy before I go. These are merely things I think you will enjoy and that I no longer have a need for."

"Thank you, Guru."

"I am proud of you as a student and as a woman, best girl. I expect I will live long enough to cuddle your child."

Toni smiled. She certainly hoped so.

11

The woman was young, maybe twenty-two, twenty-three, and dressed in jeans, a black T-shirt, and running shoes, nothing that unusual about her appearance. She was nobody you'd cross the street to get a better look at, but nobody you'd cross the street the other way to avoid because she was hideous, either. Average-looking.

The woman approached an automated bank teller, put in her card, and stood back. Apparently there was some malfunction. The woman smiled, then, without preamble, drove her fist through the teller's vid screen. Shattered glass flew every which way, and even before it finished falling, the woman was grabbing at a garbage basket on the sidewalk. She picked up the basket and began hammering at the teller, smiling all the while.

Alex Michaels leaned back in the chair and said, "There's something you don't see every day."

Jay Gridley said, "Actually, it happens quite a lot, according to Bureau agents I've talked to. Although the level of violence is usually much less. People tend to spit at the screen or camera, slam it with the edge of their fist once or twice, even kick at it. Sometimes they scratch the glass with their car keys. Nobody's ever seen one quite this . . . ah . . . *active* before."

"What happened after she trashed the videocam recording it?"

Jay said, "According to witnesses, the destruction continued until she *really* got pissed off, whereupon she somehow managed to rip the machine free of its mountings, scattering several thousand dollars in twenty-dollar bills all over the sidewalk. A small riot ensued as concerned citizens sought to . . . ah . . . recover the money for the bank."

The boss laughed. "I bet. How much of it was turned in?"

"About fifteen percent."

"Well, at least there are still a few honest citizens left. So we have another drug berserker who destroyed a bank machine. Why is this more special than the others?"

"The woman is Mary Jane Kent."

"Related to the arms and chemical companies Kents?"

"Yes, sir. She's the secretary of defense's daughter."

"Oh, my."

"Slumming in those clothes," Jay said. "Way I hear it, she could paste her diamonds all over herself and show less skin than in jeans and a T-shirt. With enough left over to make a cape."

"The family has a bit of money."

Jay nodded. *There* was an understatement. The Kent family had become modestly rich during the Spanish Civil War in the '30s, running guns into Spain via Portugal. They made out like bandits in World War II, and had done quite well in assorted revolutions and border wars, since. The men in the family generally took turns managing the family fortune and tended to became ambassadors, cabinet officers, or U.S. senators; the women did charity work, ran foundations, and tended to marry badly. Every now and then, a couple of the scions would switch roles, and the girl would manage the company while the boy ran a foundation.

Certainly, the rich had their problems, too, but Jay couldn't feel too sorry for somebody with half a gazillion dollars tucked away waiting for them to come of age. It was one thing to start poor and earn your way to luxury, another thing to be born with a platinum spoon in your mouth.

He said, "She beat the crap out of four of LAPD's finest before she ran out of steam. A passing doctor happened along during the struggle and sedated her. Hit her with a hypo full of enough Thorazine to knock out a large horse, according to the reports, and it slowed her down, but not completely. She isn't talking about what drug she took or where she got it, but she was apparently on a shopping trip, and she used her credit card until it maxed out. That was why the bank machine wouldn't give her any cash."

"Ah," the boss said. He thought about it for a few seconds, then said, "Just how much does a billionaire's daughter have to spend to max out a credit card?"

"Take a look."

He handed Michaels a ROM tag, and the boss thumbed the pressure spot and looked at the number that appeared on the tag.

"Good Lord!"

"Amen. Enough to buy a yacht and an island to sail it to," Jay said. "I got most of the credit card company's tags. If we can backtrack her and find out how and where she spent her money, the DEA guy you sicced on me says they are willing to put more bodies on the street to check everything out. It's not much, but it's what we have."

Michaels nodded. He looked at the tag again.

"Never fear, boss, Smokin' Jay Gridley is on the case." He gave Michaels a two-finger Cub Scout salute and headed for his office.

Michael's com chirped, and the caller-ID signal told him Toni was trying to reach him. He grabbed the headset. "Hey."

"Hey."

"How's Guru doing?"

"Doing okay," Toni said. "Doctor says she's gonna be all right."

"Good. I know you're relieved to hear that."

"Yes, I am. Anyway, I'll be catching a shuttle back this afternoon. I should be home when you get there."

"Great. You want me to stop and pick up something for supper?"

"Nah, we can just call the Chinese place when you get home, if that's okay."

"If you promise not to get the octopus/squid special again," he said.

She laughed. "I get cravings, what can I say? It's part of the pregnancy."

"Me eating in the other room is going to be part of the pregnancy, too, you keep slurping that slimy stuff down."

She laughed again. "How's work?"

"The usual. Got a lead on that drug thing we talked about. It's not much, but Jay is running with it. Other than that, it's pretty quiet around here. A yawn in the park. Be nice if things picked up a little."

"Careful what you wish for. I miss you."

"I miss you, too. Fly safe."

"I will. See you tonight."

She hung up, and he blew out a relieved sigh. With all the pregnancy stuff, having her *silat* teacher kick off would have been another brick on Toni's load, and she didn't need any more weight right now.

A nice, quiet evening at home with Chinese take-out would be fine by him.

"Sir. You have a call from Richard Sharone on line five."

Michaels shook off his daydream of supper and Toni. "Who is Richard Sharone, and why should I talk to him?"

"He's the president and CEO of Merit-Wells Pharmaceuticals."

Michaels blinked. Why would the head honcho at one of the world's largest drug companies be calling him?

Oh.

Michaels stared at the com's headset. He might not be the sharpest needle in the package, but he wasn't completely dull. What did Net Force have to do with drugs? Nothing, until the DEA asked for their help with this esoteric dope they were trying to find. First it was NSA, now the overlord of a drug company. Man. Somebody wanted this stuff bad.

Probably get a call from the Food and Drug Administration next.

"This is Commander Alex Michaels. How can I help you, Mr. Sharone?"

But he was pretty sure he already knew.

Net Force Shooting Range, Quantico, Virginia

John Howard stood on the line at the firing range, ready to start. He said, "Eight meters, single. Go."

A three-hundred pound crazed biker blinked into existence eight meters down the alley. The biker held a tire iron, and he lifted it and charged right at Howard, no hesitation.

Fast for a fat man, he was, too.

Howard slipped his right hand under his Net Force windbreaker, cleared the jacket, caught the smooth wooden grips of his side arm, and pulled the weapon from the custom-made Fist paddle holster. He brought the Phillips & Rodgers Model 47 Medusa up and shoved it one-handed toward the biker as if punching him.

The biker was less than four meters away now, three, two . . .

Howard pulled the trigger, once, twice . . .

The gun roared and bucked hard.

Two rounds hit the biker five feet away. The running man collapsed and slid to a stop inches from Howard's spit-shined, patent-leather-bright shoes.

Cut that a little close, John.

The biker disappeared, like turning off a lamp.

Which, in essence, was what happened. The hologram was, after all, just a particularly coherent brand of light. But the computer cams that watched it all calculated the flight path of Howard's two .357 slugs as they zipped down range, and having decided they would have struck vital areas on a real human target, gave him the ersatz victory.

Score one for the good guys.

Howard reholstered the handgun and looked at the score screen. He saw the image of the biker there and noted the pulsing red spots where the bullets hit. The one marked with #1 was in the heart, the #2 round was slightly higher and to the right. With the best .357 Magnum or .40 rounds, one-shot knockdowns hovered right about 94 to 96 percent with a solid body hit, as good as a handgun got—and it didn't even have to be to a fatal area. The first shot would have done the trick, and probably a real

attacker would be dead or well on the way there by now.
Dead wasn't the thing, though, it was the stopping power
that was important. You could shoot somebody in the leg
with a .22 and it might nick a big blood vessel and eventually kill him. Thing was, *eventually* wouldn't do you
much good if the guy kept coming, beat you to a pulp
with his tire iron or crowbar, then went home and died in
a few days, a few hours, even a few minutes. No good at
all. When you shot somebody, you wanted them to fall
down *right now;* anything less was bad. They lived or
died, that was something to worry about later. You didn't
have time to ponder on it in the moment.

Handguns were lousy weapons for instant stops, relatively speaking. A shotgun was better, and a good rifle
better still. He smiled as he remembered the old story
about a civilian who carried a handgun. A friend asked
him, "Why do you have a pistol? Are you expecting trouble?" And the guy answered, "Trouble? No. If I was expecting trouble, I'd be carrying a rifle."

Then again, it was kind of hard to slip a scoped .308
sniper rifle under your Gore-Tex windbreaker. And the
first rule of a gunfight was . . .

*Come on, John. You gonna shoot or stand here day-
dreaming?*

"Reset," he said.

The screen went blank.

"Ten meters, double. Thirty-second delay. Go."

This time, the scenario computer gave him two attackers. One looked like a pro wrestler holding a long knife,
the other an NFL lineman with a baseball bat. They
charged.

Howard drew, gave the wrestler two, shifted his hand,
and gave the lineman two. The last of the four cartridges
in the revolver left the barrel at about the same time the
lineman got within bat range.

Both attackers fell.

Howard thumbed the cylinder latch open with his right, pointed the gun at the ceiling, and used his left hand to slap the extractor rod hard enough to punch the empties out of the chambers. The hulls fell to the range floor. He pulled a speed loader with six more cartridges from his left windbreaker pocket. Reloading the P&R was trickier than doing it with his old S&W. There were spring-loaded clips in each chamber of the black-Teflon-coated P&R, to allow for using various calibers—the thing would shoot .380s, .38s, .38 Specials, and 9 mms, as well as .357 Magnums—and you had to keep the extractor partway out to make the speed loader work, and even so, it was slower than the Smith was.

Still, if you couldn't get the job done with six, you probably weren't going to be able to get it done at all.

He managed to get all six of the reloads into the chambers. He dropped the speed loader on the floor, hit the cartridges with the heel of his right hand a couple of times to get them fully seated, closed the cylinder, then brought the gun up into a two-handed grip as the third attacker appeared.

The attacker was a naked woman with a samurai sword.

Well. Somebody was getting creative with their programming. He wondered who Gunny had doing the scenarios. He'd have to ask.

Since he was ready when the woman came to life, he had plenty of time. He lined the front sight up on her nose and fired one round.

One to the head was plenty.

He looked at the score screen. Three for three. Not bad for an old man.

Gunny's voice came over the intercom, easy to hear with the smart earphones that kept loud noises out but let normal sounds in. "General, we have a troop of Explorer

Scouts coming by in a few minutes. Okay if they watch you shoot?"

Before he could respond, Gunny said, "That's 'cause we want to show them how *not* to do it."

"You want to come out here and let me show you how it *is* done, Sergeant?"

Gunny chuckled, and Howard had to smile. That was less than an idle threat. Gunny could shoot the pants off Wyatt Earp, Wild Bill Hickok, and John Wesley Hardin all at the same time, either hand, and you pick it. He was outstanding with anything you could pick up and fire. Came from being a full-time range officer and daily practice. Too bad Gunny didn't want to compete anymore. They could use him in the annual shoot against the other services. He claimed he was too old, and as he was only three or four years past Howard's age. Howard didn't much like hearing that.

Howard himself was lucky if he got to the range three or four times a month. Usually Julio came with him, but with a new baby at home, he was doing father duty, and that cut into his practice time.

Julio was about to learn that a baby changed all kinds of priorities.

Gunny said, *"Thirty* seconds for a reload? Two-plus seconds to take out two goblins you started halfway to Los An-ju-leeez? Lord, we could have gone out for dinner and a movie and gotten back before you finished. I don't guess you're about to threaten the Ragin' Cajun's records anytime soon, sir."

Howard chuckled at that. The Ragin' Cajun was Jerry Miculek, a pro shooter who'd set the modern revolver record a dozen or so years ago, down in Mississippi. Using an eight-shot .38 Special revolver, he put all eight rounds on a target in one second flat. He also fired at four different targets, two rounds each, and hit them all just

0.06 of a second slower. And with a six-shooter, he was
was able to put six hits on one target, *reload,* and put six
more there in just over three seconds. By those standards,
thirty seconds was a couple of eons.

Howard had had his revolver fitted with a set of grips
designed by Miculek, but it hadn't helped that much.

Of course, more than sixty-five years before Miculek,
the legendary Ed McGivern fired five shots from a 1905
Smith & Wesson Hand Ejector Military and Police .38
into a playing card in a mere 0.4 of a second.

No way Howard could ever get close to any of that,
not if he practiced every day of the week and twice on
Sunday. Still, for his purposes, he was good enough for
government work. Tests had shown that a fair-to-middling
shooter took between a second and a second and a half
to draw a handgun from concealment and get a shot off.
If a man with a tire tool or a knife was inside twenty or
so feet and was in a hurry, he'd get to you before you
could shoot him. If he was closer than that, and your gun
was in the holster, best you make some space or be ready
for hand-to-hand to hold him off long enough to draw
your piece.

Of course, if Howard went somewhere expecting trouble, he was sure going to be carrying a rifle. Maybe a
submachine gun, and it would be pointed in the general
direction of any trouble, too.

Then again, he had gotten shot when he hadn't been
expecting it, so this was a skill he needed to hone.

"Don't forget to stop and have your ring reprogrammed
on the way out, sir."

Howard nodded. All Net Force guns were smart technology now. You wore a ring with a code that changed
every month or so. If somebody not wearing a properly
coded ring picked up a Net Force weapon and tried to use
it, it wouldn't fire. Howard still didn't trust it, but so far

there hadn't been any failures of the system, at least not with his people. It was a good idea in theory, but if one of his team ever pointed a gun that didn't go bang! when it was supposed to, there would be hell to pay, and he'd be leading the devil's collection team himself, assuming it wasn't his gun that malfunctioned and got him killed.

"Reset," he said. "Seven meters, one."

Make it a little more challenging, this time . . .

"Go!"

He reached for his gun.

12

Los Angeles, California

The gag came to Bobby as he was driving back from the desert.

It happened because a year or so ago, he had concocted about a quarter kilo of something he called GD, short for Giggle Dust. At the time, he'd had a customer somewhere interested in it, but something must have happened, and he'd stuck it into a drawer in the RV and completely forgotten about it. When he'd been there today talking to Ma and Pa Yeehaw, who actually were married and from Missouri originally, he happened to open that drawer, and son of a bitch lookit, there it was. Eight ounces of the gray green powder, worth an easy four grand if he wanted to bother with it. Free money.

GD was a blend of MMDA—an analog of MDA, or Ecstasy—some psilocybin from a batch of dried baeocystis mushrooms he'd bought from a guy in British Columbia, and a little dexadrine. Everybody didn't react to it the same way, of course, but in most people, it tended to make for a really happy trip, laughing, giggling, speeding their asses off, beaming at everybody, and having a fun time in general. Problem was, the mix was iffy, and it was hard to get the recipe exact. This batch worked pretty good—he'd let Tad try a hit way back when—but the next mix might not. The mushrooms were the key, and they varied all over the place. Only real side effect was it tended to make you thirsty but not able to pee, so when it wore off, you'd be spending a lot of time in the john.

The gag would take all the GD he had, but what the hell, if you couldn't have fun, why bother? He had precursor for another batch of the Hammer, he already had orders for fifteen grand or so lined up, and probably another five or eight thousand would be in by the time he got ready to mix. Money wasn't a problem. He had money to burn.

The more he thought about it, the better he liked it. So he might be late for his dinner with the Zee-ster, no big deal. Zee was gonna be out of it anyhow, if he'd swung the Hammer last night. He wasn't in as bad shape as Tad, Zee was a jock, but even with chemical assistance, he was gonna be dragging ass today. And he was usually late, even when he was straight.

Drayne grinned. Yeah. He was gonna do it. He could cut over to the 405, get off at Westwood, and it would be right there, just up Wilshire, no problem. It was still early enough he could beat most of the traffic. Thirty, forty minutes, he'd be pulling up next to the Federal Building. He been there enough times when his old man had still been protecting the republic.

The building was the home of the Los Angeles office of the Federal Bureau of Investigation.

Oh, yeah, this was gonna be a hoot, all right.

Malibu

Still hardly able to move, Tad managed to sit up on the couch to stare at Bobby. There weren't many days when he thought Bobby was crazier than he was. This was one of them. He said, "You're shittin' me."

"Nope."

"You blew four thousand dollars' worth of Giggle Dust to *stone* fuckin' FBI HQ in L.A.?"

"Yep."

"You're friggin' nuts, Bobby."

"I'd have spent that much more to have been a fly on the wall. Maybe we can get one of the security recordings of it someday. See all those uptight fuckheads laughing and holding hands and being in tune with the universe and all."

"Jeez, Bobby, you have to let that go. They are just doing their jobs, you know? That's why they hire 'em."

"You don't know what you're talking about, Tad."

"Yeah, yeah. Okay. How'd you pull it off?"

"Easy. They got great security, but I went to fill out an application for a job on the floor above them. Got out to the roof, up to the air conditioners, found the right vents, moved a couple of filters, voilà! the air is full of magic."

"Four grand. For a practical joke."

"Tad, Tad, Tad. Let me tell you a story."

"Aw, geez, not another of your shaggy dog stories!"

"Shut up, Tad. Listen and learn:

"So there's this couple in Vegas, see, and after a long day, they go upstairs and go to bed. Wife drops off to sleep, but the husband can't, so he gets up, gets dressed, and goes down to the casino with ten bucks. He goes to the craps table, puts it down, throws a natural, and he's a winner!

"So he lets it ride, and wins again. And again. And yet again!

"This is incredible stuff. He's throwing naturals, he's making points the hard way, he can't lose.

"Next thing you know, the guy has parlayed his bets up to almost a million bucks. And he's feeling unbeatable, so he lets it ride one more time. If he wins, he's gonna leave rich.

"He throws snake eyes and loses it all.

"He goes back to his room. As he's getting into bed, he wife wakes up. 'Where you been?' she asks.

" 'I went down to play a little craps,' he says.

" 'How'd you do?'

"Guy slips under the covers, shrugs, says, 'I lost ten bucks.' "

The conversation sat still for a moment. Tad said, "Okay, funny. And, uh, what exactly is the point?"

"Point is, it's all gravy, Tad. This morning, I didn't know the GD existed, so when I came across it, it was like something for nothing. I used it up, I had a big laugh, it didn't cost me anything. Hell, I didn't even lose ten bucks. I came home with as much in my pocket as when I left this morning. Except what I paid for the tofu burger for lunch."

"You go a long way to make a point, man. And I don't know how you can eat that tofu shit."

"Yeah, well, getting there is half the fun, isn't it?"

Tad had to nod. "Yeah. I guess you're right. But you're still a crazy motherfucker."

"So who's arguing with that?"

"Jesus." A beat, then, "So how is the Zee-ster?"

"Probably as burned out as you are. He didn't show. How you holding up?"

"I've been worse."

"Want to eat something?"

"Nah, not yet. Maybe in a day or two. I'll just pop a few pills."

"Keep it up, Tad, pretty soon nothing short of tanna leaves is gonna bring you back."

"Karis, the mummy, with Boris Karloff," Tad said. Like half the people in L.A., Tad was an old-movie buff. He especially loved those old black-and-white Universal monster pictures.

"Well, at least part of your brain still works. I'm gonna get some champagne. You want some?"

"And rot my liver? Shee-it."

Bobby laughed and said, "I'm gonna miss you, Tad."

Tad nodded. "I know. But that was always in the cards, man. Always in the cards."

13

Hemphill, Texas

Jay Gridley hiked down a country road, not far from the Toledo Bend Reservoir on the Sabine River, just across the state line from Louisiana, a place he had once visited as a child. Long-leaf pine and red dirt and lazily buzzing flies completed the summer scene. When he'd actually been here in real time, he'd been eight or so, walking with a couple of his cousins, Richie and Farah. Richie was his age, Farah was four. They had seen a long reddish snake wiggling on the road, and all excited, he and Richie had run back to tell their parents. Jay hadn't been able to understand why his mom and Aunt Sally had jumped up in such a panic. *"Where is Farah!"*

"Hey, don't worry, we left her to watch the snake, she won't let it get away."

He smiled at the memory.

Just ahead, a white-haired old man in a dirty T-shirt and overalls—no shoes—sat in the shade of a tall pine tree and whittled on a long stick with a Barlow jackknife. Jay liked to get the small details right in his scenario work.

"Howdy," Jay said.

"Howdy, yo'self," the whittler said. A long wood shaving curled up from the edge of the knife blade.

In RW, Jay was querying a server for information that would be downloaded into his computer spool; but in VR, it was much more interesting.

"What's happenin'?" Jay asked.

"Not much," the whittler allowed. "This and that. You heard about them FBI guys got poisoned?"

"Stoned," Jay said, "not poisoned." He smiled. Yep, that had been a funny one. Something to wave at the Bureau boys when he ran into them in the cafeteria. The regular feebs were always ragging on Net Force about one thing or another, so any ammunition Jay could gather to pop off at them in return was good, especially since the L.A. incident hadn't hurt anybody, only embarrassed 'em.

"Anybody come through selling snake oil lately?"

In this case, "snake oil" was a representation of the mysterious purple cap the DEA was all hot to run down. And not just them, so it seemed.

Along his way, Jay had stopped to chat with several local characters, and so far, he hadn't turned up anything. But this time, it was different.

"Well, yes, sir, there was this fellow come through a little while ago had some of that stuff, I do believe."

Jay's laid-back Zen attitude vanished. "What? When? Which way did he go?"

Whittler spat a stream of something dark and icky and pointed with the knife. "He headed on up the road, over toward Hemphill, I reckon."

Jesus! Could it be this easy?

"Was he walking?"

"In a horse-drawn wagon."

Speed, he needed to get moving if he was going to track and run down the dope dealer. He looked around. He could drop out of this scenario and switch to another, or do it in RT with voxax or a keyboard . . . No, wait, he had a toggle he could use, a backup. He did it, and suddenly there was a moped leaning against a tree, just there.

"Mind if I borrow the bike?"

"He'p yo'self."

Jay ran to the moped, essentially a heavy bicycle with a motor that you started by pedaling the bike. It wasn't a Harley, but it was faster than a horse-drawn wagon, and a lot better on a gravel road than a hog would be anyhow, at least the way he rode, even in VR.

He hopped on the moped and started pedaling.

This contemplative Buddhist stuff was all well and good, but when things started to break, you needed to be able to *move!*

The little two-cycle motor belched, emitted a puff of white smoke via the tailpipe, and started up.

The boss would be really happy if Jay could wrap this up.

Washington, D.C.

Michaels was moving the boxes Guru had sent home with Toni when he came across a small, highly polished wooden one that gleamed, even under the dust. "Very nice," he said, holding it up.

Toni glanced over from where she was piling shoes. She already had a molehill of them in the hall, the mound threatening to become a small mountain completely blocking the door to the bedroom. "Oh, I forgot all about those."

Toni came over to where Michaels stood and took the

box from him, flipped the brass catch up, and opened the lid, then turned it to show him.

"Wow," he said.

She removed a pair of small knives from velvet-lined recesses in the box, then pulled out a shelf to reveal a hidden space under it. There was a thick leather sheath in the bottom section. It looked like somebody had chopped a third or so off the end of a banana and flattened the sides. She took the sheath out and inserted the two curved blades into it so that they rode side by side, separated only by a center strip of leather. They were all metal, the knives, and the pommel end of each consisted of a thick circle with a big hole in the middle. With a quick move, Toni pulled both blades, dropped the sheath onto the carpet, and brought her hands together. When she pulled her hands apart, each one wore a knife, with short and nasty-looking curved blades extending point forward, maybe two inches from the little finger sides of her palms. Her forefingers went through the rings on the end.

"These are a variation on *kerambits,*" she said. "Sometimes called *lawi ayam.* Indonesian close-quarters knives."

She turned her hand over, palms up, to show him.

He took a closer look. The things were short, maybe five or six inches long, and most of that was the flat handle with the hole in it. The cutting hooks themselves looked like little talons. The steel had an intricate pattern of lines and whorls in it.

"The traditional ones are usually longer and sharp on both edges. Guru had these made for her by a master knife smith and martial artist in Keenesburg, Colorado, a guy named Steve Rollert. I guess it must be ten, twelve years ago, now. They are forged Damascus, folded and hammered to make hundreds or thousands of layers in the steel. Edge is heat-treated differently than the body, so it's hard and will stay sharp, while the body has a little more flex to it.

"See, you put your forefinger through the hole and grip it so. You can also turn it around and use your little finger, with the blade coming out on the thumb side, like this."

She demonstrated the move, then moved it back to the first grip.

"And perfectly legal to carry around, I suppose?"

She grinned. "Actually, you can in some states if you wear them on your belt, out in the open. Not most places if you conceal them."

"Kind of like brass knuckles," he said. "Or maybe knuckle, singular."

"But much better," she said. "The blades are extremely sharp, and you can hit with the ring end without hurting your finger."

"Great."

She missed the sarcasm, or more likely, ignored it. "Aren't they?" She did a little series of moves, whipping the two knives back and forth.

A slight error and there was gonna be blood everywhere. His or hers. He took half a step back.

"They aren't very long," he said, and even as he spoke, he was glad they weren't longer.

" 'Cause they are slashers rather than stabbers. All the major peripheral arteries are fairly close to the skin's surface. Carotids, antecubitals, femorals, popliteals. These will reach all of those. Cut a big artery, and you bleed out pretty quick if you don't do something. Kill you quicker than not breathing will, and blood is lot harder to replace than air."

"How nice."

"I remember this guy Rollert has a sense of humor, too. These are custom work, but he makes a tool-steel version of these coated with black Teflon. He calls them box cutters, and that's how he markets them. 'Why, what's the problem, Officer? This is a box cutter, see, it says so right there on the handle.' I've got a set of those tucked away somewhere. Of course, those cost about a twentieth of what these did."

She waved the knives again, getting into it. It was spooky to watch those things blur as she whipped them around.

"What'd the cheap ones cost?"

"About fifty bucks each."

"You mean these two little pieces of steel cost a thousand dollars?!"

"Quality doesn't come cheap."

Michaels shook his head. His darling bride, carrying his unborn son, was a mistress of death and destruction. She talked about such toys the way other women talked about getting their hair done.

"You can do your *djurus* holding one of these in each hand, and with only a slight adjustment, do them the same."

"Yeah, and slice off my nose if I make a mistake."

"Better your nose than some . . . other extremity." She grinned. "Don't worry. By the time you know all eighteen *djurus,* you'll be able to use these or a longer knife or a stick, no problem. Might nick yourself if you get sloppy, but as long as you keep proper form, you won't. *Silat* is weapons-based, remember. Only use your hands if nothing better is available."

She waved the little knives back and forth, crossing and uncrossing her hands in patterns that looked damned dangerous to him.

But she was excited, and as upbeat as he'd seen her lately, and he liked seeing that.

"These were the first knives Guru showed me how to use. Traditionally, they were backup. Women carried them a lot. You could wind one into your hair or tuck it into a sarong. These have a leather sheath, but the old-style ones made in Java usually have wooden scabbards. Supposedly, there were guys in the old country who could grip them between their toes and turn your legs and groin into hamburger while you were still checking their hands for a weapon."

"Lovely."

She kept twirling and slicing the air as she talked. "They make them longer, but the short ones are best for *djurus*. Even though *djurus* are practice and knives are for application, you can do the moves with steel hands. Watch."

She stopped moving, and then did *djuru* three. Her hands didn't move any slower than they did when she did the form unarmed, at least not that he could tell. "See? You block or punch like usual, only these give the moves more of a sting."

" 'A sting,' right. I'd be careful on *djuru* two," he said. "Way your boobs are getting big, you come across your chest on that inside block, you'll shear off a nipple."

She laughed, then put the knives back into their little velvet nests. "Thanks. I feel better. Now I can go back and finish sorting my shoes."

She handed him the box. "Put these somewhere we won't forget them, and I'll show you how to play with them when we get a chance."

She went back to her chore, and he looked at the box. Well. He knew what she did for fun when he married her. She had saved his life with the art once, and he had learned enough to use it himself, a little. He had been training seriously for almost a year, and he seldom missed a day of practice, thanks to Toni's proximity. After nearly being brained once by an assassin using a cane and pretending to be a little old lady, Michaels could hardly bitch about the down-and-dirty side of fighting. *Pentjak silat* was about as dirty as it came, and when somebody was trying to bash your head in, all bets were off. When you reached into your bag of tricks, *this* was the stuff you wanted to come up with. A guy charging at you with mayhem in mind might think twice if he saw you whirling these nasty little claws around with a demented grin while you did it. He sure as hell would.

Rules? In a knife fight? No rules!

He smiled at the wooden box and went to put it on a shelf in the living room. It would make a great conversation piece at a dinner party. Or a conversation stopper, depending on what you wanted to do.

It would be very interesting to see what the two of them decided to teach their son when he got old enough to wonder about all those funny dances Mama and Daddy did. For certain, they would show him how to protect himself. Michaels's father had taught him how to do a little boxing when he'd been about six or seven, and while he'd never been very good at it, at least he had developed a sense of self-confidence in his ability to protect himself.

Once he'd started learning *silat,* he realized how much he didn't know, but since he hadn't spent a lot of time fighting, it had worked out okay anyhow.

Funny to think about, teaching your son how to fight, when he wasn't even born yet. Next thing you knew, he'd be buying him baseball gloves and electric trains.

14

Michaels had left the director's office, feeling a nagging sense of unease. Director Allison had ostensibly called him in for a progress report, but the real reason was, he was sure, that she had been given the word to light a fire under his ass. His backside certainly felt warm enough when she was done talking. She wasn't exactly dumping on him for what the agency had or had not done so far, but she must have used the term "interagency cooperation" ten times during their conversation. As much as he hated politics, Michaels knew what *that* meant.

Pee flowed downhill, and the director's drain was right above his head . . .

Unfortunately, business was slow, and because it was, this was rapidly becoming *the* case to solve, and quickly. If there had been some major e-terrorism going, some big-time computer frauds, or even more bored hackers, he could beg off, point to those, and wash his hands of this crap fobbed off on them. But his people were good, they were on top of the day-to-day stuff. Even though it was the DEA's problem, had almost nothing to do with computers, and Net Force was just helping out, if they didn't do something pretty quick, it could get ugly.

A couple more millionaires going bonzo, and the powers that be would be looking for a scapegoat to roast, and while it should be the DEA, it could well turn out to be a major barbecue, with Net Force on the spit, too.

As he got back into the hinterlands and his own office at Net Force HQ, he saw Jay Gridley standing in the door, grinning.

"Tell me you have good news, Jay."

"Oh, yeah. I think I got a solid lead on our dope dealer."

"Really?"

"Yes, sir, boss."

"How?"

"The rich man's daughter. I backtracked her spending spree. Somebody remembered that she used a public computer in one of the shops for some kind of on-line transaction. I sieved the computers she might have operated, found all the e-mail for the time she would have been in the shop, and did some cross-references and keyword hits, in case she used a phony name . . . which, by the way, she did."

"Go on, impress me."

"I had the searchbots looking for a long list of pointers, about forty keys, including Thor, Thor's Hammer, and all like that. I got a hit on one and followed it up."

"And this keyword was . . . ?"

"Purple."

"Purple?"

"As in the color of the caps. Here's the e-mail I ran down."

He handed Michaels a hardcopy print. It said, "Yo, Friday Girl—I'll have that purple thingee for you when you come by."

It was signed, "Wednesday."

"No offense, Jay, but this is a reach. A 'purple thingee'? It could be some kind of plush kid's toy for all we know. And days of the week as code names? Why would that be our rich woman and her dealer?"

Jay grinned. "That's the key, boss. *Friday* was named for the Norse goddess Frigga. *Wednesday* comes from *Woden,* which, as I'm sure you must know, is the way the Norse in the southern countries spelled *Odin.* "

"Fascinating. So?"

"Frigga and Odin were Thor's mom and pop."

Michaels thought about that for a few seconds. "Ah. That would seem to be a bit of a coincidence, wouldn't it."

"Yeah, I'd say so. Doesn't mean it's the chemist himself, but I'd bet my next month's pay against a week-old, road-killed possum this 'Wednesday' guy has something to do with this drug."

"Good work, Jay."

"I didn't spook the guy, stayed well back, but I can run him down to an addy."

"Better still."

"Well, the thing is, this is good *and* bad. If I found it, the NSA people will find it, too, if they haven't already."

"How do you figure?"

"Well, their mission is to monitor communications outside the U.S. for possible terrorist activity, assorted plots, and things it would be good for us to know in general. So they have a whole list of words which, if they come up in a telephone conversation, a com-radio, telegraph signal, or e-mail, stuff like that, it kicks in a recorder. The message is taped and downloaded into one of a shitload of mainframes NSA operates, and rescanned, then routed to a computer program that reads the message and assigns it a priority code on a scale of one to ten. Anything above five gets sent to a human, and the higher a number, the faster it gets there. So if you put the words *Suicide mission* and *bomb* into your e-mail heading in any one of a hundred major or twenty minor languages, and NSA happens across it, somebody checks it. Most of the time it's nothing, guys screwing around or whatever, but sometimes it pans out. A message that says something like 'Shoot and kill the president and blow up Washington D.C.' had better be a line from a TV show or an upcoming techno-thriller novel."

"Nobody could be that stupid."

"Oh, yeah they can. Dumb crooks are legion."

Michaels said, "All right. I know this, in general, about NSA. So?"

"So you think NSA confines its eyes and ears to *outside* our borders? Yeah, home court's supposed to be FBI territory for such things, but everybody in the biz knows which way that wind blows. NSA has the tools, and how would anybody know they were doing it if they didn't tell us? Sheeit. If they are as hot to run down these dopers as the DEA, they will have assigned anything having to do with Thor a high priority. If we want to beat 'em to this Wednesday, we better get somebody on the street PDQ. The dealer might get taken, and that'd be good, but it's better for us if we get some credit, right?"

"Right," Michaels said. "Let me step into my office and make a call. Thanks, Jay."

"Info is in your in-file under the name 'Rich Girl.' Remember me when you give out the bonuses."

Malibu, California

When Tad woke up again, he looked at his watch. Not so much for the time as for the date. Sometimes after a Hammer trip, he would be more or less unconscious for three or four days.

He had been awake a couple times before, to go pee and get some water and pain pills, and he thought he remembered Bobby telling him a story about stoning FBI HQ in L.A. all to hell and gone. Maybe that had been a dream. Make more sense if it was.

Not too bad, if the watch was right, only a couple days since he'd crashed. If he remembered the day he'd done it right.

And if it hadn't been a week and some.

He hurt all over. It was like he'd been dropped off a tall building and then bounced like a superball for a couple of blocks, slamming a different part of his body against the concrete each time. The slightest movement stabbed him with hot needles, cut at him with cold, dull razors. He managed to roll to a sitting position, then up to his feet. He swayed there for a moment, fought for balance, then headed for the shower. Moving slowly. After he got clean, he'd feel a little better, though a little better wasn't going to be much compared to how crappy he felt. Still, that was the price you paid. You could bitch after the first time, but after that, you had no excuses; you *knew* what it was gonna feel like. You couldn't blame anybody but yourself.

He managed to achieve the bathroom without falling, though he had to lean against the wall a couple of times along the way. He stripped, then got into the shower and cranked the water up full blast from all the nozzles. Had to; water coming from only one direction would probably knock him down.

Halfway to using all the hot water in the house—and that was saying something—Bobby stuck his head into the steamed-up bathroom and yelled: "Still alive? Amazing."

"Fuck you," Tad yelled reflexively.

"You okay enough to work?"

"I'm up, aren't I?" He shut off the water and stepped out, grabbed one of the beach towels, and started drying off.

Bobby watched him, shaking his head. "You look like hammered dog shit."

"Why, thank you. So what?"

"Business is picking up. I've got a dozen orders I need to send out today, eight more tomorrow, and four more the day after that."

"Got me a cap for the first run?"

"Jesus, Tad, you do want to die, don't you?"

Tad didn't answer but finished toweling off. He looked at himself in the foggy mirror. Skinny as hell, yes, but in the blurry, soft-focus mirror reflections, he didn't really look that bad.

Bobby blew out a theatrical sigh. "Yeah, I got one for you."

Tad nodded, managed a grin. He'd never gone riding with Thor twice in a week before, it always took a long time to recover completely, but with enough chemical assistance, he could get past the aches and injuries he collected while tripping. They were still *there*, of course, but he didn't feel them. Well, not as much. Thing was, he'd built up a pretty good tolerance to Demerol and morphine over the years. He could take a handful of 50 mg tabs and walk around like it was nothing, a dose that would put much bigger guys on the floor in a dreamy trance for six or eight hours. Morphine was a better painkiller than Demerol, heroin better still, but of course, those had their own problems—he wasn't a big fan of needles or gas-powered skin-poppers that blasted the drug into you. Getting addicted wasn't a problem he worried about, and he used morphine or smack sometimes, when it got really bad, but only as a painkiller, not for the high. Some people liked downers, which was what the opiates were. Tad liked uppers. Being able to *move*, to do things. The months he'd spent in a bed coughing up bloody sputum when he had active TB never left him. He didn't plan to die in bed. Live fast, die young, and if the corpse was ugly or good-looking, what did that matter? You weren't gonna be around to hear praise or revulsion, were you?

Time was running out. Take the trip now, or miss it. You get to be dead a long time, right?

Even with the Demerol tabs he'd taken last time he was up, and the shower, he felt like Bobby said he looked: like shit. So a little of the Mexican white was called for, to dull the edges. Some muscle relaxants, some steroids for the swelling and inflammation, and a little speed to balance things, he'd be able to get around. And once he picked up the Hammer again? Well, then it would all go away.

Superman don't need no pain pills.

"I'm on it," Tad said. "Give me ten minutes."

Bobby nodded. "I'm going to start final mix now."

Tad waved him off. His stash was in his car, parked at the sandwich place. He'd have to go get it, come back, and hope he could find a vein he could hit. What a bitch.

Washington, D.C.

Toni spent an hour playing with the scrimshaw, then had to quit. Her ankles were swelling, her right thumb and forefinger had gone numb from gripping the pin vise, and she was going blind looking through the magnifying lamp's lens. That stereoscopic microscope would sure come in handy.

Yeah. So would some artistic talent and a lot more patience. Putting in a thousand tiny dots, each the size of a flea's eye, was extremely exacting work. A couple of times, she had lost her concentration and put a dot outside the lines. Those would have to be sanded out and polished, and that was tricky, she'd already found out.

Maybe this wasn't such a good idea, taking up something this precise. Maybe she was just wasting her time and a lot of effort.

She went to the bathroom, washed her hands and face in cold water, and went into the living room. She sat on the couch. She could do her *djuru* hand work sitting down, most of it. The footwork was getting harder and harder to add in, and while Guru's advice had been not to worry about it, it would all come back after the baby was born, she did worry about it. It had never occurred to her it would be like this.

The Indonesian martial art had been the core of who she was since she'd been thirteen. She hadn't gotten into team sports, school clubs, or other extracurricular activities as a young woman in high school and college, not to speak of. No, she had dedicated herself to learning how to move in balance, to being able to deliver a focused attack against an aggressor, no matter if he was bigger, stronger, faster, or even well-trained. Yes, she had school, in which she did well, and yes, she had friends and lovers and a job, but in her own mind, she was a warrior.

A warrior with, she had to admit, some control issues.

Now a big, fat, pale, pregnant warrior with control issues, hey?

Shut up!

Putting scratches and itty-bitty dots on fake ivory instead of kicking ass. Some warrior.

Tears rose and threatened to spill, but Toni angrily wiped her eyes. No. She wouldn't give in to this emotional turmoil. Hormones, that was all it was, goddamned hormones! She'd learned how to control PMS, and she never let her periods keep her from work or working out. She could beat this, too! It was a matter of will!

Sure, sure, it is, as long as you watch out for peg-legged guys with eye patches carrying harpoons, whale-girl. Thar she blows!

She was more angry than she was anything, but now the tears did flow, and she couldn't stop them.

The com chirped. She stared at it. It kept on cheeping. Finally, she picked it up.

"Hello," she said.

"Hi, babe, it's me. How are you doing?"

Alex. Oh, boy. Was *that* the wrong thing for him to say.

"I hate my life," she said.

He didn't say anything, but he didn't have to say anything. She had more. Much more.

15

"You want me to go along on a *drug* raid?" John Howard said.

Michaels nodded. "Yes. We have a vested interest here, even though it is officially a DEA matter. I just got off the com with Brett Lee. They are willing to allow a Net Force liaison to tag along . . . if he's field-qualified. In the interests of interagency cooperation, of course."

"Let me see if I can translate that. We need credit for this, right?"

"Damn straight. This is going to be a high-profile bust. There is a lot of interest in catching these folks, from way up the food chain. When the media figures out what this is connected to, we don't want to be left out in the cold. You standing there conspicuously in your Net Force blues on the six o'clock news will make sure nobody accidentally 'forgets' to mention that it was us who located this evildoer and gave his location to the DEA."

Howard smiled. "You're getting a lot better at this political in-fighting, Commander."

"I'd say thank you, but I'm not sure I consider that a compliment."

Howard shrugged. "Goes with the job. Same with any organization. Once you get above the rank of major in the army, most of what you do requires one eye on the chain of command, the other eye on the internal and external politics affecting your unit. Makes it hard to see what you actually want to accomplish. You don't watch out for us, you sure can't expect anybody else to do it. Certainly not the DEA or NSA."

"I wouldn't order you to do it. Strictly voluntary, General."

"Well, sir, I'd be happy to go along and help our fellow crime fighters take down this dope peddler. It's been a little slow around here anyway."

"Knock on wood," Michaels said, rapping his desktop. "In case there are any bored angels watching who want to give us something to worry about."

"Amen."

After Howard left, Michaels's secretary told him he had a call.

"From?"

"Gretta Henkel."

"Why do I recognize that name?"

"She's the CEO and largest shareholder of Henkel Pharmaceuticals, which is headquartered in Mannheim, Germany."

Michaels rolled his eyes. Jesus, word was definitely out about this drug thing. He reached for the phone.

The conversation didn't take long, and when it was done, Michaels leaned back in his chair and shook his head. Ms. Henkel, of Henkel Pharmaceuticals, the largest European drug manufacturing company and the fourth largest in the world, had offered him a job.

Ostensibly, Ms. Henkel was looking for somebody to run their computer security department, and who better than the man who ran the computer security service for the United States government? She had, she had said, heard great things about him. Would he be interested in speaking with her personally about this? She could have one of the corporate jets pick him up and fly him to Mannheim for a chat. She mentioned a starting salary that translated to roughly four times what he was making as a government employee, plus stock options and a medical and retirement package that would, in twenty years, make him a fairly wealthy man. He could also bring two or three of his best people with him if he elected to accept the job, of course, and with hefty increases in their salaries, too.

It was tempting to think her offer was exactly what she said. A recognition of his ability to manage a complex technical operation. An offer tendered on merit. A deserved and great opportunity.

Michaels smiled at that. He had never considered himself the brightest light on the string, but neither had he thought he was the dimmest.

What this was about, of course, was this damned purple capsule everybody wanted so badly. Probably Ms. Henkel wanted it to move her company from fourth largest to third or maybe even first place. Or maybe she wanted it so the Germans could gear up for another war with supersoldiers. It didn't really matter. But she was assuming that if she paved a road with platinum for him to get there, Michaels would bring the secret of the stuff with him. It would be interesting to see if the job offer became real if he didn't happen to have that information at hand or didn't want to give it up. Or even how long his new job would last if he did.

He smiled again as he thought about telling Toni: "Hi,

honey, I'm home! Guess what. We're moving to Germany!"

Deutschland, Deutschland, über alles . . .

He chuckled at that thought.

He'd declined the offer with appropriate regrets and thanked Ms. Henkel politely.

Whatever the hell was in that mysterious capsule must be very interesting indeed.

Beverly Hills, California

He could have requisitioned a Net Force jet, but having risen on merit as a colonel in the regular army before taking command of the Net Force military arm, John Howard had a few friends still active in other services. An old Air Force buddy who had likewise risen high in the ranks got him second seat on a fighter going across the country. The training flight had to refuel midair, of course, but since it didn't land, Howard was more than two hours ahead of Mr. Brett Lee's commercial flight and waiting at the airport for him when he got off the plane. A small victory but worth the effort for the look on the face of a man who had left Washington, D.C., an hour before Howard had and well knew it.

Lee filled him in on details as they drove toward Beverly Hills.

"The suspect's name is George Harris Zeigler, age thirty-one." He looked at Howard as if expecting some response, but the name didn't mean anything to him, and Howard said so.

"He's a fairly well-known actor," Lee said. "A pretty boy who plays action heroes, has the teenage girls all hot for him. They call him the Zee-ster."

"There you go," Howard said. "I'm neither teenage nor female. And not much of a movie fan."

"In any event, we have the warrants, and our surveillance teams have him at home. He lives in a big, gated estate in Beverly Hills."

"Of course he does."

"We're going in hot and fast. We need to do this quick enough to get samples of the drug. He has bodyguards and a commercial security system. It is unlikely he is the chemist. He flunked out of high school before becoming an actor, but we think he either sells or gives the stuff to his friends, especially his female friends. He doesn't need the money; he gets fifteen or twenty million dollars each for the movies he stars in. And you've never heard of him?"

"I guess I need to get out more," Howard allowed.

Lee glared but then forced a smile. It was his operation, and he would be giving Howard his assignment. He'd have the last word. "You will be assisting the agents covering the *garage*," he said. "In case Mr. Zeigler decides to try to escape. It's a twelve-car garage, but he only has ten in it at the moment. The usual toys, including a Ferrari, a Land Cruiser, a Ford Cobra, a Dodge Viper, and a couple of antique Rolls-Royces."

"Must be nice. How many agents do you have going into the house?"

"Sixteen."

"Ah. Well, if he gets past you, we'll do our best to try to stop him."

Lee didn't speak to that, and Howard leaned back in the seat, looking out the window. *Smoggy out here today. Big surprise.*

When they got to the staging area, a local park, Howard pulled his gear out of his tactical duffel bag. He had his side arm, the Medusa, his blue coveralls, and the spidersilk vest with "Net Force" stenciled in big phosphorescent yellow letters across the back. He strapped on his revolver, slipped into the coveralls, and tabbed the vest into place. It was class-one armor with full side panels and a crotch drape. The tightweave silk and overlapping ceramic plates would stop any handgun round and most rifle bullets, assuming the shooter went for the body and not the head or legs. Somehow, he didn't think an actor who let himself be called the Zee-ster would be doing much blasting. Rich folks generally fought with lawyers, not firearms. And his chances of getting past a whole slew of DEA agents armed with subguns were slim and snowball.

Howard had wanted to bring his old Thompson, the ancient .45 submachine gun his grandfather had gotten when he was an unofficial deputy in the preintegration days, but he thought that might be a bit ostentatious in front of the cameras. And there were sure to be news copters flitting around pretty quick in this kind of operation. Dead-eye John Howard and his Chicago typewriter might not provide the image Net Force wanted.

During the briefing, Howard memorized the maps, met the two agents who'd be watching the garage with him— their names were Brown and Peterson, a tall woman and a short man, respectively. Lee, despite his quick fuse, gave a pretty good sitrep and assignment layout. Everybody synchronized their watches and slipped into tactical radio headphones set to a narrow-band opchan. Whatever the DEA's political agendas, they had done enough drug busts to know how to enter a secured residence efficiently.

They'd borrowed a tactical truck from the local police force, and it went through the heavy steel gate as if it were paper. The cars followed the truck in, five vehicles, and made for their assigned locations. Howard wasn't sure, but it seemed to him there were more than sixteen agents leaping from cars and hurrying toward the house.

Brown, Peterson, and Howard alighted and moved to the garage. Brown had an electronic master key she triggered, and the signal worked; the garage doors rolled up, all six of them.

Peterson moved to stand behind the door from the garage into the house, his handgun pointed up by his ear.

Brown crouched behind the car closest to the door, a seventies Charger, a muscle car lovingly painted in maybe twenty hand-rubbed coats of metalflake candy-apple red. *Be a shame to see that paint chipped by a bullet,* Howard thought.

He looked around. Which car would he take if he was in a real hurry? Probably the Cobra. Nah, better would be the Viper, which was essentially a rocket with wheels. They'd have to use roadblocks; nobody would be catching that sucker from behind.

He walked over to the Viper and looked into the little convertible. *Had to be a real wood dash and steering wheel. Hello? What's this?*

Lying in plain view on the passenger seat was one of those zippered plastic bags, like for sandwiches.

Inside the bag were four big purple capsules.

Howard grinned. Son of a bitch!

Brown and Peterson were intent on the door. Orders from Lee rattled over the operations channel on the headset. They had crashed the front door, after some effort, and were entering the residence.

Howard reached down, picked up the bag, opened it, and shook one of the capsules into his palm. He looked at the two DEA agents. He could have been invisible as far as they were concerned.

He slipped the cap into his coverall pocket, zipped the bag closed, and dropped it back onto the car seat.

The sounds of fully automatic weapon fire and Lee

screaming over the headset came simultaneously: "Return fire, return fire!"

Well. Looked like the bodyguards were earning their money.

More full-autos came on-line. The DEA assault team carried MP-5s, and the distinctive sound of those chattered, joining the other guns. All pistol-caliber stuff, Howard thought, nothing loud enough to be rifle. The suspect's bodyguards must have MAC-10s, Uzis, something like that. Didn't sound like H&Ks.

". . . all available agents, they're heading for the kitchen!"

The kitchen, Howard recalled from the maps, was just up a short hall from the garage.

Brown and Peterson took this as a sign they should go in. Peterson jerked the door open, Brown stepped in, pistol leading. They didn't look for Howard but vanished into the house.

Howard, whose side arm was still in the holster, considered his options. If sixteen DEA agents couldn't take out a pretty-boy movie star and his bodyguards, he wasn't going to be able to add much firepower. He'd stay right here, just like he'd been assigned.

More shots echoed from the house. Somebody screamed, two or three different voices.

"Shit!"

"Fuck!"

"Ow, ow, I'm shot!"

Ten seconds later, a man emerged from the house into the garage. In one arm gathered to his chest, he held a young woman in a maid's uniform. From her face, the girl was in mortal terror, and rightly so, since in his other hand, the guy held a short knife pressed against her neck. He was a handsome young man.

This would be the Zee-ster, Howard guessed.

He pulled his revolver, brought his other hand up, clasped the weapon in a two-handed grip, and pointed it at the knife man.

"Hold it right there, Zeigler," he said.

The man froze.

Howard forced his hands to relax a hair. Holding the revolver tightly was necessary for the shot, but clenching the thing in a death grip for any length of time past a second or two would cramp his hands pretty quickly. And he might be here a while, you never could tell.

Zeigler, with the knife held at the hostage's throat, tried to make himself smaller, but there was no way a five-foot-tall, hundred-pound woman was going to completely shield a six-foot-tall, two-hundred-pound man. Howard had all kinds of targets, including the only one that meant instant incapacitation, a head shot.

"Put the gun down! Put it down, or I'll kill her!"

He had the shot. Sights square, lined up on the man's left eye. At fifteen, maybe sixteen feet, he wasn't going to miss. Unless the guy jerked at the last second and put the hostage where his head had been. Not much risk to the woman, but some. And he'd have to kill the movie star, a head shot would do that, right into the brain.

Well, maybe not on a movie star . . .

"Listen," Howard said, "let's discuss this."

"No fucking *discussion!* Put the gun down, or I'll cut her throat!"

The maid whimpered.

"You don't want to do that. You kill her, you're standing there unprotected with a knife in your hand. Think about that. She's all that's keeping *you* alive. She dies, you die, simple as that."

"You can't do that. Do you know who I am?"

"I'm not a cop, son, I'm a soldier. They trained me to kill, not capture. I see blood on that blade, it's a done deal. I don't *care* who you are. God doesn't love men who murder innocent women, and I expect He sent me here to teach you this."

The man was on the edge of panic. "Let me go, I let her go."

"What, do I have the word *stupid* tattooed on my forehead? Put the knife down, you get to tell your story to a judge. Maybe a good lawyer can even get you off, it happens all the time. You're a millionaire. Rich and famous men don't go to the gas chamber. You cut that woman, I guarantee you'll be dead before she is. Game over."

"You might hit her if you shoot!"

Howard blew out a theatrical sigh. "Let me explain some things to you, son. This weapon I am holding in my hands is a Phillips & Rodgers .357 Model 47 Medusa. It's about as well-made and accurate a double-action revolver as you can get, and with the hammer back in single-action mode like it is now, it's *extremely* accurate. I can hit an apple at twenty-five meters all day long, and you are less than one-third that far away. You understand? You want to think about how much of you I can see that's not behind your hostage?"

Zeigler didn't say anything.

Howard continued. "There are six one-hundred-and-twenty-five–grain semijacketed hollow point rounds in this handgun. If I shoot and hit you solidly anywhere with only *one* shot—and I *will* hit you, son, you can bet the farm on that—the bullet will thump you at around twelve hundred feet per second. That means it gets there before you hear the sound of it going off. That hypersonic bullet will expand to maybe twice its size and it will put a big hole most if not all the way through you. Based on documented shootings with this caliber and particular brand of ammo, you will go to the floor ninety-six point four times out of a hundred, and no longer have any interest in anything but trying to breathe. And probably not that for long."

Zeigler swallowed dryly.

"Now, here's the deal. I don't give a rat's ass if you walk out of here or if the DEA drags your dead body out; it's all the same to me. But if I have to shoot, this gun is going to make a terrible noise inside this garage, and probably my ears will ring for a couple of days, because I didn't think to put my plugs in before I came through the door. I'd just as soon not damage my hearing any more than I have to.

"So if I have to shoot, I am going to be real pissed off. I might as well shoot again. You following me? You put the knife down right now, or I will punch a hole in you, and when you fall, I'll pump a couple more in you for making my ears hurt. Your movie career might survive an arrest. You don't put that knife down, you won't. Simple as that. Your choice. Either the knife hits the floor or you do."

Somebody was listening on the radio, because Howard heard, "Don't shoot him! Don't shoot him! We're on the way!"

Howard tongued the radio's off switch. He couldn't turn off his mike, but he silenced the earphones. He didn't need the distraction.

He took a deep breath and let part of it out, held the rest, preparing for the shot. You never bluffed in a situation like this. He put his finger inside the guard and onto the trigger. Wouldn't take much, just under three pounds, a nice, crisp pull, like breaking an icicle.

"Don't! Don't kill me! Please!"

Ziegler's left hand came away from the maid, releasing her, and made a pushing motion toward Howard.

"Come on, we can make a deal here! I'll . . . I'll give you my supplier! That's what you want, isn't it?"

The knife moved away from the maid's neck. Ziegler hadn't dropped it yet, but he was about to. His knife hand had already relaxed, and he had taken a half step away from his hostage.

Howard let out another sigh, quieter this time. *Thank you, Lord.* That would have been all he needed, millions of teenage girls hating his guts for killing their screen idol. He'd dodged a bullet himself when that knife dropped—

Somebody ran around the corner from outside and into the garage and fired a handgun twice, hitting the suspect square in the chest.

Zeigler collapsed. The maid screamed and fell to the floor, onto her hands and knees, scrabbled for cover behind the muscle car.

Instinctively, Howard spun toward the shooter, gun leading.

It was Brett Lee.

Lee quickly pointed his gun toward the ceiling, his other hand open and raised. "Easy, easy!"

Howard said, "Why did you shoot, you fucking moron? He had dropped his weapon!"

"Sorry. It looked like he was about to hurt the hostage."

"I thought you wanted him alive!"

Lee didn't say anything else. He put away his weapon.

Howard shook his head, went to check on Zeigler. One in the heart, one in the upper chest, he'd be dead before the paramedics could get him to the ambulance. Shit!

Howard stood, holstered his revolver, helped the crying hostage to her feet. "It's all over, ma'am. You're safe now." He glared at Lee. *Sweet Jesus.*

He heard the sound of helicopters moving in and swore under his breath. He was gonna take the vest off. No way he wanted the name "Net Force" to show up on the evening news after this fiasco.

Commander Michaels would surely agree with that idea.

More DEA agents boiled out of the house, guns waving around. *Day late and a dollar short.*

What a snafu.

Sweet Jesus.

16

"So, the only lead we had to the dealer is cooling on a slab at the morgue in sunny L.A.?"

"Yes, sir," John Howard said. "Apparently to the regret of teenage girls everywhere."

"Jesus," Michaels said.

"My feelings exactly. My guess is, Mr. Lee of the DEA is going to have some tall explaining to do to his superiors."

Michaels shook his head. John Howard and Jay Gridley both looked at him as if expecting some wisdom, and he didn't have any on tap. He said, "Well, at least our information helped the DEA beat the NSA to the target."

"Might have been better the other way," Jay observed. "I kinda liked the Zee-ster's movies myself. He had a certain style."

That the first part of Jay's observation was a thought Michaels had already had didn't make it sit any better. And while he'd seen the actor in a couple of movies and hadn't been that impressed, dead was dead, and shooting

somebody with his hands up was bad juju, no two ways
about it. Especially a rich and famous somebody.

He said, "Well, if you give folks a knife and they cut
themselves with it, that's their problem. The director can't
fault us for what DEA screws up. What is the deal with
NSA and DEA, anyway? Some kind of ongoing bad
blood?"

Jay said, "Not that I know of. No more than any other
interagency rivalry. CIA, FBI kind of thing. You get the
ball, you don't pass it, you shoot, even if we're all on the
same team."

"What about personal histories? Agent Lee and Mr.
George go to competing schools? Sleep with each other's
girlfriends?"

Jay looked surprised. "Hmm. Never thought of that."

"Maybe it's not relevant to the situation, but why don't
you poke around a little and see what you can find. From
our meetings, it doesn't seem as if these two have any
great love for each other, and I'd just as soon not get Net
Force splattered with incidental mud if these two are going to keep throwing it at each other."

Jay nodded. "Good idea, boss. I'll do that."

"Even though it's primarily their problem, we can't just
wash our hands of it. We have to help them keep looking,
and right now, all we've got is a dead movie star and a
dead end."

"Not altogether," Howard said. He grinned, showing
bright teeth against his chocolate skin. "There is the matter of the recovered capsules. Unfortunately, they were
near the end of their life span; the movie star could afford
to buy them and let them go bad if he wanted, and by the
time the DEA got the things to their lab, they were so
much inert powder internally."

"Which doesn't do us much good, does it?" Michaels
said.

"Well, sir, probably not. But while you'll notice that the report says there were three of the capsules, that is actually in error."

Michaels looked at him, waiting.

Howard reached out and dropped a purple cap onto his desktop.

Jay grinned. "General! You swiped one?"

"Liberated it," Howard said. "It won't do us any more good chemically than the ones the DEA's got, but I figured what they could learn from four, they could learn from three."

Michaels picked up the cap and looked at it. "Doesn't seem like it's worth all the trouble, this little thing."

"Diamonds are small, too, boss, and so are wetware and lightware chips."

"Well, as it happens, we have a friend in the FBI lab who would like to get his hands on this," Michaels said. "That way, at least we'd know as much as the DEA about what's in it, for whatever that is worth. Maybe some rare herb found only in bouillabaisse served in a certain bad section of Marseilles, France."

"Sir?"

"Sorry, General, it's from an old spy comedy vid I once saw. But the regular FBI boys have a huge database and long memories, and their lab techs are second to none. Might be they could come up with something. I'll run this past them and see what they can find. Good work."

"Thank you, sir."

"And I was very happy not to see you on the news."

"I thought you might be," Howard said.

After Howard and Jay were gone, Michaels put the capsule into an empty paper clip box and stuck it into his pocket. Chain of evidence was no good, given how they'd come by it, but he was just looking for information. This whole mess was still the DEA's bastard child, and the sooner he could get Net Force out of helping take care of it, the better. He'd drop by the lab and have a chat with the assistant section head, a man he knew from his field days. They could work something out.

Malibu, California

"Don't take the Hammer," Bobby said.

Tad, whose last little hit of heroin was wearing off, frowned through the start of a headache. "Why not?"

"Because I need you straight."

Tad grinned his lopsided grin.

"Well, okay, *relatively* straight. We got problems."

"We're rich and good-looking, how bad could it be?"

Bobby smiled, but it vanished quickly. "The Zee-ster's dead."

"No way! I just saw him. Gave him the caps from that last batch. He looked great. He can't be dead."

"I got a contact in the police who says his body's in a big drawer at the new county morgue and the doctors are flipping coins to see who gets to slice and dice him. He's past tense."

"Aw, geez, that's too bad. I liked him. He knew how to party. What'd he do, wrap one of his cars around a tree? He never could drive worth a crap."

"He was shot twice in the heart by a DEA agent leading a drug raid on his mansion."

"Whoa. You're shittin' me."

"No. Storm and Drang put up a fight when the narcs kicked in the door. Word is, the Zee-ster's house walls got more holes in 'em now than a colander. Both body-guards are shot half to pieces, too, but Storm will probably make it. Drang is still in surgery, and they don't think

he'll survive, or if he does, he'll be a big hamburger patty
. . . he took a couple rounds in the head."

"Fuck."

"Yeah, it's awful and all, but stop and think about what
that means. Why would the feds be going after the Zee-
ster? He's a user, not a dealer."

"He spreads it around some," Tad said. "I mean, he
did. Could be they caught somebody he ran with, they
gave him up."

"Whatever. But this puts us in a kind of bad spot. We
ran with him, too. Somebody might remember us."

"Remember me, you mean. You look like ten thousand
other surfer dudes. Me, I kinda stand out."

Bobby waved that off. "The point is, we let ourselves
get public with him more than we should have, because
he was a movie star and cool and all. If he had the Hammer caps on him when they took him out of the game,
they are gonna go over his background with a microscope
. . . everywhere he went, everybody he saw. A guy like
that can't move in this town anonymously unless he wears
a bag over his head, and Zeigler never was one to hide
his pretty face. The cops and the feds will burn many shoe
soles tracking every move the man made. Somebody will
cover all of the trendy places where the Zee-ster liked to
party."

Tad nodded.

"All right, here's what I want you to do. You search
your memory and dig up every time you saw Zee in public, anywhere might have had a security cam lit. Get to
those places before the feds or the local police do, get the
recordings or wipe them or whatever."

"Yeah. I can do that."

"He never came here, and when I bought drinks or dinner, I paid cash, so there's no e-trail on me. I've made up
a list of the places where I went with him alone, or where

you and him and me were. Add those to your list. Crowd
he traveled with, they don't know us well enough to send
anybody here, hell, they were usually too stoned to know
who *they* were, much less us, but vids are different. If
we're on a tape, a RAM drive or a DVD, that's bad. If
that's gone, we're clear."

Tad nodded again. "Yeah, I got it. Only a few places
they might have captured images of us."

"We can't do shit about some tourist who snapped a
few frames of Zeigler while we were at Disneyland or the
beach or whatever, but the feds probably won't find them,
either. I think we can ride this out, we do it right."

"I wonder how they did figure out to go for him?"

"He fucked up. He liked to brag about doing five girls
at a time while he was on the Hammer, and like you said,
he passed out dope to the people around him like it was
chewing gum. Doesn't matter how they found him. What
matters is, they don't find us."

"I hear that." Tad had no desire to finish out his little
remaining time on earth in a cell. He'd punch his own
ticket before he'd let that happen.

"So we're on vacation for the next couple months,"
Bobby said. "No production, no deliveries, we are shut
down. Maybe we'll go to Maui, drive the crooked road
out to Hana, kick back on the black sand beach and watch
the girls awhile."

Tad nodded absently. "Yeah." But what he was thinking was, he had Thor's Hammer in his pocket, the last
one Bobby had made, and it still had a few more hours
of shelf life left. If he didn't take it, it was going to go
to waste, and Bobby wasn't gonna be making any more
until he felt safe.

Tad might not have a couple months left in him, you
never could tell.

Should he take it? He and Bobby hadn't spent that

much time with the Zee-ster out in public. Half a dozen spots in the last couple of months, no more, and most places didn't keep vid records more than a day or two, maybe a week, before they recorded over the old stuff. He could shave it close, check out the first few places, drop the cap, and finish the last few before it came on full blast. And even after it came on, he could maintain enough to take care of the security stuff, he was pretty sure. For a couple hours, anyway.

There was some risk, sure, but what the hell, he didn't have much to lose, did he?

There was one other possibility, something he hadn't ever tried, but he'd held in reserve, just in case something happened to Bobby before it did him. He could let the cap croak, clean up the security cam stuff, and head out to the islands with Bobby. Then, in a week or two, he could find some reason to split with Bobby for a couple days. Tell him he was gonna go camp out by the Sacred Pools or something—Bobby hated camping—then catch a flight back to L.A.

He'd been with Bobby a long time. And while he wasn't in Bobby's league as a chemist, he knew a fair amount about drugs. He had managed, over the time they'd been dealing the Hammer, to be around Bobby at one point or another during every step of the creation and blending of the ingredients for the drug. Yeah, he didn't even know what they all *were,* but he knew where to find the powders and how much to use of each.

He wasn't a genius like Bobby, he couldn't create the stuff from scratch, no way. But while not everybody could create a major symphony from nothing, like Mozart, a whole lot of people could play the sucker if they had the sheet music. Tad knew Bobby's routine; he'd watched it, memorized it, and he could do that much. Ma and Pa out in the RV had all the stuff for Thor's Hammer, neatly stored in little bottles. He could pay them a visit. They'd never think twice about it. He'd collected the stuff for Bobby several times.

Of course, when Bobby found out, he'd be pissed, so maybe Tad might have to eliminate Ma and Pa, torch the RV, and hope Bobby would blame it on rival dealers or the law. Then again, maybe Tad wouldn't be around when Bobby found out. The hole he had to climb out of each time was deeper and deeper. One day, he'd hit the bottom and not be able to make it back, and that was gonna be sooner rather than later.

It was something to think about.

"You gonna sit there staring into space all day or what?"

"Huh. Oh, yeah. I'm going. I need to, uh, freshen up a bit, then I'm good."

"Fine. Do what you need to do, but don't get pulled over for a ticket or whatever, be careful, okay?"

"Yeah, yeah, don't worry."

"I have to worry, Tad, for the both of us."

Tad headed for the bathroom and another hit of the Mexican white. As he walked, he fingered the capsule in his watch pocket to make sure it was still there. As long as he took care of business, what could it hurt to take it? It would be a crime to just waste it.

And even if he did take it, a few weeks from now he could *still* come back to L.A. And if he skipped the final step when he mixed the stuff, left out adding the self-destruct catalyst, the resulting caps maybe wouldn't be quite as potent, but they wouldn't go bad, either. He could take one every day until it killed him, and that wouldn't be the worst way to go out, now would it?

He smiled at himself in the bathroom mirror.

It was like looking at a grinning skull.

•   •   •

Drayne was pissed off at himself. He knew better than to associate with people he dealt to, he *knew* better. He'd talked to a lot of dope dealers over the years, had wrangled access to a lot of FBI files via his father, without the old man knowing, of course, and he'd learned a whole lot about the biz before he had ever sold his first pill.

The upside of things were big bucks and big thrills. Dopers who were smart made fortunes, and they got to make the assorted varieties of cops look stupid while they did it. Big money, big rushes, the thrill of victory, and all that green to feed the machine.

There was a downside, of course. Stupid dopers could get killed by a rival dealer. Or ripped off and maybe killed by a customer. Or busted and sent to the graybar hotel for twenty years on a heavy federal rap. Or busted by the local yokels. Lot of minefield in the illegal trade, and you couldn't complain to the cops if somebody pointed a gun at you and stole your dope or your money.

The thing was, if you were a dealer, and if you did it long enough, and if you didn't move around a bunch while you were doing it, you were sooner or later going to get caught. Ninety-nine point ninety-nine percent of dealers who stayed in the biz for more than a few years in one place eventually got nailed. Sometimes it was a distributor who gave 'em up, sometimes it was an ex-wife or girlfriend, sometimes the cops found 'em on their own.

Once you got a lot of cash in your hands, it sometimes made you stupid. You bought expensive, flashy toys, you got to thinking because you were rich you were invincible, and just like Zeigler, all your money didn't mean squat when the bullets started to fly. You couldn't take it with you.

So Drayne had always kept a low profile. No yachts, no car that couldn't be leased by half of L.A. No bodyguards with muscles and bulges under their jackets to make people wonder who you were who needed body-guards. Absolutely minimal risks in sales, delivery, taking on new customers. Never more stuff in the house than necessary. Nobody knew what he did except for three people: Tad and the old couple who drove the RV. Tad would never give him up, and Ma and Pa Yeehaw were lifetime criminals who would go down with guns blasting before they let themselves be taken. If not, he'd have them bailed out and gone before the feds knew what they had.

Not perfect, no ironclad guarantees, but he had been very careful. Until he got sucked into the glitz of Zeigler's movie-star circles. Even then, Drayne had stood in the back on the Zee-ster's coattails, and what the hell, it had been fun, watching every door open in front of them, women falling all over themselves to get close to them, and the reflected feeling of celebrity.

It had never occurred to him that Zeigler would be the target of a raid. Feds just didn't kick in famous million-aires' doors; it just wasn't done.

Well, it was now. And while they were *probably* okay, going to ground and turning invisible until all the heat died down was the way to play it. No reason to push things. He was ahead of the game. The feds were plod-ders, but they were like the tortoise: While the hare was taking a nap, they might creep up on him and bite him on the ass. Drayne wasn't going to give them that chance, no sir, thank you very fucking much.

A month or two in Hawaii in the fall? You could do a lot worse. And worse was not the way to go.

Soon as Tad got things taken care of, they were gonna hop on one of those big honkin' jumbo jets and zip on out to the islands. By the time they got back, all this other stuff would be old news.

Old news.

17

Washington, D.C.

Toni was going stir-crazy, she had cabin fever big time, and she had to get out of the house before she went totally bonkers. Yes, the doctor had told her to stay home and confine herself to light activity. Because, the doctor had said, if there were any more problems with cramping or bleeding, and she wanted this baby, she was going to wind up spending the rest of the pregnancy in bed, so best she not cause things to get to that state by being overactive.

Toni's mother had, of course, agreed entirely with the doctor's assessment. Sure, she hadn't slacked off any when her babies were growing, Mama said, but that was different. She was healthy as a horse, and besides, all that fighting stuff Toni did was probably upsetting the baby anyhow.

Toni didn't really have any place she wanted or needed to go, and she would window-shop in the mall if nothing else, as long as she didn't have to sit here alone in the place while Alex was off at work for one more day.

She missed work more than she'd expected, and it

wasn't the same doing little piddly consulting things on the net. There was no interaction with real people, no matter how good the virtual scenarios were. Yes, the state-of-the-art ScentWare ultrasonic olfactory generators gave some pretty authentic smells. The latest-generation haptic program from SensAble Technologies allowed you to feel pressure and touch, and of course, everybody's visuals were getting better every day, but the differences between the best VR stimware and reality were like light-years compared to millimeters; there was a long, long way to go.

On a whim, Toni called Joanna Winthrop.

"Hey, Toni! How's the pregnancy going?"

"Awful. I feel like a bloated cow."

Joanna laughed. "I hear that, and I sympathize completely. No matter how many times Julio told me I was beautiful, I knew I could stand next to the hippos at the zoo and nobody could tell us apart."

"Alex doesn't understand. I know I'm whining, I can't stop myself, and as soon as I start, he runs and hides in the garage. That old car he's working on is going to be the most overbuilt classic in all creation. I think he's leaving early and coming home late from work just to stay out of my way."

"Bet on it."

Toni sighed. "So how is your baby?"

"The demon child from Hell?"

"What?"

Joanna laughed. "He's great. That's just what we call him when we can't figure out why he's crying."

"Does that happen a lot?"

"Not really. But every once in a while, none of the usual things work. He's not hungry, he's not wet, he doesn't need to burp, he doesn't seem tired, he's too little to be cutting teeth. So far, the little battery-powered swing mostly does the trick, and if that fails, we put him in the car seat and take him for a ride in the car, and that pretty much calms him down. Or Julio takes him for a long walk. By the third or fourth mile, Julio says, he's usually okay."

"Jesus," Toni said. "What have I done?"

Joanna laughed again, louder. "I'm kidding, sweetie. He's a terrific kid, worth every penny. How are you doing, really?"

Toni explained about her scrimshaw, and about how she was feeling cooped up.

"Why don't you come on over and visit us? The baby is asleep, he'll be out for another couple hours, and I'd love to see you again. I've missed the crew at work."

"Me, too," Toni said. "You're sure it's okay?"

"Of course I'm sure. I'm a new mama and you're gonna be in a few months. If we can't help each other, who will?"

Toni felt as if her load had been lightened immeasurably.

"Thanks, Joanna. I'm on my way."

Bobby's "work" phone jangled as he was looking for his suitcase in the garage. He frowned. Only a few people had the number, which was supposedly a direct line to his "office."

He went to the kitchen and touched the com's caller ID button.

Nothing; whoever was calling was blocked. Probably a wrong number. He tapped the speaker button.

"Polymers, Drayne," he said.

"Hello, Robert."

Jesus Christ! "Dad?"

"How are you?" his father said. He sounded old.

"Me? I'm fine. How, uh, are you? Everything okay?"

"I am well."

"How's the dog?"

"He's fine."

There was a long pause.

"What, uh, what's up, Dad?"

"I have some bad news, I'm afraid. You remember your aunt Edwina's son, Carlton?"

Aunt Edwina's son. He couldn't have just said, "Your cousin"?

"Yeah, sure."

"Well, he was in a boating accident yesterday. He passed away in the hospital this morning."

"Creepy's dead?" *Jesus.*

"I asked you not to call him that, Robert."

Drayne shook his head. His father would remember that. Still worried about the name, even though the man was dead.

Carlton Post had been called Creepy as long as Drayne could remember. He was three years younger than Drayne, and whenever his folks had come to visit—Edwina was his old man's younger sister by five years or so—they'd brought their four kids along. Creepy was the only boy, and Drayne had usually been stuck watching him. Drayne didn't know who had nicknamed him in the first place; the oldest girl cousin, Creepy's sister, Irene, had passed the name along to Drayne once when she and Drayne had been teaching each other how to play doctor. The name came from the way he stared at people. He'd been a shrimpy little black-haired boy who looked at you crooked without blinking for what sometimes seemed like ten minutes.

"What happened?" Drayne said. He hadn't known Creepy that well, but hearing about his death left him feeling oddly distressed.

"He was waterskiing on Lake Mead. Apparently he fell and was run over by another boat. Knocked unconscious, then cut by the boat's engine propeller. He lost a lot of blood before he was fished out, and there was extensive head trauma."

His father related the information as if talking about the weather, no excitement, no grief, deadpan and almost in a monotone. Fell. Run over. Cut. Always the cool federal agent.

"Oh, man. That's awful. How's Aunt Edwina holding up?"

"She is, of course, greatly distressed."

Creepy was dead. It was hard to imagine. The kid had grown up, gone to school at UNLV, married a girl he'd met there, gotten a degree in history, then stayed to teach high school somewhere outside Salt Lake City. Orem? Something like that? Him and—what was her name?— oh, yeah, Brenda, probably the only two non-Mormons for as far as the eye could see. They'd gotten a divorce after a couple years, and Creepy stayed there. It had been five, six Christmases since Drayne had seen his cousin. He'd actually turned out okay, a nice guy.

"The funeral will be day after tomorrow at Edwina's church in Newport Beach. I'll be driving up for it."

Edwina and her husband, Patrick, were Presbyterians. God's frozen people.

His father was coming to L.A. Well, shit. So much for jetting off to Hawaii. Drayne said, "You, uh, need a place to stay?"

"No, I'll stay at Edwina's or get a hotel room nearby. She'll need family support. The funeral will be at ten o'clock. Can you get off work to attend?"

That was the kind of man his father was. If he'd still been working for the FBI when his nephew had been killed, he would have worried about shit like that. Sure, he'd have taken a personal day and gone, but he would have fretted over missing work. Duty was his reason to get up in the morning.

Drayne said, "Sure, no problem, I can take off."

"I'm going to be at Patrick and Edwina's at nine and then drive over to the church. You can meet me either place. You remember how to get to her house?"

It had been a long time since he'd been there. "She still at that place overlooking the highway?"

"Yes."

"I can find it."

"Good. I'll see you then. Good-bye, Robert."

Drayne tapped the speaker button and shut the com off. That was his old man. Just the bare facts—who, where, what, when—and he was done. No emotion in his voice that his sister's only son, his nephew, was dead; it was just a flat recitation: *"Your cousin is dead. We're going to bury him. We'll see you there. Good-bye."*

Jesus fucking Christ.

Drayne sighed. Well, okay, this was gonna put a small crimp in his plans, but Creepy had been his cousin. He was family. You couldn't just not go, not if you ever had to bump into the rest of the family again. Traffic would be a bitch that time of day, he'd have to get up and get rolling on the PCH early, by seven, at least. Maybe six-thirty. You didn't want to be caught in a traffic jam on the way to a funeral.

Shit. First it was Zeigler, then Creepy. Bad things came in threes. He hoped the next one wouldn't be Tad.

Or himself . . .

December 1991
Stonewall Jackson High School Cafeteria, Cool Springs, Georgia

Jay Gridley stood in the cafeteria line. The woman behind

be people from all over the coun-

ayworth said. " 'N' queer Yan-

"I'm not gonna live the rest of
. I'm gonna meet people, make
where I can make a shitload of
ime I'm forty."
said.
'd heard enough of this.
o leave, he had a thought.
had been interested in debate

e a little run up to Montpelier
Easy enough to do when you
virtual space and time.

the counter slopped a big ice cream scooper full of
mashed potatoes onto his compartmentalized baby blue
Melmac plate, turned the scoop over and pressed it against
the creamed spuds to make a concave indentation, dipped
the scoop into a pan of greasy brown liquid, and said,
"Chon'tgravyth'thet?"

Jay made the translation mentally: *"Do you want gravy
with your mashed potatoes?"*

By the time he'd figured out what she said, the server
had already poured the warm goo all over the plate, slop-
ping into the green beans, the hamburger steak, and the
little empty slot where Jay had planned to have a piece
of cherry pie. Forget that.

"Uh . . . sure," he said, way late.

She handed him the plate back, under the angled glass
sneeze guard.

This was where Mr. Brett Lee of the Drug Enforcement
Administration had gone to high school, graduating at age
seventeen, third in the class of '91, before going off to
Georgia Tech to get his master's in criminology. He'd
gone to work for the DEA the year after he had graduated
college and had thus spent nearly thirteen years working
for them.

In the real world, Jay would be looking at the school
yearbooks, talking to teachers and fellow students, down-
loading pictures and stats, and putting together an education history of Mr. Lee. In VR, he had built a scenario
that would let him walk through the school itself—or
rather what he imagined a place named after a Southern
Civil War hero might look and feel like—and absorbing
the information in a much more interesting manner.

Lee had been well-liked, had gotten good grades, and
had hung with jocks, having been a middle-distance runner on the school's track team.

Jay had come as far back as high school because he

had not been able to discover any connection between Brett Lee and Zachary George either in their work careers or college. While the two men were only a year apart in age—George was thirty-seven, Lee, thirty-six—Lee had been born and raised in Georgia, while George had grown up in Vermont. When Lee was at Georgia Tech, George had been at New York University. They had not crossed paths that Jay could tell until they were both working for the federal government, and while there was no record of their first meeting there, there was some kind of friction apparent by the time both had been in harness for a few years.

Jay had all that—the two didn't like each other, maybe they just rubbed each other the wrong way or something— but the cause of the conflict had not come to light. He could pass on what he'd come up with to Michaels, but it didn't tell them anything they didn't already know.

The young Lee, sitting at a table with four guys and two girls from the track teams, dipped a French fry in catsup and ate it as Jay moved to sit at a conveniently empty table behind the group.

Convenient, hell. He had designed the setup that way himself.

The conversation was hardly enlightening. They talked about things of interest to teenagers: music, movies, who was going out with whom, teachers they hated, the usual. And in the twenty-year-old jargon, it was pitifully dated. Lee was close to Jay's age, and if he'd talked like this, he must have seemed a terrible dweeb to any passing adult. Or dork. Or dickhead. All phrases the boys used fast and furiously, mixing and matching as needed:

"Yeah, well, Austin is a dickhead dweeb," one of the boys said. "He gave me a fuckin' C on the midterm because I didn't use the right color ink!"

"Yeah, Austin's a dork, all right," another boy said.

18

Michaels walked into the Columbia Scientific Shop, not expecting much from the small size of the storefront. An error, he quickly found.

The place didn't have much frontage, but it opened up once you were inside. It wasn't the size of a Costco or anything, but it was a lot bigger than he'd expected.

There were racks and racks of items, ranging from Van de Graaff generators to home dissection kits to chemistry sets to huge telescopes.

Lord, he'd wander around in here forever.

"May I help you, sir?"

Michaels turned to see a woman who looked as if she might be the perfect TV grandmother smiling at him. She was short, slight, wore her gray hair in a bun, a pair of cat's-eye reading glasses hung from a string around her neck, and she had a white sweater draped over her shoulders. The blue print dress she wore went almost all the way to the floor. She looked to be late sixties.

"Yes, ma'am," he said. "I'm looking for a stereomicroscope."

"Ah, yes, aisle nine. What kind of working distance would you need between the lens and object?"

Michaels didn't have a clue. "I don't know."

"Perhaps if you told me the purpose?"

"Um, it's for my wife. She's pregnant and has to stay at home, so she's taken up scrimshaw."

Granny beamed and nodded. "Congratulations! Your first child?"

"Yes." Well, it was his and Toni's first child. And their last, too, according to Toni.

"If you'll follow me."

He did, and in due course, they arrived at aisle nine and a rack of optical equipment, most of which he couldn't put a name to. None of it looked cheap, however.

Granny said, "Your wife will need a focus distance at least the length of her inscribing tool, eight or nine inches. This unit here will give her a foot, so that will do it. It's a Witchey Model III, and it comes with ten times and twenty times. Much more power than she needs, but if you put an oh point three times auxiliary lens on it, right here, that will give you three times and six times, which should be sufficient for scrimshaw. Just to be sure, we can add in another lens that will ramp it up to five times and ten times."

Michaels nodded, not really understanding what she was talking about.

"We could use an articulating arm, but probably a standard post mount would be fine." She looked around and leaned a little closer toward him. "My supervisor would just as soon I sell you a fiber-optic shadow-free ring light to go with it, but frankly, you can get a gooseneck lamp and a hundred watt bulb and save yourself three hundred dollars."

Michaels blinked. "Uh, thank you."

She gave him a perfect grin, full of smile wrinkles and

dimples. "The basic scope is eight hundred dollars, and the two lenses normally retail for about one hundred dollars each, but I can knock a bit off that. Say, nine hundred and fifty dollars all total? And I'll throw in a gooseneck lamp at a discount, too."

Michaels blew out a small sigh and nodded. The profit he'd made on the Miata rebuild was pretty much shot after the honeymoon and the Chevy, but he had a thousand or so left. Toni wanted this but wouldn't buy it for herself, and the truth was, he was feeling guilty about not being more supportive about the pregnancy. It was his son she was carrying, after all, and the least he could do was try to make her enforced inactivity more bearable.

"I'll take it," he said.

Granny laser-beamed another smile at him. "Excellent. If you'll follow me, I'll have one brought up to the checkout counter."

Michaels followed her toward the front of the store. On the way there, a pair of small boys ran past on the cross aisle in front of them. A second after they passed, there was a crash, yells, then what sounded like glass shattering.

Granny said, "Shit! You little bastards! You're *not* supposed to be running in here!" Whereupon she herself took off at a good sprint. The long dress's hem kicked up enough for Michaels to see that Granny wore a pair of flaming red Nike SpringGels, high-end running shoes that went for almost two hundred bucks a pair.

He had to smile. Another example that things were not always what they appeared to be.

Quantico, Virginia

John Howard, in shorts, a T-shirt, and his old sneakers, was working up a pretty good sweat on the obstacle course near Net Force HQ. There were a few Marine officers he recognized running the course, a few FBI types, and there, just ahead on the chinning bars, none other than Lieutenant Julio Fernandez.

Julio saw Howard but kept doing his chins, palms forward and hands a little wider than his shoulders.

Howard stopped and watched. He counted eight before Julio gutted out the last one and let go, then leaned forward and started rubbing at one bicep.

"How many did you do?"

"Twelve," Julio said.

Howard raised an eyebrow.

"Yeah, yeah, I know, I used to do fifteen, sometimes twenty on a good day. I haven't been getting out here as often as I should."

"The joys of family life," Howard observed.

"Yes, sir, that's for sure. I wouldn't trade it for anything, but it does change things some. Before I met Joanna, if I woke up in the middle of the night and felt like it, I could suit up and hit the gym or go run a couple miles, whatever. Now when I wake up in the middle of the night, it's to the sound of a crying baby. Changing a diaper full of gooey yellow poop at three in the morning was never in my flight plan. I don't think I've had three hours of sleep at any one stretch for three months."

"How'd you do it, John? How'd you live through a tiny baby?"

Howard laughed. "I stopped working out. I stopped going to have a drink with the boys after dinner because I was falling asleep in my chair watching TV. You have to change your priorities."

"Yeah, I hear that. I can see it all now: I'm gonna wind up like a certain fat old general, too stiff and tired to walk from the couch to the bed. It's a pitiful thing to think about."

"Fat old general? You want to run the course, Lieutenant, and see just how fat and old I really am? Perhaps I should give you a handicap. Ten seconds? A minute?"

"Your ass, General, sir. I might be in terrible shape, but that's compared to a twenty-five-year-old SEAL, not a man your age."

"I'm not a man my age, Julio. I'm getting better every day."

"You got your stopwatch?"

Howard smiled. "As it happens." He pulled the watch from under his shirt where it hung on a loop of old bootlace.

"Start it. I'll see you at the end. Time you get there, I can probably shower, shave, and catch up on my sleep."

"Go, Lieutenant. The clock is ticking. But be careful of your heart."

Julio smiled, and took off.

On the way home, Michaels's virgil played a few bars of Franz Liszt's *Les Preludes,* a somber, regal musical sting that, according to Jay Gridley, was the basis for the theme that announced the Emperor Ming in the old Flash Gordon movie series in the '30s. Buster Crabbe, the swimming champion, had starred in those, Jay had told him. Jay had been to what had once been Buster's house, as a boy in SoCal. It had a big swimming pool in the backyard. Talking a bigggg pool . . .

It was Susie. He saw her tiny picture appear on his virgil's screen, and he activated his own minicam so she could see him.

"Hey, yo, Daddy-o!"

" 'Daddy-o'? What happened to 'Dadster'?"

"Oh, that's *so* yesterday," she said. "You really did go to school with the dinosaurs, huh?"

"It's true. I had to hike a prehistoric trail ten miles long every morning, in the tropical heat, uphill both ways, and be careful of stepping into the tar pits. You have it easy, kiddo."

"So Mom says."

"How are you?"

"Fine."

"Everything going okay with, ah, Byron?"

"Yep. He's a good guy, really."

Michaels felt his belly clutch. He had thought he was going to lose contact with her after the nasty business with Megan, but somehow, his ex-wife had relented. Thank God for large miracles.

"I'm glad to hear it," he said. Boy, that came hard.

"He argued with Mom something awful about letting me see you."

Michaels felt the heat begin in him, threatening to rise and shut off his breathing and vision. *That bastard!*

"Didn't like the idea, huh?" he managed to say, faking a smile. She could see him, after all.

"Oh, no, Daddy-o, it was *Mom* who didn't like it. Byron said it wasn't right to keep a father from seeing his daughter. He wouldn't give up until she agreed."

Michaels's anger turned to wonder. "Really?"

"Yeah, he doesn't like you much after you insulted Mom and knocked him down, but he tries to be fair. He's just not you. I miss you, Dad."

As always, that broke his heart. "Me, too. You tell Byron thank you for me, would you?"

He debated for a moment about whether to tell his pre-teen daughter that she was going to have a new little brother. Well, half brother. Then he decided she ought to hear it from him.

"I have some news for you. Did you know you're going to have a baby brother in a few months?"

"Mom told?" she said. "She told me I couldn't say anything to you. But it's not a brother, it's a sister."

For a moment, he couldn't track what she said, it was as if she had spoken words he understood but arranged them wrong. What she said made no sense.

Then it came to him:

Megan was pregnant!

"Daddy-o, where'd you go?"

"Huh? Oh, sorry, sweetie, I'm in my car, I had to, uh, switch lanes."

"Pretty cool, huh?" she said. "A baby sister. Almost none of my friends have any that little. Chellie's got a brother who's two, and Marlene's got a sister who's like one, but nobody else's mom is preggers."

"Pretty cool," he said. "Congratulations."

Susie's slip brought up a whole wave of things he didn't want to think about. He loved Toni, and she loved him in a way Megan never had. He was over his ex-wife, finally. Well, almost over her. There was always that little wonder about the road not taken, even though the roads they had traveled the last few years had been pretty ugly. But she was Susie's mother, and there had been some good times. Wonderful times, at the beginning.

Now that she was having another man's baby, the old jealousy tried to rear its viperlike head, and for a moment, he almost let it.

No. That serpent was dead.

And now what did he tell Susie about her half brother? Should he say anything? He didn't want to get into any kind of competition with Megan for his daughter's affection as much as he didn't want to lose it.

And yet, if he was going to continue to be part of Susie's life, Toni was also going to be a part of it, as would their unborn child.

Sooner or later, word would get back to Megan; somehow it always did, and he would rather Susie hear it from him.

"Well, Li'l Bit, it looks like you are going to be *really* cool."

"Huh?"

He smiled into the virgil.

19

The Safari Bar and Grill was first on Tad's list. This was an old but little-known watering hole not far from Santa Monica City College. The food was good, the drinks generous, and the place was far enough off the main drags so the locals had mostly kept it hidden from the tourists.

Tad approached the assistant manager on duty and gave him the bullshit story he'd worked up.

"Say, man, I got a problem maybe you can help me with?"

The assistant manager, a smiling black guy of thirty with nice teeth, dressed in khaki safari shorts and matching shirt, said, "What's the problem, bro?"

"Okay, look, a while back, my brother and his wife were having some difficulties. I uh, got together with her to, you know, help them out. We had lunch here a few times."

"Uh-huh, so?"

"One thing kinda led to another. My sister-in-law and I, well, we, ah, stepped over the line, you know what I mean?"

"You punching your brother's wife? That's bad biz, bro. Gonna make Thanksgiving dinners a bitch."

"Yeah, yeah, I know. It just happened, you know. Anyway, they got their shit worked out okay, they're back together. But my brother, he's a jealous type, and he suspects that while they were on the outs, his wife maybe did some stuff she shouldn't have done."

"He's right, too, idn't he?"

Tad looked at his boots. "Yeah, and I feel like shit about it, okay? But he only suspects, he doesn't *know,* and he sure as hell don't know about *me.* The thing is, my brother is big and kinda mean, and he's with the cops, and if he starts poking around and finds out his wife and I spent any time together, I'm fucked."

"I hear that."

"So like I said, we were in here a few times, had a few drinks and a few laughs, and if he shows up here somehow and gets his hands on your security tapes, I could be in deep shit."

The assistant manager smiled. "Not to worry, my man. You here further back than a week, he won't find nothing. We record three days at a time. Nobody sticks up the place or starts a fight the police need to see, we start the disk over again. No permanent records."

Tad smiled. "Hey, man, I appreciate you tellin' me this." He pulled a couple of tightly folded twenties from his pocket and extended his hand. When they shook hands, the twenties pressed into the assistant manager's palm, and he grinned and nodded. "No problem, bro. You be more careful now, you hear? That pussy will kill you, you not careful."

After the Safari, Tad rumbled the big Dodge along surface streets to two other restaurants within a few miles of each other and ran the same story.

At the Sun 'n' Shore, it played pretty much the same, except for the time. The security cams there recorded over the old stuff after only twenty-four hours. Not to sweat it.

At the Irish Pub, they had cams, but all they did was feed a couple of show monitors, no tapes or disks.

Tad was feeling pretty good about this. He had three more places to hit, and he was done. He could take the Hammer cap and get the trip rolling, they were all gonna be this easy.

But of course, just to fuck up that plan, the Berger Hotel, on the hill overlooking the ocean, was more of a problem. A lot of well-off people with well-known faces came here and got a room to get laid in, and the bar was dark and quiet. And when you had folks with fame and money in your house, you were smart to spend a little more on security to make sure the rich and famous didn't get ripped off. That was bad for business.

So at the Berger, they kept their recordings for a year on long-running superdense video diskettes, SDVDs. The system wasn't full-frame twenty-four-a-second vid, but blink cams that snapped stills every few seconds. You didn't get full motion stuff that way, but you could store a lot more time on a lot less space, and the cams were set to take snaps often enough so you couldn't walk across the lobby without being caught. A still picture that showed faces would do the trick.

Tad ran the sister-in-law number on the assistant manager of the hotel, some kid who looked like he was just out of college with a degree in hotel management, and got sympathy, but that was all.

The kid, a pale, green-eyed, dishwater blond in a dark suit and tie, said, "I'm sorry, sir, it is against hotel policy to allow anybody to see the security recordings."

"Even the cops?"

"Well, of course, we cooperate with the police in criminal matters."

"So if my brother shows up and flashes his badge, he gets the SDVD? And my sister-in-law and I get drummed out of the family? Not to mention by brother kicks the shit out of me, maybe breaks an arm or two?"

"I . . . I wish I could help, really."

"Look, if I knew the date we were here, couldn't you get that diskette out and, uh, misfile it? Accidents happen, right? Somebody could have put that into the wrong file drawer or something, couldn't they? It would have been like a month ago. If anything had happened on that day, the cops would have come looking for it by now, right?"

The kid was wavering.

Tad brought out the heavy artillery. "C'mon, man, I made a big mistake, but it's done. Nobody got hurt, and as long as it never gets out in the open, nobody ever will. I love my brother. What he don't know won't hurt him. Or me. Put yourself in my shoes."

The kid wanted to help, but he was skittish.

Tad went for the throat: "Enter it . . . nobody will ever *know*. I sure won't tell, and it's not like you'd be doing anything *criminal*. It would be worth a lot to me to keep my brother from finding out. Look, I just sold my car. I got enough for a down payment on a new one, plus about a thousand bucks extra. You get me the diskette, I give you the thousand. Everybody comes out ahead. My brother doesn't find out I screwed up, he and his wife live happily ever after, and even if anybody ever comes looking for the recording—which they probably won't—all they'll think is that it got mislaid. Hell, you could even put a blank one in the slot, and they'd probably just think the cams were out of whack . . . if anybody ever bothered to look. Cut me some slack here, please."

Everything Tad said made a certain kind of sense. And

the bottom line was, who would know or ever find out? Not to mention that a thousand bucks tax-free cash was surely more than this kid took home in a week. A week's pay and then some for a thing nobody would ever miss? How tempting was that?

The kid licked his lips. "What was the date?" he asked.

Tad kept his face serious, even though he wanted to smile. One born every minute.

When Tad got back into the Dodge and cranked it up, he had the SDVD, a little silver disk about the size of a half-dollar coin. He broke it in half, broke those pieces in half, and stuck them in the ashtray. He lit a cigarette with a throwaway Bic, dialed the flame up to high, and torched the diskette pieces. They smoked but didn't catch fire, just melted into sludge after a minute. The greasy smoke coming off the molten diskette did stink up the car something fierce, so he rolled down the windows to let the smoke escape.

So much for that.

Two places left on Bobby's list, and neither one of them was going to be as tough as the hotel. One was a movie house the Zee-ster rented to show one of his pictures to a hundred of his closest friends at the moment, the other was a gym where Bobby and the Zee-ster had worked out together a couple of times. Probably neither of them even had security cams, but if they did, between his sister-in-law story and a pocket full of cash, he didn't foresee any problems. People would help you out if the story was good enough, and if they were a little reluctant, a fat wad of green went a long way to moving things along. Everybody had a price; you just had to find it.

So there was no reason not to pick up the Hammer that Tad could see.

He swallowed the big purple cap, washed it down with a swig of bottled water, and headed for the movie theater.

April 1992
Washington, D.C.

The ballroom at the hotel was crowded, mostly fairly
well-dressed teenagers, with a sprinkling of teachers and
employees here and there. Jay walked through the twenty-
year-old scenario, looking at the students as they headed
for their seats.

This was the quarter-final round for the debate, whose
topic this year was: "Resolved—Imminent Threats to National Security Should Supersede Habeas Corpus."

Boy, didn't that sound exciting?

Jay had learned in his research that debate teams were
given an issue at the beginning of the year, and that this
issue would be the same nationwide. The teams—two on
a side—had to be able to argue both sides of an issue,
and the reason for that was that sometimes they might not
know which side they were going to be assigned until the
last minute. The topic, which certainly sounded like ends-
justify-the-means to him, spoke to the idea of the scope
of legal protection, habeas corpus, being a shortened version of the full term habeas corpus ad subjiciendum. Technically, he had just learned, it meant something like, "You
can have the body to undergo the action of the law," or
some such. What it meant was, you couldn't be thrown
into jail without due process of the law. If you were suspected of a crime, then you had to be arrested, charged,
given access to legal counsel, arraigned, and eventually
brought to trial. The authorities couldn't just throw you
in a jail cell and leave you there without offering a reason.
As such, habeas corpus was the cornerstone of British and
U.S. law.

To Jay, such a debate was a yawner, about as exciting
as eating a bowl of cold oatmeal while watching paint
dry, but the buzz in the room was certainly enthusiastic.

The reason Jay was here was because the DEA agent Brett Lee and the NSA agent Zachary George had both attended this conference as teenagers. It could have been a coincidence—there were hundreds of students here, one team from the small states, and multiple teams from the bigger ones—but maybe this was where the two had run afoul of each other originally.

That would make sense, Jay reasoned. Being on opposite sides of a debate would mean that one would lose and the other would win, and maybe arguments had gotten heated to the point of personal anger.

However, a check of the records once he got to looking revealed that Lee and George had not been on teams that debated each other. In fact, neither of their teams made it to the finals. Georgia got blown out in the first round. Vermont did get to the quarter-finals, and had argued the affirmative position against a team from Nebraska, the result of which was that they had also been eliminated. Georgia and Vermont had not even been staying on the same floor of the hotel.

Jay's scenario was based on old news footage, hotel records, and camcorder tapes and photographs taken by students and teachers, as well as the official society recordings that had been compiled and sold commercially. The net was still in its infancy in the early nineties, but there were some old debate web pages in WWW archives, and some BBSs. Jay had set his searchbots and blenders and strained it all, feeding it into a simple WYSIWYG view program. Added a few bells and whistles, of course.

So there he sat, with the Nebraskans and the Vermontians—the Vermontinese? the Vermin?—about ready to go at it.

Zachary George was the leader of his duo, and he was the opening speaker for the round.

He got up, defined terms, and began his introduction to his reasoning.

George said, "In times of war or national disasters, the country as a whole must come before individuals. While we are a nation based on liberty for all, destruction of the national structure could easily result in liberty for none.

"If a man has a cancerous finger, is it not wiser to cut off the finger than allow it to spread and destroy him? Is a single finger worth the whole man? No, of course not. Likewise, if the life of the nation is threatened, a single or a few individuals cannot be allowed to cause such destruction. As the great Roman general Iphicrates said two thousand years ago, 'The needs of the many must outweigh the needs of the few.' "

Huh. Jay thought that quote came from the Vulcan *Star Trek* character Spock, in one of the old movies from the eighties or nineties.

George continued in this vein, but Jay was busy looking around, trying to spot Lee. It didn't take long. The young Brett Lee, looking much as he had in Jay's earlier scenario at Stonewall Jackson High, watched George from a third-row seat, leaning forward eagerly, hanging on every word.

Jay got up and moved to get a better look at Lee.

George droned on: ". . . and did not Plato say, 'No human thing is of serious importance'? How then can the temporary suspension of liberty by a man or even a small group of men compare to the liberty of millions?"

Jay walked to a point where he could see Lee's face.

Hmm. Lee's expression certainly did not seem like that of a young man who scorned what he was hearing. It was more like a believer hearing a sermon by his favorite preacher. Or a young man listening to the words of his beloved. Could these two have been friends who later had a falling out?

This definitely needed more exploration, Jay decided.

But scenario could only do so much. As the speech continued, Jay's attempt to learn more was frustrated by the facts—or lack thereof. Whether in scenario or RW, if it wasn't there, any speculation about an event was just that, speculation. The program would let Jay make anything he wanted to happen in VR happen, but it would not necessarily be what *actually* happened.

Despite Jay's best efforts, he could not put the two boys together at the debate conference outside the presentation done at the quarter-final competition. Sure, it was likely both Lee and George had been at the semifinals and the final team debate. Both the Vermont and Georgia teams had stayed until the conference was over; the records reflected that. They almost certainly would have been in the audience watching, and it was not inconceivable that they had somehow met before or after that.

There were a few records after the quarter-finals on both boys, but nothing that put the two of them in any closer proximity than they were in Jay's scenario.

Maybe wasn't the same as *for sure.*

Even so, Jay felt as if there was something buried here, something he needed to uncover.

The problem was, how?

20

When Toni walked into the kitchen, she saw the microscope. It sat on the table, a red bow stuck to it.

She was stunned. A total surprise.

"Alex! Where are you?"

After a moment, he came into the kitchen, grinning.

"You shouldn't have done this." She waved at the scope.

"Yeah, I should have. I've been slack in my husbandly duties lately."

"I hadn't noticed that."

"Not *those* duties. The, uh, expectant father ones."

"It's a beautiful piece of equipment," she said, touching the scope mount with one hand. "But we can't afford it."

"We can. I had enough left in the car account to get it. You deserve it."

"It was a want, not a need," she said.

"Nah, you *needed* it. I could tell."

She smiled, and realized she hadn't been doing enough of that lately. "Thank you, darling."

"What, you aren't going to make me take it back?"

She laughed, and she knew he'd said it to make her laugh.

"I got two lenses to do whatever it is it is supposed to do so you can work under it," he said. "Supposedly you'll have a foot between the lens and the work object. I hope that's enough."

"It is. My pin vises are only about seven inches long or so."

"Yeah, mine, too," he said, waggling his eyebrows.

Again, she laughed.

"I should buy you one of these every day. Well, go set it up and see how it works."

"Later," she said. "I have something else in mind first."

"What else could be more important?" Butter wouldn't melt in his mouth.

"Come along, and I'll show you."

Now it was his turn to laugh. And even if she was pregnant, they were still newlyweds, right?

Toni headed for the bedroom, and Alex was right behind her. No farther than seven inches, the way she figured it.

Jay was deep in cyberspace, working a scenario that involved hunting something big and mean with a pack of dogs, when a disembodied voice said, "Honey, I'm home!"

He dropped out of VR, blinked, and beheld Saji.

Saji, stark naked.

"Whoa!" he said.

"Sure, now you notice me. I've been here for half an hour. If I were a thief, I could have walked off with everything in the place, including you, and you'd have been oblivious."

"Uh . . ."

"What's the matter, goat-boy? Cat got your tongue?"

"I hope," he said, grinning.

John Howard and his wife Nadine were about to take a shower together, something they hadn't been able to do much in the last ten or twelve years with their son running around the house. But now that he was in Canada, well, it was time to make hay while the sun shone.

"I'm fat and ugly," Nadine said. "I don't know why you want me around."

"Well, you're a pretty good cook," he allowed.

She threw her shoe at him, but he was expecting it, so he managed to dodge it.

"Of course, you also have lousy aim."

She reached for her other shoe.

The phone rang.

"Let the robot answer it," he said.

"This from the master of duty? It could be Tyrone."

Nadine picked up the phone. The extension in the bathroom was a faux antique dial phone that didn't have a caller ID screen. "Hello? Oh, hey, baby!"

Yep. Tyrone.

Howard had mixed feelings about the call. Of course he was happy to hear from his son. He'd have been a little happier if the boy's sense of timing wasn't so lousy. Half an hour earlier or an hour later, those would have been better. People who didn't have children didn't know what happened to their sex lives after the little ones got big enough to pad down the hall and shove the bedroom door open, looking for Mama and Daddy.

"Yeah, sweetie, he's right here. I'll put him on."

Howard took the phone. Unfortunately, he stopped paying attention to Nadine as soon as Tyrone said hello. A mistake.

The second shoe hit him on the butt.

"Hey, ow!"

"Dad?"

"Nothing, son. Your mom is just being cute."

Santa Monica, California

The Hammer was coming on by the time Tad left the movie theater. Like he thought, there hadn't been any surveillance cams set up in the theater proper. There was one installed in the redi-teller in the lobby, but neither he nor Bobby had used the money machine when the Zee-ster had done his private showing. There wasn't any need; everything had been on the tab Zeigler ran.

By the time he got to the gym, the chem was working pretty good in Tad. It had come on faster than usual. Maybe it was because he had tripped such a short time ago and was still wrung out, or maybe it had to do with the other dope he'd been taking to stay ambulatory. Whatever. Thor was on a roll, urging Tad to join him in a night of ass-kicking and taking names, and it was all Tad could do to maintain control.

Steve's Gym was an upscale place just off the PCH that catered to serious jocks. Tad pushed open the door, got a blast of frigid AC in the face, and almost had an orgasm from the cold rush.

Lifting weights had never been Tad's thing. As a kid, his lungs had been too bad to let him do squat physically. Between the bronchitis and asthma that later opened him up for tuberculosis, and his naturally skinny frame, he was never gonna be able to bulk up, so he hadn't ever tried.

With the Hammer working, he could probably go over and grab one of those big barbells and twirl it like a drum majorette's baton if he wanted to, but why bother? Nobody here he wanted to impress.

"Can I help you?" came a deep voice from off to Tad's right.

He looked. There was a woman there who looked like the Incredible Hulk's sister: She was big, heavy, ugly, and looked as if she needed a shave. But she had tits—fake ones—and the red leotard she wore showed an absence of male equipment down south. A definite woman, sort of.

Tad smiled, enjoying a particularly nice rush of something in the chem cocktail. "Steve around?"

According to Bobby, Steve was the owner of the gym. He was a former Mr. America, Mr. Universe, and Mr. Whatever Came After That, past his prime but still as big as a rhino and plated with slabs of steroid-cured muscle. Maybe six two, two sixty, down twenty or thirty pounds from his competition days, Steve was still as wide as a door with arms as big around as most guys' legs. Bobby wasn't in the same class as most of the bodybuilders who came in to move mountains of iron plates, but he was buffed enough so nobody laughed when he took off his shirt, and in better shape than most of the celebrity jocks who made it a point to be seen here. Guys like the Zeester, who had personal trainers the way most people had toothbrushes, would stop by, do a few sets, work up a sweat, and have their pictures taken by their publicity guys as they left, all pumped up and manly.

Anyway, Bobby had told him to talk to Steve, who'd be happy to help out any friend of Bobby's. Bobby dropped a lot of money in this place, doing private sessions, buying T-shirts and vitamins and shit.

The Amazon said, "He's with a client right now. Maybe I can help you?" Her expression at seeing his pipe-stem frame in his black clothes said she didn't really think she could help him, that God Himself would have trouble helping such a pencil-necked geek.

Tad smiled, his mind zipping along quickly, making connections and drawing conclusions that were usually beyond him. The Hammer made you strong as Superman, but it also gave you Lex Luthor's brainpower. That wasn't just subjective on his part, either, he had done some things that convinced him the increase in processing power was real.

He said, "Nah, it's personal biz."

"He's gonna be about an hour," the woman said. "You can wait if you want."

Normally, Tad might have gone for that. An hour was nothing when he was straight—well, more or less straight. But when the Hammer was pounding in your brain, doing nothing for an hour when you were in the gotta-move stage was pretty much impossible.

Another body rush swept over Tad, and as it did, he got an erection, a woody that came up all of a sudden, like a switchblade opening, *boing!*

He looked at the woman bodybuilder. She probably outweighed him by thirty or forty pounds, and no way, no how was she his type, but she was female and she was right here. He said, "You want to screw? I bet I can wear you out in an hour."

The woman laughed, a deep, resonant rumble way down in her belly. "Oh, wow, that's really funny. You and me? Ha!"

Tad smiled pleasantly.

"Even if I was into men, which I'm not, you'd be the last guy I'd choose, fuzz-brain. I'd want somebody who could pick me up and put me down easy, and you don't look like you could pick up an empty beer bottle without help."

Tad continued to smile. Quickly, he stepped up to her,

scooped her up, and held the startled bodybuilder cradled in his arms like a baby. "You mean like this? So, I passed the test, right?"

With that, he used his left arm to support her weight, reached over with his right hand, caught the leotard between her breasts and ripped it down the front, all the way to the crotch. The cloth fell away like tissue, showing the muscular nudity underneath.

The woman was still behind the curve, so startled by what he had done and probably that he had been able to do it, her mouth just gaped.

"Nice hooters," Tad said. "You get a good deal on 'em?"

He stuck his hand between her legs, and whatever surprise she felt faded enough for her to scream and punch him at the same time.

Tad ignored the loose fist she threw as it bounced off his cheekbone, and sought to explore the area his hand had found. She started kicking and screaming, and even with the Hammer, he was having trouble keeping her still.

The cavalry arrived then, three guys who together probably weighed as much as a small car.

"Hey! What the fuck are you doing?!" one of them said. "Put Belinda down, asshole!"

"You got a security cam setup in here?" Tad asked.

"You're damned straight we do, you fucking psycho!"

"Where is it?"

"Charlie, call the cops. And call an ambulance for this moron," the guy said.

"You must be Steve, right?"

"That's right, dickweed, and you're dead. Put her down!"

Tad grinned. As it sometimes did when he got excited, the drugs in the Hammer came up full blast, roaring in like a tornado.

"Here," he said. He threw Belinda at the three. Charlie had stepped away, heading for a phone, but Belinda hit Steve and his Neanderthal buddy hard enough to knock them over. All three of them tumbled to the floor, hard.

Tad leaped at Charlie, grabbed him under the armpits, and lifted him into the air until his feet cleared the floor. Charlie had to go about two fifty, maybe two sixty, a nice hefty lad. "Which way is the security cam control room?"

Charlie, who hung there like a kid's doll, stammered, "Th-th-there!"

He pointed.

Since Steve was almost back on his feet, Tad turned and threw Charlie at him. The collision of beef was pretty hard.

Tad ran for the unmarked door, didn't bother to use the knob, and knocked it open. There was a video monitor and a computer set up, a big hard drive working.

Tad glanced around. No diskettes stacked up anywhere, no removable drives on the shelves. He moved closer and divined that the security device was no more than it appeared to be: a short-time recorder that ran a cycle, recording over and over, using the same storage device.

He grabbed the thing, smashed it against the floor, and shattered it into several pieces. The HD disk popped out, and he picked that up and broke it in half, then stuck the pieces in his back pocket. Never knew but what they could recover stuff even if it was busted.

All done now.

He started for the door.

Steve, too stupid to know when he was outmatched, came at Tad, swinging a steel bar. Even without weights on it, the bar had to go fifteen pounds, and it would have broken something had it hit him.

Tad dodged, ducked, and the bar whistled over his head, slammed into the wall, and punched a long hole in the Sheetrock. The force of Steve's swing buried the steel rod half its length in the wall.

Tad drove his knee into Steve's kidney, and the big man went down as if his legs had suddenly vanished.

Nobody else got in Tad's way as he left the building.

He headed for his car.

Nobody came after him. Just as well, too. He had enjoyed wrestling with the folks in the gym, and if they'd come out for him, why, he would just have *had* to oblige 'em.

Now that that was over, he could relax and let the Hammer swing him along.

Gonna be a good night, yessir, he could tell.

Let's move it, Thor!

21

The Newport Beach Community Presbyterian Church (USA) was not as ostentatious as, say, the Crystal Palace, but certainly it was L.A.: in your face enough so it wouldn't pass for a church most other places. Philosophically, God's frozen people tended to have conservative views on politics, conservative views on social issues, and of course, conservative views on religion. They were very liberal on converting the heathen, though, and never let a chance to start up an overseas mission pass by unmolested. An old running joke in the church was, the Presbyterians had offered to completely fund the Red Cross and CARE, provided those organizations would let them pack a dehydrated minister in with each big shipment of blood or food. They were mostly Republicans, Drayne figured out back when he was still going to church, mostly white and old Republicans, at that. His family had been members since Grandpa Drayne, a deacon of his church back home in Atlanta, had moved out here eighty years ago. The synods were different, but California and Georgia weren't that far apart as far as the basics were concerned.

The building itself had a lot of glass, giving it a light and airy look, and the air conditioning unit out back, roaring to keep the assembled cool, was the size of a half-ton pickup truck. Drayne figured the reason the Baptists always preached about hellfire was because in those un–air-conditioned Southern churches, the congregation could relate to the concept. If the AC went out during a mild spring hot spell in a Presbyterian church, services would be canceled for fear the assembly would all die of heat stroke.

The place sure didn't seem somber enough for a funeral, and most of the mourners were wearing anything but black. Looked like a flock of parakeets, all the pastel colors. What could you expect? It was L.A., wasn't it?

Drayne's father had been a deacon at one time, though his FBI travel had cut into that, but last Drayne knew, the old man still attended church every Sunday down in Arizona. If he wasn't a true believer, he sure gave that impression.

Drayne himself had skipped every Sunday when his father hadn't been around to make him go, and hadn't been inside a church except for a couple of weddings since he'd left home for college. Oh, and that once when he made a major chemical sale to somebody who thought a Catholic church in Berkeley would be a safe place to do a dope deal. Turned out the buyer was wrong. He got busted after a fender-bender accident leaving the parking lot.

Drayne had managed to dig up a dark suit, a white shirt, and a plain tie that were all five or six years old, unworn for almost that long, knowing that if he came in a T-shirt and shorts, his father would probably pull his gun and shoot him. And even though he was retired, the old man always carried a piece when he went out, a habit he couldn't let go of. He'd still be protecting the republic when he was in a wheelchair and blind.

Despite the fact he was pushing seventy, the old man still looked pretty healthy. His hair was white, and his fair skin, pale most of his life, was now a ruddy color that was almost a tan, from spending more time out of doors in the Arizona sunshine. Drayne knew he looked just like a younger version of his father. The family resemblance had always been strong, even though he had refused to believe it for a long time. Then one day he'd caught sight of himself in a rest room mirror as he was washing his hands, and lo! there was the face of his father staring out at him. Assuming he lived so long, the old man was what Drayne was gonna look like at his age.

Amazing, that.

His father stood outside the church, looking at his watch, waiting for Drayne. He wore a black suit, probably one of a dozen black or dark gray ones he owned, and since he hadn't gotten fat after he retired, it still fit. A better fit than the suit Drayne himself had on.

"Robert," his father said.

"Dad."

"Let's go inside. We'll sit with Edwina."

People were still filing in. The service wouldn't start for another twenty minutes. Drayne knew that his father would be early, and that he expected everybody in the family to be early, and so it was.

Drayne offered condolences to his aunt and uncle and cousins. Irene, the girl who had showed him hers while he showed her his when they'd been nine, had grown up to be a good-looking woman, though she was married with three kids of her own now, and a little on the hefty side. Sheila, the middle girl, wore dark-rimmed glasses and a black dress with long sleeves, and had also gotten a little chunky. But Maggie, the youngest, who'd been a little geeky-looking girl with thick glasses, was now a beautiful redhead of twenty-five who, he had heard, taught aerobics somewhere in the Valley, and looked as fit and as tight as a violin string.

"Hey, Maggie. I thought you wore glasses. I don't see any contacts. You have the laser surgery?"

"No, I'm on the NightMove system. You wear these hard contact lenses to bed, and when you wake up, you can go without glasses or contacts all day."

"No kidding?"

"Yeah, it's called Ortho-K. Been around for a while, but they finally got it pretty much perfected. You can go sixteen, eighteen hours, and in my case, I have twenty/twenty without glasses."

"Great. Hey, I'm sorry about Creepy."

"Thanks, it's such a shock. Can't believe he's really dead." She leaned over and kissed him on the edge of the mouth.

Definitely a cousin worth kissing, Maggie. If it hadn't been her brother's funeral, he would have thought about hitting on her, though the family would have howled at that. Shoot, he wasn't going to marry her or have kids, what did it matter if they were cousins? He'd seen the way she looked at him, she'd be up for it.

His father said, "How are things at work, Robert?"

He came away from his mild sexual fantasy. "Fine. I'm up for a promotion. They are considering me for head of Polymers. Be worth another ten thousand a year."

"Congratulations."

"How is Arizona? The dog okay?"

"Fine. The dog is fine."

That pretty much exhausted everything Drayne and his father usually said to each other. But sitting here waiting for some preacher, who at best probably had not seen

Creepy in ten years, to talk about what a wonderful boy he had been and God's plans and all, Drayne felt an urge to poke at his father. He said, "You hear about what happened at HQ in L.A.?" There was no need to identify HQ, that was all it had ever been called in their family.

"I heard."

Drayne wanted to grin, but of course, that would have been inappropriate in this place at this time.

"Sounds like something you'd pull," his father continued.

For a second, Drayne felt a cold splash of terror. "What?"

"I haven't forgotten the incident in your English class." His tone was stern, disapproving.

He felt a sense of relief, and at the same time, of irritation. *Jesus Christ! The old man was still pissed off about that?* Drayne hadn't thought about it in years.

It had been nothing. He'd made a little stink bomb, one with a kitchen match and a cheap ballpoint pen, the kind of things kids did. You took the ink cartridge out, put the match inside the body of the pen, and rigged a bobby pin in the spring, then screwed the thing back together. The bobby pin stuck out where the ballpoint tip had been, so when you pulled it back and let it go, it thumped into the head of the match, lighting it. But since the flame didn't have anywhere to go, it flared up and down the pen's barrel and vaporized some of the cheap plastic before it went out. The result was a short blast of godawful smelly smoke; that was it.

Drayne had been fourteen, in the eighth grade, when he'd dropped one of the pen stink bombs into the garbage can next to the English teacher's desk when she hadn't been looking. It had been a hoot, that stinking smoke belching from the trash, but some goody-goody had seen him do it and ratted on him. He'd gotten two days off to consider the heinousness of his crime, and the old man had taken his belt to him when he found out. And never let him forget it.

"I'm not fourteen anymore, Dad. That was a long time ago."

"I didn't say you did it. I said it sounded like the kind of childish prank you used to do."

Drayne didn't say anything, but it pissed him off that the old man was still throwing up ancient history in his face. Even though he *had* done the FBI prank, that shouldn't have been the first thing out of the old man's mouth.

"Nobody got hurt, did they?" Drayne finally said.

His father had been thinking about it. He came back fast: "But they could have been. People unwittingly exposed to drugs are at risk. Somebody could have been injured. What if some of the agents or staff had been allergic to the drug? On medication that it might have interacted with? What if there had been some kind of emergency needing a prompt response? A fire in the building, maybe a bank robbery or a kidnapping, and they had been unable to respond properly? The idiot who thought it was funny to chemically assault an office of federal agents didn't think about those things, you may be sure. It was an irresponsible, criminal act, and he'll be caught and punished for it. I hope they lock him up and lose the key."

Drayne gritted his teeth. It would be a bad idea to say anything. Just let it go. *What did you expect? The old man was gonna express admiration for the cleverness of the stone job? C'mon, Bobby, you know how he is. Now is the time for all good men to shut the fuck up.*

But he couldn't help himself. Drayne said, "Maybe not. From the reports, it didn't sound as if they had any leads. Maybe the guy was too smart for them."

The old man turned to look at Drayne, blinking at him as he might at seeing a dog turd dropped into a church social punch bowl. "If he had been *smart,* he would have known better than to assault agents of the FBI. They'll get him." He paused a second. "Do you *admire* this criminal, Robert? Is that what you are saying? Didn't you learn anything from your upbringing?"

Drayne flushed but finally realized it was time to keep silent. He just shook his head.

Yeah, Dad, I learned plenty. Much more than you will ever know.

But then the minister arrived, a guy who looked to be about a hundred years old, and it was time to get down to the business of burying Creepy.

Malibu, California

Tad was still up, though about to crash, watching the morning bunnies and studs jog along the beach. The early fog had mostly burned off by nine or ten A.M., showing the brilliant blue hiding behind the gray.

Man, he was wasted. As the chemicals of the Hammer faded and lost their grip on him, he felt a bone-deep weariness begin to claim him. This was gonna be a hard one to recover from, he knew. Best thing to do would be to take a shitload of downers and sleep for as long as he could, twenty-four, thirty-six hours, let his body get as much enforced rest as he could. Couple of the long-lasting phenobarb suppositories, some Triavil, maybe some Valium mixed in, to keep the muscles relaxed. Some Butazoladin for the joints, Decadron for the inflammation, Vicodin and little snort of heroin for pain, Zantac for his stomach, maybe even a little Haldol, just for the hell of it.

Bobby, off at his cousin's funeral, wasn't gonna be too happy with him when he found out about Tad busting up the gym. Probably they wouldn't want to be seen hanging together for a while, in case ole Steve the bodybuilder ran into them somewhere and made the connection. Tad didn't think the gym rats knew he was tight with Bobby, he was pretty sure they didn't know, but book it, they weren't gonna forget him after last night.

It would probably be in the papers and on the tube, about the gym, but Bobby wasn't plugged into the news, only what he caught on the radio when he was out driving, so maybe he wouldn't hear about it until Tad had a chance to break it to him, put a little spin on it.

He managed a grin, even though his face was sore from the drug rictus he'd worn for most of the night. Yeah, spin, right. How much spin could you put on trashing a place and beating the crap out of folks because you had suddenly gotten horny?

Well, at least there weren't any public recordings of the Zee-ster and Bobby floating around, Tad knew that. That was the important thing. Maybe Bobby was right. Maybe they should jet over to the islands and mellow out for a few weeks, come back when things settled down. Way he felt right now, the idea of swinging the Hammer again any time soon didn't really appeal. Of course, if he lived through the recovery and got to feeling better, the desire would come back pretty quick. It always did.

Being able to do what he had done last night when he looked like a male version of Olive Oyl? That was a big fucking draw.

Hell, after he'd left the gym, he'd lost interest in sex, but he had driven up to the Hollywood sign, hopped the fence, and climbed up to the top of the big *H*. Sat there watching the city for a while, climbed down, and driven to Griffith Park, where he'd roamed for hours, just enjoying the green. Hadn't gotten home until after Bobby left, which was a good thing, 'cause he'd probably have told him about the gym, being fearless at the time.

No, better he learns about it in a couple, three days, back when I'm straight again and it's all past tense. Bobby could go to World or Gold's or one of the other upscale places to work out, it was no big loss.

"Time to get the doc-in-a-box out, Tad m'man," he said aloud. "And settle down for long nap."

22

Michaels put a pair of dollar coins into the soft drink machine and pushed the button marked Coke. Change clattered into the return as the plastic bottle hit the bottom slot and rolled into view. He had pretty much given up drinking fizzy sugar water, but now and then he indulged. His father had liked the stuff; he drank three or four a day.

It brought back old, pleasant memories from his childhood to sit and sip one.

He took the Coke out, fed the change back into the machine, added another dollar coin, and looked at Jay Gridley.

"Club soda," Jay said.

Michaels pushed the button. Three bucks for two soft drinks. What a racket.

"So you can't come up with any history on Frick and Frack other than they were at a conference at the same time twenty years ago as teenagers?"

Jay took his bottled drink and popped the cap off, then

swigged from it. "Nope. I know there's something there, but I haven't found it yet."

"Well, don't kill yourself looking. It probably doesn't mean anything anyway. Better you should concentrate on the drug thing. We find what they want, they are off our back. Any leads there?"

"Nothing to speak of. The local cops and the DEA are all over Zeigler's place like white on rice. He had to get the drug from somewhere, and they figure if they back-track him enough, they might find something."

"You don't?" Michaels drank some of the Coke. Okay, so it was bad for you, but sometimes you just had to indulge. He didn't smoke, or drink more than the occasional beer or glass of wine. He ate pretty well; he worked out every day. A bottle of Coke now and then ought not to kill him.

Famous last words.

Jay said, "Maybe, but I wouldn't bet on it. Guy like that, big-time movie star, he probably didn't play golf with his connection. I'd be real surprised if he had a listing in his address book under Dope Dealer."

Michaels shrugged. "So how do we run the dealer? Wait for somebody else to go berserk and backtrack them?"

"Don't have to wait," Jay said. "Apparently some guy walked into a gym in Santa Monica last night and laid waste to the place. Threw some guys bigger 'n Hercules around like rag dolls when they objected to him feeling up the woman working the desk, who apparently was pretty well-built herself. Knocked doors down, punched holes in the walls, like that."

"The police have him?"

"Nope, he got away. We got the description—he sounds like a beatnik from what the witnesses said—and we have the police sketch."

Jay grinned, and Michaels joined him. Police sketches all seemed to look alike, and not very much like any of the guys they were supposed to represent. Plug a saint into an ID kit, he'd come out looking like a thug.

"According to the reports, after he got working, this guy went to the security cam setup, tore up the recording device, and made off with the disk drive medium."

Michaels considered that for a few seconds. "So he was not so stoned he couldn't think about covering his ass."

"Maybe. Or maybe there was something on the disk he wanted, though it probably wasn't him. According to the complaint, all the people involved swear they would have remembered this guy if he'd ever been in their place. Guy was built like a toothpick, bodybuilders notice such things. That he was the proverbial ninety-seven-pound weakling made his rampage all that much more amazing. The bodybuilders couldn't believe it. Got to be our friend Mr. Purple Cap responsible . . . or a major number-busting coincidence."

"So what good does this do us?"

"Well, we know that three of the dealer's customers live in or around L.A. The rich woman, the dead movie star, and the live beatnik. I'm thinking maybe our dealer might like the sunny lifestyle. The shelf life of this mojo drug is pretty short, it rots in a day or so, and for the Zeester to get stuff himself, then to the rich girl, and for her to have time enough to use it? I'm thinking maybe the guy who supplied Zeigler is not halfway around the world. FedEx, or even a paid courier, are limited by the speed of a jet. The farther away he is, the narrower the window when the drug will still work."

Michaels nodded. "Okay. So hypothetically speaking, *maybe* he lives within spitting distance of SoCal. Does that help us much?"

"Narrows down the search. I can start checking chemical companies, drug supply houses, running lists of convicted dealers, like that. And maybe the cops will turn up something on the late Mr. Zeigler's travels."

Michaels said, "Good a direction as any, I suppose."

Jay took another long swallow of the club soda. "Anything new on the drug itself? How'd that cap assay out?"

Michaels frowned. *Crap!* He'd tucked the thing into his pocket and forgotten about it. Those trousers were in a heap on the floor in his closet. He hoped Toni hadn't sent them to the laundry yet.

He smiled at that thought. The only way Toni was going to do his laundry was if he specifically asked her to, and he hadn't done that. The pants would still be there when he got home. She hadn't signed on to be his maid, he'd found that out pretty quickly. Nor had he expected that.

"Boss?"

"Nothing. I mean, nothing on the capsule. I haven't had a chance to get by the lab yet."

It was Jay's turn to shrug. "I got the DEA's breakdown of what ingredients they could find. I'll use those for a starting point. If the guy is smart, he'll buy his chem for cash, and far away from home, but you never know. Sometimes it's the little things that trip you up. Remember Morrison, the HAARP guy?"

Michaels nodded. How could he forget that? "Yeah, I remember."

"He had all the big stuff worked out but slipped up on something as simple as a night watchman. Him and the Watergate guys."

"Well, do what you can do, Jay. Keep me in the loop."

"Sure thing, boss."

Michaels looked at his watch. Getting close to noon. Maybe he'd stroll on down to the gym and do a little workout. That way he could take a break when he got home without Toni making him practice his *silat* first. She'd work him harder than he'd work himself, but if he'd already done his *djurus* for the day, she'd let him slide.

Newport Beach, California

Drayne came away from the funeral experience pretty depressed.

The church service had been fairly saccharine, like he'd expected. The old minister, if he remembered Creepy at all, couldn't speak in anything other than platitudes and generalities, and he put in a pitch to save souls while he did it. Neither Edwina nor Pat could bring themselves to get up and say anything, and Creepy's sisters and ex-wife managed some personal stuff that was touching and surprising. Drayne never knew that Creepy had a collection of Star Wars cards, nor that he coached a boy's soccer team in Utah.

The procession to the graveyard and the internment service at the family plot was no more fun. While he was standing there, a sudden flash of déjà vu hit Drayne. Another funeral he'd gone to when he'd been ten or eleven popped up in his mind, something he had completely forgotten about. A kid a year or so younger than Drayne who lived across the street and down a couple of houses, Rowland, his name was, had been killed in a gruesome freak accident. Rowlie's father had worked at a small private airport somewhere. Rowlie and his two brothers had gone with their father one Saturday to the airport. The boys had been playing chase in and around the hangars. Somehow, Rowlie had run in front of a small plane that was about to taxi out for takeoff. The plane's propeller had hit him. He'd been killed instantly. The coffin had been kept closed because he'd been almost decapitated and chopped up pretty good; at least that was what Drayne had heard.

Jesus. He didn't need another reminder of death, not with Creepy just lowered into the ground.

There wasn't an official wake, though family and friends were welcome to stop by Pat and Edwina's, so of course Drayne had to do that. What did you say at such times? People standing around, drinking coffee or tea, talking about the recently departed as if he'd gone on some kind of trip?

Drayne got out of there as soon as he could. His old man was busy, taking charge, making sure everything was shipshape, and they didn't really have much to say to each other, Drayne and his old man. They never really had. The old man had never thought much of his only son, never seemed interested in what he did, always expected perfection. He brought home a report card with five *A*s and a *B*, the old man didn't say, "Hey, good job! Congratulations!" No, he said, "Why the *B*? You need to apply yourself more."

Once, when he was about twelve, he'd been visiting his grandma, out in the Valley. He found some old photo albums and started digging through them. In the back were a stack of his old man's report cards. The son of a bitch had made straight *A*s through high school. Had been valedictorian of his class before he went off to college and law school, and eventually the FBI. Jesus. Drayne couldn't even bitch about the old bastard holding him to a higher standard than he'd achieved on his own.

Oh, yeah, Drayne had been a whiz in chemistry. It had been his natural element. And he was smart enough to get good grades in his other subjects without having to crack a book most of the time. He just didn't see the point in working his butt off to learn stuff like "Tippicanoe and

Tyler Too!" when it wouldn't ever be any part of his life.
Who gave a rat's ass about gerunds and split infinitives,
or ancient Greek history, or what the current names for
countries in Africa were? Drayne was going to be a chemist, he was going to make his fortune playing with things
he wanted to play with, and to hell with the rest of it.

No, they had not gotten along for as long as he could
remember, his old man and him. And yet he felt some
kind of perverse need to demonstrate to his father that he
was competent. Which was kind of hard to do when what
you were most competent at was mixing and selling illegal drugs, and your old man was a pillar of law enforcement who put people like you away.

The drive back to Malibu was bright and sunny. The
fog had long since burned off, and traffic wasn't too bad.
Neither the weather nor the lack of usual stop-and-go traffic lifted his mood.

He hadn't seen Tad last night or this morning, and he
suspected that was because Tad had taken another Hammer trip, even though Drayne had told him not to. The
Hammer was Tad's reason to get up in the morning. Tad
was a full-time doper, he could mix and match his chems
to suit his needs better than anybody Drayne had ever
known, and for him, Thor was the ultimate party friend,
the guy Tad had been looking for all his life. And Thor
would be the guy who'd kill him, too.

Then again, in his own way, Tad was fairly reliable. If
he had swallowed the cap and gone hyper, it had probably
been after he had done the job Drayne had sent him to
do. It was rare if Tad came home and hadn't done whatever Drayne had sent him to do, and even when that happened, it was due to something Tad couldn't control.

He didn't really know why Tad was so important to
him. They had run into each other doing biz, and something about the reedy guy in black had tickled Drayne.

Nothing sexual, they were into women—though Tad pre-
ferred drugs to pussy, mostly—and not as if Tad were
some kind of sparkling conversationalist or brilliant intel-
lect. But he was loyal, and he did think Drayne was a
genius. And he got the job done. If he wanted to go out
in a blaze of Dionysian glory, that was his right. Tad was
pretty much the only friend Drayne had. Making and dealing illegal chem didn't open you up to a whole lot of deep
relationships with honest people. When Tad croaked, that
was going to leave a big hole in the list of people Drayne
could relax around.

Of course, he had enough money now that if he in-
vested it right, he could almost live off the interest. Another year or so of thousand-buck-a-hit sales, he'd be set.
Then he could retire if he felt like it, maybe move into a
better class of people, make some friends who started out
thinking he was a dot.com millionaire, or had made a
killing in the market or something, who'd take him at face
value. Live his life out in the open, perfectly legal, no
looking over his shoulder.

That made him grin. Yeah, he could do that. Would
he?

Not an ice cube's chance in a supernova he would.
Because it wasn't just the money, it was the *game*. The
ability to do what he did, to do it better than anybody
else, and to get away with it. Hell, if he wanted to, he
could take his formulas to the legitimate drug companies,
and they'd fall all over themselves to shovel money at
him. A lot of what Drayne had discovered and created
was what the pharmaceutical giants had been researching
for years. Got a patient with muscle wasting who is bed-
bound and on the way down? What would it be worth to
him to enjoy some mobility in his final days? Got a guy
who can't get it up, and Viagra doesn't work for him?
How much would he spend to get an erection so hard it

would hum in a breeze? You about to take the GRE to
get into graduate school? What would adding fifteen
points to your IQ for a couple hours be worth? Stuff
Drayne worked with could do that and more.

Drayne could have gone to work for those guys a long
time ago. He could have brought just part of what he
knew to the table, and they would have kissed his shoes
and given him a blank check to get it. But there wasn't
any *challenge* there, not to be straight.

Not to be like his father.

He sighed. He was smart enough to know he was a
little fucked up when it came to such things. Had done
some reading in psychology, knew all about Oedipus and
shit like that. But he was what he was. However he had
gotten there, it was his path, and he was going to walk it,
and the devil take the reasons.

Jesus, he was tight, wound up like a spring. Maybe he
should stop at the gym on the way home, loosen up a
little, take it out on the weights. He'd feel better if he did.
A good, hard workout was the cure for a whole lot of
things, tension, stress, it would mellow you out almost as
much as champagne.

Yeah. Maybe he'd do that. It would be relaxing.

23

Drayne couldn't remember the last time he had been so pissed off. He pounded the steering wheel of the Mercedes hard enough to crack it, and he wished it was fucking Tad's head!

Jesus Christ!

By the time he got home, however, he had calmed down somewhat. He was almost detached, almost fatalistic about it when he pulled into the garage and shut the engine off. He had always known this was a possibility, though he hadn't expected it would ever really happen. He was too smart to be caught by the plodders; he'd been giving them fucking *clues* and they couldn't do it. Only, Tad wasn't. And the boy had stepped in it good this time.

Tad was out cold on the couch, and even the pitcher full of ice water hardly roused him. He mumbled something.

Drayne started slapping his face. Eventually, his hand got sore and tired, but Tad came awake, sort of.

"What?"

"You idiot! You don't have *any* idea what you did, do you?"

"What?"

"The gym! You trashed the gym! I stopped by there to work out, and that was all anybody was talking about! Even if I hadn't sent you, I could recognize you from their descriptions! You moron!"

Groggy, Tad sat up. He rubbed at his face. "I'm all wet," he said.

"You got that right. Christ on a pogo stick, Tad!"

"I don't understand, Bobby. I got the disk from the security drive, the job's done, we're free and clear, nobody has anything to link us to Zeigler. There's no proof of anything."

"You really don't see it, do you?" Drayne sat heavily on the couch next to his partner. Of a moment, he felt sorry for Tad. He kept forgetting most people didn't have his horsepower when it came to cranking up the mental engines. "Obviously, the smart drugs hadn't kicked in when you decided to feel up Atlas's sister. Think about it."

Tad shook his head, still not tracking.

"Look, I know you're tired and stoned, and ordinarily I'd let you sleep it off, but time just got to be a problem. You made a mistake."

"I don't see it. They don't know who I am. No way."

"Okay. Let me explain it to you." He looked at Tad, who made death warmed over seem the picture of health, and realized he had to take it slow for him to keep up with it. He eased off his anger a little. "Let me tell you a story. Just sit back and listen carefully, okay?"

Tad nodded.

"When I was in middle school, they had us in an arts and crafts track. We got three months each of music, art, and speech in one bundle, and three months of drafting, shop, and home arts in another.

"So the first day I show up in music class, and sweet little old Mrs. Greentree, had to be about a hundred and fifty or so, has us all sitting there, and she says, 'What is the universal language?' And of course, none of us have a clue. And she says, 'Music. Music is the universal language. The notes are the same in Germany as they are in France or America.'

"Right, okay, so we got it. Music is the universal language.

"So later that day, we get to to the first section of second bundle, which turns out to be drafting class. This is taught by Coach. Back then, every other male teacher in the school was Coach.

"So we're sitting there, and Coach says, 'Okay, what is the universal language?'

"So anyway, being as how I am newly educated and eager to impress, I shoot my hand up and Coach grins at me. 'Yeah?'

'Music, Coach,' I say. 'Music is the universal language!'

"Coach just about kills himself laughing. 'Music?! Haw! Music ain't the universal language, you dip, *pictures* are the universal language! You in China and you run into some Chinaman and you want to ask him where the toilet is, what are you gonna do, *sing* to him? "Oh, mister Chinaman, please tell me, where is the toilet, la la la . . . ?"

" 'Jesus, get your head out of your butt, son! You draw him a *picture!* Music! Haw!'

"A couple years later, that same question came up in math class, and guess what? I kept my hand down and my mouth shut. Same thing happened when I got to basic computer class. Music, pictures, mathematics, binaries, they are all considered universal languages."

Drayne shut up and looked at Tad, who shook his head.

"Okay, so what's the point?"

"*Context* is my point, Tad. *Context.*" He spoke slowly, as if talking to a retarded child. "Not just what gets said or done, but *where* and *when* it happens is critically important."

Tad frowned, and Drayne could see that he still didn't get it.

"Let me tell you another story."

"Jesus, Bobby, okay, I get it that you're pissed—"

"Shut up, Tad. Once upon a time I knew a guy who was a bouncer at a titty bar. One night, he and some of his friends went to a heavy metal rock concert, you know the kind, head-bangers, primal rock, big crowds standing on the floor screaming to the music, half of them stoned or drunk. So in the middle of the concert, a girl who is sitting on her boyfriend's shoulders decides to pull off her top and flash the crowd, or the band, or whoever."

"I've seen that a few times," Tad said, trying to follow him.

"Right. So'd my bouncer friend, and no big deal. And normally, the way it works is, the girl waves her hooters around, then puts her top back on, a fine time is had by all, and that's that. But this time, while she was unbound and waving in the breeze, her boyfriend reaches up and grabs her breasts, starts rubbing them. Now, she doesn't slap his hands away, she laughs, and next thing you know, she's pulled off her steed and felt up by thirty or forty heavy metal fans. We're talking mob mentality here, and the atmosphere is ripe for trouble. My friend the bouncer is too jammed in to help, and the crowd is so thick that concert security can't get there, either. The girl vanishes.

"Fortunately, aside from getting passed around and fondled against her will, it didn't go any further. They let her go, she gets her clothes back, her nipples are sore, end of event.

"So, whose fault was it she got mauled, Tad?"

"Hers. She should have kept her top on."

"Yes. And people shouldn't get drunk or do drugs and go to rock concerts, and we should always look both ways before crossing the street. No, it's the *boyfriend* who set it off, and the girl, who could have stopped it, made it worse. See, soon as he laid a hand on her boob, she should have slapped the shit out of him. The implied message when somebody flashes in such a situation is 'Look, but don't touch.' When the boyfriend broke the implied rule, the others assumed that a girl who'd do that in public, who was willing to allow touch along with the looking, well, she might be willing to let somebody else play, too, so they helped themselves."

"Not right."

"Nope, it wasn't. But given the circumstances, a bunch of stoned mouthbreathing head-bangers, you can understand how it might progress to that, or worse. There's the way things *should* be, and the way things *are*. You might not like it, but you ignore the way things *are* at your peril."

"And you are saying that I fucked up even though I got rid of the evidence. That it is going to progress to something else?"

"That is exactly what I am saying. See if you can stay with me here: The police and the feds will *know* you were on the Hammer, because nothing else can explain a burned-out matchstick like you kicking major steroid ass like you did. And the bust at Zeigler's was a major deal and on the minds of the cops. And if they dig just a little, they'll come up with the Zee-ster working out at Steve's, and *zap!* A light will flash over their heads and they'll think, 'Hmm. Big movie star shoots it out with the DEA, and they find this superguy drug in his house. Then, within a real short time, somebody trashes a gym where the big movie star works out, obviously on the *same* superguy drug. Say . . . isn't *that* a funny coincidence?' And somebody . . . somebody in the FBI or the local police . . . they are gonna ask themselves the big question: Why? Why'd the guy—that's you—why'd the guy come in and steal the security cam's recording device? Other than coming in to feel up Brunhilda and kicking the crap out of a few bodybuilders, that's all you did. And they are gonna come up with, 'Hey, maybe there is something on that disk the guy doesn't want us to see. What could it be?' And somebody is gonna take it one step further and make an assumption, since they know the Zee-ster worked out there, and that somebody is gonna say, 'Hmm. Maybe because the big movie star was there *with* somebody who really doesn't want to be seen?' "

"But the recording is gone—" Tad began.

Drayne cut him off, but his voice was quiet. "So it is. But the people who work there aren't. I know Steve, the owner, and he might remember that a couple of times when Zeigler was there, he and I came or went together. And if Steve or Tom or Dick or Harry or anybody else in the place remembers that, then my name is gonna come up in a conversation with the feds or cops. And even if Steve *doesn't* remember, the cops *will* get a list of members and go looking for a connection. This is a cop lesson I learned at my daddy's knee: When you don't have anything, you check *every*thing. And sooner or later, they are gonna send somebody out to talk to folks on the list, just routine, and there will be a knock on our door. And I have a nice made-up job that fortunately I didn't mention on my application at the gym, one that's all nice and electronically vouched for, so maybe they can poke at it a little and it might even hold up, but . . . *What is the fuck-ing job, Tad?*"

"Oh, shit."

"Oh, shit, yeah. I'm a *chemist.* Think that'll, you know, raise any red flags or ring any bells? Illicit drugs and a chemist? There are millions of test tube jockeys in the world, but how many of us working out at the same gym as the dead guy they are investigating up the wazoo? Even the stupidest cop alive could run with that one.

"The feds might not be the fastest mill wheels in the world, but they grind exceedingly fine. They are plodders, but that's what they do best, and if they get this far, we are fucked. Even if the house is as clean as a wetware assembly room. If they can't *prove* anything, they'll know who I am, and that will throw a big rock into the gears. I won't be able to go pee from now on without seeing an underwater camera lens in the toilet bowl looking up at me."

Tad shook his head. "I'm sorry, man."

Drayne shook his head in response. "I know, Tad, I know. And it's done. Now, we have to see if we can manage some kind of damage control."

"How?"

Drayne looked at him. "You know the guy in Texas, down in Austin?"

"The programmer who buys two caps every three or four weeks, for him and his girlfriend."

"Yeah, him. I read about him in *Time.* He's supposed to be a genius, supposed to be able to make a computer sit up and bark like a dog, if he wants. Got his start hack-ing into secure systems just for the fun of it."

"So?"

"So, we make him a deal. He does us a favor, we sup-ply him with whatever rings his bell, for free."

"Dude is richer than Midas, he doesn't need the money."

"But I know how geniuses think," Drayne said. "Especially outlaw geniuses. He'll do it so we'll owe him, and in the doing, he can prove he's still got the chops he started out with. He gets to exercise the old muscles and feel like a badass outlaw again."

"What is he gonna do that'll help?"

"He's going to make us invisible. Get ahold of him."

"Now?"

"Right now."

The more he thought about it, the better he liked the idea. It could work. If they moved fast enough, it definitely could work.

24

Sweat ran down John Howard's face.

In the heat of battle, the SIPEsuit's polypropyl/spider-silk layers didn't get rid of the perspiration nearly fast enough to keep you dry. The weight of the ceramic plates wasn't bad, but it didn't help cool things any. Even during a tepid night, such as it was now, the helmet's sweatband quickly got soaked, and you had to blink away the moisture that oozed down into your eyes. And you couldn't raise the clear face shield to let some air in, because the heads-up display wouldn't work without the shield, and neither would the seventh-gen spookeyes built into the armored plastic.

The good thing was, night was no cover for the bad guys. The latest-release intensifiers in the starlight scopes were powerful enough to let you see with the slightest city glow, and the suit's computer false-colored the images so they didn't have that washed-out, pale green look. The blast shield cutouts had been upgraded so that if some yahoo threw a flare or a flashbang, the filters would pop

on-line within a hundredth of a second, saving you from
a sudden nova-lume that would sear your eyeballs blind
in a heartbeat. Though this was something of a mixed
blessing.

"You can run, Abdul, but you can't hide," Howard said.

From the LOSIR headset, Sergeant Pike's voice: "Sir?"

"Disregard that," Howard said. He shifted his grip on
the tommy gun. His good-luck piece wore the pistol grip
forestock and a fifty round drum, weighed a ton, and it
took a little practice to use properly, especially if you were
used to the cheek-spot-weld, right-elbow-high, left-hand-
under-the-foregrip the Army liked to teach long-arm
shooters when Howard had gone through basic all those
years ago.

"Sir, I make it nine ceejays coming in through that alley
to the left."

Howard's own heads-up display verified that. "Copy,
Sergeant. That's two each and one left over. Wake up
troops and mind your fields of fire."

The other three men with Howard did not respond.
They knew what they were supposed to do.

Howard clicked the selector onto full auto and raised
the finned barrel with its Cutts compensator over the top
of the rusty oil drum he had chosen for cover. The old
drum was full of what looked like brick and concrete frag-
ments, so it was cover and not just concealment. If the
enemy spotted him and directed fire his way, he did have
some protection.

The first of the nine soldiers appeared at the mouth of
the alleyway. They stopped, and the leader held up his
hand, signaling for the others to halt. He looked around,
didn't see Howard or the rest of his quad, then hand-
signaled for the rest to advance.

Howard touched a recessed control on his helmet and
shut off the spookeyes. The bright-as-noon scene went

immediately dim, but there was still enough ambient light to make out the shadowy forms of the enemy troopers. He slitted his eyelids, to make the scene even darker, forcing his pupil to dilate wider.

When the ninth soldier appeared, one of Howard's quad tossed a five-second photon flare. Bright, actinic white light strobed, casting tall, hard-edged shadows from the startled soldiers.

Howard waited a beat, then opened his eyes wider.

His men let go with their subguns, and the enemy soldiers returned fire, yelling and blasting away.

Howard indexed the two in his assigned field of fire and gave them each a three-round burst.

In the light of the still burning photon flare, the nine went down like pins in a bowling alley. The scene fell quiet. The five-second flare winked out, and it went dark, much darker than before. Even though he had been using hardball .45 auto ammo with low-flash powder, the afterimages of his fire decreased his vision. Howard touched the control, and the spookeyes turned night into day again. The heat sigs on the downed soldiers showed no movement. Good. A perfect ambush.

"End sim," Howard said.

The Baghdad street scene vanished, and John Howard removed the VR headset and leaned back in his office chair. The exercise had been designed to practice with the spookeyes, and it had gone as planned. The ability to see in almost total darkness was a great help, but there were some drawbacks. Because of the automatic filters built into the scopes, any scenario that included random, repeated weapons fire effectively rendered the spookeyes useless, just as it did wolf ear hearing protectors.

With a single bright flash of light, the scopes' filters would kick on long enough to diminish the light to safe levels, then open back up. This worked great for an explosion. However, with multiple flashes of bright orange muzzle blasts going off all around you, the filters would kick on and off, going from light to dark so fast it was extremely disorienting. The effect was rather like being surrounded by strobe lights all timed differently. Early sims showed the accuracy rate of troopers firing in such a scenario dropped dramatically.

So different tactics had been employed to get around the problem.

At first, the scientific types had tried to rig the scopes to drop filters and leave them down for five or ten seconds. Unfortunately, this made the scene too dark to see anything except much-dimmed muzzle flashes, your own or the enemy's. Spray and pray was a sucker's game.

They tried adjusting this, but since firefights sometimes lasted for five seconds, sometimes a lot longer, the results were less than satisfactory.

They also tried raising the gain threshold, so it took more to cause the shields to deploy, but even an amplified kitchen match in the dark would be enough to temporarily blind a soldier.

The scientists and engineers scratched their heads and went back to their CAD programs.

It fell to the men and women in the field to come up with a better way, like it usually did. Using the scopes to find and track an enemy, then reverting to the old-fashioned method seemed to be the best approach. At least it worked in VR scenarios and at the range. How it would work in the real world remained to be seen, at least for his units.

Howard sighed. He had run dozens of war game scenarios over the past few weeks, and there was only so much of that a man could take. In his time as the commander of Net Force's military arm, there had been slack periods, but never as slow as it had been these last few weeks. He knew he was supposed to be happy about that, the idea that peace was better than war, and he was, but—

—sitting around and doing nothing but figurative paper clip counting was boring.

Of course, he wasn't as likely to get shot sitting around and doing nothing, and that had been on his mind lately, too.

Washington, D.C.

Toni tried doing her *djurus* while sitting on the couch, just using her upper body, as Guru had told her. Yeah, she could do it, and yeah, it was better than nothing, but it was like taking a shower with a raincoat on. You couldn't really feel the water.

She stood, moved the coffee table out of the way, and did a little stretching, nothing major, just to limber up her back and hips some. The doctor hadn't said she couldn't stretch, just nothing heavy-duty, right?

The elastic of her stretch pants cut into her belly as she sat and bent over to touch her toes. Damn, she hated this, being fat!

After five minutes or so of loosening up, she felt better. Okay, so she could do a few *djurus* with the footwork, the *langkas,* if she went real slow, right? No sudden moves, no real effort, it wouldn't be any more stressful than walking if she was careful, right?

For about ten minutes, she practiced, moving slowly, no power, just doing the first eight *djurus*. She skipped the forms where she had to drop into a squat, number five and number seven, and she felt fine.

Then, of course, she had to go pee, something that happened five times an hour, it seemed.

When she finished and started to leave the bathroom, she looked into the toilet.

The bowl had blood in it, as did the tissue she had just used.

Fear grabbed her in an icy hand.

She ran to call the doctor.

Austin, Texas

Tad drove the rental car, Bobby riding shotgun and giving him directions.

"Okay, stay on I-35 going south until we cross Lake Whatchamacallit, and look for a sign says Texas State School for the Deaf. We have to find Big Stacy Park— as opposed to Little Stacy Park, which is just up the road a piece—then Sunset Lane, then we turn onto—you piece of Chinese shit!"

This last part was accompanied by Bobby slapping the little GPS unit built into the car's dashboard.

"What?"

"The sucker glitched, the map disappeared!" Bobby hammered the malfunctioning GPS unit again. "Come on!"

"I don't see why we had to come here in person," Tad said. "We could have called or done this by e-mail over the web."

"No, we couldn't have. The feds can monitor phones and e-mail, even encrypted stuff. They were able to do it for years before the public even realized they could and already were. Besides, this guy wants an insurance policy. He wants to see our faces. He'll know the name, and he can use that, but we could change our identities."

"We could change our faces, too."

Bobby hit the GPS again. "Ah, there it is. I got the map again." He looked at Tad. "Yeah, we could, and he'll know that. But the thing is, he wants us to come to him with our hat in our hand and say please. Then he dazzles us with his techno-wizardry, and we owe him big-time and forever. It's an ego thing. Besides, as long as we're in business, he'll have something on us, doesn't matter what our names are or what we look like. We have the market cornered on Thor's Hammer, remember? Whoever is selling it is gonna be us, no matter what we call ourselves."

"Yeah. I have to say, though, this might be out of the frying pan and into the fire, man. Even if it works, we're trading one problem for another one."

"I don't think so," Bobby said.

Tad said, "There's the lake, up ahead."

"Okay, watch for the deaf sign, should be just after we cross over that."

"I'm watching. Back to this *maybe* biz. The guy will have something to trade if he ever gets busted. You think he wouldn't give us up to save his own ass?"

"Don't think that for a second. I'd give him up, if positions were reversed."

"Jeez, Bobby—"

"C'mon, Tad, think a little bit past the end of your nose. The clock is running at the cop shop. This computer dick-wad can get into the gym's computer and the police system and make my name go away. He does that before they get to me, we're clear."

"If the cops didn't just get a hardcopy."

"They didn't. Steve told me they downloaded his membership files into their system over the wire. Nobody uses hardcopy for this kind of stuff anymore. I didn't even fill out a treeware registration form when I signed up; I just logged it all into a keyboard at the gym.

"So the *immediate* threat, the law, is taken care of. Mr. Computer Geek is a *potential* problem, but that's down the line. He isn't going to run to the cops and turn us in now, not if he wants help from mighty Thor to keep wearing blisters on his wang with his lady friend. You see what I'm saying?"

"Yeah, but—"

Bobby cut him off. "You know about Occam's Razor?"

"No. You not gonna tell me another fucking story, are you?"

Bobby laughed. "No. It's a way of looking at problems. A rule that basically says, don't get complicated when simple will do the job. The simple thing here is, if the cops don't know about me, they can't come looking for me."

"Okay, I can see that. You buy some time, get out from under the immediate threat. But you still got the potential thing later."

"Well, if you just let it hang out there, yeah. But this computer guy could, you know, have an accident. He could slip in the bathtub and dash his brains out or get hit by a bus crossing the street or maybe an allergic reaction to shellfish, and just up and die. There are certain chemicals that can kill somebody and make it look just like anaphylactic shock. And hey, stuff like that happens all the time, right? Cops would investigate, but if it was an *accident*, that would be the end of it, right?" Bobby grinned, that all-his-shiny-teeth smile that showed he was really amused.

Tad got it, finally. He nodded. "Oh. Oh, yeah. I see what you mean."

"There's hope for you yet, Tad m'boy—there, there's the sign, pull off at that next exit!"

Tad nodded. Bobby was almost always a step ahead of the game, even when things got creaky. Push him out a window, and he would land on his feet every time. He had it under control. It felt good to know that.

25

Washington, D.C.

Jay sat *seiza* and tried, like the old joke about the hot dog vendor and the Zen master, to make himself one with everything.

He was having some problems with it. First, the sitting-on-your-heels position was very uncomfortable. They might do it in Japan, where everybody was used to it, but in America, you didn't normally sit that way, or knotted up in a lotus pose, or even on the floor—not without a cushion or pillow to flop on.

Second, while he was supposed to be concentrating on his breath, just sitting back and watching it come and go without trying to control it or count it or anything, that was almost impossible to pull off. As soon as he became aware of his breathing, he kept trying to slow it and keep it even and all, and that was a no-no. And counting just came naturally for him, it was automatic. So he had to make a conscious effort *not* to count, and that was a no-no. Don't count, and don't think about *not* counting.

Third, you weren't supposed to think of anything at all,

and if a thought came up, you were supposed to gently move it away and get back to nothing but breathing. Thoughts were products of the monkey brain, Saji had told him, and had to be quieted to achieve peace and harmony with one's inner self.

Yeah, well, in his case, the brain was more like a whole *troop* of howler monkeys all hooting and dancing through the trees, and quieting that jabbering bunch was a tall order.

His knee hurt. That last inhalation turned into a sigh at the end. The thoughts about work, dinner, Saji, and how stupid he felt sitting here just *breathing* rolled in like a storm tide, as unstoppable as if he stood on the beach waving his arms at the ocean and telling it to hold it right there.

Get a grip, Jay. Millions of people do this every day!

Who knew that meditating would be so difficult? Sitting here and doing nothing was harder than anything Jay had ever done, or in his case, *not* done.

In the back of his mind, nagging at him, was something about work, some little thing flitting up and around like a moth, something he couldn't quite pin down. Something about the drug thing, and the DEA and NSA agents Lee and George . . .

No. Push it away. Get back to that later. For now, just *be* . . .

Lee and George. Not much to know about them. Close to the same age, both career men, both lived in the District. Both of them married briefly but divorced, no live-in girlfriends at the moment. A lot alike . . .

Don't think, Jay, you're supposed to be meditating!

Oh, yeah. Right. Breathe in. Breathe out. Breathe in . . .

Lee's ex-wife was originally from Florida, now a lawyer in Atlanta who also taught law at a local college. She and Lee had met in law school. Jay had checked her out, and while she was well-regarded as a teacher, she was also considered something of a radical. She was a member of the Lesbian Teacher Association or some such, big on women's rights. A no-fault divorce, no hard feelings, at least not in any official records or interviews. Still, that must have made Lee feel weird. You get a divorce, your ex-wife switches her sexual preferences to the other side of the street. Might tend to make you doubt your masculinity a little.

George's ex was a stockbroker. A law-school graduate who didn't practice but who worked for one of the big trading companies on Wall Street, did well enough that she had a two-million-dollar condo overlooking Central Park, single, no significant boyfriends five years after the divorce, didn't seem to date much, according to what Jay had uncovered about her. Like Lee with his ex-wife, George apparently got along famously with his ex.

We're all very civilized here . . .

Thoughts, Jay, watch it!

Okay, okay! Breathe in, breathe out, breathe in . . .

Kind of made you wonder, though, how a woman who was rich enough to afford a condo that expensive didn't have guys lined up waiting for her favor. Good-looking woman, hair cut short, built like a dancer.

Well, it didn't really matter, did it?

Breathe out, breathe in, breathe out . . .

The next thought that swung down from the monkey tree and chittered at Jay so startled him that his eyes popped open, and he said, "Oh, shit!"

Sitting *seiza* on floor across from him, Saji came out of her own meditation. "What? The place on fire?"

"No, no, I just had a thought—"

"Don't worry, it's part of the process—"

"No, I mean, an idea. About the dope case!"

"Let it wait, it will keep."

"No, it won't. I have to get to my computer *now!*"

"Jay, this is not how to meditate."

"I know, I know, but I have to check this out."

Saji sighed. "Fine. Do what you have to do." She closed her eyes and went back to her sitting. Jay was already up and hurrying from the bedroom to his terminal.

Michaels took the day off to be with Toni. She was still in bed, sleeping hard, and he planned to let her sleep as long as possible. The spotting the day before wasn't a sign of fetal distress, the doctor had told them, but it had caused Michaels more than a little dry mouth and nervousness. By the time he had gotten to the clinic, Toni had already been examined, was getting some blood tests, and the doctor had pulled him aside to talk to him.

The doctor, a tall, very dark, and spindly gray-haired man of sixty or so with the unlikely name of Florid, was blunt: "Listen, Mr. Michaels, if your wife doesn't sit down and prop her feet up and do a lot of nothing for the next four months, there is a chance she is going to have a preterm birth and lose this baby."

"Jesus. Have you told her this?"

"I have. She's still relatively young and healthy, and the baby seems fine, but her blood pressure is up a little. Normally she's one twenty over seventy-four, but today she's at one thirty over eighty-six. That's not technically considered high, but we always watch that, especially in a primagravida . . . that's a first-time pregnancy."

"Why is that?"

"There is a condition called preeclampsia that happens in around five pregnancies out of a hundred. Usually it's mild, and by itself it usually doesn't cause problems, but sometimes it can cause what is known as *abruptio placentae,* which is a spontaneous separation of the placenta from the uterine wall, not a good thing. Usually this is in the third trimester, sometimes at delivery, and we can work around it, but it makes things hairy.

"Worse, sometimes preeclampsia can progress to full eclampsia, which, while very rare, involves seizures, coma, and sometimes, a fatal event."

A fatal event.

Michaels swallowed. Now his mouth was *really* dry.

"Is this what's happening to Toni?"

"Probably not. There isn't any albumen in her urine, and she doesn't have much edema, and usually you get those with the rise in BP, but better safe than sorry."

"Toni is the toughest, strongest, healthiest woman I know."

Dr. Florid smiled. "Yes, I expect she can bend steel in her bare hands. Normally, pregnancy is not a medical problem, women can go about their business and do everything they were doing before they got pregnant. Most women. But interior plumbing isn't the same as voluntary muscles. No matter how strong-willed you might be, you can't toughen up the inside of a uterus. Toni's is fragile; likely she was born that way. Now, she could go on to deliver this baby without any more problems, but I'd be a lot happier and that would be a lot more likely if she took it easy. You need to impress on her how important it is for her to relax. After the baby comes, and assuming she has time, she can go swing on a vine like Sheena, Queen of the Jungle, and kick the crap out of lions and rhinos for all I care, but for now, *no strenuous exercise.* What I think is strenuous and what she thinks that means are probably different. I don't want her doing any heavy lifting, jogging, horseback riding, or deep knee bends, and I don't want her doing those martial art dances she can't seem to live without. She can lie in bed. She can sit in a chair or on a couch, she can walk to the kitchen to take her vitamins, but that's about it."

Michaels nodded. "I understand."

"If we have another epsisode of second-trimester bleeding, I am going to confine her to bed for the duration. I know she won't like that."

Michaels had to grin. "No, sir, that's for sure."

He had another question, started to speak, but decided that maybe it was selfish to ask it.

The doctor read his mind: "Sex is permissible, assuming you don't like to pretend she's a trampoline while you do it."

Michaels flushed, embarrassed.

The doctor laughed. "Listen, I know this all sounds very dramatic and scary, but you need to remember that in medicine, we have to plan for the worst-case scenario. Chances are very good that nothing bad will happen to your wife or your unborn son. But we have to let you know the possibilites, no matter how small. We have to cover all the bases."

"So you don't get sued," Michaels said.

"Hell, son, I could give my patients and their families movies, recordings, documents, a degree in medicine, and get 'em to sign a paper saying they understood them all and would never even talk to a lawyer in church, and we'd *still* wind up in court if anything went wrong. We always get sued when something goes wrong."

"Must be awful."

"Catching babies makes up for it. The look on the new mama's face when she sees her child for the first time is priceless. Pure joy. Long as my malpractice insurance and my hands hold up, I'm going to keep doing it."

He clapped Michaels on the shoulder. "What I personally think is that this pregnancy is going to do fine, if your wife will just kick back and let it roll along."

"Thank you, sir," Michaels said. "I appreciate it."

Now, as Toni slept and Michaels puttered around the

condo, he hoped the doctor had been right in his assessment. Toni wanted the baby, and he did, too. It was going to be the center of their new family and life together, and it would be devastating to lose it.

Him, not it.

In the living room, he came across the box with the two *kerambit* knives. He took them out, put one in each hand, got a feel for how they worked. Odd, to be playing with knives and thinking about a new baby.

Well, maybe not, given the boy's parents.

He moved the knives slowly and carefully. It probably wouldn't do Toni's stress level any good at all for him to accidentally slice his wrist open. Not to mention his own health. Still, the little blades seemed familiar in his grip, comfortable, and the *djuru* moves didn't seem to put him in any danger of cutting himself. At least not this slowly and carefully. One hurried wrong move could put the lie to that quick enough, though.

He put the knives up, and tiptoed back in to check on Toni.

26

On the flight home, Drayne felt pretty good. The computer guy was as good as he'd been cracked up to be. The police in SoCal and Steve's Gym no longer had any reference to one Robert Drayne in their systems. More, the techno-whiz was able to determine that they hadn't gotten around to where his name had been to assign anybody to check it before it had magically vanished. Nor had it been printed out to a hardcopy. The list had been renumbered, and unless you knew somebody had been erased and knew precisely where to look and *how* to look, you wouldn't be able to tell it had been done. And even if you *could* tell that, you wouldn't know who was gone.

Once again, Drayne was golden. And all it had cost was a promise of free dope as long as the guy lived. Cheap beyond measure, even if he had to pay it.

Drayne smiled as the flight attendant walked along the first class rows, asking if anybody wanted complimentary champagne. Probably the stuff was Korbel, or at best one of the California domaines owned by the French. Not bad if you had no experience with the really good stuff, but as far as Drayne was concerned, he wouldn't use it to clean the chrome on his car bumper. Still, the attendant was a babe, not wearing a wedding ring, and the flight from Dallas–Fort Worth to LAX was still hours out from landing. He could strike up a conversation with her, maybe get her number. *Say, have you ever considered acting? You have great bone structure. . . .*

The attendant stopped to talk to a woman Drayne thought he recognized as somebody in L.A. politics, a city council member or maybe a spokesperson for the mayor's office. Drayne glanced at his watch.

About now, Tad would be buying the computer whiz a dinner at a great little out-of-the-way Italian restaurant locally famous for its fresh produce, ostensibly to make arrangements to deliver a dozen caps of the Hammer as a first payment of a lifetime drug supply. The computer geek, a health nut, had raved about the place. The salad that came with the meal featured fresh wild greens, mushrooms, and other local herbs, and was terrific, he'd said.

Drayne had smiled, regretting that he had to be back in L.A. and would have to miss that, but hey, Tad loved salad!

The last time Tad had eaten a salad or anything remotely healthy had probably been twenty years past. Anybody who looked at him could see that. But a guy as full of himself as Mr. Computer Wizard would skate right past that obvious fact without blinking. People saw what they wanted to see, not what was really there.

So the guy had chosen his own exit and made it easy for them to hold the door open.

If everything went as planned, just as the computer geek was about to lay into this garden delight, he was going to get a call on his com. Tad had the number programmed into his own com, and a touch of a button would do the trick. While Mr. Wizard was distracted, Tad was going to add a couple of different kinds of sliced mushrooms to the man's salad that weren't on the menu. These grew wild in places as hot and damp as Austin still was this time of year, easy to find if you knew where to look, and once they were sliced were virtually identical to any other small, white-fleshed mushrooms.

The first variety of these particular 'shrooms contained heavy concentrations of amatoxins and phallotoxins, either of which could be fatal, and both of which would almost certainly destroy liver and kidney functions, leading to death within a week to ten days 80 percent of the time.

The second variety was chock-full of Gyromita toxins, which, while not quite as nasty as the others, also attacked the liver and kidneys, plus the circulatory system, leading to heart failure in extreme cases. Mostly Gyromita poisoning was uncommon in the U.S. because cooking these mushrooms usually mitigated the toxin. Nice, crisp, raw ones in a salad would still pack a nasty punch, however.

Mr. Computer Wizard would enjoy his meal. He and Tad would part company on the best of terms. A day later, maybe two, Mr. Wizard would come down with flulike symptoms: nausea, vomiting, diarrhea, cramps. His doctor would probably miss the diagnosis at first, but even if he didn't, the only way to keep the victim alive would be a liver and maybe a kidney transplant, and even then, the heart was still at risk.

No guarantee, of course, but eight chances out of ten he would croak weren't bad odds. And if he made it, he'd be a long time recovering, on immunosuppressive drugs if they could find him a new liver, and unable to screw with his body chemistry if he wanted to stay alive. And if he made it that far? Well, they could always pay him another visit.

If he died, it would be due to mushroom poisoning, a terrible tragedy, a freak accident. Bad for the restaurant's reputation and insurance carrier, but, hey, that was how life went sometimes. You want an omelette, you gotta break a few eggs.

The flight attendant approached. "Care for champagne, sir?"

"That would be nice. Look, I don't want you to think I'm hitting on you, but I'm a movie producer. Have you ever considered acting?"

He held up his producer business card and smiled.

She took the card, looked at it, and smiled back. "I've thought about it. I was the lead in my high school play."

Life was very good.

Life is crappy, Toni thought. Nobody had told her what might happen when she got pregnant, nobody had said she'd be reduced to the mobility and muscularity of a slug. She hated this.

Alex had hung around to take care of her, but she had made him leave. He was sweet, but she wasn't going to be pleasant company, and she didn't want him thinking of her as a constant bitch. Better he should see her smiling and at least offering some pretense of being happy once in a while.

"You sure?" he'd asked, after three exchanges on the subject.

"I'm positive. Go."

And he had, and that pissed her off, too. Yes, she had said for him to, she had insisted that he do so, but she hadn't really wanted him to leave. Why didn't he know that? How could he just . . . take her at her word that way? Why were men so stupid?

Yes, yes, all right, she knew it was illogical, but that was how she felt.

Now that Alex was gone, she was at a loss for what to do with herself. The doctor had made it crystal clear she was on light duty from now on, and since a big part of her had always been physical, this was proving to be intolerable. She couldn't move, she might as well put down roots and turn into a fucking houseplant. She *really* hated this.

She didn't feel like sitting at the scrimshaw project. She didn't feel like watching television or listening to music or reading. What she felt like doing was going for a five-mile run to clear her mind. Or a half hour of stretching and then *silat* practice. Or anything requiring sweat and sore muscles.

No point in even bothering to think about such things. It would only make her feel worse, if that was possible.

Other women must have gone through this. She could do it if anybody else could, she kept telling herself. But that didn't help.

The house was clean. She had spent way too much time doing that lately, wiping counters, sweeping floors, rearranging shelves. You could eat off the floor—if you were allowed to bend over and take the risk.

She wandered into the bedroom. The bed was made. The bathroom was clean. Nothing.

The floor in Alex's closet by his shoe rack had some clothes piled up to be dry-cleaned. Well, she could do that. Surprise Alex, given as how she didn't usually fool with his chores.

She picked up a suit, a sports jacket, a couple of good silk shirts, a few ties. The laundry-to-go basket was in the garage, where Alex would usually notice it when it got full, toss the dirty clothes into his car, and drop it off at the Martinizing place run by a family of Koreans on the way to work.

As she started dropping the clothes into the hamper,

she automatically went through the pockets. Being raised in a family full of brothers had taught her that when doing the wash. Boys left all kinds of crap in their pockets, and a handful of coins clattering in the washer or dryer would drive you nuts, not to mention chipping the inside of the machines. Ink pens could ruin a load of whites, and it was no fun picking lint from a washed, shredded, and dried paper napkin from a load of dark shirts, either.

In the suit trousers, Toni found a paper clip box, and inside that, the capsule.

She knew what it was from Alex's description, it being big and purple and all, and it puzzled her as to why it was in his pocket. But maybe it was important. She seemed to recall the stuff had some kind of timing chemical in it, and it would be inert after a day or so. Alex hadn't worn this suit yesterday, had he?

She reached for the phone on the workbench, looking at the capsule. She put it down next to the scrimshaw piece she'd been working on as Alex's com bleeped.

"Hey, babe, what's up? You okay?"

"Yeah, I'm fine. I was taking your dry cleaning out to the hamper—"

"You were what?"

"Don't sound so amazed."

"Sorry. Go on."

"Anyway, I found this purple capsule in your pocket."

"Ah, damn. I keep forgetting about that. I was going to take it by the FBI lab and have somebody look at it. That's the one John got on the raid I told you about."

"I can do that for you, run it by the lab."

"No, you can't. You aren't supposed to be driving, remember? Hang on to it for me, I'll do it tomorrow."

"Fine."

"Uh, thanks for calling me about it."

"You at work yet?"

"Almost there."

"I'll see you later," she said.

After she broke the connection, Toni stared into space. She sure hoped this baby was worth all this crap. He'd better be.

She wandered back into the house. All of a sudden, she was tired. Maybe she would lie down and take a short nap. Might as well. She couldn't do anything else.

Jay shook his head, feeling stupid. It had been right there in front of him all along, and he had just skipped over it. He had narrowed his focus too much and missed the connection.

Maybe all this navel-gazing was good in the long run, learning how to clear your thoughts, to relax your mind, but the old Jay Gridley wouldn't have let this slide past unseen.

Maybe it wasn't a good idea to be too relaxed mentally in his business.

He ran it down. The most important piece took a while, but finally, he got it. Wasn't proof of anything, of course, but certainly it was a circumstantial lump that would choke an elephant.

Jesus.

He needed to fly it past the boss, to get his hit on it, but he was pretty sure it meant something important. He reached for the com to call, then decided maybe it would be better to avoid using the phone or net. Net Force's coms, especially the virgils, were scrambled, the signals turned into complex binary ciphers that were supposedly unbreakable by ordinary mortals. That little episode in the U.K. with the quantum computer had cured Jay of his faith in unbreakable binary codes, however. And given the people with whom they were dealing, maybe face-to-face was better.

"I have to go into HQ," Jay said to Saji on his way to the door.

"This late?" She opened her eyes and stared at him, still seated in her meditation pose.

"It's important. I love you. See you later."

"Drive safe," she said.

He thought about his discovery all the way to Net Force HQ. Boy, wasn't the boss going to be surprised at this twist!

27

Tad sat at the gate, slouched in a chair, waiting for his connecting flight back to LAX. Even full of painkillers, speed, and steroids to the eyeballs, it was all he could do to hold himself up. Every muscle, every joint, every part of him he could feel ached, a bone-deep, grinding throb that resonated through him with every heartbeat. The best dope he could get only dulled the pain, it didn't come close to stopping it. He was so tired he could hardly see straight, and the way he felt, if he sneezed, his head would fall off. But his fuck-up was fixed, and, yeah, okay, he'd had to ice some poor sucker to wrap it. At least Bobby wasn't pissed at him anymore. He hated to disappoint Bobby, who put up with a lot of his crap without kicking him out. Only friend he'd ever had, Tad knew, and the only person on earth who had ever given a shit about him. You just didn't let people like that down.

A goth girl of eighteen or nineteen walked by and slouched into the bank of chairs across from Tad, eyeing him. She wore a torn black T-shirt under a distressed black leather jacket with the sleeves cut off, black sweat-pants, and pink tennis shoes. She had short hair dyed pur-ple, a nose ring, lip ring, eyebrow ring, and nine ear studs showing. Tad would be real surprised if she wasn't wear-ing more gold and steel in her belly button, nipples, and labia. She gave him a twist of a smile—yep, there was the tongue stud—and he managed a lifted lip in return. Probably saw him as a kindred spirit, and what the hell, probably he was. Some of the kids who dressed the part were wanna-be's, some of them were nihilists, some of them true anarchists. You could usually tell after thirty seconds of conversation which they were, but right now, he couldn't summon the energy needed even to wave her over and see. Not that it much mattered if she did come over; he wasn't in any condition to slip off to the john to snort some coke, smoke a joint, or screw, if any of those were her pleasure. Truth was, he liked Bobby's kind of woman anyhow, the pneumatic bunnies who pumped dick as well as they did iron. Not that he'd had much interest in that area lately. Well, except for that royal fuck-up in the gym with Wonder Woman.

The announcer came on and garbled something out. Tad didn't have any idea what she'd said, but people started to get up and shoulder their carry-on bags or tow them behind them on little leashes, like Samsonite dogs who didn't want to go for a walk and had to be dragged. Tad didn't have any luggage. If he needed clean clothes, he bought them and threw the old stuff away, shirts, pants, underwear, socks, whatever. It was a trick he'd learned as a street kid in Phoenix a thousand years ago. If you have to travel, better to travel light. If you don't have nothin', nobody can steal nothin' from you. You don't have to remember anything, and if you have to split, you can do so without looking back. He had his e-ticket printout, a wallet, five hundred or so bucks in it, a couple of credit cards, and his ID. That was his luggage, and it was zipped into a back pocket. Unless somebody came up and did a butt slash and rob, he wasn't gonna lose that. And if he did? Fuck it. It didn't really matter, did it? You could get another wallet, more cards, more money. None of that was important.

The goth girl got up and sidled in behind Tad as he moved toward the woman taking tickets. She said, "I got some coke. You wanna do some, head to the bathroom when you see me go there."

Tad lifted his lip in his half-assed grin. "Cool," he said.

But he doubted he'd see her when she went. He was in first class, and he'd bet she was in tourist, unless she was slumming, and he didn't think she was. Besides, he had his own coke, and he knew how pure it was. Street drugs were always risky. Maybe if he felt better in a little while, he'd share that with her. Find out what she could do with that tongue stud.

He planned to crash when he got back to Malibu, and sleep for a week. Maybe by then, he would have recovered enough to pick up the Hammer again. Now that everything was copacetic with Bobby, there was no need to fly to Hawaii or even slow down biz. Life was normal again, such as normal was, and he could get back on the road to Hell as soon as he was able.

Quantico, Virginia

Jay was almost hopping up and down he was so full of whatever it was that he had to say.

Michaels smiled and waved at the seat. Jay headed in that direction, but he didn't sit.

"Okay, tell me. You caught our dope dealer?"

Jay frowned, as if that thought was the last thing on his mind. "What? Oh, no. If we were doing a movie, that would be the A story. What I did is figure out the B story. Well, at least part of it."

"You want to run that past me again?"

"Okay, okay, look, I was all over the DEA guy Lee and the NSA agent George. Nothing, no connection. But I expanded the search, and I came up with Lynn Davis Lee and Jackie McNally George."

"Who are—?"

"The ex-wives. Lee and George met their wives in law school, got hitched, went their separate ways a couple years later. Both are divorced."

"So am I, Jay. So is roughly fifty percent of everybody who got married in the last twenty years."

The younger man grinned. "Yeah, but Lynn Davis and Jackie McNally were roommates in law school."

"Really? That is an odd coincidence"

"It gets better, boss. Lynn Davis—she dropped her married name after the split—is a lawyer and part-time teacher in Atlanta. From what I was able to determine, she . . . ah . . . prefers the company of women to men."

"How shocking. So?"

"Same deal with Jackie McNally. She is very low-profile about it, but apparently she is also a lesbian."

Michaels thought about that a second. "Hmm."

"Yeah, you see where I'm going here? Doesn't that seem, well, *queer,* that two guys married and then divorced college roommates, both of whom are lesbians?"

"Doesn't speak highly of the boys' lovemaking skills, but it also doesn't prove anything, does it?"

"Nope. But what if Ms. Davis and Ms. McNally had the same sexual preferences *before* they got married? From what I can tell, that was the case."

Michaels chewed on that for a moment. "Ah," he said, beginning to understand.

"It makes sense," Jay said. "There are a lot of places where—laws notwithstanding—being gay is still a problem. Federal agencies aren't allowed to discriminate about such things, but you know how it is. Come out as gay, you put a glass ceiling over your own head."

Michaels nodded. That was true, like it or not, especially in security agencies. The theory was, an openly gay operative wouldn't be a problem, but somebody in the closet might be a candidate for blackmail, if he or she didn't want to be outed. And he had a pretty good idea of where Jay was going with the rest of it, but he didn't say anything, just waved for him to keep rolling.

"So, consider this scenario. Lee and George are . . . well, let's say, men's men. They know that being that way is likely to top them out at a low level in a lot of agencies. And lesbians have the same problems."

"So you think we have a case of two gay men marrying two lesbian women to provide each other with solid heterosexual backgrounds?"

"It wouldn't be the first time," Jay said. "Having an ex-wife or husband on paper would forestall some tongue-wagging, especially if you were discreet from then on. Only now, Lee and George, who maybe aren't so close anymore, really don't like each other. Might explain some things."

Michaels nodded again. "That could be. You did good, Jay. Thanks."

After Jay was gone, Michaels thought about it some, then reached for the com. He wanted to talk to John Howard. An ugly idea had just entered his mind, and while he hoped things wouldn't go down that road, he had to check it out.

•   •   •

Howard nodded at Michaels. He'd been figuratively shuf-
fling paper clips when the commander called, and any
excuse to get up and move was good.

"No doubt in your mind?" Michaels said.

"No, sir. Lee flat assassinated the man. Zeigler was
clearly about to drop his knife. He had started to step back
from his hostage, and when Lee fired, he was no more
than twenty-five feet away. Plus, my radio mike was still
on. Lee heard Zeigler say he was surrendering. No, sir.
This guy was a DEA field agent for years, he went on
scores of raids, some of which had gunplay on both sides,
I checked his record. When he pulled the trigger, he had
to know the situation was under control."

"Okay, let's assume for a moment that he didn't panic
and do it by accident, he iced the man on purpose. That
brings up a big question, doesn't it?"

"Yes, sir. Why would he do that?"

"Any theories you want to share?"

"I have been thinking about it. Assuming there was no
personal hatred of the man, the only thing I can come up
with is that he didn't want Zeigler giving up his dealer."

Michaels said, "That doesn't make any sense, because
the whole purpose of the raid was to bust the guy hard
enough so we could find that out."

"Yes, sir. Thing is, Zeigler was in a panic, and he was
about to spill his guts when Lee double-tapped him."

Give the commander credit, he picked up on it right
away. "Where somebody other than Lee could hear him.
You."

"Yes, sir, me. And the maid."

Michaels shook his head. "I don't like this worth a
damn, John. Something stinks here."

"I do believe so myself."

The commander steepled his fingers and leaned back in

his chair. "If it had just been Lee there, he could claim he shot Zeigler to save the maid."

"Who speaks about five words of English and was so terrified she didn't know which way was up," Howard added. "Not a great witness either way."

"So come the shooting review or whatever it is DEA does, anything you have to say is going to make Lee look real bad. He had to know what he did was going to cost him big time."

"I'd assume so, yes, sir. If they believe me, it ought to be worth his job. If he was one of mine, I'd kick him out and tell the local DA to burn him, manslaughter at the very least, maybe murder two."

"Which he has to know, and even so, he's willing to horizontal somebody in front of a witness."

"Maybe he thinks he can blow enough smoke to get past it."

"I wouldn't underrate yourself, John. You are the military commander of Net Force, a general. You can shine a lot of light on him."

"Yes, sir. So we're back to the big question. Why'd he do it? What did he have to gain that was so important he'd risk his job?"

"I don't know. But I certainly think we need to find out."

"Yes, sir, I believe that's true."

"There's one other thing we need to think about here, too, John."

"Sir?"

"Maybe Lee loves his job and is willing to do anything to keep it." He raised an eyebrow.

Well, Mama Howard didn't raise any stupid children, either. Howard said, "Bit of a stretch, isn't it?"

"He killed a world-famous movie star in front of a witness who, at the very least, can get him fired and maybe charged with a nasty felony. Maybe if something happened to the witness, he might not be so worried."

Howard nodded. "I take your point. I'll make sure my brakes are working before I go for a drive."

"And make sure nothing is attached to the ignition switch, too, John. I'd hate to have to break in a new military commander."

"Yes, sir, I'd hate to put you to the trouble."

They smiled at each other.

But when Howard left, he considered what Michaels had said. Lee did seem to be something of a loose cannon. He didn't want to be in front of him if he went off.

28

Drayne was not a man to make the same mistake twice, especially on something that, in theory, could cost him his freedom. As soon as he was back on the ground in L.A., still in the car on the way home, he made a call to a real estate agent he'd never met. He got her name out of the phone directory and picked it because he liked the sound of it.

"Silverman Realty," the woman said, "this is Shawanda speaking."

Shawanda Silverman. What kind of intermarriage produced such a great name? He loved it.

"Yes, ma'am, my name is Lazlo Mead, and I'm going to be living here in the Los Angeles area for about a year or so for a project I'm just starting to work on."

"Yes, Mr. Mead?"

"What I want is to lease a three- or four-bedroom furnished house not too far from things, but in a nice area, you know, maybe out a little ways, in one of the canyons?"

"Certainly I can help you with that. What . . . ah . . . price range are we talking about?"

"Well, the company is paying for it—I'm in aircraft supply and maintenance—so maybe you could find one where the rent was somewhere around eight to ten thousand dollars a month?"

He could hear the cash register in her voice: "No problem with that," she said too quickly. "I can make a list of a few places, and we can get together and view them."

"Well, here's the thing. I'm kind of in a hurry, but I'm up to my eyeballs in work. Somebody gave me your name as having done this kind of thing for people before, so maybe you could just, you know, pick a place that would work for me and my wife and just go ahead and lease it for us. I'll e-mail you a transfer, you know, first month, last month, cleaning and security fees, whatever—say forty thousand?—and e-sign any paperwork to get the ball rolling. We can get together later. Sooner I get out of the hotel and into a real place, the happier I'll be."

"I understand that, Mr. Mead. I'm sure I can find a house that will work for you. Any preferences as to furniture or schools or such?"

"Well, my wife likes modern stuff, so we want to keep her happy. No early American or like that. No kids, so schools don't matter."

"I'll see what I can do. I'll e-mail you pictures, if you want."

"That would be good." He gave her one of the remailing addresses he used. She probably already had caller-IDed the number of the clean phone he kept for just such transactions, the one made out in the name of Projects, Inc. Now there was a term that could be stretched to fit virtually anything. What did it mean? Nothing. He gave her the number. Soon as she found something, she said, she would call. He got her e-mail address and promised to send a fund transfer first thing in the morning.

After he broke the connection, he felt a lot better. In a day or two, he'd have a hideout, so if he had to leave the Malibu house in a hurry, there would be a place he could run to where he could sort things out. He had a big, fat, five-hundred-pound gun safe bolted to the concrete floor in a U-Store-It place way out Ventura Boulevard; he'd drive over the hill and move most of the cash from the beach house to that tonight, as a matter of fact. Maybe some of the better champagne. The locker, which was eight by ten feet, was air conditioned, he'd made sure of that. With his money safe and a place to hide if it came to that, he would be halfway ready.

Lazlo Mead was about to come into full existence, too. Drayne had a wonderful, illegal software program and card stocks for making phony IDs. A couple of hours and a good color laser printer, a few watermarks and holograms, and presto! Mr. Lazlo Mead would have a driver's license from, oh, say, Iowa; a social security card, maybe a library card, and a couple of credit cards that looked perfect, even if they weren't valid. The program would also print out pictures of a mythical wife and parents, if he wanted.

That would take care of the basics. When Tad got home, he could do the other part, the hired muscle. A few armed bodyguards could buy them enough time to haul ass if somebody came calling, especially if Drayne gave them the right story. *"Somebody yells 'Police!' they are lying,"* he'd tell the shooters. *"It's guys trying to rip us off."* Tad knew people who wouldn't care if whoever hired them were dope dealers or gunrunners, long as they got paid. Guys who'd shoot it out with cops anyhow, if the pay was rich enough.

Maybe he ought to get a gun, too. He'd never had much use for those, but after the Zee-ster bought it, the thought had popped up. He didn't have any training, but you didn't have to be a rocket scientist, now did you? Any fuzz-brained gangbanger in East L.A. could use a gun, how hard could it be? Point it and pull the trigger, it went bang. Wave it, and it was like a magic wand; people sat up and paid attention. Something that looked cool, one of those stainless steel movie guns the action adventure guys used, pearl handles or something.

Of course, all this would tap into his money pretty good, forty grand for the house, probably fifty or sixty more for five bodyguards, just to get started. But it had to be done. He'd been lax before, but not anymore. All this had been a wake-up call, and he didn't want to be caught by surprise. It had been a big game, really, but when customers started getting cooked by feds, the seriousness factor went way up. He hadn't really believed he'd ever be caught, not really, and the idea of spending years in a federal prison somewhere fending off some big horny con named Bubba did not appeal at all. So it would cost, big deal. Money was the easiest part. If he put the word out, he could move fifty or sixty hits of the Hammer a week, easy. Couple, three months of doing that every week or two, he'd make expenses and a whole lot more. Clear, say, half a million in the next few months, then take a break?

Cross that bridge when he got to it. It had been a close call, that business with the Zee-ster. He would not get that involved with the customers again. He was smarter than most people, he knew that, and he knew he could see things better, but when you were moving in a hurry, you had to watch your step. All kinds of things out there that could trip you up.

The "office" com number went off. He frowned at it. Saw there was no caller ID sig lit. He knew who it had to be.

"Polymers, Drayne."

"Robert. This is your father."

Jesus. Didn't the old man think he could recognize his fucking *voice* after all these years? "Hey, Dad. What's up?"

"I'm leaving your aunt's to go back to Arizona tomorrow. I thought we might get together for breakfast before I go."

Drayne felt a cold finger along his spine. His father wanted to see him? That was very strange. "Sure. I know a couple of places near Edwina's that are pretty good."

"Give me the name, and I'll get directions from Edwina."

"Sure."

"We'll meet at seven A.M.," his father said. It was not a question.

"Seven sharp," Drayne said. Which, when speaking to his father, was redundant. He gave him the name of a good breakfast place just off the Coast Highway.

Drayne frowned again as he severed the connection. Well. His father was leaving town, and it might be a year or two before they saw each other again. Breakfast was not such a big deal. Except that his old man had not invited him to such an event in what, ten years?

Maybe he just wants me to help Edwina out, Drayne reasoned. *Or maybe he felt the clammy hand of death touch him while he sat in the church and wants to tell me about his will.*

Drayne laughed aloud at that thought. *That would be the fucking day.*

Washington, D.C.

Toni, feeling better after an afternoon mostly spent sleeping, listened to Alex's day. At least he thought her brain was working well enough to ask her advice about work. Of course, she had been his assistant for a long time, she knew the game.

"So that's what we've got on our friends at the DEA and NSA," he finished. "What do you think?"

She considered what he'd said. "Well, you know the classic motives for crime: passion, thrills, revenge, psychosis, personal gain. On the face of it, Lee wouldn't have any particular reason to want Zeigler dead for any kind of personal vendetta, unless maybe he *really* hated his movies. I don't think he was that bad an actor. From what you've said, he doesn't seem like a thrill-seeker or a psycho. So what's the personal gain?"

"I don't see any right off," he admitted. "Killing a big movie star doesn't win you friends or money."

She said, "You remember those calls you got offering you work with the pharmaceutical companies?"

He chuckled. "Yeah."

"Well. From what you've said, there seems to be a lot of interest in this drug. We're talking about big money. Maybe somebody convinced Mr. Lee he could cash in big time if he got the dealer and delivered him—or his formula—to the right party. He wouldn't want Net Force getting to the guy first, so he wouldn't want John to know the dealer's name, right?"

He stared at her. "Wow."

"Don't you *dare* sound so surprised, Alex Michaels," she said. "My mind does still work from time to time, when my hormones aren't blowing my head apart."

"You said that, not me." He grinned.

She pretended to glare but couldn't hold onto it. She smiled in return.

"Anyway, it's a good theory. Maybe Jay can make a connection, some record of contact or something."

"These guys would be pretty good at covering their tracks," she said, "if they've had years to practice it like Jay thinks."

"Still, it's a place to look. Even though it is all moot if we can't run the dealer down."

"You'll find him," she said. "I have great faith in you."

"You'd be the only one."

"How many do you need?"

He smiled again. "Why, ma'am, I do believe one will be just exactly enough."

29

Howard was tired of running scenarios, more tired of sitting around. He was itchy to do something, and he was considering running some real-world field exercises just to clear the cobwebs from his brain. Get the troops sharpened up; even though there was nothing to get sharp about now, there would be, eventually. He hoped.

"Love to see a man hard at work."

Howard looked up and saw Julio standing in the doorway of his office. "Lieutenant Fernandez. What brings you here?"

"I believe that would be my size-eleven combat boots, sir."

"And is there a purpose for this visit?"

"Why, good news, General Howard, sir."

"Come on in, then. I can use some news. Any news, good or bad, would be a change."

"I think you're gonna like this."

Howard looked at the flat-black hard case Julio held. It was about three feet long, half that wide. "You have my attention, Lieutenant."

"Sir. You might recall the Thousand-Meter Special Teams Match for United States Military Services held at Camp Perry every November?"

"Oh, I recall it, all right. That would be the match where Net Force's sharpshooters always come in last place . . . behind the Marines, the Army, and even the *Navy?*"

"Only because you won't order Gunny to enter. He'd beat 'em. And we did beat the Navy that one year," Julio allowed.

"Because their shooter lost his hearing protection in a freak accident and blew out an eardrum is why."

"Still beat 'em. Take it any way you can."

Howard nodded at the case. "This a secret weapon?"

"Well, a weapon, yes, but not so secret. Just new. Take a look."

Julio set the case down on the old map table across from Howard's desk, popped the latches on the case, and clamshelled it open.

Howard walked over and looked at the components inside the case.

"Why, it is a gun. It appears to be a bolt-action five-oh BMG rifle," Howard said.

"Yes, sir, but not just *any* five-oh. This is a prototype, one of only two built, of the upcoming EMD Arms Model XM-109A Wind Runner, designed by Bill Ritchie himself. Third generation."

Julio reached into the case and pulled out the stock and receiver assembly. "This here receiver is made of 17-4 PH stainless and, with improved heat-treating, now Rockwells out at forty-five-plus. Sixteen pounds, wire-cut, tolerances you wouldn't believe, and with the fully adjustable stock here retracted, a mere twenty inches long. Stock is equipped with a carbon-fiber polysorb monopod recoil pad and nice cheek piece incorporating no-tear bio-gel."

"You have to go looking for your shoulder after you fire it?"

"No, sir, it kicks about as hard as a stout twelve-gauge. Of course, it will shove you back about a foot if you shoot it prone, and you will want to be lying down behind it and not firing offhand."

"I bet."

"Speaking from experience, sir. You'll notice the M-14 bipod and mounted scope, the latter of which is a U.S. Optics adjustable, 3.8X–22X, very nice optical gear, sighted in for a thousand meters. And here is a nifty little red dot switch, automatically adjusted for parallax, that gives you short-range capabilities. Short range in this case being three to four hundred meters. Put the dot on the target, that's where the bullet goes, plus or minus a few inches.

"Might as well throw it as shoot that close, though.

"The new model Son of Wind Runner here uses a five-round magazine like the older models, and has a Remington-style adjustable trigger, set to three pounds. Uses your standard MK211 caliber .50 multipurpose cartridge as the primary tactical round, though match-grade handloads are the ticket at Camp Perry, of course." Julio held up a box of ammo. "Like these."

He opened the bipod and set the receiver and stock up on the table. He reached back into the case and came out with the barrel.

"Your barrel here is a twenty-eight-inch fluted match-grade graphite from K&P Gun, with an eighty-port screw-on muzzle brake, the holes set at thirty degrees. You secure the barrel to the receiver like so, using an Uzi-style nut and a self-locking ratchet, right here."

Julio put the barrel into the receiver and tightened it. It didn't take long.

"Total weight, thirty-four pounds. Insert a loaded magazine, and there she is, ready to rock 'n' roll."

"Very nice," Howard allowed.

"The original XM 107 was designed for use by the Army, particularly the Joint Special Operations Forces, and the Explosive Ordnance Disposal teams. And, theoretically, the Infantry, though the groundpounders didn't get too many copies. SOF uses 'em against soft or semihard targets out to seventeen hundred meters, and EOD uses 'em to blow up unexploded ordnance from a long way outside proximity fuse range."

"Like I said, a nice toy. How much?"

"These things are like hen's teeth, sir. The waiting list is a mile long, and how can you put a price on this kind of quality?" He stroked the barrel with one hand. "There are only two of them exactly like this in all the world."

"Let's try, shall we? How much?"

"Well, with our discount, a hair over five thousand dollars each."

"That actually sounds pretty reasonable." Then, knowing Julio for all the years he'd known him, he said, "A 'hair over' you said. How thick a hair we talking about?"

"Call it three thousand and change," Julio said. He grinned.

"What? For eight thousand dollars, this beast had better dance and whistle 'Dixie,' Lieutenant!"

"Well, I wouldn't know about that, sir. But EDM Arms guarantees one-minute-of-angle accuracy at a thousand meters right out of the box."

Howard raised his eyebrows at that. "One MOA? Guaranteed?"

"Just as you see it. I thought that would get your attention. But that's only to keep the lawyers happy. EDM

Arms has got *verified* five-round groups at a thousand meters of *one-half MOA*. They say they got a couple groups that good at seventeen hundred meters, even a little longer."

Howard looked at the weapon again. "Good Lord. That's a tack-driver."

"Yes, sir. And Bowens, our newly recruited ex-Army shooter, has been doing just that with this very piece, starting yesterday. Talking about a pie-plate-sized group from a mile away. He didn't want to let me take it long enough to show it to you."

Howard grinned.

"So, come next month, Net Force's little piece of the National Guard is going to shoot the living asses off the Navy, the Marines, *and* the Army."

"If one of them doesn't get his hands on the other one," Howard said.

Julio grinned real big.

Howard stared at him. "You didn't."

"Well, sir, yes, sir, I did. If something broke on this here weapon—highly unlikely, I know, given the fine, fine quality, but if something *did* break—we'd want proper backup, wouldn't we?"

Howard shook his head. "I'll have to beat the budget to cover this."

"Not the way I figure it. We do it right, we can make our costs on side bets. I can get three to one against us, easy. I wouldn't be surprised to even make a small profit."

They both grinned at that.

"Anyway, I thought you might like to take it to the outdoor range and put a few through it. That is, if you aren't too busy here." He looked around.

"You missed your calling, Lieutenant. You should have been a comedian."

"Yes, sir, I believe I could have sparkled in such a profession."

Howard looked at the weapon. Why not? He didn't have anything better to do.

"You coming along?"

"No, sir, I have diaper duty, starting in—" he looked at his watch "—forty-six minutes. Best I not be late."

Howard chuckled. "No, I understand. It has been a while since I had such duty myself, but one cannot stress the importance of it enough."

"If one's wife is Lieutenant Joanna Winthrop Fernandez, one can sure as hell stress it high, wide, and repeatedly," Julio said. "You want me to show you how to break it down? Where the cartridges go?"

"I believe I can manage on my own, thank you."

"Have fun."

"Oh, you, too."

"Yeah, right."

Howard looked at the rifle after Julio was gone. Well, why not? He was the commander of Net Force's military, he ought to know how the hardware worked, right? It was training. He could justify that.

Besides, blowing holes in a target three-quarters of a mile away sure beat sitting here doing zip.

The Texas Panhandle, North of Amarillo

Jay Gridley walked along the trail, cutting sign. This was an exercise Saji had taught him when he'd been recovering from his electronically induced stroke, how to track somebody. A bent twig here, a blade of grass lying there, the signs were there if you knew how to look.

In the real world, he was backtracking e-sig, net and

phone and globeSat connections, but here, he was after a
bad man on foot, Hans, a notorious drug seller.

It was hot, and Jay paused to take a swig of tepid water
from his canteen, the fabric of which was wet to allow
some small cooling from evaporation. He thought that was
a nice touch, even though he wasn't sharing the scenario
with anybody. Those little things counted. Anybody could
plug off-the-shelf view- or feelware into their computer
and walk through VR; a pro had higher standards.

He took off his broad-brimmed planter's hat, wiped his
sweaty forehead with a red bandanna, replaced the hat,
and stuck the handkerchief back into his pocket.

There, just ahead, he saw something. Or rather, he
didn't see something. He bent and looked at the hot
ground from only a few inches above it. There weren't
any real tracks, but the dry ground was too smooth.
Carpet-walker, turned and headed that way.

Jay kept walking. Ahead and in a little declivity was a
stand of cottonwood trees and what looked like willow.
Water, a pond, or an underground stream come up to the
surface, he figured. He could almost smell the moisture.

Sure enough, there was a small stream, maybe as wide
as Jay was tall, clear water bubbling over a rocky bottom.
The stream wound away, and Jay stepped into the water
and started to follow it. A man looking to hide his tracks
would use such cover, probably staying with it until he
found a rocky enough spot to exit where he wouldn't
leave footprints.

Jay enjoyed the feel of the water around his ankles as
he moved slowly along. Half a mile ahead, he paused.
There, to the right, were six or eight big rocks leading to
a patch of gravel. That's where he'd leave the water, if
he wanted to get back on his previous heading.

It took him more than a hundred yards before he spotted something. Another flat patch of dirt, too smooth.

There were no wind riffle marks, no raindrop patterns, none of the natural weathering signs that ought to be there. Jay grinned. Bad man Hans had been here; he was sure of it.

In the distance, Jay saw a small village. That it had a Germanic look to it didn't really fit the Texas panhandle, but it was okay to mix scenario now and then. It kept you from getting into a rut.

He'd bet diamonds against dog doo that Hans was in that village, smug in his belief that nobody could track him there.

Why didn't these fools ever learn they couldn't screw with Lonesome Jay Gridley? Must be some kind of genetic defect that ran in bad guys.

He picked up his pace a little. He didn't need to worry about the signs now, he knew where Hans was. All he had to do was go and identify him. Once he was sure of that, the game would be over.

30

Toni felt terrific. She and Alex had a great night together, and when she awakened this morning, she'd been rested and much refreshed. Being able to help him with the case he was working on, that had been something, too. For a few moments there, she hadn't felt totally useless. She hadn't lost all her chops. Maybe that was a good sign.

After Alex left for work, she felt creative. She decided to go and work on her scrimshaw for a while.

At the bench, she turned on the gooseneck lamp, gathered her tools, and was about to get started when she saw the purple capsule lying there where she'd put it and forgotten all about it.

She reached for the cap, looked at it, and decided what the hell, as long as she had it in hand . . .

She put the cap on the table in her work field and adjusted the lamp to shine on it. Focused the stereoscope on it . . .

Ah. Here was a major discovery. It was a purple gelatin capsule with some kind of pale powder inside it. *Oh, boy. Way to go, Sherlock.*

Maybe something inside was more interesting. If she opened it very carefully . . .

"Shit!" she said, as the powder, which was a kind of bubble gum pink, spilled all over the table. She dropped the halves of the cap and grabbed a little paint brush she used for dusting the ivory. She swept the pink powder into a little pile, then onto a sheet of paper. There it was.

As she picked up the larger of the now mostly empty capsule segments to reload the powder, she noticed an odd strip of coloration on one end, just inside the edge. Hmm. What was that?

She held the cap under the scope, couldn't quite make it out. It looked almost like some kind of pattern. Well, we'll see about that. She put the cap down, removed the auxiliary lens, and brought the scope's magnification to 10X. Let's have another look, shall we?

Jesus! What was that? She fiddled with the light, turned the cap this way, then that, and got the shadows just right so she could make it out.

Etched into the material of the cap were tiny words. "Hi, Feebs! Want to find me? Ask Frankie and Annette's grandkids, they know where! Sincerely Yours, Thor."

Hello!

She reached for the phone on the end of the bench. She had to get Alex. He was going to want to hear about this.

Newport Beach, California

The restaurant, Claudia's Grill, was half a block off the highway and slightly up the hill, so it had a nice view of the water. Drayne pulled his Mercedes into the parking lot, gave the key to the attendant and got a parking stub, then went inside. It was three minutes to seven, and the place was pretty full. They served a good breakfast here, and it was a great location.

His father sat alone in a booth, staring out through a wall of glass at the Pacific, the waters already changing from gray to blue as the sun began to burn off the morning fog.

"Hello, Dad."

"Robert."

Drayne slid into the booth. "What's up?"

"Let's order first."

The waitress came by. Drayne ordered poached eggs, chicken apple sausage, and whole-grain pancakes. His father asked for white toast, corn flakes, and decaf coffee.

When she was gone to put their order in, his father cleared his throat. He said, "I'm glad your mother isn't alive to see what you've become."

Drayne stared at him as if his father had just sprouted fangs and fur and might start baying like a werewolf. "What?"

"How stupid do you think I am, Robert? Did it never occur to you that thirty years with the Bureau might have taught me something?"

"What are you *talking* about?"

"PolyChem Products," his father said.

Drayne felt his belly spasm, as if he had just gone over the big drop on a roller coaster. "What about it?"

His father looked disgusted. "There is no 'it.' It's a paper corporation, a phantom. The bank records, the history, none of it is any deeper than a postage stamp. You thought I might look at it, but not too closely, didn't you? *You* are PolyChem Products."

Drayne couldn't think of anything to say. He was cold, as if he had suddenly found himself shoved headfirst into a refrigerator. He'd never expected this.

The old man looked away from him, out at the ocean

again. He said, "I have friends, boy, people who owe me favors. I know where you live, and I know you live well, but I also know that you don't have any visible way of earning money. So that means you are into something illegal or immoral. Probably both. From the way you talked about admiring that criminal who assaulted the agents and staff at HQ recently, I surmise it probably has something to do with drugs."

"Dad—"

His old man turned back to face him, held up his hand to silence him, and in that moment, he was Special Agent in Charge Rickover Drayne of old, steely-eyed and fierce, one of the most stalwart protectors of the republic. "Don't say anything. I don't want to hear about it, I don't want to *know* about it. You're an adult; you can make your own choices. I expected better of you, that's all."

Drayne lost it: "You expected me to turn into a fucking robot without feelings who would grow up to be just like you." He was amazed at the sudden venom in his voice. "You wanted a carbon copy of yourself to send forth, a grown-up Boy Scout who was trustworthy, loyal, friendly, obedient, who would cog his way into the system and stay there smiling until he wore out, just like you. You never once asked me what I wanted to be when I grew up or cared what I thought about anything."

The old man blinked at him. "I wanted the best for you—"

"*Your* best! What *you* thought I should be! Face it, Dad, you were always too busy saving the country from the forces of evil to give a shit what I did, as long as I kept my grades up, my room clean, and I didn't bother you."

"Robert—"

"Jesus fucking Christ, listen to yourself! Everybody in the world calls me Bobby except for you! I asked you to do that a hundred times! You didn't listen. You *never* listened."

Nobody said anything for a long time. Finally, Drayne said, "So, what are you going to do? Give my name to your friends who owe you favors? Have them investigate me?"

The old man shook his head. "No."

"No? Why? Because I'm your son and you love me? Or because you wouldn't want your old FBI chums to know *your* son was anything less than the soul of respectability?"

The old man was spared whatever answer he might have made as the waitress returned with their breakfast. Drayne had never felt less like eating in his life, but both he and the old man smiled at her.

When she was gone, the old man said, "You can think whatever you want. You . . . You're a brilliant man, son. Smarter than I ever was. I always knew that. You could have gone into legitimate business and made a fortune. You could have been somebody important."

"What makes you think I can't do that now?"

"Oh, you could. I don't think you want to. You were always more interested in pulling my chain than anything else, weren't you?"

And I still am, Drayne was smart enough to realize. But he didn't want the old man to walk away with any kind of victory, no way, so he said, "No. All I wanted was to get your attention. Any attention, good or bad, was better than indifference. That's what you gave me, Dad. Indifference. So now you finally notice me, enough to bust my balls. Thank you so fucking much. You want to turn me in for being a criminal, go ahead. I don't care." *And if you do turn me in, I win,* he thought.

Drayne stood, dropped a fifty on the table, and said, "I'm not hungry, but you enjoy your breakfast. It's a long drive back to Arizona. Give my regards to the dog."

Drayne turned and stalked off. Dramatic, but he'd made worse exits. Let the old bastard chew on that for a while.

Once he was in his car, he realized how shaken he was. Even after all the years of layering scar tissue and callus over it, on some level, he still cared what the old man thought of him. Amazing to realize that.

Tad couldn't sleep. He was topped off with enough drugs to put a stadium full of rabid football fans into a trance, but his mind wouldn't go down.

He had taken a hot shower. He had tried to blank his mind. He had gotten up and eaten another phenobarb, and while he was so stoned he could hardly move, he was no way about to sleep, and he needed that, bad.

Bobby had told him about the new operations plan, the safe house, moving the money, and wanting to hire some armed muscle to ride shotgun. Tad had shrugged that off. Whatever Bobby wanted was fine. Tad had made some calls. Some guys were coming by to see Bobby later, shooters who didn't care who they cooked, long as the money was good. It wouldn't cramp things here, they had five bedrooms, plenty of space. Bobby was thinking he could post one as a lookout, have him watching the road, scanning police radios, shit like that. Somebody came calling, they'd hit the beach before the visitors got to the door, jog a ways down to the parking lot where his car was already parked, ready to roll. Could maybe leave another ride in the opposite direction, at the bed-and-breakfast place, slip the owner a few bucks for parking. Maybe even have a jet ski or something, take to the ocean. Maybe rig a bomb to the front gate or something.

Bobby got into the details of stuff like this, and once he did, he covered it pretty fine.

Tad didn't think it was gonna come to that, but that

last biz had put the fear of God into Bobby a little, so that was cool, whatever.

Tad went out on the deck, sprawled in the padded lounge chair, lit a cigarette, and blew smoke at the ocean. The wind blew it back in his face, and he smiled at that. Bunnies in thong bikinis jogged past, guys with tans dark as walnuts, all going about their boring lives. Tad waved at them, some of them waved back. Jesus.

A helicopter zipped by a few hundred feet up, probably looking for people caught in the rip and pulled out beyond the surf. Welcome to the Promised Land, folks. Sun, water, beautiful people, even airborne lifeguards to make sure you don't venture too far away from paradise by accident.

Tad finished the cigarette, ground the butt out on the arm of the chair, then snapped it out toward the water using his thumb and middle finger. This was what his life had come to: There was the Hammer, and then there was waiting for a chance to grab the Hammer; that was it.

Except for the waiting part, it was okay.

He leaned back and watched the seagulls wheel and work the uncertain air currents over the beach, diving and rolling, sometimes hovering almost still against the force of the wind. Some real intricate patterns there, those flights.

The aerobatic dance of the gulls was what finally lulled him to sleep.

31

Michaels said, "Mean anything to you?"

Jay shook his head. "Nope, not right off, but I've turned the searchbots loose on it. I should be getting a first-hit list any moment."

Howard came into the conference room. "Sorry I'm late. I had to park in the secured lot. There's some, ah, hardware I was checking out locked in the trunk of my agency car I didn't have time to return yet. I wouldn't want to lose it."

"No problem. Do you recognize the names Frankie and Annette?"

"No, sir."

Michaels slid a hardcopy printout across the conference room table to Howard, who picked it up and looked at it.

Howard shook his head. "And this came from where?"

Michaels explained how Toni had discovered the hidden message inside the capsule. He was feeling a certain sense of pride when he told them.

Jay said, "Tell Toni that's nice work. Nothing in the

DEA reports about this. Somebody there is maybe sitting on this information?"

"That's what I thought," Michaels said. "I asked the director to pull some strings, and she's gotten the original lab reports from DEA. They went over the caps they've recovered with a fine tooth comb. None of those have this little grandkids riddle inscribed in them."

"We think the DEA might be hiding things from us?" Howard said.

Michaels nodded and brought him up to speed on what Jay had discovered.

"And there's one more little tidbit," Jay said when Michaels had finished. "I have a record of a telecon between Hans Brocken and our Mr. Brett Lee, of the DEA, from three months back. Herr Brocken is the chief security officer for Brocken Pharmaceuticals, of Berlin, Germany."

"Careless," Michaels said.

"I did have to look for it. It wasn't something you'd stumble across accidentally. They made a pretty good effort to hide it."

Howard said, "You really think Lee is in bed with a drug company? Looking to sell the formula for this stuff?"

"It makes a certain kind of sense," Michaels said. "We talked about reasons for him shooting the movie star before, remember."

"And you think Lee is in league with the NSA?"

"Only with one particular person there. No point in casting aspersions on the entire agency," Michaels said. "It seems that Mr. Lee and Mr. George have history about which they have not been entirely forthcoming, though this is still circumstantial evidence."

"I'll get harder stuff eventually," Jay said. "Oops, speaking of which—" He tapped keys on his flatscreen. "Okay, here's what the Sherlock searchbot has to say about my query . . ."

Jay frowned at the flatscreen.

"You want to let us in on it, Jay?"

"Huh? Oh, sorry." Jay tapped a key.

The flatscreen's vox began reading aloud in a smoky, sexy woman's voice:

"Frankie Avalon and Annette Funicello, teen singing and television idols from the late 1950s and early 1960s, first appeared together in the low-budget movie *Beach Party*, from American International Pictures, 1963, co-starring Robert Cummings, Dorothy Malone, and Harvey Lembeck, and featuring musical roles by Dick Dale and the Del-Tones, and Brian Wilson and the Beach Boys. The movie was the first of several in the chaste surf-and-sand genre, which was to remain viable and popular for the next two years.

"Avalon and Funicello were paired in several additional surf movies, including a distant sequel, *Back to the Beach*, Paramount Pictures, 1987, also starring Lori Loughlin, Tommy Hinkley, and Connie Stevens."

The computer's voice went silent, and the three men looked at each other.

Michaels said, "The stars of fifty-year-old teenybopper movies? Fine. Who are their grandchildren?"

Jay shook his head. "I'm cross-checking here, but it does not appear that the two had any off-screen relationship that would have resulted in children together. They were both married to other people."

"Not having children would make it hard to have grandchildren, wouldn't it?" Howard observed.

Michaels said, "Maybe we aren't talking about literal grandchildren. Maybe movie grandchildren?"

Jay tapped away at the keyboard. A moment passed. "Nope, nothing that fits. Nobody ever did another beach movie with the actors who played their children in the '87 picture."

"Maybe the message is speaking metaphorically?" Howard said.

Jay looked at him.

Howard said, "Anybody make any similar kind of pictures recently? Celluloid grandchildren, so to speak, of the originals?"

Jay smiled. "Well, film isn't made out of celluloid anymore, but that's pretty good, General. Let me see . . . Okay, here we are, under Beach Movies, there are several, hmm . . . ah. I think I found it!"

A few seconds passed while Jay read to himself.

"Jay?"

"Sorry, boss."

The flatscreen's vox said, "*Surf Daze*, an homage to the surf movies of the early 1960s, Fox Pictures, 2004, starring Larry Wright, Mae Jean Kent, and George Harris Zeigler. Set in Malibu in 1965, *Surf Daze* chronicles the adventures of—"

"Stop," Michaels said.

Jay paused the recitation. "What?"

Howard beat him to it. He said, "George Harris Zeigler."

Jay nodded. "Oh, yeah. The Zee-ster."

"The recently departed Zee-ster," Michaels said.

Jay said, "This was, um, seven years ago. Before he hit it big. He'd have been about, what? Twenty-four or -five then. Thing is, where he's gone, I don't think he'd be telling us anything useful."

"This is too much of a coincidence. This dope dealer is pulling our chain. We need to talk to the other actors."

"You gonna turn it over to the regular feebs?"

Michaels took a deep breath and let it out. "No. I think maybe we ought to go check this out ourselves."

"Not in our charter," Howard said.

"The current waters are very murky," Michaels said.

"Given the capabilities of the DEA and NSA, I'm not altogether sure just who we can trust. Sure, the FBI are our guys, and they love us—in theory, anyway—but we can't cover any leaks on their part. We don't want to be behind the eight ball on this, do we?"

"No need to convince me, Commander," Howard said, smiling. "I'm going senile from boredom in my office. The drug raid was the most interesting thing that's happened in three months. I'm game."

"Me, too," Jay said.

"I thought after your last adventure in the field you'd want to avoid it," Michaels said.

"I was alone then," Jay said, "and dealing with a militant gun dealer. With the general here and you, I'd feel secure enough to interview a drop-dead gorgeous movie star. Did you see Mae Jean in *Scream, Baby, Scream*?"

"I must have missed that one," Michaels said.

"Me, too," Howard said.

"I'm telling you, she's got lungs could raise the dead, aurally and, um, visually. One of the great on-screen screamers of all time, right up there with Jamie Lee. And did I mention she was drop-dead gorgeous?"

"I thought you had a pretty intense relationship going, Jay?"

"That's true, boss, but that doesn't mean I'm gonna do anything. I can look, can't I?"

Howard and Michaels grinned at each other.

Howard went back and collected his staff car, then headed for home. He didn't want to take the time to return the rifle right now, but it would be safe enough at his home; safer, in fact, than in the general access parking lot at Quantico. Since they weren't going to drop everything and rush over to La-La Land in the next few minutes, he'd have time to pack a bag and tell Nadine good-bye.

They'd be flying commercial—Commander Michaels did not want to attract any attention by cranking up one of the Net Force jets—and they'd be flying incognito, on open-ended agency tickets, so they wouldn't have to put any names on a passenger list until just before boarding, and those would be cover noms anyhow.

Given that he'd just been out to the left coast, it might not be as big a thrill for him as it was for Jay Gridley; still, it would get him out and moving, and at this point, anything was better than spending another day doing make-work.

He headed out toward the freeway and the drive back to the city.

Normally, the drive was a straight run up I-95 and into the District, loop around the belt and to the north end of town where he lived.

But after a couple of miles, he spotted what he thought was a tail.

A lot of people drove this stretch of road, and there were scores of cars and trucks heading in the same direction, so there was no way to be sure, but he first saw the car as he changed lanes to pass. A little way farther, when he pulled back over into the right lane, the car did likewise.

Big deal. This was hardly conclusive evidence. But he had been through the standard Net Force surveillance course as part of his in-processing, and something one of the sub-rosa guys from the FBI who'd taught the class had said always stuck with him: *"If you think you're being followed, it is easy to check, and very cheap insurance. If you're wrong, you might feel a little silly. But if you are right, you might keep yourself from winding up in deep shit."*

Maybe he was overly cautious, but as a professional military man, Howard had learned long ago that being prepared was not the same as being paranoid. And like the instructor had said, checking it out was easy enough.

There was a little state road running northeast to Manassas not far ahead, and Howard eased over into the exit lane. If the car behind him—looked like a white Neon—kept going, he'd catch the next on-ramp and head on home.

Six cars back, the Neon reached the off-ramp and exited a couple hundred yards behind him.

Well, well.

That didn't prove anything for certain. Two or three times, he remembered the FBI guy saying, it could still easily be a coincidence. *"Think about it. What would happen if one of your neighbors heading home happened to get behind you on the freeway? They'd make every turn you would, right? Could be perfectly innocent. Don't jump to to a conclusion until you are sure."*

And there were several simple ways, Howard remembered, to be sure.

He tooled along on the state road, which was narrow but scenic, heading away from the suburbs toward the more rural country. There was an intersection ahead, and apparently the Occoquan Reservoir was to the left. *Fine, left it is.*

He went maybe a quarter of a mile, didn't see the white Neon turn behind him.

So, okay, he was paranoid. He'd find a place to turn around and go home. He was relieved.

There was a little gas station minimart a half mile or so ahead, and Howard pulled in there, stopped, and went inside. He used the bathroom, bought a pack of Corn Nuts and a can of root beer, and headed back to his car. If anybody had been following him, he'd had an excuse to stop. The idea was, the surveillance guy had told them, not to let the people following you know you knew they were there. Better the tail you know than one you don't.

He kept going the way he'd been going, figuring to loop back around to a main road or the freeway eventually.

Five hundred yards out of the minimart, he caught sight of the white Neon in his rearview mirror. The car was a ways back, maybe half a mile, but he was pretty sure it was the same vehicle.

Hmm. He was pretty convinced, but a few more tests should make it interesting.

Howard made a series of turns as he came to little branching streets, right, left, right, right, driving several miles until he was on a nice little country road—and thoroughly lost. He was going to need to use the GPS to find his way out of here. He had no idea where he was.

Eventually he found himself on another road that led, so the sign said, to the Civil War battlefield of Manassas. The two big battles there had been originally named, he recalled, for the little river that went through the area, Bull Run.

Several times, the Neon disappeared from sight, sometimes for as long as two or three minutes, and it seemed to Howard that the guy tailing him had an uncanny ability to guess the right way to turn.

Then it dawned on him that there might be some kind of bug on his vehicle, and all the guy had to do was follow the signal.

Damn, he should have thought of that sooner.

But after half a dozen random turns, there was no doubt in his mind that the Neon was shadowing him. Now, the questions were, who was it, and why were they following him?

He could have called the highway patrol, had a few beefy state troopers pull the Neon over and politely ask those questions. Of course, if the shadower turned out to be Lee, he'd just as soon not air that laundry in front of Virginia authorities; best to keep that in house. Or he could have scrambled a Net Force military team and had them brace the driver, but the truth was, he could take care of his own business. He had his side arm right here, and as yet there was no reason to call out the troops, especially if this turned out to be a huge coincidence. Somebody lost trying to find their way out by following him.

Yeah, right.

He was mindful of what Michaels had said about the DEA agent Brett Lee. After that shooting in L.A., Howard could cost the agent his job, maybe even cause him to face a criminal prosecution. And since the man seemed to be involved in something illegal besides that, he might not be too unhappy if Howard were to run his car into a tree somewhere and not survive the accident.

Of course, it was a long way from following somebody around in your car to premeditated murder, and maybe that wasn't what this was all about. Maybe it was somebody else altogether. Somebody Howard had run afoul of and didn't recall, out stalking for other reasons entirely.

So, the thing was, he needed to box up whoever it was tailing him, stroll on over, and have a few words with him and find out.

Out here in the country, among all the trees and fields and pastures, he ought to be able to find a place to do that.

He started looking.

32

Drayne was not surprised when Shawanda Silverman got back to him within a day. She had a nice place all lined up, and any time he wanted to come by and take a look, she would make herself available.

Times must be hard in the real estate biz, he figured.

He got the address and information and said he'd be by to pick up the keys soon. All the legal stuff had been handled over the net, e-sigs and the money transfer from one of the blind-alley addys. It was a done deal.

He wouldn't go himself, of course, he didn't want his face to stick in her mind. Normally, he would have sent Tad, but Tad was still zoned out on the deck. Drayne had tossed a blanket over him when it got dark and cool, then put a beach umbrella up to shade him when the sun came up. Old Tad might not move for another day or two, if ever he moved again at all.

Fortunately, the bodyguards had shown up, and while two of the four he hired weren't the sharpest knives in the drawer, the other two were fairly bright. All were armed with handguns, they had a couple of pump shotguns in a big case, and all claimed fighting expertise in some Oriental martial art or another. The biggest of the bunch was six two and two fifty, easy, and had a face that had stopped a few punches. One of the smarter ones was Adam, a tall and muscular dishwater-blond in his late twenties who looked as if he might have done some surfing at one time.

Drayne decided to send Adam to meet with Ms. Silverman, to collect the key for the new place.

"Your name is Lazlo Mead, M-e-a-d, and you work for Projects, Inc.," he told Adam. "If she says anything about your voice sounding different, tell her you had a cold when you talked on the phone."

"Won't be a problem," Adam said. He took a breath, blew half of it out, then said, "Hello there, Miz Silverman. I'm Lazlo Mead."

Drayne had heard his own voice on recordings enough to recognize that Adam's impersonation was dead-on. "Jeez, that's good."

"I do a little stand-up now and then," Adam said. "Unfortunately, it doesn't pay real well. Not yet, anyhow."

After Adam was gone, Drayne pondered the bodyguard situation a little. He wasn't planning on telling any of them the location of the safe house, just in case push came to shove and they got left behind when he took off. Adam was smart enough to figure it out, and if he wanted to bother, he could con it out of Silverman easily enough. After all, he would be Lazlo, wouldn't he? That might be a problem, so if things went into the toilet, he'd have to make sure Adam either got clear with him or wasn't going to be able to tell anybody what he knew about the hidey hole.

Maybe it was time to get that gun, Drayne figured.

But at least things were on the move, his insurance was in place, and he felt a lot better.

He had put the word out to his customers that the Hammer was going to be available with the timer starting in forty-eight hours. Within a matter of a few minutes, he had twenty orders, and an hour after that, twenty-five more. That was forty-five hits of the drug, plus one for Tad, if he was awake by then. And since Tad was out cold, Drayne would have to do the deals himself, but that wasn't a problem, he'd use net cutouts and FedEx Same Day only, no Zee-ster face-to-face to worry about. Now all he needed was some chem.

With the guards, he didn't want to start out too wild, so he decided to go to the RV to do his mixing when it came time. He wouldn't need them to go with him, they were mainly to protect his castle and his retreat if he needed to run. Nobody would know him from, well, Adam out in the desert where the RV would meet him.

He grinned. Yep, things were back on track. Except for that crap with his old man. Well. He could sort all that out later. Come up with some story that would make the old man feel bad, like maybe he was a spy or an undercover cop or something. Yeah. Wouldn't that be poetic justice? Having his father think he was serving his country while being accused of doing something illegal and immoral. That would be a hoot.

For now, maybe it was time to pop a cork and have some bubbly. And maybe get one of the new bodyguards to show him about guns, too.

Washington, D.C.

"You are leaving me here and going *where?*" Toni said.

"Hey, you discovered the clue," Alex said. "We need to follow it up."

"*We* need to do that? Net Force doesn't do that kind of field work, that's for the regular FBI."

"Yeah, well, I don't know how secure that would be now. If Jay's suspicion is right, we have two guys who are capable of getting information not normally available. NSA has ears everywhere."

"Come on, you couldn't figure a way around that? Couldn't you hand-carry this info to somebody in the shop and have them check into it without exposing it to outside ears?"

Alex continued packing his overnight bag, tucking his bathroom travel kit into the case. "If I knew who to trust, sure. The director is on our case about this. If it goes wonky, even if it's not our fault, you know who will get the blame. Much easier to shove it off on Net Force than to admit problems in her house. Or worse, making accusations against a brother agency without ironclad proof. You've been around long enough to know which way that wind blows."

"It sounds like rationalization to me," she said. "An excuse to get out of the office. And out of here."

He stopped packing and looked at her.

"I'm fat, hormonal, pale, and pregnant," she said. "And I'm driving you crazy."

He came over and caught her shoulders. "No. You are carrying our child, and I love you. You are the most beautiful woman in the world, more so now than ever."

"You're just saying that to make me feel better."

"Well, yeah," he said. But he grinned.

She grinned back at him. "You're a bastard."

"Take that up with Mom. She never told me, and I'm sure my father would have been surprised to know that."

"A smart-ass bastard at that."

But she grinned, too.

"I'm meeting Jay and John Howard at the airport in about three hours. We have time for a shower and a proper good-bye, don't we?"

"A smart-ass goat-boy bastard."

He laughed, and she did, too.

The area around Manassas was, like much of northern Virginia, rolling hills, suburbs and mini-malls, and roads that gridlocked during rush hour. Still, there were areas where the pine and oak trees still held their own, and there were a few stone fences and old houses standing against the weather.

Howard had driven for about thirty minutes, until he found an empty, tree-lined rural road narrow enough for his purpose. He drove along until he was a half mile or so ahead of the Neon, then turned right into a narrow tractor path leading to a cattle-guard gate in a barbed wire fence. He shut off the engine. There were no houses nearby, just some brown and white cows grazing in the pasture.

What he planned to do was get out, head through the cow pasture and into the little patch of woods opposite it, and then circle behind the Neon, which he figured would stop and wait to see what he was up to. Once he was behind the shadower, he'd creep up on him with his revolver in hand, and find out exactly who he was and what he wanted. A simple plan, but one that should work.

Behind him, the Neon pulled off the road about four hundred meters away, turned sideways with the passenger side facing Howard, and stopped.

Howard waited a few seconds, then got out of his car.

He was still on the driver's side closing the door when there came a *chink! chink!* as the passenger's and driver's side windows shattered, followed by the sound of a rifle shot. The bullet, traveling faster than the sound, missed him by maybe two inches.

Shit!

Howard took two steps to the front tire and dropped into a crouch behind it. He pulled his revolver. The engine was the best protection, and the heavy steel wheel would probably deflect a sniper's bullet aimed lower.

Another shot, another round pierced the car's doors, through and through, and if he'd been there, it would have gutted him.

This was bad.

There was no other cover nearby. It was fifty meters through an open pasture to the tree line, and trying to cross the road the other way would be equally stupid, he'd be exposed. A decent shooter could nail him. And his handgun, while a fine weapon, was not going to do the job at four hundred meters unless God intervened in his favor.

He risked a quick look.

Another shot echoed over the pasture land, and the round smashed into the car's side above the front tire but stopped when it hit the engine. Made a terrific clang.

If the guy came toward him, he'd still have the advantage for another three hundred, three hundred fifty meters, and if he circled around, Howard was really in deep shit.

He could call for help, but it would never get here in time. What the hell was he going to do?

Memory was a funny thing. Up until that moment, he had forgotten what he had in the car's trunk. He felt a sudden surge of hope and possibility flow over him when he remembered.

Howard scooted toward the rear of the car.

Another shot hit the car amidships and must have struck a frame support or something in the door; it didn't go all the way through to his side.

He reached the back tire. He had his keys, and the trunk release was on the electronic alarm and opener. He took a deep breath, put his revolver over the car's trunk, pointed it at the Neon, and triggered off three shots as fast as he could.

At the same time, he popped the trunk control, lunged under the still-rising lid, and grabbed the hard-shell case inside. He jerked it out and fell back behind the tire.

The sniper's next shot was great; it hit the passenger-side tire, lanced through the steel-belted radial, hit the driver's side tire and penetrated that, then punched a hole in the corner of the hard-shell carrying case, almost jerking it from Howard's grip.

The car dropped to its rims, and he wasn't going to be driving it anywhere any time soon.

Howard popped the latches and dumped the parts of the .50 BMG rifle onto the ground. The bullet had missed anything important. He put his handgun down and, with a speed aided by adrenaline, assembled the rifle in what had to be record time. He loaded the magazine with five cartridges of the match-grade ammo, chambered a round, and lit the red-dot attachment on the scope. It was sighted in at three hundred meters, he recalled, so he'd have to adjust his aim a bit. Or maybe not. This thing shot pretty flat for a long way.

Time to make an assumption here. The shooter was probably using a scoped deer or sniper rifle, 30-6, maybe .308, something like that, and if it was, it would likely be a bolt action. So he was going to have to manually chamber a round after each shot, which meant that Howard would have half, maybe three-quarters of a second between shots.

Not much time to get set up. And if it was a semiauto, that would be really bad. But it was what he had.

Howard took a grip on the heavy rifle. He stuck his head up, held it there for an agonizingly long time, maybe half a second, then ducked.

The shot came, hit the trunk, zipped through, but missed by a good six inches.

Then Howard leaped up, dropped the .50's bipod on the trunk's lid, slamming it shut, and put the red dot on the middle of the Neon. He squeezed the trigger, a shade too quickly, and the recoil from the weapon knocked him back and almost off his feet. The blast of sound was like a bomb; it deafened him. Even as he fought to regain his position, he chambered another cartridge, the empty extracted and smoking to his right.

That would give the son of a bitch something to think about! *Not so much fun when the victim can shoot back, is it?*

Howard looked through the scope. On high magnification, he could see the bullet hole where the side of the Neon had buckled in around it; it had blown paint off in a hand-sized crater, but there was no sign of the shooter. If the guy had any brains, now *he* would be behind the front tire with the engine block protecting him. When the .50 went off, it sounded like the wrath of God, and the assassin would know that the odds had just shifted dramatically into Howard's favor.

Howard's ears were ringing and he couldn't hear anything over that. He looked down, saw the earplugs that came with the rifle, and risked the second it took to scoop them up. He shoved them into his ears.

No sign of the shooter.

Fine. Let's see how *you* like being dinner, asshole.

He put the red dot on the top of the front tire and squeezed a shot off, more careful now.

The bullet hit a few inches high and must have shattered and sprayed the engine compartment. Vapor came out from under the hood, maybe from the radiator, maybe coolant for the AC. He'd bet that car wasn't going anywhere, either.

Now it was time to get the troops out here. He pulled his virgil and hit the emergency sig control in a rapid sequence.

"Sir?" came a voice.

Howard smiled. *Gotcha now, sucker.*

"Hold on a second." Howard shot the Neon again. Hit the front tire this time. The car sagged.

"I want a helicopter with a squad of troops ready to shoot landing twenty meters east of the GPS location of my virgil in fifteen minutes maximum. This is not a drill."

"Yes, sir!"

"Here is the situation. . . ."

But when the chopper from Quantico arrived and a dozen of Net Force's finest hit the ground, fanned out, and surrounded the mortally wounded Neon, the shooter was nowhere to be found. The car was much closer to the tree line than Howard's car was, and somehow, the would-be assassin had managed to slip away without Howard spotting him.

Damn!

33

Jay looked up from his flatscreen at the boss and the general. "The shooter's car was stolen," he said.

They were in the airport, in one of the VIP lounges that the boss had access to, waiting for the flight to L.A. If John Howard was rattled about somebody trying to shoot him out in the boondocks where Stonewall Jackson had earned his fighting nickname, you couldn't tell it by looking at him.

As a licensed federal agent, however, Howard would be carrying a gun with him onto the plane, this at the boss's insistence. Both Michaels and Jay had their air tasers with them, too, though Jay had only fired his in the required semiannual qualification sessions, and the last of those had been four months past. He didn't try to kid himself that he was any kind of gunfighter, even with the nonlethal shock 'em and drop 'em tasers most Net Force personnel outside the military arm were issued.

"A stolen car. Not a major surprise there," Howard said. "It would have been too much to hope for that he'd use his own vehicle. I don't suppose the lab rats managed to get any fingerprints or DNA for a match?"

"Not yet, sir," Jay said.

"That isn't a surprise, either," Michaels said. "Not if it was who we think it was in that car. How about Lee's whereabouts?"

"That's a little trickier," Jay said. "We couldn't just have the FBI hunt him down and grab his ass, not without tipping our hand. According to a sub-rosa contact we managed with the DEA, Mr. Lee was today taking some personal time. He was in Maryland, visiting his paternal grandmother, who is in a nursing home just outside Baltimore. Accessible on-line records at the Sisters of Saint Mary's Home for the Aged indicate that Mr. Lee did sign in about an hour before the attack on General Howard, and he signed out ten minutes after the attack. Nobody has gone in and done a face-to-face with the staff to check that yet, however."

"How easy would it be to fake the in and out signatures and records?" Howard asked.

"I could do it with both hands tied behind me and a cold so bad the voxax could only pick up every thirteenth word," Jay said. "While blindfolded and in my sleep."

"That hard, huh?"

"Shoot, boss, *you* could do it."

"All right, so we get an investigator out there to see if Lee actually did go visit his old granny."

"If he was there, that would make it impossible for him to have been the shooter," Jay said.

"Let's just see before we try to cross that bridge."

"I'd be very surprised if we can find a nurse or ward clerk who remembers seeing Lee there today," Howard said.

"Anything on other forensics at the scene?" Michaels asked.

"Nothing to write home about," Jay said. "No empty shells lying on the ground, no blood, no hair, no dropped bar matchbooks or IDs or maps showing how to get to the perp's house. Shoe prints are a popular brand of cheap sneaker. Fibers from where the shooter kneeled appear to be lightweight gray cotton, probably sweatpants."

"And the clothes and shoes and no doubt gloves are probably in a trash bin or burned to ash by now," Michaels said.

"This was a pro," Howard said. "If I hadn't had that portable cannon, I think he might well have taken me out."

"You tell your wife about it?" Michaels asked.

Howard looked at him. "Would you have told yours?"

The boss looked uncomfortable. "Maybe. Toni was a Net Force op, she knows how things go sometimes. Of course, she's pregnant, and I wouldn't have wanted to upset her once everything was over with."

"The local cops weren't called in, the media doesn't have it, we're keeping it in house," Howard said. "I didn't want to worry my wife, either. I'll mention it to her later. After we catch the son of a bitch who did it."

Jay didn't say anything. He'd have told Saji, but she was a Buddhist, they were into the real world and all. He looked around. Technically, they weren't supposed to be doing this, since it wasn't really part of their mission statement. Plus they weren't supposed to be flying on the same jet. If the flight went down, it would take out the commander, the military chief, and the head of Computer Operations, which would be bad for Net Force. The director would be royally pissed; then again, Jay wouldn't much care about that, being dead and all. What the hell.

Jay wasn't worried about flying, that had never bothered him. A plane went down now and then, that was awful, but it was like being struck by lightning. If it happened, it happened. What were you gonna do, stay home all your life?

He was looking forward to visiting Hollywood. Outside virtual visits, he had only been there once in real time, on a trip when he'd been in high school, part of a computer team entered into a national contest. They'd come in second and should have won, except that one of the twits on his team had flubbed an easy program a third-grader could have managed. As much time as Jay did creating scenario in VR, he felt as if he'd be right at home among the moviemakers. It would be the middle of the night before they got there, and they'd head straight for the hotel, but tomorrow would no doubt be sunny and delightful.

He spun up the flatscreen's power, hit the wireless airnet key, and logged via an encoded sig into the Net Force mainframe again. He had VR gear in his bag, but he didn't like to do VR work in a public place, too many people, no telling who might decide to come up and swipe your luggage while you were sensory deprived and deep in scenario. Probably they'd be okay here in the VIP lounge, but no sense in developing bad habits. He'd just have to do it the old-fashioned and boring way, using the vox controls and hand-jives, a pain, but there it was.

Banning, California

Drayne had the air conditioner going full blast in the RV, and Ma and Pa Yeehaw had unshipped the little car they towed behind the RV and gone into town to do a little bar hopping or whatever, while Drayne mixed up a new batch of the Hammer. He'd hold off on adding the final catalyst until he got back to town. Now was a good time to check out the new safe house, and nobody would be looking over his shoulder there while he did the final mix. Once the clock started running, he'd send one of the body-guards to FedEx with the packages, and that would be that, another forty-five thousand into the secure e-account, and wasn't life beautiful?

He grinned. *I wonder what the poor folks are doing now?*

Beverly Hills, California

Mae Jean Kent was an impressive-looking woman, Michaels noted, oozing sexuality, and however powerful her lungs might be, they were certainly augmented with a major pair of headlights, double-D, at least. Toni had been quick to tell him these weren't real, but nonetheless . . .

She was beautiful, blond, tanned, fit, and wore a halter top and hip-hugger pants and sandals. She also wore big sunglasses. She agreed to meet them at some local restaurant that was apparently *the* place to meet locally, and she was constantly waving at people who passed the outdoor table at which she, Michaels, Jay, and John had been situated.

"Hi, Muffy! Hey, Brad! I'm sorry, Alex, what was that again?"

"Ms. Kent—"

"Oh, please, call me MJ, everybody does!"

Michaels guessed her age at thirty, judging from her hands, but she was acting more like eighteen. Part of the youth culture out here, where you might be over the hill at twenty-five.

"MJ. So tell me about this beach picture."

"Oh, it was a terrible shoot! First thing was, Todd—that's Todd Atchinson, the director?—was having a major crisis and he ran out of Paxil and was a bear to work with. He just kept *yelling* at everybody. Then Larry—that's Larry Wright—had a major fight with his boyfriend, he's gay, such a waste of a perfect bod, you know? Anyway, Larry was so depressed he just moped around like an old hound dog. And George—I was so sorry to hear that he died, so sorry, but he was a major doper, major—kept getting a, you know, a *woody* every time we shot a scene together, and they had to shoot around it because his bathing suit was, you know, bulging all the time!" She giggled and took a deep breath, showing off the results of what must have been expensive plastic surgery.

Michaels wished Toni were here, so she could see just how vapid and unattractive this woman was, despite her looks and attempt at what she thought passed for sophisticated animation.

Michaels glanced at Howard, who kept a straight face but offered no help. Jay seemed entranced by the rise and fall of MJ's hooters under the barely-able-to-hold-them halter top.

"Is there anything you can think of that might have a connection to something called Thor's Hammer?"

She turned and waved at somebody passing the tables. "Hey, Tom, baby! How *are* you!" She made a kissy face at Tom baby.

Michaels caught the hint of a grin on Howard's face, but when he looked closer, the grin vanished.

"MJ?"

"What? Oh, no, I don't remember anything about a sore hammer."

"Where was the movie shot?" Jay asked. Apparently his breast-induced trance was not as deep as Michaels thought.

"Where?"

"Yes. The location."

She glanced upward, as if expecting the answer to be written on the underside of the big umbrella sheltering their table. Then she looked at Jay and gave him her full-wattage smile: "Malibu," she said. "On the beach."

Michaels got the gist of Jay's question and followed it up. "Anything unusual about the location?"

"Unusual? No, I don't think so. It was kind of like a private beach, Todd knew some of the owners who had houses right next to it, so they roped it off for the shoot. A lot of tourists came by every day and asked for autographs between setups. I have a lot of fans."

"I heard a critic say your performance in *Scream, Baby, Scream* was first-rate," Howard put in. He smiled.

Michaels looked at Howard. Butter wouldn't melt in his mouth.

"Really? I tried hard to get some subtext into that, but the script was, you know, just full of major problems. Writers just don't understand what a proper vehicle should be like for actors. They are all hacks out here."

Probably used too many big words, Michaels thought. *Those two- and three-syllable ones must be killers.*

That was unkind, Alex. This is Hollywood, remember, it's all about what looks good. It's not her fault how it works.

"Well, we thank you for your time, MJ," he said. "You've been a great help to us."

"Hey, no problem. I'm glad to cooperate with the government any way I can. If you get a chance to talk to the IRS, tell them to quit auditing me, okay?" She flashed the smile, inhaled deeply, and then turned to wave again. "Barry! How are you!"

Waiting for the parking lot attendant to fetch the rental car, Howard said, "Well, that was helpful in a major way, you know?"

Michaels said, "And when did you see *Scream, Baby,*

Scream, John? Dial it up on your room cable last night?"

"Just my bit to keep the conversation moving," he said. "Besides, I didn't say I'd *seen* it, I said 'a critic said.' That would be our staff critic here. I was just taking Gridley's word for it."

"Well, I suppose we should go try Larry," Michaels said. "And hope that he and his boyfriend have patched things up since *Surf Daze.*"

"Or Todd," Howard said. "Maybe he's gotten his Paxil refilled."

"Maybe we don't need to," Jay said.

Michaels and Howard looked at him.

"The inscription in the capsule said the grandchildren would know where to find him. I think MJ might have told us."

"The beach at Malibu," Michaels and Howard said together.

"Big-time drug dealer could afford to live there."

"It's a long stretch of coastline," Howard said. "Hundreds of homes."

Jay said, "But movie shoots in cities have to have all kinds of permits. I can access the records for the surfer pic and find out exactly where the location was. That would narrow it down to a handful of houses. We could check ownership records on those, eliminate some of them."

Michaels said, "That's good thinking, Jay."

"I didn't think you were paying full attention to your work back there," Howard said.

"Silicone doesn't do it for me," Jay said. "Besides, she's much smarter in her movies, which ain't saying much."

"Okay, get on-line and find out what you can."

"One other thing," Jay said. "I got a blip during the interview." He waved the flatscreen, looked at Howard.

"Several witnesses, a couple of them nuns, attest that Brett Lee was in the nursing home yesterday when you were being shot at. It couldn't have been him."

"Damn," Howard said. "Then who?"

"Maybe your dog crapped on somebody's lawn," Jay offered.

"I don't think so," Howard said. "We don't have a dog."

"Maybe you should get one. One with big teeth."

The car hop arrived and pulled the rental car to a stop. Michaels took a five from his wallet and gave it to the man, who looked at it as if it were a piece of used toilet paper. Lord, what kind of tips was he used to getting?

Inside, Michaels said, "Find us a place to go, Jay."

"I'm on the case, boss."

34

When Tad woke up, he noticed a couple things: First, he was on the deck, with the beach umbrella doing its best to keep him in the shade, but starting to lose that battle.

Second, there were some men with guns wandering around in the house.

Fortunately, he recognized one of the gunslingers, so he realized the bodyguards had showed up, and Bobby must have decided to hire them.

Shit happened when you went into hibernation. You got used to it.

He looked at his watch, and the date showed he'd been out for a couple of days. Not too bad.

His head felt as if somebody had opened it with a dull shovel and poured half the beach into it. He was way beyond grainy. All the rest of him just hurt. Bad.

He managed to get to his feet, using the umbrella for support, and headed toward the bathroom. Once, after sleeping for a couple of days, he had stood over the toilet peeing for more than a minute, on and on, must have pissed half a gallon. For some reason, his bladder never let go while he was out, and he counted that as a blessing.

The guy with the gun that Tad recognized nodded at him. "Hey, Tad."

Tad nodded in return. The name came to him, slow, but there. "Adam. How's it going?"

"Good. Bobby's out. He's supposed to be back in a while."

"Cool."

He shambled into the bathroom, cranked the shower up, then stripped. He waited a few seconds for the water to heat up, then stepped into the shower. He stank, and he could pee just as well in the shower.

He needed to get to his stash. He wasn't gonna be able to function real well for a couple of days yet, no matter what, but certainly not straight.

He opened his mouth, let the needle spray rinse the taste of tar and mold out, spat three or four times, then swallowed a couple of mouthfuls of the hot water. He knew he was dehydrated, and if that got bad enough, his electrolytes could get wacky enough to stop his heart. He'd known guys on speed who hadn't eaten or drunk anything for a couple of days who'd died that way. Heart just stopped beating.

He stayed in the shower for ten minutes, letting the spray pound him. He felt a little better when he stepped out onto the cool tile floor and started drying himself with the big fluffy beach towel. A little better wasn't going to cut it.

His stash was in the wheel well of his car's trunk, and the car was parked in the lot of the sandwich place two down from them. When Bobby was running in paranoid mode, which was most of the time, he wouldn't let Tad keep anything in the house that might get them busted. Not even in the car, if Tad wanted to park it in the driveway or garage or anywhere inside the security gate. Nothing more than you can swallow, Bobby told him, and close enough so you can do that if somebody crashes the gate.

Tad mostly tried to do it that way. For a while, he buried his drugs on the beach. He had kept his stuff in a mason jar with a plastic lid so no coin-hunter or narc would find it with a metal detector. He would sneak out late at night and bury the jar in the sand. But he'd lost one that way, completely spaced out on where he'd hidden it. And another time, somebody's dog had dug up one of the jars, so he'd stopped that. The walk to the car wasn't that far, half a block, but of course, it felt like a thousand miles after a session with the Hammer.

Well, there was no help for it. He wasn't going to send Adam or one of his hard-ass friends to collect his dope. He didn't trust anybody that much except Bobby, and Bobby wouldn't do it anyway.

Tad slipped on a pair of raggy black sweatpants, a black T-shirt, and a pair of black zorrie sandals. Might as well get to it. It was gonna take a while.

"I'm walking over to where I parked my car," he told Adam. "Don't fucking shoot me when I come back."

"Why waste a bullet?" Adam said. "You look like somebody could kill you with a hard look. Hell, you look dead already."

"You need to work on your material, Adam. I heard that one already."

"Lots of times, I bet."

Tad thought about his route for a minute. Out the front gate and along the road was longer. But walking along the beach through the sand would be harder. The road would be noisier, all the traffic. The beach would be hot. He'd have to walk around cars parked on the highway. He didn't need any more obstacles at the moment. Until he got his medicine mixed and working, just breathing was an effort.

Okay, the beach. He headed for the deck stairs.

Michaels said, "One of those three or four houses?"

Howard drove, Michaels rode shotgun, Jay sat in the back. As they idled slowly along the highway, looking toward the beach, Jay said, "Got to be. Permit specifies this part of the beach. That sandwich shop over there is in the movie. I pulled it up and scanned location shots. That house to the far left was built two years ago, so it wasn't there then."

"Do we have owners on these?"

"Yes. The pinkish one is owned by the actress Lorrie DeVivio. She got it in the divorce settlement with her fifth ex-husband Jessel Tammens, the movie producer."

"DeVivio is what . . . sixty and rich? Hard to image her making and peddling dope," Howard said.

"Ah, you know the old movie stars, eh, General?"

"She won an Oscar," Howard said. "And not for her looks."

"What about the other houses?"

"Second one belongs to the chairman of the board of the Yokohama-USA Bank. He's also sixty-something and also richer than God.

"Third one, the pale blue and white one, is owned by a corporation called Projects, Inc. Some kind of corporate retreat, maybe. I'm running down the incorporation stuff now. They are out of Delaware.

"Fourth one belongs to one Saul Horowitz. Don't know who Solly is, and the searchbots haven't been more forthcoming so far."

"That sounds promising. Pull over there, into that restaurant lot, and let's think about this for a minute," Michaels said.

All four of the houses had security gates and fences, at least to the road side. As Howard parked the car, a Mercedes convertible arrived in front of the third house and pulled up to the gate. The car's top was down, and a sunbleached blond, deeply tanned young man in a Hawaiian shirt who looked like a surfer held up an electronic remote and pointed it at the heavy steel gate, which slowly swung open to admit his car. He pulled into the drive, and the gate started to close behind him.

"Yo, kahuna dude!" Jay said, in a valley-boy voice, "Surf's up!" Jay held up his hand, the middle fingers closed, his thumb and little finger extended. He waggled his hand back and forth. "Mahalo!"

"Thank you, Brian Wilson. You get the license plate number?" Michaels said.

"Crap! I'm sorry, boss—"

"It's a vanity," Howard said. "P-R-O-J-E-C-T-S."

"Run it," Michaels ordered.

Jay, chagrined at his failure to catch the number, dialed up the California DMV and logged in, using his Net Force access code.

A few seconds later, he said, "Car is owned by Projects, Inc.," he said. "Big surprise there, huh? Looks like you get wheels to go with the house. Nice perks."

"So, what do you think?" Michaels said.

"Either it's that one or the Horowitz place," Howard said. "Rich bankers and rich movie stars might use dope, but they don't need to sell it."

"Just FYI, General, they found a bug on your car. That's how the shooter kept from losing you." Jay pointed at the flatscreen. "Also, Mr. Lee, who as we all know couldn't have been said shooter, called in sick today."

"Something fatal, I hope," Howard said.

"And to keep things interesting, Mr. Zachary George is on vacation this week and next," Jay said.

Michaels said, "Anything on the searchbots for Mr. Horowitz here yet?"

"Nope," Jay said. "But I don't think we need it."

"And why would that be?"

"Take a look at the death-warmed-over stick in black walking along the road there, coming from the sandwich place," Jay said.

"So?"

"Look again, boss."

Michaels did. He frowned.

"Yeah," Jay said. "Kind of hard to picture him beating the crap out of a room full of bodybuilders and trashing a gym, isn't it?"

Michaels nodded. "But that's the guy."

"Never thought I'd see an actual match to a police ID composite," Jay said. "All we have to do is watch and see if he chooses door A or door B. Whichever one he picks, I'd bet my next month's salary against a bent quarter that's our dealer's house."

The three watched the man, who looked as if he might fall down any second, as he shambled along. It took him a while to get there, but he finally did.

"And we have a winner," Jay said. "It's the surfer dude's pad. Net Force rules!" He looked at Michaels. "Now what, boss? We gonna go kick ass and take names?" He held up his air taser and waggled it.

Both Howard and Michaels laughed.

Michaels said, "I see your experience in the field didn't teach you anything. We're not going anywhere. We're calling the FBI. They'll go in."

Drayne parked the car and went in. He saw one of the bodyguards skulking behind the banana and short palm trees nod and wave at him. Good to know they were watching the place like they should.

Inside, Drayne walked out to the deck. Adam was there, looking at the ocean. "Where's Tad?"

"He stepped out, said he was going to his car," Adam said. "Said he'd be back in a few minutes."

Drayne nodded. Tad would be self-medicating as soon as he was ambulatory again, and his pharmacy would be in his car, parked away from the house. It better be.

The front door opened, and speak of the devil.

"Hey, Bobby."

"Tad. You all right?"

"Will be in about half an hour." He headed for the kitchen.

Drayne followed Tad into the kitchen, watched as Tad counted out ten or twelve pills, caps, caplets, and tablets, filled a glass with water from the tap filter line, and washed the drugs down in one big swallow.

"While you were napping, I set up some things," Bobby said. "I was gonna send one of the bodyguards, but now that you're awake, you can make the FedEx run."

"Okay."

"We're moving forty-five hits of the Hammer."

Tad raised an eyebrow.

"Might as well make hay while the sun shines," Drayne said.

"You mixed it already?"

"Yep. Did the final at the new house, so the stuff is just under an hour old."

"Got mine?"

"It's too soon, Tad, you ought to sit this batch out. I'll be doing another bunch next week."

Tad didn't say anything, and Drayne shook his head. "It's your ass."

"Such that it is, yeah," Tad said. "Give me thirty minutes for the stack to kick in, I'll be ready to roll."

Drayne shook his head again. "Your funeral."

*   *   *   *

"Geez, Boss, you don't think the three of us could take one surfer dude and a zombie?"

Michaels had already put in the call to the director, and she in turn had called the local FBI shop and started the ball rolling. He said, "Isn't this the zombie who wiped up the floor with a gym full of guys strong enough to pick up tractor trailers? Didn't you just bring that up?"

"Yeah, but—"

"And don't you recall the recordings of a white-haired old man who shrugged off a cloud of pepper gas and air tasers like they were mosquitoes and tossed guards and cops around a casino like a kid throwing toy soldiers? Or a woman who ripped an ATM machine out of a wall with her bare hands?"

"Yeah, but he can barely move now. He can't be on the drug."

Howard said, "There are too many things we don't know here, Jay. Think about it. What is the lay of the house? Can they sneak out the back while we're climbing the front gate? Are they armed? Who else is in there with them? I'm the only one with a gun here, so do you and the commander run around back and make sure they don't escape with your tasers while I try to kick in what might be an armored front door? Not to disparage your shooting ability, but even if you hit something, you've only got one shot before you have to reload, and the fastest AT reload I've ever seen took almost two seconds. I'd guess you couldn't do it in five or six. In two seconds, a man can run twenty, twenty-five feet, knock you down, and take off. In six seconds, he could be down the road having a beer, figuratively speaking. And that's unarmed. If the surfer or the zombie have weapons, what do you think they'll be doing with them if you miss? Or if you yell 'Stop!' and they shoot first? They could have a submachine gun in there, and they could take out twenty civilians out there on the beach. That would be after they cut you down."

"Mm," Jay said. "That would be bad for public relations, not to mention my personal love life. So why didn't we call in Net Force troops? We can trust them."

"That would have been my choice," Howard said, "but the commander is right. We found them, but it isn't our operation, we aren't supposed to even be here, we're outside our job description. If we had a dozen Net Force military troops kick in the door of a Malibu beach house, we'd all be looking for jobs. Assuming we could even get our people here in the next couple of hours, which we could not."

Michaels said, "By rights, this belongs to the DEA. Even if the director decides to let FBI agents make the arrests, it's still a hot political potato. The director can risk pissing off a brother agency, we can't. We can't even get warrants, so even if we were willing to get fired, the capture wouldn't be legal. Even an ambulance-chaser lawyer with a lobotomy could get them off. The arrests would be completely illegal."

"Yeah, okay, I can see all that," Jay said. His voice was reluctant.

Michaels looked at his watch. "We should have agents showing up within thirty or forty minutes, if we're lucky. We do it by the numbers, get part of the credit, and most importantly, the drug dealer is off the street. The end result is the same, no matter who hauls them off."

"For how long is he off the street?" Jay asked.

"Excuse me?'

"This guy is carrying around a secret that is worth millions, maybe tens of millions, you said so yourself. Won't the drug companies be falling all over themselves to be first in line to hire him the best legal team in the world? How high can his bail be?"

Michaels nodded. He knew what Jay said was true. "Probably. But that's not our worry. We were supposed to find him. We found him. We did our part. What happens to him after they catch him isn't our problem, we don't have any control over that. We're just a cog in the big machine, Jay. We do our job, we have to hope the rest of the system does its job. Can't be everywhere."

"That sucks," Jay said.

"Welcome to the real world, son," Howard said.

35

Drayne gave Tad the minipackets with the Hammer caps, the list of addresses, and pointed him at the door. By now, most of the payments would have already been transferred electronically into the safe accounts. Before Tad stuck a packet into the FedEx clerk's hands, he'd check again to make sure the payment for it had cleared.

As the door closed behind Tad, the phone rang. It was the business line.

"Polymers, Drayne—"

"If you have a lawyer, call him," came his father's voice. "You'll need him soon."

His father hung up without identifying himself, and Drayne felt a rush as cold as liquid nitrogen envelop him.

"You!" he said, pointing at the nearest bodyguard. "Go get Tad! Don't let him outside the gate!"

The bodyguard hurried away.

Drayne's fear, cold at first, now flushed into an uncomfortable warmth that suffused his whole body.

The old man had turned him in!

No. If his father had done that, he wouldn't have had

any second thoughts. The old man never apologized for anything once he decided it was the right thing to do. And though he hadn't said anything specific, it didn't take a rocket scientist to read the volumes between those lines.

Drayne was about to be busted. The old man had found out about it, and he'd called to warn him.

Son of a bitch.

Almost more important than getting arrested was that his father had gone against thirty years of duty to tell his son he was in trouble. Couldn't bring himself to give it all away, of course, but even this much, knowing how smart Drayne was, and that he would figure it out, was nothing short of a miracle.

Son of a bitch.

Drayne went to the security console in the kitchen and looked at the camera focused on the front gate. Nothing there. He touched the controls. The cam was mounted on a gimbal, could look pretty much in any direction. He put the cam into a slow 360-degree pan.

Across the street at the Blue Gull, a car was backed into a parking slot, and a man sat in the passenger seat, the window down, looking in the direction of Drayne's house.

Drayne stopped the pan and focused the cam on the car.

Okay, that could be somebody waiting for his wife to come out of the bathroom or something.

He hit the zoom. The glare on the windshield wouldn't let him see inside, but the security folks knew about glass glare, and a dial let him polarize the lens. The windshield cleared to show a second man in the driver's seat and a third man in the back.

Shit! They were already in place!

Tad came back into the kitchen. "What's up?"

"Company," he said. "Look."

Tad looked at the screen. "So? Some guys in a car. Don't mean nothing."

"Yeah, except that my father just called and told me to call my lawyer."

"Your father? Oh, shit."

"Exactly." Drayne took a deep breath. He said to Adam, "Go see if anybody is hanging around out back."

Adam returned in thirty seconds. "Nope. Couple of girls with their tops off lying facedown on beach towels next door, that's it."

"Okay, they haven't covered the rear of the house yet. Tad, Adam, we're going for a walk. The rest of you stay here. If anybody comes to call in the next five minutes, don't let them in. After that, it doesn't matter. You don't know anything. Not who I am, not where I've gone. You got that?"

There was a murmur from the guards. They pulled their pistols out.

To Adam, Drayne said, "You have an extra one of those?" He pointed at the gun in Adam's holster.

"Sure."

"Give it to me."

Adam did so. The gun was kind of squarish, black, and made out of some sort of polymer. Drayne said, "What do I do?"

"It's a Glock .40," Adam said. "Point it like you would your finger and pull the trigger. It's ready to go. You have eleven shots."

Drayne hefted the black plastic gun, then tucked it into his pants in the back, under the tails of the Hawaiian shirt.

"Let's go," he said.

"Here comes the cavalry," Howard said.

Three unmarked late-model sedans cruised slowly up

the highway from the south. The cars turned into their parking lot and pulled to a halt.

"More behind us," Jay said.

Howard looked around and saw three more cars and a van convoy into the lot.

A tall man in a gray sweatsuit got out of the lead vehicle and walked to the passenger side of their car. "Commander Michaels? I'm Special Agent in Charge Delorme."

Michaels waved at Howard and Gridley. "SAC. General John Howard and Jay Gridley."

"No offense, sir, but isn't Net Force supposed to be a computer-based operation?"

"It is."

"With all due respect, sir, once you located the suspects, you should have called the proper agency in right away, not come out here on your own."

Gridley leaned forward and said, "Yeah, well, last time we found a suspect, the proper agency rolled in like gangbusters and shot him dead. We were kinda hoping to avoid that this time."

Howard grinned a little. He was a mouthy kid, but he did put his finger right on the problem from time to time.

"Thank you, Jay," Michaels said. To Delorme, he said, "Don't worry. We'll sit right here out of your way while you do your job."

"Sir," Delorme said. He stood and waved his hand in a circle, index finger pointing up at the sky. Three of the cars pulled out of the lot and across the highway, skidding to stops on either side of the target house. Doors opened, and agents in body armor with FBI lettered in big Day-Glo yellow on their backs, armed with assault rifles and wearing goggles and LOSIR headsets, boiled out of the cars. Delorme pulled a headset on, caught a vest somebody tossed at him, and moved toward the highway.

Other agents alighted from the cars still in the lot and ran across the road.

Two cars rolled toward places where the beach was accessible from the road, and more agents leaped out and hut-hut-hutted toward the ocean, to circle around behind the house.

"Not bad deployment," Howard said, after watching them move into position outside the gate. "A little slow, kind of sloppy, but not bad for civilians." All the high-tech gear in the world, and when it came right down to it, it was still going be the ground troops who had to gain the territory.

"Might as well sit back and enjoy the show," Michaels said. Then he said, "Shit!"

"What?" Howard and Jay said together.

Michaels pointed. A big Dodge rolled out of the sandwich shop parking lot and roared away, heading north.

"Sir?" Howard said.

"The zombie is driving that car!"

Howard didn't hesitate. He started the rental car's engine and pulled out onto the highway.

Jay said, "Why don't you get closer, General? We might lose them!"

Howard said, "If they see us behind them, we'll sure as hell lose them. We're going up a hill here. This gutless piece of crap rental can't begin to keep up with that hot rod they are in. So far, they are obeying the speed limit, but if they see us and decide to run, we can't keep up with them."

Michaels was on his virgil, trying to call the SAC running the bust.

The man wasn't answering.

"Come on, come on!"

"He'll have his com shut off, tactical channels on LO-

SIR only," Howard said. "You don't want to have to answer the phone in middle of a firefight."

The boss swore.

"Try FBI HQ," Jay offered.

Michaels shook his head. "Probably half their guys are on this raid already, and it's gonna take anybody else as long to get here as it did to get to the beach. Maybe longer."

"What about the local police?" Howard said.

"Who *are* the local police? Where are we? Who has jurisdiction?"

"Call CHP," Howard said. "Probably they can get here fastest. Put up a roadblock. Better than nothing."

Michaels nodded. He tapped a button on the virgil, waited a few seconds, then started talking. The woman's voice coming from the virgil was calm enough, but her news was bad:

"Sorry, sir, but we have a major traffic accident on the Ventura, ten cars and a semi full of hazardous chemical that's on fire, all available officers are there or on the way there. I can put you through to the county sheriff's patrol."

"Damnit!" Michaels said. He shut the virgil off.

"We're okay," Howard said. "We stay with them, they'll stop sooner or later. When they do, we'll get whatever police agency that covers the area to roll."

"If we don't lose them," Michaels said.

"If we don't lose them," Howard agreed.

"Close," Adam said. "FBI assault team, looked like. What did you guys do?"

"Don't worry about that," Bobby said from the backseat. "Close only counts in horseshoes and hand grenades. They didn't follow us, right, Tad?"

Tad looked into the rearview mirror, but anything more than a few feet back was a blur. He hadn't gotten his stack

just right; he was having a little trouble focusing his vision. But nobody was within a block of them, and if the
feds were there, they'd have already zoomed up and tried
to run them off the road by now, right? Out here on a
road over the hill with nobody around, that was the way
to do it. There was a curve maybe a quarter mile back,
and if he squinted hard, Tad could see that the road was
empty at least that far.

Tad said, "No. Nobody followed us."

Adam, in the front, turned around and looked. "Looks
clear." He rolled the window down and stuck his head
out, glanced around, then pulled his head back inside. "No
helicopters. Where are we going? The safe house?"

"Yeah. For now. After that, I think maybe we need to
take a nice long trip somewhere out of the country."

"All of us?"

"No reason for you to go," Bobby said. "Nobody
knows who you are. We'll give you a nice bonus, you
can get back to your life."

Fuzzed as his brain was, Tad didn't think that was a
very good idea, but he didn't say anything. Bobby knew
what he was doing. Bobby always knew what he was
doing.

"Fine by me," Adam said. He turned around to watch
the road in front of them again.

Bobby said, "Loud noise, Tad."

Tad didn't have time to think about that when two
bombs went off—*Boom! Boom!*—that fast, and the windshield spiderwebbed on the passenger side.

"Fuck!" Tad screamed. The car slewed onto the shoulder, hit a couple of rocks, and jounced hard. He fought
the wheel, managed to get it back on the asphalt.

Tad looked into the mirror, saw Bobby just leaning
back into the seat, that black gun in his hand. He glanced
over at Adam. There was a bloody splotch on his chest

and more blood oozing from a hole right over his heart. His left eye and part of his nose was also gone, shredded, gore running down his face. He was slack, only the seat-belt keeping him upright.

It took a second for Tad to get it.

Bobby had just shot Adam. Twice. In the back and in the back of the head. One of the bullets had gone right through him and through the windshield, which was now whistling with the breeze coming through it—what he could hear with his ears ringing from the noise.

"Jesus fucking Christ, Bobby!"

"He was a liability," Bobby said. "He knew where the safe house was. He knew you personally. We have to make a clean break here, no loose ends."

Tad nodded. "Yeah, okay. Whatever you say."

"What was that?" Jay said. "Sounded like some kind fire-cracker—look at the car!"

Howard eased up on the gas pedal and the rental car slowed dramatically. The little four-cylinder gas-alkie en-gine with battery backup was barely able to move them uphill.

The Dodge ran off the road, hit something and bounced, then scraped and skidded back onto the tarmac.

"Gunshots," Howard said. "Two of them. Pistol cali-ber."

"They shooting at us?"

Michaels said, "No, not us. Somebody in the car."

"Why?"

Michaels looked at Jay over the back of the seat. "Did I get here before you? What can I see that you can't? I don't know."

The three men stared at the car, which rounded another curve in the wavy road and disappeared.

Howard shoved the accelerator pedal down. The little

car moaned, and not much else. Their speed picked up slowly. He pounded the steering wheel. "Piece of Japanese crap! Go!"

Michaels reached for the in-dash GPS, thought better of it, and pulled his virgil. Its GPS would be more accurate. Better find out where they were. Maybe they could get a helicopter from somewhere.

Los Angeles DEA had those, didn't they? All the drug raids they went out on, they'd have to have air cover.

Could he risk calling the DEA in?

Well, why not? Lee wasn't the guy who shot at Howard, he had witnesses saying he was elsewhere. And he didn't have to call Lee back in D.C., just the local HQ.

He didn't want to do it. But what was more important here? Letting the DEA get the credit? Or maybe losing the drug dealer altogether?

Crap—

The decision was interrupted by his virgil beeping. Michaels pulled it from his belt. The ID showed it was the director. He tapped the link-on, and the vid control, held the virgil up so the cam could see his face.

"Yes, ma'am?"

"My SAC tells me that the drug dealer was not in the house they raided, nor was the other man. What is the situation there, Commander?"

"Three men managed to escape by car just as the raid went down, ma'am. The agents didn't see them. General Howard, Jay Gridley, and I are in pursuit. We are heading east over the mountains at the moment. We have been unable to contact SAC Delorme's team."

"I'll have them spot on your GPS signal," she said.

"I was thinking we might call in the DEA," he said. "They'll have air support."

"Already done, Commander. They should have a helicopter in the air by now, and they are also tracking your virgil's GPS, have been all along."

Howard nodded. "I see."

"We have to let them in, Commander. There is no choice in the matter, you understand?"

He understood, all right. "Yes, ma'am."

"Try to maintain your surveillance. I expect you'll be seeing the DEA forces show up soon. Call me when you have something to report."

"Yes, ma'am."

Michaels discommed. Howard glanced over at him.

"You heard the director. Try to stay with them. DEA is in the air."

But that wasn't quite true, Michaels realized a few seconds later. The DEA had a helicopter, all right, he saw it not more than a block ahead as they rounded the next curve.

The copter was parked across the middle of the road.

36

Drayne saw the helicopter blocking the road a good two seconds before Tad's drugged reaction time finally kicked in and he slammed on the brakes. The big Dodge's wheels locked and the car skidded to a rubber-burning stop.

Adam's body twisted out of the seat belt's shoulder strap and he thudded against the dashboard, then slid sideways into the door, smearing blood all over the window and door post.

"Shit!" Tad said.

"Turn around, turn around!"

But as he said it, Drayne looked over his shoulder in time to see a car a hundred feet behind slew to a stop and turn so it blocked the road.

Tad saw it, too. He hit the brakes again.

To their left was a rocky slope, the wall of the mountain. To the right, a fairly steep drop down the hillside into a valley of rock, dried brown bushes, and eucalyptus.

A half-dozen men with guns were crouched around the copter, pointing their weapons at the Dodge. Drayne looked back in time to see three men pile out of the other side of the car behind them. They came up behind the hood and trunk, and pointed weapons, too.

Well, *shit.*

"Fuck! What do we do?"

Drayne thought fast. There was a dead body in the front seat of their car. Tad had enough drugs to stone a parade, not even counting the scores of Hammer caps. This was bad.

Drayne leaned forward and gave Tad the pistol he had. "Here, take this."

"We'll get slaughtered," Tad said.

Drayne reached around the seat and took Adam's pistol from the dead man's holster. "Maybe not, I've got an idea. Stick the gun out the window and shoot it into the air."

"Why?"

"Just do it."

Tad did, the sound loud in the quiet afternoon.

The men behind the copter ducked, but they didn't return fire.

Drayne almost smiled. Good, that was good. They wanted him alive. Alive, he was valuable. Dead, he was worthless.

And now Tad, bless him, had powder residue on his hand showing he had fired a gun.

"Okay, okay, let's think about this. We got their attention, but we're boxed, so we're gonna have to do this with lawyers. We have money, and we have power. The pharmaceutical companies want what I have. So we get out with our hands up, and surrender."

"You sure?"

"Trust me, I know what I'm doing. One phone call, we'll have some very heavyweight people lined up to help us."

"Okay, man."

Of course, Tad would have to take the fall for killing

Adam. And since Tad would get shot resisting arrest or trying to escape, he wouldn't say otherwise. Drayne could pull that off. If he yelled, "Hey, don't shoot, Tad! Put the gun down!" at the right moment, the feds would hose Tad. DEA rules of engagement wouldn't be that different from the FBI rules when facing an armed perp. Too bad, but Tad had one foot in the grave anyhow. He liked him, but his death might as well count for something. No point in Tad being dead *and* Drayne being in jail, was there?

Drayne climbed over the seat.

"What are you doing?"

"I want to be right behind you when we get out, we don't want them to think you're reaching for something when you move the seat to let me out."

"Oh, yeah."

"Tuck that gun into your belt and keep your hands in the air when you get out."

"Okay."

"Let's do it. Just stay cool. We'll walk away from this, believe me. Once we're out on bail, we can take off and stay gone forever." Not that they would get bail with a corpse in the front seat of their car. Judges frowned on that.

Tad nodded. "Okay."

Howard had braked and turned the car to block the road, and the three of them jumped out on the driver's side, away from the stopped Dodge.

"Get those tasers out, for all the good they'll do," Howard said. He pulled his gun from under his jacket, crouched behind the front wheel, and pointed the gun over the hood. "See if you can get the DEA there on your virgil's emergency band and tell them not to shoot us."

Michaels nodded. He was the commander of Net Force, but he was willing to defer to the general in this kind of situation. He wasn't going to to let his ego get them killed.

He hit the emergency call button, got the Net Force operator, and told him to patch them through to the DEA team. The FBI Director should have their number.

Crouched behind the trunk, his taser clutched in both hands and pointed at the Dodge, Jay nervously said, "I think . . . I think I'm gonna throw up. And I gotta pee, real bad."

"It's okay," Howard said, "we all feel like that."

Oddly enough, Michaels didn't. He felt relatively calm, almost as if he were watching and not participating. His mouth was awful dry, though.

Behind them, a car approached. Howard turned and waved at it frantically. "Stop!"

The car, a dark minivan, did stop. The passenger door opened and a man jumped out and ran toward them.

He had a *gun* in his hand.

Howard swung his revolver around and almost shot the guy—then they all recognized him.

Brett Lee, of the DEA

Lee crouched into a duckwalk the last few steps. "What's the situation?" he asked.

"What the hell are you doing here?" Michaels responded.

"I was following you," Lee said.

They all stared at him.

He said, "Look, okay, I screwed up on the bust at the movie star's house, okay? My job is going away, at the least. I need to help catch this guy so I don't leave in total disgrace. I need a little victory."

That made sense. Before anybody could speak, Michael's virgil started its musical sting. No ID sig. That damned thing was practically useless. He thumbed the connect button. His camera was still on, but the incoming screen was blank, no visual transmission.

"Commander Michaels? Riley Clark, DEA. Is that you in the car behind the suspects?"

"Yes. And I have Brett Lee here with me."

"Hold your positions, and please don't shoot unless you are fired upon—"

As if his words were a signal, a gun went off. Michaels ducked instinctively.

From the virgil, Clark's excited voice came: "Negative, negative, do *not* return fire, the gun was pointed into the air, repeat, hold your fire!"

Michaels raised from his squat and looked. The driver's side door opened, and two men stepped out, their hands in the air. The zombie and the surfer. What an odd-looking pair they were together.

"Which one is the chemist?" Lee asked.

Jay said, "Gotta be the surfer."

Drayne felt tight, knowing all those guns were pointed at him, but he also knew he was the golden goose, and while the DEA field guys might want to burn his ass, the higher-ups would know which way the political winds blew. Sure, he might have to do some time at one of those country-club honor farms somewhere, working on his tan and Ping-Pong game, but in the end, he was going to cut a deal, and he was going to walk away rich. Guys worth tens of millions of dollars didn't go to jail very often, almost never, and he'd be very cooperative. The feds would bargain with him, because he had something everybody wanted. He could turn people into superhumans. Hell, the Army would be first in line, if the Navy and Marines didn't beat them to it.

He was smarter than the guys they sent against him, always had been, always would be. He could think circles around them. This was a temporary setback, that was all.

He was a genius, and he'd show them just how smart he was.

He smiled. "Don't shoot!" Drayne yelled. "We give up!"

Something was wrong, Howard felt, but he couldn't put his finger on it. Lee was right here next to him; Howard didn't trust him, and if Lee raised that pistol, he was going to bat it down, but that wasn't it, it was something else.

Then he knew. It hit him like a lightning bolt.

Lee had gotten out on the passenger side!

He twisted around, looked at the van, said, "Shit!"

The driver's door was open, and a man was behind it, a rifle resting on the windowsill, but not aimed at Howard or Michaels or Jay or Lee.

Howard swung his revolver around.

The rifle went off.

Tad was looking right at him when Bobby's head exploded. The skull deformed in front, like it was plastic, and Bobby's whole forehead spewed into the air, blood and bones and brain in a greasy fluid like a water balloon bursting, spraying every which way.

Fuck. They shot Bobby.

Tad didn't even think about it, he bolted, ran straight for the only way not full of guns, right over the side of the hill. He hit five or six yards down, his legs collapsed, and he rolled himself into as much of a ball as he could, bouncing and smashing into creosote bushes and rocks and dirt, until he hit something so hard it took his consciousness.

Michaels watched in slow motion as John Howard shoved his handgun forward and started pulling the trigger. There were orange flashes from the muzzle and smaller flashes from the cylinder, but the sound was oddly quiet, like a cap pistol.

Brett Lee screamed—Michaels saw his mouth open—and he tried to point his pistol at Howard.

He's going to shoot John, Michaels realized.

Michaels lunged, slamming into Lee. They both sprawled on the road. Lee dropped his gun to break his fall, hit, rolled up, and kicked at Michaels.

Without thinking or pausing, Michaels swept his right hand down and up again in an arc, caught Lee's ankle and, at the same time, dropped into a low position and shoved with his left hand at Lee's chest.

Lee fell backward, hit the road flat on his back, and his head thumped the asphalt and bounced. He was stunned enough so he didn't move.

Michaels blinked and realized he had just done an *angkat*, a throw against an unweighted leg. Huh.

Jay, who probably didn't have any more of an idea of what was going on than Michaels did, stepped up and shot Lee with his taser. Lee juddered and jittered on the dusty road as the electrical charge spasmed his muscles.

Michaels turned to look at Howard, who was up and moving toward the minivan, gun still extended in front of him. Michaels didn't see his taser, he must have dropped it, but he hurried to join Howard.

Behind the still-open driver's door, which had several holes in it, a man lay on the ground, bleeding, a rifle next to him. His chest was a ruin, dark with arterial blood, and Michaels knew the man had been shot in the heart. He'd be dead soon, if he wasn't already.

He couldn't see the man's face until Howard kicked the door shut, and when he did, it was not really all that much of a surprise:

The heart-shot man was Zachary George of the NSA.

37

When Tad woke up, he didn't know where he was. Outside, somewhere, and buried in some kind of sweet-smelling brush. He had cuts and bruises he didn't remember, and felt like crap, but that wasn't anything new, it had happened before. Lots of times.

He tried to sit up, couldn't make it, then fell back and gulped for air.

This might be it, Tad, old son. The last roundup.

Damn. How'd he get here? Where *was* here, anyway?

The sight of Bobby's head blowing apart filled his memory.

Aw, *shit!* Shit, shit, *shit!*

It all came back to him in a jumbled rush of pain and emotion. Killing Adam, the helicopter in the road, the leap he'd taken to get away—

Bobby's head exploding. In slo mo and Technicolor.

Jesus!

He looked at his watch to see how long he'd been out, but the crystal was shattered, the minute hand bent to the face and stopped, the hour hand gone completely. The feds would be coming for him, they might be almost here, and he had to get up, he had to get moving, or they'd catch him. Probably none of them would have just jumped off the fucking cliff like he had, but they'd figure a way down soon enough to grab his ass. He didn't know how long ago it had been. It felt like it was still afternoon going into evening, so maybe he'd only been out for a few minutes.

He wasn't going to get far in his condition, he knew.

He reached into his pocket and came out with one of the Hammer packets. A couple of them fell on the ground, but it was too much trouble to bother picking them up. Well, he sure wasn't going to be making any deliveries anytime soon, and the clock was running on this batch. He had until tomorrow around noon before the stuff would all go sour. Use it or lose it, and he couldn't take them all.

He tore open the packet and dry-swallowed the Hammer cap. Thought about it for a few seconds, then ripped open another packet and took that cap, too. It would be a while before the stuff would kick in, and he couldn't sit here waiting for it, no matter how much he hurt.

The gun he'd had tucked in his belt was gone. His car was God knew how far up the hill, surrounded by feds. He was screwed.

And Bobby was dead. That hadn't really sunk in, it didn't seem real. They'd killed him, they'd fucking *executed* him, he'd had his hands up, and they had blown his head off!

Tad felt a surge of anger well up, filling him with murderous rage. He wanted to run back up that hill and tear them apart with his bare hands, rip their arms and legs off, stomp on the bloody torsos.

The anger was good, but it was barely strong enough to get him to his feet and moving. If he could stay clear long enough for the Hammer to kick in, he'd be okay. Once the drug took hold, he'd be able to travel at speed.

And go where?

The safe house. They didn't know about that. Bobby had the place stocked, there was some running-away money stashed there, more in the safe at the storage space.

Bobby was dead.

Tad couldn't believe it. Bobby was smart, good-looking, rich, he had everything going for him. And they cooked him, *blam!* Just like that.

Tad stumbled, fell, and managed to get back to his feet. Oh, they were gonna pay for killing Bobby.

He was fucking going to *make* them pay.

"No sign of the zombie?" Jay said.

"The DEA people haven't found him yet. Local deputies will be joining the search soon," Michaels said. "General Howard went down with them and found this." He held up a purple capsule. "There were several of them under a bush down there. DEA got the rest, but it doesn't look as if they have turned sour yet. So this is still an active capsule."

"No great loss. We got the chemist."

"We have his body," Howard said.

Jay nodded and blew out a sigh. What a fuck-up this had been.

"I bet forensics will match that rifle George had to the bullets they found in my agency car at Manassas," Howard said. "George was the shooter. That's why Lee had such a great alibi."

"So they were in it together all along. But why shoot this guy Drayne?"

"I don't know," Michaels said.

Lee had recovered from the fall and taser shock and was handcuffed and sitting in the back of one of the DEA vehicles that had finally arrived. He was more than a little distraught when he saw the body of George covered up and waiting for the coroner.

He'd sobbed and begun crying. Not really the kind of reaction an op from one agency usually had for an op from another agency, certainly not the same sex. Something there, all right.

"Bastard," Lee had said to Howard. "You *killed* him!"

"Damn straight," Howard had replied. "I only wish I'd shot him two seconds sooner."

"Bastard. You're a dead man."

"Not by your hand, pal. You're an accessory to murder and attempted murder, probably seven kinds of conspiracy, and God knows what else. You're going away for a long, long time."

"Maybe not. Maybe I have something to trade."

"Better be damned good, whatever it is," Howard said. "And between you and me and my colleagues here, if I see you on the street anywhere close to me or mine, I'll drop you and worry about the consequences later."

"You threatening me, General Howard?"

Michaels said, "You must be mistaken, Mr. Lee. I didn't hear any threats. Jay?"

"Nope, I didn't hear anything at all."

Howard nodded at Michaels and Jay.

Jay smiled. Well, what the hell, they were a team, right?

On the drive down the hill, Michaels called Toni.

"Hey," she said. "How's the glamour there in Tinseltown?"

"Great, if you like chase scenes and shoot-outs."

"What?"

"We tracked down the dope dealer. He's no longer with us, however."

"What happened?"

Michaels filled her in on the operation.

When he was done, she said, "That's good work, Alex. Nobody got hurt except the bad guy, and Net Force gets the credit. How are they going to play it with the media?"

"Straight, I hope," he said. "But I wouldn't bet on that. Camera teams were all over us ten minutes after it happened, news choppers circling like mechanical vultures. I let Jay talk for us and he kept it vague, but I don't know what the DEA and FBI guys had to say. Rogue operatives are never a good spin for any agency. You can say, 'Yeah, we had a problem but we cleaned it out,' but the first question from the reporters will be, 'How'd you get a problem like that in the first place?' It's a no-win situation."

"Not for Net Force."

He grinned at the small image of her on the virgil. "Well, yes, that's true. We get off smelling like roses."

"So, when are you coming home?"

"Probably tomorrow morning. We need to file reports with the local FBI and DEA offices, talk to their supervisors, like that."

"Couldn't you file those reports on-line from here?"

"You know how that is, they want to see us when we tell it. Won't take long, but by the time we get done, it'll be late, and we're flying into a three-hour time difference. Might as well wait until the morning."

"At least it's all wrapped up."

"Not completely. The zombie—that's Thaddeus Bershaw, we got that from his car registration—got away."

"That's not major, is it?"

"Not that we can tell. We don't know for sure what his part was in things, but he wasn't the brightest bulb on the string. Jay dug up his background, and he was an uneducated street kid. Probably no more than an errand boy. The dealer was Robert Drayne; he had a degree in chemistry. Also had a father who was with the Bureau for thirty years, retired to Arizona."

"Interesting."

"DEA and FBI put out an APB net and street on Bershaw. They'll find him eventually. Anyway, he's not our problem anymore."

"I miss you," she said.

"Yeah, I miss you, too. See you tomorrow. I'm thinking maybe I'll take a couple personal days and we can do something."

"I'd like that."

Michaels discommed and leaned back in the seat. It had been a long day, and he wasn't looking forward to the double debriefing. It would be nice if they could do it once, with ops from both the DEA and FBI listening together, but that wasn't how it was going to go, of course. That way would make too much sense.

They were way too slow coming down the hill to find him. By the time he heard them yelling at each other, Tad was six hundred yards away, and the double-hit of magic purple was coming on *strong*. Ten minutes after that, he was feeling good enough to jog, and ten minutes after *that,* he was able to run like the wind, hopping over rocks and bushes in his path, covering ground much faster than any normal man would be able to do on foot in the gathering darkness. He could run faster, see better, and make quicker decisions, and no way were they going to catch him from behind, if they even had a clue which way he had gone. Probably still looking for his body under the bushes back there.

Three miles or so away, he angled back up toward the road, then paralleled it for half a mile until he came to a tiny shopping center. He found a motorcycle chained to a light pole, and it took all of thirty seconds to find a rock big enough to smash the lock. The owner had trusted the lock and chain, and so he'd left a spare ignition key under the seat, tucked in the cushion springs, where Tad and ten other guys he knew always kept their spare bike keys, and the sucker, a midsized Honda, cranked right up.

They'd probably have roadblocks set up on both sides of the hill looking for him, but he could dance that or maybe go off road and around it. Now that it was fully dark, he would have an advantage: He didn't need to use the headlight; there was enough city glow for him to see the road. Time they spotted him coming, it would be too late.

The double dose of Hammer was something. He had never felt so strong, so fast, or so quick-witted. They didn't have a chance. If they did stop him? Well, he would just kill them all.

Tad sailed eastward down the hill in the dark, hitting speeds of eighty, ninety miles per hour with the lights off, whipping past startled drivers who heard him but couldn't see him him until he appeared in their headlights. Must have scared the crap out of them.

If the fed had roadblocks, they must have been closer to the place where the copter had been, which made sense, sort of. They weren't figuring on a guy who could run three miles in the dark before he got back to the road. They didn't have the Hammer and he did.

Once he was down and in the flats around Woodland Hills, he flicked the headlight on. He didn't have far to go now.

He made it to the safe house without incident. Inside, he flipped on the television and tuned it to CNN *Headline News*. He didn't feel like eating, but he knew he needed fuel and liquid, so he grabbed a big can of ham slices and a six-pack of Evian water. He peeled ham slices off two at a time and washed them down with water as he watched the news. He needed information as much as he needed fuel.

The info wasn't long in coming. A local camera crew had gotten to the site of the shooting, and while most of what the reporter had was probably total bullshit, there were a couple of things that stood out: The drug dealer who had been slain had been located through the efforts of the FBI's computer arm, Net Force; the leader of that organization, Commander Alexander Michaels, had come all the way from Washington, D.C., to be in on the raid. The newscam had footage of Michaels, right out there on the road, looking down at the body of some agent who had been killed by the drug dealers during the raid.

Yeah, well, if one of theirs was dead, the feds had done it themselves. Bobby hadn't done it, and except for that one shot Tad put into the sky, he hadn't fired, either. Lying fuckers.

There were interviews with local DEA and FBI agents, as well as some computer geek for Net Force. It had been a coordinated operation among the three agencies, so it seemed, but Net Force got the big pat on the back for coming up with the information that led to the suspected drug dealers. One of said drug dealers had escaped, was still at large, and considered armed and dangerous. They flashed a picture of Tad, along with his name. Driver's license photo. So they had IDed him, no big deal.

The news moved on, and he shut it off.

When he looked down at the ham can, it was empty. He had eaten two pounds of ham and downed six bottles of water, and he didn't even feel full. Probably his last meal.

Tad thought about it for a few seconds. Commander Alexander Michaels. Net Force. Washington, D.C. A long way to travel for somebody in his shoes. And nothing he did would bring Bobby back, dead was dead. Why bother?

Yeah, well, fuck it. He'd almost reached the end of his string anyhow.

He went into the bathroom. Bobby had stocked the place with all kinds of shit they might need if they had to run. He found scissors and an electric razor with a trim attachment and cut his already-short black hair into a flat-top. The Hammer made him want to jump up and down, but he held himself steady by force of will so that the do wasn't too ragged. He used half a bottle of hair coloring on his new cut. He shaved off his lip-hanger goatee. Pulled out his earrings and tossed them.

After the hair color was done, bleached to an ugly yellow, he showered. Got out, and rubbed himself down with bronzing gel, applying it carefully with the little sponge thing.

Okay, so he wasn't gonna pass for a surfer, but he wasn't the same fish-belly white beatnik in the picture, he was blond and tanned. He found some slacks, a dress shirt, socks, and running shoes, all in pale gray or white, not his look at all. There was a pair of wire-rimmed glasses with plain glass lenses, and he put them on. He could almost pass for normal.

There was about fifty thousand in cash in frozen food packages in the freezer. He took about ten grand. He didn't expect he'd need that much, and if he somehow got back here—unlikely—he could get the rest then.

There were some fake photo IDs in a desk drawer, three or four sets each for him and Bobby. Tad picked up a set, looked to see that the driver's license was from Texas, and that the name was Raymond Selling. Bobby's little joke: Selling was the winner of last year's Los Angeles Marathon race. He'd done one for Richard Kimball, too, from the old TV series, *The Fugitive*. The last one was for Meia Rasgada, which was Portuguese for "torn stocking," yet another kind of runner.

Bobby was a riot.

Had been a riot.

He needed to move, he really *needed* to move, but he had one more thing he had to do before he could. He took one of the clean digital phones in the kitchen and punched in a number from memory. His memory at the moment was excellent; he could draw on anything he had ever seen, smelled, tasted, heard, felt, or done if he needed it, and he knew it would be there.

"Yo," came the deep voice.

"Halley, it's Tad. I need something."

"Yeah, me, too. Your money in my pocket. Go."

"I want an address for Commander Alexander Michaels, M-i-c-h-a-e-l-s. He's the head of Net Force."

"I can give you that without having to burn an electron, dude. Net Force HQ is in Quantico, Virginia, part of the new FBI complex next to the Yew-Nite-Ted States *Muh*-rines—"

"No, I want his *home* address."

"Ah. That'll take a little more. They'd keep that buried pretty good."

"How long?"

"Ah, forty, forty-five minutes."

"Call me back on this number when you get it."

"Cost you five hundred."

"Not a problem."

"I'm on it, dude."

Tad took his new self outside. There were two cars in the garage. A year-old tan minivan with a Baby on Board sticker on the back window, and a three- or four-year-old Dodge Dakota. Both had keys in the ignitions. He paused long enough to grab the rear bumper of the truck, to squat and lift the tires clear of the pavement a few times, to burn off some of his excess energy. Then he climbed in and cranked the engine.

He pulled out of the driveway and headed for the airport. On the way, he called and booked a first-class seat on the next nonstop flight to Washington, D.C. The plane wouldn't leave for three hours. Another five or so hours to fly there, figure on maybe two more to find the place. Call it ten hours all totaled, be there by eight or nine A.M. at the absolute latest. He'd be riding the Hammer for that long, and when he started to come down, he had a whole shitload of caps that would be good until noon, and another twelve hours of Hammer to ride after he took it. Midnight tomorrow, easy.

That should be more than enough time to have a long chat with Commander Alexander Michaels of Net Force, and to teach the fucker what a bad mistake he had made in helping get Bobby Drayne killed.

Plenty of time.

38

Los Angeles, California

Michaels had just finished shaving and was getting dressed when there came a knock on the hotel room's door.

It was Jay. He said, "FBI got a lead on Bershaw."

Michaels waved Jay in as he continued to button his shirt. "Yes?"

Jay held up the flatscreen so Michaels could see the image thereon. A blond-haired man with glasses, dressed in casual sports clothes.

"They sure this is him?"

"Check the side-by-side."

A magnified image of the blond appeared next to an identical-sized head shot of Tad Bershaw. Overlay grids appeared, numbers scrolled, and yellow highlight outlines pulsed over the features.

"The feeb surveillance matchware doesn't worry overmuch about hair, eye, and skin coloring, it compares ear size and lobe shape, nose length and nares spacing, eye spacing and brow angle. Plus somatotypes, though those can be altered by shoe lifts and padding. This is him."

"Where was this taken?"

"LAX, last night. The matchcam sent a sig to FBI HQ, but the priority tag imprint apparently was malfunctioning; instead of an A-1 stamp, the file was batched with a bunch of routine no-hurry PPOIs . . . that's possible persons of interest. So they should have seen it last night, but nobody got around to scanning the file until a few minutes ago."

"So much for infallible technology," Michaels said. He sat on the bed, pulled on his socks. "So where did he go?"

"According to the gatecam at CrossCon Air, he took a nonstop red-eye to Washington, D.C. Plane landed around two A.M. this morning, eastern time. Dulles matchware showed him getting off the jet, but that's the only image they got. FBI checked the rental agencies, he didn't get a car, and they are talking to bus and limo drivers and cabbies. No hits yet. From the passenger list, they know he's using the name Raymond Selling."

"Like the marathon runner?"

"Who?"

"Selling is the fastest long-distance man in the country, probably the world."

"I don't follow the sport. Running for twenty-six miles hurts me just to think about it."

"Why Washington?"

Jay shrugged. "Why not? Maybe he's got an old girlfriend there, somebody he used to run with. Easier to disappear in a big city than a small one."

"Well, maybe we'll bump into him when we get home."

"I hope not," Jay said. "If he's got any of that dope left, he's not somebody I want to meet face-to-face."

Michaels tied his shoes, stood, and reached for his sport coat, which hung on the bathroom door. "What time does our flight leave?"

"Couple hours. Be back in Washington about seven P.M. Five-hour flight, add three for the time zones."

"Well, let's go have breakfast and enjoy the L.A. sunshine. It'll probably be raining when we get back to the East Coast."

Jay closed the flatscreen, and they started for the door. He still had a worried look.

Michaels said, "Something else?"

"Yeah, a major problem. In-house Security says somebody got past the Net Force firewalls and into the mainframe last night."

"I thought that wasn't possible."

"It's not, for most people. I could do it. And if I could, some others could. A handful."

"Was anything damaged or stolen?"

"Fortunately not. The file protection programs make that real hard without the encryption keys. Even I might have trouble wrecking any big part of the system from outside. Security says the probe rode in on a GAO line and managed to get into the personnel files. It didn't damage them, they are read-only for the GAO auditor, who, by law, we have to let in. Somebody had to know about that to use it."

"Who would know?"

"Ex-programmer, maybe ex-ops, FBI, GAO. Maybe even Net Force."

"Really?"

"We've had people quit. Fired a few, too. Programmers always leave themselves a back door when they are building secure systems. We vetted ours, and I had our people checking, but the guy who builds it can hide a few things when you are talking millions of lines of code."

"So what now?"

"We'll run down all ex-employees with enough skill to pull it off. My hope is that it'll turn out to be some kid hacker counting coup. But that wouldn't be the way smart money bets."

"Mm. Stay on it, Jay. In the meantime, let's don't keep General Howard waiting."

On the way to the elevator, something about what Jay said bothered him. He couldn't quite nail it down as they stepped into the lift. Jay pushed the button for the lobby; they were on the sixteenth floor.

As the elevator descended, pinging as it passed each floor, Michaels said, "That intrusion last night. Do we know where it came from?"

"Not really," Jay said. "It bounced off a couple of satellites. We were able to track it as far as the West Coast, that's it."

Michaels thought about that for a second. "Why would anybody capable of breaking into a secure system like Net Force's mainframe want to look at our personnel records?"

"If that's what they planned to do, boss, rather than just stumbling into those records by accident."

"Just for the sake of argument, let's assume they meant to go there."

Jay shrugged. "Who, where, what, when, why," he said. "Find out if somebody works there, what they do exactly, how long. Maybe how much somebody gets paid."

"You skipped one," Michaels said. "Find out where somebody lives."

"Yeah, that could be."

Michaels felt a sudden chill frost him.

Jay said, "I see where you're going here, but it's probably just a coincidence."

"What if it isn't? What if it's Bershaw? What if he is looking to even the score for the death of his friend?"

"That's a reach, boss. Guy who pulled the trigger on Drayne is dead."

"Bershaw wouldn't know that. He went over the side of the hill as soon as the shooting started."

The elevator reached the ground floor and opened. The two men stepped out and walked toward the hotel's coffee shop.

"He could have heard or watched news reports about it," Jay offered.

"You were on CNN's coverage. The FBI and DEA weren't saying much. Nobody said who shot Drayne, only that he was killed. And who was getting most of the credit for finding the drug dealers?"

"Uh, that'd be us," Jay said.

"Yes. And there were only three of us there: you, me, and General Howard."

"Still a reach," Jay said. "It doesn't necessarily follow."

"Bershaw escapes. Somebody on the West Coast gets into Net Force's personnel files within a few hours. Bershaw disappears, then shows up on a flight to Washington. I don't like it. If you were him and you were pissed off because somebody had murdered your friend, blasted him while he stood there with his hands up, and you wanted to do something about it, who would you go after?"

Jay didn't say anything.

"Yeah. That's what I thought. The man in charge, who was right there on the scene. You could be waiting for him when he got home. Only thing is, Toni is already there."

He pulled his virgil, hit the voxax, and said, "Call home."

The virgil made the call.

After five rings, the message recorder came on. "Hello. You've reached area code two-oh-two, three-five-seven . . ."

"Toni, if you are there, pick up or call me back ASAP."

Michaels felt a sense of panic threaten to take him as

he ended the call. He tapped the resend button and selected five-minute intervals, to repeat until a connection was made or he shut it off.

"She's not answering."

"She could be asleep. Outside watering the plants. A dozen things," Jay said.

John Howard stood in the short line of people waiting to get into the coffee shop. He saw Jay and Michaels approaching, smiled at them. Michaels didn't feel like smiling back.

Howard caught it. "What's the matter, Commander?"

Michaels ran through it, feeling more and more nervous as he laid it out.

Howard said, "Jay's probably right, it's probably nothing. But just to be on the safe side, how about I have a couple of my people drop by and check."

"I would appreciate that." Being all the way across the country made him feel helpless. Once he knew Toni was okay, he'd feel a lot better.

Howard looked at Michaels a moment longer. "One more thing, Commander," he said. "Jay's the one who got all the attention on TV. It might not be a bad idea for him to get hold of Saji and tell her to get somewhere safe."

Michaels nodded, but Jay was already pulling out his virgil. A few seconds later, Saji answered, and everyone relaxed a little.

Howard pulled his own virgil and spoke quietly into it, muted the sound so he had to hold it to his ear like a mobile phone to hear the reply. When he was done, he turned to Michaels and said, "Somebody will be there in twenty minutes. They'll call you back or have Toni call you."

Michaels nodded. "Thank you. Call home yourself, John, just to be sure, then we might as well go have breakfast." But until he heard from Toni, he wasn't the least bit interested in eating.

Washington, D.C.

It was almost noon, and Toni was in the kitchen and about to fix herself some lunch when there came a terrific crash, as if a truck had slammed into the house.

She knew who the intruder was as soon as he came through the side door—a door he opened by kicking it, smashing the lock, and almost tearing it from its hinges. Splinters of shattered wood flew everywhere, and the door slammed against the wall hard enough for the knob to break the spring stop and punch a hole in the Sheetrock.

She didn't recognize him, but it had to be the drug guy who had escaped. His hair and eyebrows were bleached and his skin color was dark, but it was him.

As she stood there in her nightgown and ratty bathrobe, she knew she had only one advantage: What he saw was a small, pregnant woman who couldn't possibly be a threat to him.

And in truth, she wasn't much of a threat. Any strenuous activity could cause her to lose the baby. A full-out hand-to-hand fight would certainly do it. Even if her skill at *silat* was enough to overcome his drug-induced strength, she couldn't risk applying it. She had to fall back on one of the first principles of her art: deception.

So she played it as he would expect: "Who are you? What do you want?"

"Alexander Michaels," he said.

"He's not here."

"I figured that. He's still in Los Angeles, isn't he?"

She didn't say anything. She couldn't make it too easy.

He grinned, a maniacal, over-the-edge expression. There was a wooden coat tree by the door. He grabbed it, turned it sideways, brought his knee up and the rack down, and snapped it over his thigh as if it were a twig. He dropped the broken halves. "Don't fuck with me, lady, I'm not in the mood, okay?"

It wasn't hard to act afraid. She had never seen anybody do anything like that before. The man was a scarecrow missing half his stuffing, and no way should he be able to do what he had just done.

"He . . . he won't be home until tonight. His flight gets here around s-s-seven o'clock."

Bershaw—that was the name Alex had told her—grinned his mad smile again.

"Ah. Good. That will give us plenty of time to get acquainted. What's your name?"

"Toni," she said.

"Wife or girlfriend?"

"W-w-wife."

"Well, don't worry, Toni, I'm not gonna hurt you." He looked at her. "Got a bun in the oven. How far along are you?"

"Five months."

"Congratulations. You do what I tell you, you and the kid will live to get to know each other. You can call me Tad. Why don't you take me on a tour of the place, since we have some hours to kill?"

"Okay."

The com chirped.

"Don't answer it," he said.

Toni's thoughts ran at top speed, banging into each other as she tried to keep them straight. She had to get word to Alex somehow. This man had come here to kill him, she was certain of that, and he might or might not

kill her and the baby. She had to go along with whatever
he wanted until she could figure out a way to stop him.

Tad followed Michaels's wife as she led him through the
condo, where he made sure there weren't any surprises
waiting for him. It was an okay enough place, nothing
special, and there were some pictures of her and her husband here and there, other images of their families, easy
to see the resemblance in those.

Every five minutes or so, the phone would ring, and
he'd just shake his head at her. He didn't want her talking
to anybody, especially her husband, and maybe giving
him some secret code kind of clue.

In the garage was an old Chevrolet convertible, the
hood up, and parts of the engine laid out on a workbench.

"Very nice," he said. He walked over and put one hand
on the car's fender, rubbed it lightly. "Your old man is
into cars."

"Yes. He rebuilds them. It's his hobby."

Tad needed to work off some of the Hammer's bubbling and insistent energy, and while he was horny again,
a pregnant woman didn't do it for him. He looked around
for a pry bar or a hammer. A little drum work on the
Chevy would do fine. He'd be sure to let Mr. Michaels
see his project car was gonna need a lot more effort to
bring back to cherry condition before he did the same
deconstruction on *him*.

He saw a ball peen hammer hung on pegs over the
workbench and went to get it. The Hammer working a
hammer, he liked the symmetry in that.

But when he got to the bench, he noticed something
else. Little pieces of ivory, needles, a microscope. Scrimshaw.

"Your husband has a lot of time on his hands," he said.

He nodded at the bench. "Cars and art. That's when he's not having guys murdered."

"My husband doesn't have people murdered," she said. She glared at him.

He smiled. She had balls, this pregnant woman did. She'd seen what he could do, and she knew he could kill her with a backhand, but here she was defending her old man anyway. Tad had never heard his mother ever say a kind word about his father. "That fucking asshole," was about as good as it ever got. Give Toni here a point for loyalty.

"Tell that to my friend Bobby," he said. "He was standing in the middle of the road with his hands in the air, and the feds gave him an instant craniotomy. *Blam!* Blew his head apart."

"My husband didn't order that. Net Force does computer investigation, they aren't field operatives on drug busts. And they'd never shoot a prisoner, anyway."

"Yeah, well, he was there, I saw him on the evening news. He should have stayed at his desk on this one."

He twirled the hammer in his fingers, was about to go do the car, when he saw the capsule. He looked at it, saw that it was open under the microscope, and the powder emptied out. He put the ball peen hammer down and moved to look.

He shook his head. "That fucking Bobby. He was too smart for his own good sometimes." He turned to look at her. "You know about this? Your old man talk to you about his work?"

"Yes. Sometimes."

"Bobby was a genius, you know. Certifiable, high MENSA grade, smarter than almost everybody. Even when I'm Hammering and all my edges are sharp, Bobby could still think circles around me. He had contempt for the feds, 'cause of his father. You don't know about that part, but his father was with the FBI for like a hundred years. He and Bobby didn't get along. So Bobby left clues in every fifth cap: little riddles, each one different." He waved at the cap. "That's how they found him, isn't it? Some geek at your husband's computer farm turned the machines loose on this and figured it out, didn't he?"

She didn't say anything.

"C'mon, you might as well tell me. I can't kill him any deader than dead, can I?"

"Please don't kill him."

"Bobby might have fucked up and gotten caught because he underestimated his opposition—you tend to do that when you are always smarter than them—but he should be alive. Somebody has got to pay for that."

He was really ready to pound the car now, and he reached for the tool to do it with, when the doorbell rang.

"Don't answer it," Bershaw said. "They'll go away." He considered it for a second. "No, maybe we ought to see who it is."

The security cam Alex had installed showed two men in uniform, with holstered pistols. Net Force troopers.

"Cops?"

"Net Force Security."

"I thought your husband was a desk jockey."

"He is, but they have some special teams for certain situations."

"Yeah, like executing drug dealers."

The two at the door rang the bell again. And again. They weren't going away, and she wondered why they were here. The missed phone calls, maybe.

Toni felt a surge of hope, but she quickly quelled the feeling. The two men at her door were in immediate danger. Bershaw was a killer, and he had a drug-driven rage that couldn't be easily stopped. A wrong word, and he might go off like a bomb.

"Get rid of them, some good reason to go away, and you better not give them a fucking hint," Bershaw said. "You do, they die, you and the kid die, and I might get bored waiting here alone for hubby to come home, but that's how it will go down."

"I understand."

Bershaw stood behind her and to one side, out of sight, as Toni opened the door. He didn't have a weapon that she could see, but he didn't really need one.

"Yes?"

"Mrs. Michaels. We're sorry to bother you, but Commander Michaels has been trying to contact you."

"Oh. Oh, yes, I'm sorry about that. I was working out, doing my aerobics, and then I took a long hot bath to relax." She was in her bathrobe. "I turned off the ringer and let the computer take messages."

"Yes, ma'am. If you would call Commander Michaels at your convenience, that would be very helpful."

"I will. I'm going to go take a nap, and I'll call him when I wake up. Sorry to have caused you any trouble."

"No trouble at all, ma'am. Have a good day."

When they were gone, Bershaw said, "That was all right, except for the part about calling your husband. Now you'll have to do that. But I'm gonna write a script for you. You will make the call, and you will say exactly what I tell you to say, not one word more or less, you understand?"

"I understand."

"Good. We have a little time to work on it, since you are going to take a nap and all. Tell me about your family, brothers, sisters, like that. I've seen some of the pictures, so don't lie to me. If I think you're lying, I'll just kill you, okay?"

Toni felt her heart pounding harder than usual. He was being very cautious, and she might not get another chance to warn Alex. She had to hope he would get the message she had been able to send.

Los Angeles, California

They had almost finished breakfast when Michaels's virgil announced an incoming call. He had it off his belt and thumbed to receive in two seconds. "Yes?"

"Sir, this is Chris Carol, military ops. We just spoke to your wife at your house. She seems fine, sir."

Michaels blew out a sigh. Thank God!

"Did she say why she wasn't answering the phone?"

"Yes, sir. She was taking a bath, sir, and had the ringer turned off."

He shook his head. Of course. It had to be some piddly thing like that.

"We'll remain in the area on surveillance, sir, as per General Howard's orders."

"Thanks," he said. "Ask Toni to call me as soon as she can, will you?"

"She says she will call you, sir, after she has a nap. She must be tired from her workout."

"What? What did you say?"

"Sir?"

"About her being tired?"

"Sir, I just assumed she might be. She said she had been doing her aerobics, before her bath, sir."

Michaels felt a shard of icy steel stab deep into his bowels. He looked at John Howard. "He's there," he said. "He's got Toni."

39

The general had pulled strings in a hurry and gotten them
fast rides. The National Guard fighters had zipped from
Los Angeles to the East Coast at speeds more than twice
supersonic most of the way. By the time they were on the
ground again, the trip had only been a little over two
hours. It was almost two-thirty in the afternoon when the
escort picked Michaels, Howard, and Jay up at the air base
and took off with lights flashing and sirens screaming.
They'd shut those off before they got to his neighborhood.
Howard had set up a command post a half mile away from
the house, and there were more Net Force people on the
scene, far enough back to stay hidden but close enough
to see if anybody left.

An hour into the flight, Toni had called, and it had
twisted his stomach to hear her speak the words that Bershaw must have made her say:

They exchanged greetings, he'd asked how she was doing, and she'd said she was fine, then she said, "I'm sorry
I missed your call earlier, I didn't mean to make you

worry. Listen, I can't talk now, I've got my mother on the other line, some crisis with my sister-in-law she has to settle. Call me when you get to the airport tonight, okay? Bye."

He put in a call to Toni's mother in the Bronx. She was surprised to hear from him, and he pretended he was calling to check on Toni's *silat* teacher. Guru was doing okay, his mother-in-law told him. Say hello to Toni when he saw her, tell her to call and visit.

If he needed any confirmation, that did it. Toni wasn't talking to her mother. And she was being held hostage by some psychotic drug fiend who almost certainly blamed Michaels for his buddy's death. It was a nightmare.

"How do you want to play it?" Howard asked, as the Net Force car careened toward the city. "You want to call in the FBI kidnap teams?"

"Would you call them in if it was your wife?"

"No, sir."

"We have snipers, don't we?"

"Yes, sir. A couple of very good ones."

"Have them meet us at the staging point. I'll try to get him in front of a window. If they have a shot, tell them to take it. It will have to be in the spine or the head to be sure to drop him."

"Yes, sir." Howard didn't say anything about job description or rules of engagement. He pulled his virgil and made a call.

"You're not going in there alone are you, boss?"

"Toni's my wife. It's my house. I know them both better than anybody else. Damned right I'm going in."

"Jesus, you've seen what this guy is capable of. Even if you shoot him, you can't be sure of stopping him."

"I know that. What choice do I have? I'll have surprise on my side. Maybe that will be enough."

"We could storm the place, hit it with fifty guys—"

"And he could break Toni's neck before they got through the door. No. It's me he wants, so if he spots me alone, he'll have what he came for. If he's in my face, Toni can get clear."

"And you might get dead."

"Yeah, well, that's how it is. Better me than her."

What he didn't say was that he still had the capsule Howard had found at the shooting site in his pocket. And that if he took it before he went in, he'd be more than a match for the zombie. He was in better shape, he had some training as a fighter, and he was motivated. The drug would cancel Bershaw's advantage.

But there was a big problem. It was risky. He didn't mind the jeopardy to himself, but what if the drug didn't do exactly for him what it did for Bershaw? What if he went crazy like some of the other druggies who used it? Saw snakes coming out of the walls or thought he was being chased by demons or whatever those people who had gone mad and committed suicide had seen?

Could he risk Toni's life and the baby's life like that?

Six of one, half a dozen of the other, his little inner voice said. *If the zombie goes through you like Sherman through Georgia, he'll probably kill Toni anyway, don't you think?*

Michaels stuck his hand into his pocket and fingered the capsule.

Devil or the deep blue sea, Alex. And you better decide soon. You don't know how long it'll take before the stuff kicks in if you decide to go that way. It might not help in time, even if you do eat it.

Shit.

"Ten minutes to the staging point," Howard said. "My snipers will be there. If they can see him, they can casket him."

Michaels nodded. He fingered the capsule.

. . .

Toni was sure Alex had gotten her warning. She could hear it in his voice when she called, and she was fairly certain the rumbling noises in the background had been a jet engine and wind noise. That meant he was on his way home, and he'd be here sooner than Bershaw expected him.

What was he going to do when he got here? Would he bring in the regular FBI hostage negotiators? She tried to put herself in his position, and that answer came up a solid no. He would know Bershaw was desperate, probably know he was on the mind-altering drug that made him fast, smart, and strong. Alex wouldn't take the risk that Bershaw would hurt her or the baby.

What would he do?

And her greatest fear was that he would try to sneak into the house and take on Bershaw alone. It wasn't a macho thing but just how Alex was. He would see her as his responsibility, and his coming in alone as the best chance of drawing the killer's attention away from her.

If she had not been pregnant, she would have already tried to take Bershaw down herself. He was fast and strong, but she had more than fifteen years of *pentjak silat* training and practice, and she would risk that her skill could offset his drug-powered strength.

Silat was a weapons-based art. Toni was comfortable with a knife, a stick, a sword, whatever came to hand. A knife from the butcher block rack wouldn't take a second to pull. No matter how resistant to pain, no matter how strong a man might be, he couldn't walk if he had no blood circulating or if the tendons controlling his feet or legs were cut or if his spine was severed.

But in her condition, the slightest mistake would cost her. She wouldn't risk the baby unless there was no other way. If it came down to it, she would not let this psychotic kill Alex, even if it meant she and the baby didn't make it. You didn't stand by and allow the man you loved to die if you could prevent it, no matter what it cost you.

She had already rehearsed grabbing the knife in her mind a dozen times, never looking at it so as to give it away, but planning how to step, what to throw to distract him, what her targets might be.

She had to expect Alex to show up hours before he was supposed to show up. She had to be ready.

Right now, she had to pee. And she didn't much want to do that with Bershaw watching her, but better that than to wet herself.

"Tad?"

"What?"

"I need to go to the bathroom."

"Let's go."

He followed her down the hall. "Go ahead."

"Can I close the door?"

"No. Just pee. I'll look the other way."

"Thank you."

She thought she might be able to use that, somehow, if she could think of a way.

While the woman was on the john, Tad turned away and dry-swallowed two more of the Hammer caps. He could feel the first ones start to wane, and a few seconds later, he took a third. He had built up a tolerance to the stuff by now, but it didn't matter; the remaining caps were all going to be deactivated soon, anyhow, and any way you looked at it, this was going to be his last Hammer ride. When Ma and Pa at the portable lab heard about Bobby getting killed, they would get rid of the RV and hit the road for parts elsewhere. The plan he'd had of getting to the lab and mixing his own caps wouldn't happen now. He could mix the stuff, but some of the chem was just beyond his ability to create from scratch. Bobby had never written his formulas down anywhere, figuring if the cops ever grabbed him, those would be his best bargaining chip.

He heard the toilet flush, turned and saw the wife stand up, her robe falling to cover the short nightgown. She had good legs under that rounded, pregnant belly, and he caught a quick glimpse of her bush. Maybe that was worth exploring, even though it wouldn't be his first choice. Any port in a storm.

But there was something else he wanted to do first. That car was still in the garage. The wife could watch him trash her husband's toy.

"Come on," he said. "We have stuff to do in the garage."

He led her down the hall.

"Sir, the snipers are set. We've got three, two in front, one in back. They know what our man looks like. If they see him, he's history."

"Thank you, John."

Howard handed Michaels his revolver. "Point it at his head just like you would point your finger at his nose and pull the trigger. It will kick some and buck, so hold it two-handed if you can. A head shot is the only way to be sure to stop him."

Michaels took the heavy black handgun and hefted it.

"Is your ring updated?"

"Yes."

"You have six shots. If he's still coming after that, reloading won't help. Aim for the head. Don't say a word, don't hesitate, if you get a shot, take it. If you don't, he'll kill you."

"I got it."

"Leave your virgil on and sending. We won't try to call, but we'll monitor you. As soon as we see Toni, or you indicate that she is clear, we'll come in."

Michaels nodded. His mouth was dry, and his stomach fluttered.

"Whatever happens, he won't be walking away from this."

Michaels looked at Howard, realizing what he was saying. "Thank you."

"Good luck, Alex."

Michaels nodded. He took a couple of deep breaths and let them out, rubbed his eyes, and started toward his home to save his wife.

He was half a block away from where Howard and Jay were when he realized he had made his choice about taking the Hammer cap. No. His mind was his best tool, and he did not want to risk Toni's life on his mind being fuzzed, even if it gave him the strength of Hercules to do so.

He would have to do it the hard way.

Toni watched, feeling detached, as Bershaw swung the pry bar and punched a bar-shaped hole through the safety glass windshield. Little squarish chips of glass flew like jewels under the garage lights as he pulled the bar back and struck with the ball peen hammer he held in his other hand. It took four or five hits, and the windshield was gone.

He had already done the headlights and taillights.

After the windshield, he walked around the car and shattered all the remaining glass, the sides, the rear, scattering glittering shards in all directions.

Then he started on the front fender, alternating the hammer and pry bar like some kind of mad drummer following a tune only he could hear.

It wasn't until he started on the metal that Toni got an idea of just how much power he had. The heavy gauge steel of the car's fender and hood not only buckled like aluminum foil, several times he actually punched holes right through, trapping his tools so that he had to yank

them free. The impacts were loud, the *grinch!* of a pry
bar pulled from a car's hood sounding like Toni imagined
the unlubricated gates of hell might sound when opening.

The destruction was terrible to watch. More terrible was
Bershaw's expression. He was laughing, having the time
of his life.

The effort had to be burning him up, tearing muscles
and tendons, doing major damage to his very bone structure, but he kept laughing and pounding, hitting with such
force that the fiberglass handle of the hammer finally
splintered and broke, leaving the rounded nose of the
hammer buried in the passenger door, and the pry bar's
loop bent almost closed.

Toni realized that attacking this man physically would
be suicide if she made even the tiniest mistake. Even with
a knife.

After what seemed like a long time, he dropped the bent
pry bar, rolled his shoulders, then turned to look at her.
He stared at her for a few seconds, unblinking.

He looked like a raptor about to swoop down on prey.

"What would you do to save your husband's life?" He
finally said.

"Anything."

He grinned. "Good. I have something in mind. Let's go
to the bedroom."

Toni felt a small surge of hope. If he wanted sex, he
would have to put himself into a more vulnerable position.
He would have to allow her to get close. *Silat* was an in-
your-face art. If he let her get close, she would have a
chance. A small chance, maybe.

If she had the shot, she might be able to take him.

Michaels tucked the gun into his back pocket as he slid
open the garage window. He had heard the noise half a

block away, and by the time he got to the garage, he had a pretty good idea of what he would see.

He was wrong. What he saw was much worse than he'd expected. Jesus Christ, how could a man built like Bershaw do this much damage with a hammer and pry bar? The Chevy looked as if it had rolled off a cliff.

He saw that the door into the house was open, and he climbed through the window, pulled the revolver out, and made his way across the floor, trying to avoid stepping on all the shattered bits of glass. A head shot. Point the gun like your finger, and pull the trigger. Hit him in the head with a bullet, and it was all over.

Michaels edged into the doorway and into the house.

In the bedroom, Tad said; "Get on your hands and knees."

The woman climbed onto the bed and did what he said. He moved to stand behind her. "Back up a little."

He reached out with both hands, caught the middle of her robe, and ripped it apart, exposing her bare bottom. He reached for his zipper.

Toni gathered herself as she heard the sound of his zipper going down. A twist, a hard fist to the testicles, grab and rip them off, roll to the side and onto the floor—

Michaels stepped into the bedroom, saw Bershaw's back to him, Toni beyond him on the bed. The years of law and order training tried to assert themselves. Maybe he should give the guy a chance to surrender.

Hell with that. The bastard was about to rape his wife, he was tanked on drugs that made him the most dangerous person Michaels had ever seen. He pointed the gun at the back of Bershaw's head and started to squeeze the trigger.

•   •   •

Tad heard something, or maybe he felt the air pressure in the room change. Suddenly, he knew they weren't alone. He spun. There was the husband, with a gun.

Good! Tad lunged.

Michaels saw Bershaw spin, his speed was incredible, and leap at him. He was halfway though squeezing the trigger. Fast as Bershaw was, Michaels was ahead of him. The gun went off.

Bershaw tried to duck, but the bullet hit him. Michaels saw it plow a furrow into his skull, just under the hairline, but then the mirror on Toni's closet door shattered.

Bershaw kept coming, but the bullet's impact changed his angle a little, so he veered to the left slightly. Michaels dodged to his right, and Bershaw almost missed him.

Almost. His flailing hand smashed into the revolver and tore it from Michaels's grasp. The gun flew, and Bershaw slammed into the dresser and landed on his hands and knees. But he looked up at Michaels and smiled—smiled!—with blood oozing from the head wound.

The bullet hit at an angle and glanced off, Michaels realized.

He had to get this maniac away from Toni, who was on the floor next to the bed.

Michaels grabbed the small television set on the stand next to the door and threw it at Bershaw, who reached up and batted it aside like it was a pillow. The TV set hit the floor and ruptured into three pieces.

He had to lead him out of here! Away from Toni!

Michaels backpedaled through the door.

Bershaw came to his feet, wiped the blood from his eyes, stuck one finger into the gory groove on his forehead, and looked at his finger. "Close, but no cigar."

Michaels turned and ran for the living room. "Come and get me, asshole!"

Michaels risked a glance at his virgil. As soon as Bershaw came after him, Toni would be safe. The general's men would be ready to hit the door when they heard Michaels yell for them.

Oh, shit! It was gone! The virgil was gone! Where had he lost it? The window?

He didn't have time to worry about that now.

He made it to the living room, and he looked around frantically for a weapon, something to throw, anything!

He saw the little wooden case with the two *kerambit* knives in it. He grabbed it and jerked the lid off just as Bershaw came into the room. The man was moving a little slower, he was a little unsteady on his feet. The bullet glancing off his head must have had some effect.

Bershaw grabbed the end of the couch as Michaels ran around behind it, trying to slip the rings of the little curved knives onto his index fingers. Bershaw heaved, and the couch came off the floor and twisted, flew five feet, and landed upside down with a crash.

"You can run, but you can't hide. Joe Lewis said that, did you know?"

Stall him! "What do you want?"

"You killed Bobby. I kill you. Even trade."

"I didn't kill him. He was shot by a rogue NSA agent working for the drug companies! That man is dead, too!"

"Doesn't matter. You pointed the shooter at him. You get to pay."

Bershaw moved in, his hands held out to grab.

Michaels had the little curved-bladed knives gripped solidly now, hidden behind his forearms and closed hands, only the forefinger rings showing. If Bershaw saw that, or cared, he didn't give any indication, he just kept coming, moving like some Frankenstein's monster that couldn't be stopped.

Michaels took a deep breath and held it.

It might be his last.

40

Toni hurried down the hall. In her hand, she held the *kris* that Guru had given her, the wavy-bladed Javanese dagger that had been in the old lady's family for years. Such daggers had been more ceremonial than used for a long time, but it was still a knife, when stick came to stab, and it was the only weapon in the bedroom.

She heard a loud noise, felt the floor shake as she reached the living room and saw the two men there.

Bershaw advanced on Alex.

Alex stood in a *djuru* stance, and Toni immediately realized he had the *kerambits* in his hands, even though they were all but hidden.

Even with a head wound, the man was supernaturally fast. He lashed out with one hand, and before Alex could move, he caught him with a slap that knocked him backward into the bookcase, showering him with hardbacks.

"Hey!" Toni yelled.

Bershaw turned, smiled at her. "I'll take care of you later. Better put that down before you cut yourself, honey."

The distraction was enough for Alex to recover a little. He grabbed several books from the shelf behind him and threw them at Bershaw.

Tad turned back to finish Michaels. He saw three books coming at him in slow motion: a red one, one with a dark dust cover, and one that opened so that the pages were flapping in the air. He dodged the dark dust covered one, backhanded the red book, and let the flapping one hit him on the chest; it was nothing.

Michaels was right behind the books, though, and just quick enough to get a punch in on him before Tad could block it. No big deal, he would absorb that and crush the fucker.

His vision went out on the left side, just flashed red and . . . went away.

Tad frowned and backhanded Michaels, knocking him sprawling over the overturned couch. He put his hand to his face, and it came away covered with blood and some kind of clear gel. His mind made the connection.

The son of a bitch had ripped his eye out!

How?

Michaels came up, and Tad saw how he'd done it. He had a little knife in his hand. Looked like a claw.

Tricky shit, hiding that.

Well, fine. He'd just step in, break that fucking arm, and shove that little sticker up the man's ass, that's what—

Tad moved in.

Something hit him in the back, and he felt a stab of minor pain.

He reached around, realized the wife had thrown that fucking curvy blade and stuck it up in the middle of his back. He grabbed the thing by the blade, pulled it out, and brought it around in front of himself. The blade was black with funny little patterns in the steel. He waved it at the woman. "Thanks. Just what I needed."

He turned in time to see Michaels come over the couch, that little knife leading.

Tad grinned. He still held the wavy knife by the blade, only a few inches of it sticking out, but he jammed the somewhat dull point at Michaels's forearm, drove it into the muscle, felt it grate on bone, to stop only when his hand hit Michaels's arm.

Michaels's hand spasmed open. So much for his little claw.

But the knife didn't fall, it was as if it was glued to his fucking hand.

Fine, fine. You want to play? Tad jerked his own weapon free, shifted his grip, and figured he'd just get a good swing and take the whole arm off. *That* would get rid of the little knife damned quick. After that, he'd just carve the bastard up in little chunks.

Michaels felt the *kris* go into his right forearm, felt the tip hit his radius and then slip past and saw it come all the way through, just an inch or so of the point sticking out.

His hand opened on its own.

Bershaw jerked the *kris* free and lifted it past his ear like an ax, and he knew the man was going to chop down. Knew with his maniacal strength, the man might cleave right though the muscle and bone and slice Michaels's hand completely off.

But he had the other *kerambit*. And now he was close, inside, right where a *silat serak* player wanted to be when it all came down. He had one chance, maybe, and he took it. He lashed out in a punch at Bershaw's neck, a short left hook, twisting his fist as he threw it.

The tiny blade of the *kerambit* bit into the right side Bershaw's neck a couple of inches below the jaw and ripped a channel all the way to his Adam's apple.

The man frowned and paused in his downstroke.

Michaels collapsed, just let his legs go limp. It was the fastest way to get clear, and as he fell, he punched with the knife again, scoring a nasty slash across Bershaw's thigh, just below his groin.

Bershaw drew back his unwounded leg and kicked. His foot took Michaels in the side, just under the armpit, and he felt and heard ribs crack, a wet *snap-snap* that stole his breath.

Blood fountained from Bershaw's neck, jetting out with each pulse, spewing with his trip-hammer–fast beat like a torn garden hose spraying water under pressure.

Bershaw kicked him again, but not as hard. Michaels managed to turn a little, so he caught it on the shoulder. Muscle tore, but he didn't think the arm broke, even though the force of the kick turned him a hundred and eighty degrees around.

Michaels hooked his right foot behind Bershaw's right ankle, then drove his left heel into the bloody cut on Bershaw's thigh.

Bershaw lost his balance and fell backward, slamming into the couch.

Michaels rolled away and up. He held the *kerambit* in his left hand up point-first at Bershaw.

The right side of Bershaw's body was soaked in blood from the carotid artery Michaels had sliced open. The blood still pulsed out, but much slower and with less force now.

Bershaw came up, grinned, and took two steps toward Michaels. But now it was his turn to move in slow motion.

Michaels stabbed at him. Bershaw put up an arm, and the blade scored a line from the wrist to the elbow, but it hardly bled at all.

• • • •

Tad suddenly felt tired, so very tired. Yeah, he had to kill this guy, for Bobby, but as soon as he did that, he was gonna have to go sit down. The Hammer was slowing, he could feel it, and it wasn't time yet. Not yet. Just this one thing left to do first, then he could take a break. Go see Bobby.

Bobby?

Something about Bobby . . .

Fuck it. Kill the guy, then worry about it.

Bershaw grabbed Michaels's knife arm with both hands and squeezed.

Michaels felt his wrist crack, and in desperation he snapped his other elbow out in a horizontal shot, right out of *djuru* one, out in front of him like Dracula behind his cape, only with all his weight behind it. He hit Bershaw square on the temple.

Man! Who would have thought this guy could hit so hard? He'd have to tell Bobby about this.

But he felt so tired. So weak. It was so much trouble just to stand here, and why should he even bother?

The Hammer left him then, all by himself here with this stranger who hit him. The gray closed in on Tad.

Bobby? Is that you, man?

The light in Bershaw's remaining eye flickered as he let go of Michaels's arm and stumbled back a step.

Then the light went out, and Bershaw fell, a puppet with his strings cut.

Michaels turned and saw Toni, a book gripped in her hands, advancing toward them. In that odd interplay that sometimes happened in scary situations, he noticed the title of the book, and he started to laugh.

Toni stopped. "Alex? Are you all right?"

He waved at the book. "You were going to hit him with that?"

Toni looked at it.

It was *How to Win Friends and Influence People*.

EPILOGUE

Washington, D.C.

Michaels's arm itched, and he wanted to tear off the plastic flesh bandage and scratch the cut. The surgical glue was holding the wound closed just fine, and he had pain medicine if he needed it, for the broken wrist that ached dully and the cracked ribs that hurt every time he breathed, but nothing seemed to help with the itching.

He sat in the kitchen nook at the table, looking at Toni as she came back from the fridge with a beer for him.

"Thanks," he said. "You should have let me get that."

"I'm in better shape than you, pregnancy notwithstanding."

He took a sip, put the bottle down on the table.

"So what's the latest from the office?"

"Well. It turned out that Lee and George were working for the drug company, like we thought. Lee is trying to cut a deal, but I don't think he has enough leverage."

"So why'd they kill the chemist?"

"That's the twist. The pharmaceutical house they were in cahoots with—"

"Did you just say, 'in cahoots with'?"

"You want me to tell this story or not?" But he grinned.

"Go ahead."

"It turned out the drug company already had a similar line of research going, upon which they had spent a lot of money, and in which they had a lot of confidence. Not as extensive as Drayne's, but going in the same general direction. They were far enough along that they had already started some testing protocols, gotten some government approvals, and they didn't want somebody stealing their thunder."

"They were trying to *suppress* Drayne's stuff?"

"Yeah. George and Lee had been given big blocks of stock to make sure Drayne's formulas didn't wind up on anybody else's table. If their company reached the market first, they'd be millionaires."

She shook her head. "Huh. Didn't see that one."

"Nobody else did, either."

"What about John Howard?"

Michaels took another sip of his beer. "He says he is gonna retire. Says life is too short, and he wants to be around when his son graduates from school and goes out into the world on his own."

"I don't blame him for that."

"Me neither."

"Jay Gridley still a Buddhist?"

"Mostly lapsed, if there is such a thing. He can't sit and contemplate his navel and stay sharp enough to run with the bad boys on-line, he says. He'll have to work all that out. But he and his girl are going to get married."

"That's great."

"Going to honeymoon in Bali, so he says."

"And what about us?"

"Us? We're fine. I guess I won't be spending much time in the garage until the Chevy gets back from the body shop. Incredible what damage he did."

"Yes, it was. I can see why so many people wanted to get their hands on this drug. If he had been a jock on the stuff, he could have taken the entire house down to the foundations."

He nodded. "Tell you what. If I ever complain about things being slow at work again? I want you to slap me upside the head."

"My pleasure," she said.

They smiled at each other, and despite his aches and itches, Michaels was very happy to be able to do that.

It sure beat the other options.